THE RANCHER'S LADY

"You're cold," Cord said softly, his lips near her ear. "You really should get out of these wet clothes."

Eliza could not bring herself to move, but Cord's nimble fingers, dancing like hot coals across her body, rapidly undid the buttons of her jacket and shirt. She felt helpless to resist as he undressed her, leaving her wearing only her soggy petticoat. Cord stood up to spread her clothes out in the sun and Eliza closed her eyes. It was one thing to stare at him in fascination while she was safely dressed, but it was quite another to do so when her own body was perilously close to being stripped of its protective covering.

"It ought not take your things more than an hour or so to dry," Cord said as he settled down beside her again.

"An hour? What are we going to do for an hour?" She could read the answer in his eyes.

Cord moved closer and gathered her in his embrace. He kissed her tenderly, then with fierce, possessive energy. Eliza melted into his arms, not questioning why she was there, only glad that she was. Any lingering doubt was gone. She knew that whatever the future held for her, she must give all she had and was into his safekeeping. That was the way she wanted it. That was the way it *had* to be. . . .

Leigh Greenwood

Wicked Wyoming Nights

LOVE SPELL BOOKS　　NEW YORK CITY

To Fran and Karen

A LOVE SPELL BOOK®

April 2002

Published by

Dorchester Publishing Co., Inc.
276 Fifth Avenue
New York, NY 10001

ISBN 0-505-52478-3

Visit us on the web at www.dorchesterpub.com.

Wicked Wyoming Nights

Chapter 1

Wyoming, 1891

Moonlight flooded the wide plain, but failed to reveal the three horsemen moving purposefully in and out of the canyon's deep shadows. Their bridles wrapped with flannel to prevent any betraying sound, they herded the two dozen steers out of the draw and toward the low hills in the distance, away from the buildings of the Matador Ranch that lay five miles down the creek. They were most vulnerable on the open plain—one chance rider could spoil weeks of careful planning—but the only living creatures they encountered were a pair of coyotes feeding on the carcass of a jackrabbit and some sage hens startled from their roost in the cottonwood thicket along the creek edge.

Three pairs of eyes peered nervously about them trying to see around rocks and through ridges; three pairs of ears strained to hear the slightest sound in the vast silence of the night; three bodies sat tautly erect in the saddle ready to respond to the first sign of danger. The slow minutes crept by, one after another, until they were tantalizingly close to the safety of the hills; then a hair-raising yell shattered the quiet of the night, and five men burst from ambush.

"Don't let a single one of the thieving bastards get away!" The rustlers recognized the voice of Cord Stedman, owner of the Matador, and terrified of what they knew would happen if they were caught, they abandoned the steers and fled across the plain.

But they were neither such excellent riders nor so well

mounted as those who followed, and the pursuers were upon them before they could reach the cover of the canyon. A tall man riding a huge black gelding overtook the leader, and the two of them went down in a short, brutal fight. Similar battles took place nearby, but the odds were uneven, and within minutes the nearly unconscious rustlers were tossed into a pile.

"Try this again and we'll break your necks," warned a deep voice laced with raw fury. The cowboys herded the steers back toward the Matador headquarters, leaving the would-be rustlers to ruminate on the folly of attempting to steal from a young, vigilant rancher who never seemed to sleep or leave someone else to do his work for him.

"This is the best piece of land I've seen since we reached Wyoming," Ira Smallwood said to his niece, looking about him at the thick grass and tall hay. "And that willow thicket is the perfect spot for a house."

"But Uncle Ira, you vowed we would live in town this time."

"It's got plenty of water, a little wood, and even hay for winter feeding," he continued, ignoring her. "With a little bit o work we could sell it for a tidy bit of cash in a few years."

"Maybe it's already been claimed. The good land usually is."

"They'll have to prove it," her uncle barked, thinking of the arrogant ranchers who mercilessly drove off any homesteader who tried to settle on their grazing lands. "I won't give up so easily this time."

He pulled the wagon into the long shadows cast by the willows, climbed down with stiff muscles, and walked across to the stream. A wet spring and a heavy snow melt caused the water to rush over debris and around rocks with a deep-throated gurgle. "We could grow anything we wanted here," he shouted back to his niece. "There's enough water in this creek for three farms."

A tiny sigh escaped Eliza Smallwood, and her long, slender hands twisted in her lap as she bit her lower lip. This *was* good land, but she dreaded to see her uncle take up farming again. In the past ten years he had discovered one perfect spot after another, but each time he would grow restless and decide he had been mistaken. She climbed down and began to gather wood. Her graceful movement and elegant carriage were at variance with her faded brown dress and the wide-brimmed bonnet she had left on the wagon seat. She was a tall girl with thick black hair swept back from her face. Her nearly black eyes and lashes stood out vividly against skin that was smooth and white in spite of the brutal effects of the sun and wind.

Her loveliness was unmarred by any trace of the hardships she had endured, but she wore an expression of stoic resignation. Her uncle's inability to settle anywhere for more than a year denied her friends or companionship, and a succession of troubles following Ira like a raccoon's tail caused her to wonder if life would ever hold out the promise of anything beyond dismal failure and deadening loneliness.

"Hurry up with that fire," her uncle called impatiently. "I'm starved."

She walked down to the stream to fill a wooden bucket with water for coffee and the inevitable stew. "I don't think this pot is going to last much longer," she said, settling it into the bed of coals. Nearly everything they owned was torn, chipped, or worn thin, but her uncle refused to part with the money to replace it.

Ira had killed a young antelope that morning and the stew, seasoned with onions and the last of her potatoes, was eaten in silence. She washed up while he drank his coffee. The night air was cold and the warmth of the fire felt good on her skin.

"I think I'll open me a saloon," Ira announced without preamble. Pausing in the act of climbing into the wagon to prepare for bed, Eliza waited for her uncle to explain his bald statement, but when he didn't continue, she climbed back down to wait. "You can help me run it," he said at last, looking up. His harsh features, illuminated by the feeble glow, were without warmth and the brooding eyes without love or understanding.

"Maybe they already have enough saloons."

"Then I'll open one anyway. I'll see that mine's better than all the rest."

"But I don't know anything about running a saloon," she

objected. "How can I possibly be of any use?"

"You can serve the men their whiskey." He studied her dispassionately. "You'd be pretty enough if you'd wear something besides that old, faded dress."

"You know strangers frighten me," Eliza said, skipping over the fact that, despite her pleas, her uncle had refused to replace her worn-out clothes. "I never know what to do."

"Then it's time you learned. You're not much good to me just sitting around waiting to cook supper."

"But you promised Aunt Sarah to take care of me." Eliza had always depended upon Ira's veneration of his wife to protect her from his strange fits and starts. "And you know she wouldn't approve of me working in a saloon."

"There's nothing wrong with working in your own uncle's place," he responded roughly. "Especially not as long as I'm there. Besides, why should I have to do everything when your face could make more money than a dozen farms?"

"I couldn't do it," she protested. "I know I couldn't."

"Stop whining and go to bed," Ira ordered irritably. "You'd think I was asking you to do something sinful. Any fool can serve whiskey and sing a few songs. And you're no fool for all the crazy notions in your head."

Eliza flushed in the darkness. At twenty she was a grown woman, but virtually cut off from social contact since she was ten, she had built her expectations of marriage on her dimly remembered parents' devotion to each other. One particularly melancholy night she had confided her dreams of love to her uncle, and she had never ceased to regret it. He had torn her illusions apart fragment by fragment and then laughed at her, not in sympathy or amusement but with a cruel, taunting rasp that scoured her tender soul.

She had thought of running away, but there was nowhere for a girl without a husband or family to go and no way for a respectable female to earn a living. She was just as firmly bound to her uncle by circumstances as she was by her vow to her aunt.

Sarah Smallwood had loved her husband deeply, but she was well aware of his shortcomings. "Promise me you won't ever leave him," she had begged Eliza when she knew she was dying. "He can't manage by himself." Neither then nor now did Eliza understand how she was supposed to help her uncle, but her resolution to honor her vow never wavered, not even when Ira was about to embark on a scheme no more likely to prosper than any of the others he had taken up and discarded over the past ten years. It never did any good to try and reason with him, so she started to prepare for bed.

"Are you sure it's safe to sleep on the wet ground?" Eliza asked. He had been coughing a lot recently.

"Don't worry about me. Just make sure breakfast is ready on time."

"It always is," she whispered under her breath, and closed the flap behind her.

Eliza felt more hopeful next morning. The ground was stiff with frost, but the sky was clear and the greening plains stretched limitlessly before her. The icy coldness of the stream felt good to her skin. Her uncle was up and gone without telling her when he'd be back. It was always this way, she thought, yet he expected his breakfast to be ready the minute he returned. She worked silently, never once feeling the hopeful excitement of new surroundings or untested opportunity. Her world was bound by work and fear of the unknown, so much so that when she looked up to see two horsemen approaching she was immediately filled with misgivings.

"Uncle Ira!" she called in a long, drawn-out wail, but he was nowhere in sight. She was going to have to confront these men alone, and her heart started beating so hard it hurt. She faced them across the fire not knowing why they were bearing down on her at a gallop or what she could do to defend herself. Her mind was so paralyzed with fear she didn't notice their faces were not those of hardened of murderers, but of boys no older than herself. In her distraught mind they looked like the type of terrifying enemy her uncle had warned against for the last ten years.

The riders slowed their approach, and she dashed behind the wagon; they divided, one on each side, and with a shriek she tried to take refuge inside, but the shorter man leapt from the saddle and grabbed her by the waist. She whirled, confronting him with the terror-filled eyes of a cornered animal. The shock of finding a beautiful woman in his arms so

11

stunned the young attacker he loosened his grip long enough for Eliza to break away, and she made a desperate dash for the willow thicket.

"Now look what you've done Royce," yelled his disgusted companion. "I'd be ashamed for anyone to know I couldn't hold on to a girl, even if she was bigger than me." This dig at his short statue helped Royce recover his tongue.

"Did you see her, Sturgis?" he asked earnestly. "There ain't no angels prettier than she is."

"You'll *be* an angel if we don't get these squatters out of here before the boss hears about it. He's still so worked up over them rustlers he's liable to take the hide right off your back." Royce climbed back into the saddle.

"But I had her in my arms," he stressed.

"Use your rope if you're afraid to touch her." Sturgis looked around, but Eliza had disappeared among the drooping branches. "Damn, now we've lost her. Mr. Stedman will turn us off for sure if we don't do no better'n this. Keep an eye out for her husband while I circle around the other side. Now where'd she get to?" he called when he couldn't find her. "Did she come out your side?"

"No, she's still in there."

"I'll be damned if I can see her. See if you can flush her out." The boys circled the thicket, peering into the heavily budded branches. "There she is, between those two trunks."

"Please go away," Eliza begged when Sturgis dismounted. "I haven't done anything to you."

"We just want to talk to you, lady." Eliza was faster in moccasins than Sturgis was in his high-heeled boots, and she scampered out of his reach. "Use your rope, fool," he yelled at Royce. The bemused young man quickly looped his lasso and threw it with a quick, practiced motion that settled it about Eliza's waist. Her fingers clawed wildly at the tightening ring, but it clamped down on her just as inexorably as it had on hundreds of calves.

"Please don't dishonor me," she entreated. "Let me go." The boys gaped at each other.

"Nobody's going to do anything like that," Royce stammered, embarrassed at being thought to harbor such wicked designs on the person of a female. "This is Matador grazing land, ma'am, and Mr. Stedman don't allow nobody on it."

But Eliza couldn't have been more frightened if she had been captured by painted savages, and she prepared to fight for her very life. When Sturgis approached her, she charged him like a demented virago, and Royce had to pull the rope taut to prevent her doing serious damage to his face.

"Whee!" gasped Sturgis when he was safely out of range. "I think she's crazy."

"Uncle!" shrieked Eliza, thoughtlessly giving warning of Ira's approach. Cursing his niece's stupidity, Ira headed for the wagon and his rifle at a dead run, but Sturgis had time to mount his horse and throw a second rope over him.

"You simple-minded fool!" Ira howled, struggling so fiercely he fell to his knees. "If you'd kept your mouth shut, I could have put a bullet through both the bastards."

"Nobody's going to shoot anybody," Sturgis said sternly, recovering his balance now that he faced a hostile man instead of a frightened woman. "We just came to say you can't settle here."

"This is government land," growled Ira, struggling to his feet. "It's free to anybody who'll work it."

"It's in the middle of the Matador, and Mr. Stedman won't allow any squatters on this creek." Ira battled the rope, but Sturgis's pony kept it taut. Too dazed to struggle for her own release, Eliza watched wide-eyed as her uncle unexpectedly sprinted toward Sturgis's horse. The rope went slack, and free of the noose, Ira headed for the wagon as fast as his legs would carry his thin, aging body.

"He's going for his rifle," Sturgis yelled, discarding the now-useless rope. Royce threw himself from the saddle, and in seconds the three men were rolling in the dust. The boys were young and strong, but Ira fought with the strength of rage. Eliza, watching with terror-stricken eyes, slumped to her knees when they at last pinned the bloodied and exhausted man to the ground.

"You'll pay for this," Ira panted through gritted teeth. Unable to break the hold on his arms and neck, he relaxed and Royce, inexperienced and out of breath himself, was caught off guard. With a yell of triumph Ira whipped over and around on top of him, but Sturgis dealt him a heavy blow to the back of his head and Ira subsided, too stunned to move, his eyes blazing with hate.

"Tie him up before he jumps me again."

"If you weren't so careless—"

"Shut up and get your rope." Ira's feeble struggles were to no avail and he was soon bound securely. "What are we going to do with her?" Royce asked getting to his feet. "She might fetch help if we let her go."

"Where from? There's nobody for miles, and even if there was, she wouldn't know where to find them."

"If you're so smart, then *you* decide what to do with them." Sturgis studied the two for so long Royce became impatient.

"Let's put them in the wagon and chase them off," he suggested.

"I'll be back with the sheriff before nightfall," bellowed Ira. "Then we'll see who stops me from homesteading this piece."

An angry, goaded look settled over Sturgis's young face. "Won't be much use in coming back if you don't have nothing to set up housekeeping with," he said, glancing significantly at the wagon and the animals tied behind. "Come on, Royce. Let's have a little fun."

"Don't you touch that wagon," shouted Ira, but Sturgis ignored him and climbed inside with the excitement of a little boy about to enjoy a forbidden treat.

"I can't see what anybody would want with these," he said, pulling out Eliza's battered pots. "Ought to be gotten rid of," and he pitched them, one after the other, into the dirt, where Royce stomped them into an unusable mass of crumpled metal. Plates and cups followed until the ground was littered with breakage. Next he found Ira's bedroll and scattered its contents; finally he turned to their trunks and ransacked them for shirts, pants, and underwear. "Look here," Sturgis chirped. "Have you ever seen anything like this?" He pranced out holding up a chemise.

"Woo-wee!" whistled Royce, dancing away with it in his arms like it was a girl. Sturgis tossed out some more of Eliza's underthings, and soon the two boys were cavorting about like idiots dressed in garments that would normally have caused them to blush just to mention. Eliza, frightened and humiliated, could hardly see for the tears in her eyes.

"Just look what your stupidity has done," Ira lamented, casting all the blame on her.

"I couldn't help it. They came up so suddenly."

"You wasted our last chance standing there like a block while they tied me up. You could have shot them both."

"I couldn't," she shuddered, shrinking from the idea of shooting anyone.

"Don't talk to me," he said peevishly. "It puts me out of temper just to hear your voice. Stop, you devils!" Ira yelled as Sturgis tossed out a book. "I'll have you hanged for this."

"There's enough for a real blaze," Sturgis called gleefully to Royce.

With a shriek that penetrated even the boys' destruction-drunk brains, Eliza pitched herself at Sturgis, and pushing him as hard as she could, knocked the book from his hands and snatched up the volume from the dust, but Sturgis pushed her to the ground with complete disregard for cowboy chivalry. Meanwhile, Royce gleefully scooped up a pot of live coals and threw them at the canvas cover of the wagon causing it to burst into flames. With a sob, Eliza scrambled to her feet in a vain attempt to reach her precious books, but Sturgis imprisoned her arms and laughed at her struggles.

Immobilized by the ropes that bound his hands and feet, Ira watched in helpless rage as the leaping flames consumed the canvas, but he fell into a ranting fury when Royce released their pig and aimed his rifle squarely between the horns of their milk cow.

Chapter 2

"What in hell do you think you're doing?" thundered a voice that stopped the two arsonists in their tracks. Eliza spun around to find a tall man on a huge black gelding less than twenty feet away.

Eliza would have been frightened by Cord Stedman on foot, but on horseback he looked bigger than life and she felt ready to faint. Here was the cowman her uncle had warned her about for so long; Eliza felt sure she was facing the Devil himself. Sturgis and Royce could see their wrathful employer in a more rational perspective, but at the moment their view was not very far from Eliza's.

"W-we were just c-c-chasing some h-h-homesteaders off the creek," Sturgis managed to say while Royce stood with slack jaw and staring eyes.

"Put out that fire, you young fools, and the first one to shoot a cow will be digging a bullet out of his own hide."

For a fraction of a second the boys stood paralyzed, then almost simultaneously they sped into action. The fire had gained a strong hold, and even soaking their shirts in the creek couldn't keep it from consuming the last of the canvas. The sight of the dreadful, smoldering mess was too much for Eliza's nerves and she sat down on the ground with a hiccuping cry.

Cord quickly dismounted and reached out for her hand. Eliza's sobs stopped with jarring suddenness when she felt his touch; she yanked her hand back and stared at him with alarm in her eyes.

"You don't have to be frightened," he said softly. "I won't hurt you." Gently he pried her hands apart and lifted her to

16

her feet. Eliza tried hard to pull away, but his strength was amazing and she was helplessly forced to do as he willed. She knew she ought to run, but her legs wouldn't respond. Instead she gaped foolishly, afraid of what he would do next, unable to believe he had come in the guise of a friend.

"How's she supposed to believe you when your hooligans have just about destroyed everything we own?" Ira bellowed furiously. "You're a bigger villain than they are."

Cord turned his hard, measuring gaze on the bound man "Didn't the boys tell you to move on?"

"They came prancing in here, like every other cocksure cowboy I ever saw, trying to lay claim to the whole county."

"Then you've had your warning, so you've got no one to blame but yourself."

"You can't keep me off this land," Ira exploded.

"I don't want trouble, but I can't have rustlers settling in the middle of my herds."

"I'm not a rustler," Ira swore wrathfully.

"That's what every squatter says, but the soil is never turned and the cattle keep disappearing."

"We're from Kansas," Eliza said, as though that alone would clear them of suspicion. "Uncle would never steal, even if we were starving."

"I'd like to believe you, but I can't take the chance on seeing my profits disappear into another man's pockets," Cord said in a completely different voice from the one he'd used for her uncle.

"All you ranchers are greedy, thieving liars," roared Ira as waves of remembrance welled up within him. "You ride over farms destroying crops and bringing disease to kill our livestock and families."

"Move on and I won't do either," Cord responded. "Sturgis." The young man named stepped forward hesitantly. "Put everything that's not ruined back in the wagon. Then take these people into town and have Ed Baylis replace the rest. I'll let you know how many months it'll take you to pay for this foolishness when I see the bill."

"But sir?" gulped Royce in shocked protest.

"I hope you're not going to try to excuse your conduct toward this young lady." Cord's eyes and voice were set in an uncompromising scowl.

17

"No, sir." The chastened young men began their dispiriting task.

"There are several places you can homestead within easy riding distance of town," Cord said, turning to Ira.

"I'll not be told where I can live."

"Suit yourself, but next time you may not be so lucky." Ira looked mulish. "The other ranchers don't treat you this well. The big ones won't, and the small ones can't afford it. Take my advice, for your niece's sake if not your own, and stay away from grazing land."

"Does the sheriff of Buffalo let you ranchers make your own rules?"

Cord's eyebrows came together in a forbidding frown." He can't protect every settler all the time, if that's what you mean." It wasn't, but it answered just as well.

"Let's go, Uncle. Can't you see it's no use?"

Ira glared uncertainly at Cord as the boys finished reloading the wagon.

"I have other hands just as loyal and considerably more experienced," Cord informed him, quite aware of what the furious little man was thinking. "I don't give a second warning."

"You haven't heard the last of me," Ira said sullenly.

"Uncle, don't," entreated Eliza.

"Suit yourself," Cord replied nonchalantly, turning to his men. "Are you done?"

"Almost."

"Then hitch up the team. We don't want to slow their departure. I haven't asked your name," he said, turning back to Eliza. "I'm Cord Stedman, owner of the Matador Ranch."

"To hell with you and your ranch," roared Ira. Eliza was too mortified by her uncle's outburst to speak.

"You'll be a welcome addition to the female population of Buffalo," Cord added.

"Don't get any notions about my niece. Remember, she bears my name."

"I was never one to hold a child responsible for somebody else's name," Cord stated with excruciating directness. He mounted easily and turned his horse away from the gathering. "I want to see you boys before dinner. And don't forget to bring the bill."

18

"Yes, sir," they answered in chorus. Cord chucked to his horse and cantered away.

"I'm going to kill that man," Ira vowed half to himself. "I swear it on Sarah's grave."

"You'd never live to tell of it," challenged Royce with a deadly calm that belied his eighteen years. Ira was taken aback; there was no doubt Royce meant what he said. The look on Sturgis's face said the same.

"He can't be all bad, Uncle. He did stop them from burning our books. And he is going to replace everything."

Eliza continued to watch her uncle anxiously. His oath had filled her with uneasiness. His wife and son were the only things he held sacred, and there was a strange look in his eyes that hadn't been there before.

It was easy to find Baylis's Dry Goods Store, but it was a little harder to make the irascible owner understand their errand, what with the boys not wanting to reveal what they had done to cause Stedman to take such an unprecedented step and Ira Smallwood refusing to talk at all. However, it wasn't long before Ed Baylis had the whole story, and it didn't please him one bit.

"With all this scaring and murdering of anybody who gets in your way, you boys are becoming a real aggravation to decent folks," Ed said irritably.

"We never murdered anybody," insisted Sturgis. "Mr. Stedman would have our hides if we even shot one of 'em by accident."

"I don't know why I have anything to do with you," Ed grumbled, "but a man's got to make a living, and Cord Stedman does pay his bills on time. Which is more than I can say for most of the law-abiding citizens in this town," he added bitterly. "Are you boys positive he said to replace everything? That's going to take a right smart piece of change."

"Everything," Royce confirmed, trying not to think of such a large sum of money. "You're to consult the young lady if you have any questions, but Mr. Stedman don't want any arguments over anything." Baylis whistled through his teeth, and the sound apparently made the boys so uncomfortable

19

they disappeared after telling him they'd come back to pick up the bill. Shortly after that, Ira struck up a conversation with a complete stranger and left Eliza to finish up by herself.

"She knows more about these things than I do," Ira had said with total unconcern, but Eliza was too ill at ease to keep her mind on shopping until Ed's wife volunteered to help her.

"There's no point in sparing a rancher's pockets," Ella declared, insisting Eliza choose the best of everything. "They own just about the whole state, and a more selfish passel of men you'd be hard pressed to find. Cord Stedman just may be the best of the lot, but that isn't saying much."

"I was scared of him at first," Eliza ventured timidly, "but he was really quite nice."

"There's no need I ever heard tell of for a woman to be scared of Cord Stedman, but he doesn't treat men the same, and he hates homesteaders with a passion. He might not have burned you out, but he's done that and worse to others." After that alarming speech, Eliza dared not ask Ella to tell her anything about the man who had so unexpectedly sparked her interest, but instead directed her attention to the wholly pleasant task of filling her newly covered wagon with shiny pots and cups and plates without chips.

"What about your clothes?" Ella asked after several crates of crockery had been settled into the wagon.

"They didn't get hurt. Just a little dirty."

"Then let him pay for a new dress. Or at least a length of cloth," Ella urged, moving to where several bolts of bright material were laid out for easy inspection. "That'll teach him not to bully helpless women." Eliza looked over the bolts with growing interest. "A girl can never have too many dresses, even out here," Ella hinted encouragingly. But Eliza lost interest in the material when her eyes came to rest on a gown of dark blue satin trimmed with white lace. "Do you like it?" Ella asked unnecessarily when Eliza's whole face lit up.

"It's the most beautiful dress I've ever seen," Eliza told her, enthralled.

"Then take it."

"Oh, no, I couldn't."

"Yes, you can. You deserve it."

"No, I don't. I don't have anything half as pretty. I couldn't possibly let Mr. Stedman pay for it."

"Then I'll give it to you."

"But why?" she asked in wonderment.

"Because there's nobody around here who'll look half as good in it. Besides, it's been here for six months and I'm sick of looking at it."

"But I don't have anywhere to wear a dress that fine."

"You'll find someplace," Ella assured her, closing the discussion. Eliza resisted the temptation to indulge in daydreams of being admired by everyone who saw her in the dress, and concentrated on finishing her purchases so she would be ready when her uncle returned, but Ira didn't reappear at the appointed time, and the steady flow of strangers entering the store, especially the men who stared at her with open curiosity, made Eliza terribly self-conscious. Ella took compassion on Eliza and carried her off to her own house for a bite of lunch. There she soon coaxed her whole history out of her.

"I'm not used to talking so much," Eliza apologized.

"You haven't said a word I haven't had to pry out of you."

"Uncle doesn't like it when I chatter."

"I never met any girl less given to chattering. I suppose it comes from being by yourself so much."

"It does get lonely sometimes. I've wanted to live in a town for such a long time, but now that uncle intends to open a saloon, I'm not sure I want to anymore."

"You'll get used to people around here in no time. We're just plain folks. We don't get up too much out of the way. Certainly not like those painted hussies at Lavinia's," she added inconsequentially. "What do you plan to do with yourself?"

"Uncle Ira says I'm to help him in the saloon, but I'd rather teach school."

"I shouldn't think you'd like working in a saloon very much. You're not the type. But whatever would you want to teach school for?"

"I like children, though I must admit I haven't been around them very much."

"That probably accounts for it," decided Ella.

"I know I would like teaching. Aunt Sarah used to teach me, and it was the thing I looked forward to most each day. I've read all of her books." Her enthusiasm waned. "Some got lost, and we had to sell a few of the others."

"We don't have a schoolhouse or a teacher anymore," Ella informed her. "The schoolhouse burned down last winter after some shiftless cowboys spent the night there. Then they had those killings over Newcastle way, and the schoolteacher packed her bags and skedaddled back to Ohio."

She broke off, distracted by a strident voice in the front hall; then before either of them could move, Ira pushed his way into the parlor.

"I might have known I'd find you sitting about doing nothing," he barked, glaring angrily at his niece.

"Don't you come barging into my house and shouting at my visitors," Ella challenged, firing up instantly. "Your niece worked herself silly while you were wetting your whiskers in some saloon." No female had ever talked back to Ira, but there was something about Ella's heaving bosom and the martial light in her eyes that persuaded Ira this was not the time to do battle for his male prerogatives.

"Come on," he said curtly to Eliza. "I've found us a place to settle."

"You come back whenever you get the chance, child," Ella offered. "Maybe something will come of your teaching. We certainly could use a schoolmistress around here."

"You back to that school nonsense again?" her uncle asked as they drove out of town.

"You know I've always wanted to teach."

"Put that idea out of your head for good. You'll be too busy in the saloon to have time to worry about teaching anybody's snotty-nosed brats."

"But we don't own a saloon."

"We do now. Well, almost," he corrected himself. "I haven' t been wasting my time regardless of what that old hellcat thinks. I've found us a place to live close to town and a man who's willing to take me on as a partner."

"What's it like?"

"It's not as large as I'd like, but it's got a nice big room and a bar that goes the whole length."

"I don't mean the saloon, I mean the land. Do we have a well, or is there a stream nearby? How long will we have to live in the wagon?"

"There's already a well and a house on it," her uncle replied, pleased with himself.

"Can we move in right away?" she asked hopefully.

"Sure. Croley says it was abandoned last week and nobody's moved to claim it yet."

"Is there something wrong with it?" she asked with dwindling enthusiasm.

"Of course not. There's just so much land around here nobody has to take seconds."

Eliza wondered why they always had to be the ones to take seconds. The *house* was no more than a dilapidated cabin, and she knew from experience her uncle wouldn't do anything to make it more comfortable until winter. The land didn't appear to be very fertile and the outbuildings consisted of a lean-to and a sagging chicken coop. There wasn't a cooking stove either, but she tried to hide her disappointment and think of how nice it would be not to have to live in the wagon. After all, she sighed, they might not even be here come winter.

The trip from town had been miserable; Ira had recounted every story of lawless cowboys he'd heard in the twenty years since leaving Indiana. Eliza had hoped coming to Wyoming would help him forget what happened in Kansas, but the ruckus at the creek had merely served to refocus and intensify his hatred. It had angered Eliza at the time too, but her fear had passed, and Mrs. Baylis's comments about Cord had only succeeded in increasing her curiosity about this puzzling young man.

As she began to lay the table for supper she found she remembered him in surprising detail. No one could forget his enormous size or the air of command that was so much a part of him she knew he owned the land even before he spoke. But it was his eyes she found most striking; those cool, penetrating gray-blue orbs, so well matched by his grim, determined mouth, missed no detail. Yet she felt certain some cache of humanity lay hidden behind his mask of brusque efficiency.

His coarse bushy hair was brushed back from a high forehead, and thick eyebrows nearly joined over the bridge of a strong nose. She wished his jaw were not so set — it gave him an inflexible appearance — but the face was more to her liking than any she could remember. He might not be all that handsome, but the more she thought about him the less she found she would alter.

"Have you gone to sleep in there?" her uncle shouted through the window, causing her to start violently. "When is dinner going to be ready?"

"It won't be long, Uncle," she promised, realizing she had spent twenty minutes staring vacantly into space.

She busied herself with her preparations, but Cord's image wouldn't go away. She couldn't help contrasting the erect, well-muscled body that sat so easily in the saddle, strong hands holding the reins and powerful legs wrapped about the barrel of his horse, with her thin and slightly bent uncle. She wondered if she would ever see him again. He looked so big and frightening it was a wonder she hadn't fainted when he took her hand. Just the thought of it made her light-headed.

You don't know the first thing about that man, or any other, she told herself severely. You ran from those two boys like they were murderers, yet you didn't even back away from Stedman, and he looked fierce enough to murder a dozen people. Still, Stedman saved our wagon, she thought, shaking her head.

Her uncle's angry face appeared in the doorway. "I'm going to take a willow switch to you if you don't get moving. I've never known you to act like this. Are you ailing?"

"I am a little tired," she murmured, moving quickly to set the food on the table.

"Then get yourself to bed after you clean up. There's too much work to be done for you to take sick."

24

Chapter 3

The Matador ranch house was unusually large for Wyoming. It had been built by the previous owner at the insistence of his demanding wife and ambitious daughter, but Cord was now its sole occupant and the few rooms he used were streamlined for business. He believed a cowman who lived in the saddle needed few possessions, and he didn't burden himself with anything he considered unnecessary.

The front porch sheltered two wooden benches too uncomfortable to encourage long stays, while the entrance hall served as a business center for the ranch and contained nothing more than Cord's rolltop desk and a small iron stove for warmth. The kitchen and dining room were the province of Ginny Church, his foreman's wife, and were run with an efficiency that rivaled Cord's. But with the exception of a single bedroom furnished with a narrow bed and a trunk, the rest of the house stood empty, stripped bare of its luxurious furnishings.

"This bill looks mighty large," Sturgis said for the fourth time as he paced up and down the porch.

"What do you think he'll say about it?" asked Royce, becoming increasingly nervous.

"It's what he's gonna *do* that has me worried," replied his friend, and a thoughtful silence fell between them.

"He *did* tell us to get rid of squatters."

"Well, it's plain as a pimple on your backside he didn't like the way we did it."

"But what did we do wrong?"

"He'll tell us soon enough." The sound of a leisurely tread approaching the door caused them to freeze, but it was

Franklin Church who stepped out into the twilight.

"Come inside," he beckoned, laughing softly when he saw the boys standing like stone sentinels. "The boss is expecting you. In fact, he's downright impatient to see you." The color drained from their faces, and try as he would, Royce found he could not swallow.

A single oil lamp cast Cord's rugged features into unsympathetic relief as he sat at his desk adding a column of figures. In the dancing shadows the lines of firmness showed hard and unbending, and the boys' courage faltered despite their determination to take their punishment like the men they hoped to become. Cord finished his figures and, apparently satisfied, entered the results in a ledger. Then he blotted the page, put the ledger away in a drawer, and turned to face his quaking hirelings.

"Where's the bill?" In the boys' keyed-up state, the paper seemed to grow longer and the total more enormous as Cord painstakingly checked each item. "It's a right sizeable figure," he remarked, looking up. "You can't make a practice of this, or you'll be in debt for the rest of your lives."

"No, sir," Sturgis acknowledged, crestfallen.

"But you did tell us to keep everybody off the creek," Royce reminded his boss, and received a paralyzing elbow in the ribs from his friend.

"I don't remember telling you to rope women or burn their books."

"We were only trying to scare them," Royce explained, rubbing his side and glaring angrily at Sturgis.

"Is that why you were wearing Miss Smallwood's clothes?" Royce flushed crimson at the memory. "Never mistreat a woman in my name again. Now, do you have the money to pay this?" The boys hung their heads knowing they didn't have five dollars between them. "I didn't think so. I'll withhold your wages until it's paid."

"That'll take months!" Royce exclaimed, unable to restrain himself.

"Almost until Christmas from the looks of this."

"We won't get any money at all?"

"I can lend you something along, but it'll just take you longer to pay it off." The depressing vision of Saturday nights in the bunkhouse with no cigarettes or whiskey took all the

26

spirit out of Sturgis.

"It won't seem like living without no pleasures."

"Maybe next time you'll be more careful," cautioned Cord, folding the bill and putting it in a drawer. "One day someone's going to use a rifle on you, and that can't be fixed by withholding wages. Now get along. Franklin's waiting for you in the bunkhouse." The boys shuffled toward the door, shoulders drooping and their youthful optimism utterly crushed. Cord watched with an unchanging expression until the door was just about to close behind them, then he called out, "Come back a minute." As they retraced their steps, they wondered what further calamity could befall them.

"I can't allow you to take all the blame," Cord told them. "You were protecting my property, and it's my fault if you didn't understand my orders."

"We should have known better, sir."

"You're young yet," Cord continued, "but you've got promise and I don't want to discourage you." He took out the bill. "I don't think I should have to pay all this," he said, grimacing at the total. "Let's say you'll get your wages, but not your bonus. Does that seem fair?"

"Yes, sir!" the two replied in chorus, reviving miraculously.

"Be off then and don't keep Franklin waiting." The boys stumbled over themselves in their haste to leave. They were afraid if Cord had to look at their ugly, stupid, guilty, vastly relieved faces a moment longer he would change his mind.

"He never objected when Franklin turned that squatter's wagon over and ran off his stock," remembered Royce when they were well out of earshot.

"Nor any other time," allowed Sturgis, "but I'm not asking any questions."

"You're lucky," Franklin said when they reached the bunkhouse. "No other owner would have paid that bill."

"Or cared what happened to a squatter as long as they were gotten rid of," added a veteran hand.

"Mr. Stedman's not like the other ranchers," Franklin informed them with a slightly scornful manner.

"Just the same, I don't think he would have replaced a single cup if it hadn't been for that girl. He's got some mighty gentlemanly notions about females."

27

"What did she look like?" asked Franklin.

"Royce thinks she looked like an angel," Sturgis laughed.

"Married?"

"No. The man was her uncle."

"That must account for it then, but I don't understand it. Mr. Stedman never gives the time of day to those women in town." No one was prepared to debate the point. Something had to account for Cord's puzzling leniency toward the Smallwoods.

Ira rolled a cigarette and lighted it with a quick flick of the match head on his rough pants. "I was lucky to get the chance to buy into a place like the Sweetwater."

"I suppose," Eliza answered mechanically, but the thought of serving liquor to dozens of strange men petrified her. Fatherly Ed Baylis made her edgy, while the bold men who had shamelessly eyed her that morning made her want to hide under the counter. A sharp knock at the door caused her to glance inquiringly at her uncle.

"Don't just stand there," he grumbled. "Open the door."

"But who would be wanting to see us at this time of night?" Eliza asked anxiously. "We just got here."

"If you'd open the door, we could both find out," he said sarcastically. Eliza was even more unsettled by the man standing in the doorway.

"Is this Ira Smallwood's place?" he asked in a reedy, clipped voice. "I'm Croley Blaine." Hard, calculating eyes swiftly examined Eliza from top to bottom in an appraisal so cold and unnerving she could only point to her uncle.

"Come in," Ira invited, glad of a break from the monotony of his niece's company. "Don't mind her. She's just skittish around strangers." A man of medium height, Croley still retained much of the trim, muscled physique of his youth, but Eliza disliked him instantly and her flesh quivered under the impact of his flinty, inquisitive gaze. She felt immodestly clothed despite a collar that reached to her chin.

"Go along to bed," Ira ordered impatiently. "Mr. Blaine and I want to talk business, and I don't want you dragging tomorrow."

Eliza almost ran to her small room, hiding behind a

rickety door that muffled the sound of the men's voices while providing a feeling of safety. She knew it was unfair to dislike Mr. Blaine before she even knew him, but she couldn't help it. She undressed quickly in the shadow-streaked light of the moon and climbed into the cold bed. She tried not to think about the saloon, but it appeared to be settling over her head like a malignant destiny, while her ambition to become a schoolteacher was moving farther and farther away.

"That girl's got to be part of the bargain, or the deal's off," Croley said to Ira.

"She will be."

"She doesn't look like the type. If she's that jumpy over one stranger, how will she keep her head when some drunk makes a grab for her?"

"She hasn't been around people much. She'll get used to it."

"I don't know. I'm not giving you half my place for nothing," stated Croley, unconvinced.

"You're not *giving* me anything. I paid you good money."

"Not as much as it's worth."

"It's not worth half of that unless you start getting more people inside your doors, and my Eliza is the only way you'll do it."

"In the right getup she could draw bees from a honey pot," Croley agreed thoughtfully. "Take her over to Lavinia's tomorrow. She's got a house full of gals she dresses fit to get a man's blood riled up. Your niece won't do a thing for business in a dress that covers up everything from her chin to her toes. She's not sweet on anybody, is she?"

"We just got here. She hasn't set eyes on more than a dozen people."

"Well, people have set eyes on *her*. They're already asking after the black-haired beauty who went riding out of town with an old weasel."

Ira liked being called a weasel about as much as anybody else, and he glowered fiercely. "Don't go telling everybody where I live. I don't want the place swarming with a bunch of thieving cowboys." The fury blazing in Ira's eyes captured the interest of his new partner.

"For a man fixing to make his living in a saloon, you don't seem too fond of our best customers."

"Actually I don't mind cowboys too much, but I won't have

anything to do with those high and mighty ranchers."

Croley's eyes grew bright with interest. "You had a run-in with one of them?"

"I have cause from years back to want them all dead."

"Who'd you cross up this way?"

"You ought to be asking who crossed *me*," Ira erupted. "I was minding my own business too, which is more than can be said for the swaggering hellion who owns the Matador."

"So you've run up against Cord Stedman, have you?" Croley asked, his eyes narrowing.

"If he's the big bruiser with bushy hair and eyebrows and a cocksure way that makes you ache to fill his ass with lead, then that's the one," Ira ranted.

Croley's expression was unreadable, but a trace of a smile showed fleetingly at the corner of his mouth. "He's pretty well thought of in these parts. Even the small ranchers usually find a good word for him."

"Then they haven't tried to homestead Bear Creek," snarled Ira.

Croley's grin was unmistakable now. "So you made that mistake, did you?"

"It's not private property."

"It might as well be. There's only a couple of pieces along the creek from here to North Fork not already in Stedman's name."

"He'll learn his mistake before long."

"What are you planning to do about it?"

"I don't know," Ira acknowledged lamely. "I haven't had time to think about it yet."

"You'll be wasting your time if you keep trying to claim that land. Stedman won't let you live on it, not even if they let you record it at the land office, and the sheriff won't help you."

"Doesn't anyone stand to up these ranchers?"

"There're other ways to hurt Stedman if you're really interested," Croley said deliberately.

"I want to see his pride in the dust."

"I don't know about that, but it's possible to do him a serious hurt."

"How?"

"There're people about who don't like him any more than

30

you do, but it's not safe to let it be known in some quarters. His crew is a rough lot."

"I'm not backing away from anybody," Ira declared pugnaciously.

"Save your boasting for the saloon," Croley said, rising. "Some of the boys get right frisky when they get a little liquor under their belts."

"I'm not forgetting Stedman."

"Didn't think you would. But the first thing you have to do is turn your niece into the kind of looker that'll fill the house every night. Arnett's got himself a dancer and Lavinia's girls get their share of the trade, so that doesn't leave much for us. You sure she won't quit on us?"

"No Smallwood backs down. She'll look smart enough to pop the eyes right out of their heads. She can sing right pretty too, but she can't dance."

"If she can pull in a dozen extra cowboys a night, there'll be time enough to worry about that. Now I'll say good night. I don't trust Luke not to put his hand in the till when I'm not looking over his shoulder.

The two men parted, each pleased with the agreement. Croley's cold eyes glittered with avarice when he thought of what Eliza's success could mean, but he didn't like the frightened look in her eyes. Maybe she would get used to it, but he had never known a girl to be good with men who didn't come by it naturally. Drinking cowboys didn't come down easy on anybody. If a girl started scared, she stayed scared, but it was worth a try. With Eliza's looks she'd attract attention just sitting in the corner. Besides, if things didn't work out, he could always get rid of Smallwood. The man was a fool to let hate cloud his judgment, but maybe Croley could find a use for that too.

Ira went to bed with even more sanguine hopes. He never doubted Eliza would do anything he wanted. She might be as shy as a hummingbird, but her mother had plenty of backbone and there was no reason to think once Eliza got used to the job she couldn't give as good as she got. The costume did worry him, though. Eliza was tiresomely modest, and likely to balk at anything she considered improper. He hoped Lavinia could talk her into the right kind of clothes. He could force her out on stage, but it wouldn't be any use if she was too hysterical to perform. And cringing and pulling at her dress wouldn't help either.

He'd worry about that tomorrow, but anything was better than trying to make a living from the soil. He had grown to hate the dry, powdery earth almost as much as he hated ranchers. Years of struggling against drought, sun, and grasshoppers to eke out a living had left him bitter and disillusioned. Eliza could grow a few vegetables and keep a cow and some chickens if she wanted, but soon there'd be enough money to buy anything he wanted without ever having to wonder whether the frost would kill his crop before it grew, or the rain ruin it before he could gather it.

Involuntarily Ira's mind reached back to the years when his wife and son were alive. In vain he tried to drive away memories that still had the power to splinter his self-control, but he couldn't break their grip, and the angry, belligerent man he had become dissolved into the memories of a younger self in whom laughter and happiness had, for one brief span, dwelt companionably. Blighted crops had had no power to depress him when Sarah's gaiety was there to lighten his spirits and her hopefulness to keep fear at bay. The unquestioning love of an adored son had been all the more reason to dwell beyond the crippling reach of failure. Those had been golden years, when tomorrow could always be depended upon to erase the misfortunes of today.

Then suddenly both wife and son were dead, and it was as if every light in the world had gone out. He felt cast loose, his anchor lost, but whenever he might think to embrace the comforting blackness with welcoming arms, Eliza would not let him die. Her existence tied him to an older brother who was everything he wasn't, to a time before those brief years when Sarah brought the warmth of love and happiness into his bleak life. It was hard not to hate Eliza, to blame her for still being alive, for forcing him to go on living a life that every day became a more onerous burden. She was all he had in the world, but she was a bitter exchange for what he had lost.

Chapter 4

A heavy thunderstorm struck during the night. Awakened by an ear-splitting crash of thunder, Eliza found the roof leaking and puddles of water forming on the dirt floor. Repressing a strong desire to pull the covers over her head and ignore the whole thing until morning, she stepped gingerly across the cold ground and peeped into the main room. The fire had gone out and the room was in pitch-black darkness, but she could hear the unmistakable plop of dripping water. She moved in the direction of her uncle's muted snores and bumped into the table. The snoring ended with a guttural snort, but they resumed their even rhythm as she massaged her throbbing side; her uncle had gone to sleep on the table and was completely dry. She stumbled back to her room and climbed between the damp sheets. For one who could remember nights in the rain with only the wagon for cover, she was comfortable enough, but unfortunately wide awake.

Her mind wandered, browsing through her past. She recalled the warm comfort of her Aunt Sarah's presence and the laughter of the little boy her uncle worshipped. She would never forget that bright summer day when they were both laid under the Kansas sod. Overnight she had been catapulted from irresponsible childhood into the assumption of her aunt's duties. With wrenching suddenness life had become difficult and unhappy. She was not a selfish girl or one given to expecting special attention, but she found it more and more difficult to accept her uncle's harsh treatment and disregard for all that she did. There was something stirring within her, a restlessness that made her peevish and impatient, suddenly unhappy with things she'd previously accepted without question. On several occasions recently she'd had to bite her tongue to keep from talking back, but she had never stood up to her uncle and she doubted she ever would.

The image of Cord Stedman rose up unbidden to tempt her mind from the blighting hopelessness of her life. She tried to push it aside, but it wouldn't go. No man had ever disturbed her virginal thoughts, and to discover one had taken up abode there, not to be dislodged, was bewildering. She ought to be afraid of him, but even as she had snatched her hand away from him that morning at the creek, she'd realized she was drawn to him instead of fearing him, and that had made her feel guilty.

She thought of his powerful chest and arms, only partly hidden by the sheepskin jacket, and a tremor of excitement coursed through her. How could anyone so big and powerful not be dangerous? Even now those sultry eyes, screened under craggy brows that acted like a protective barrier against intrusion, agitated her peace. The outline of his heavy beard on smooth-shaven, tanned, and weathered skin only served to heighten the impression he was outside the limitations that fettered and confined more ordinary mortals.

Yet she sensed that behind his cold, efficient exterior there burned a fire of unfathomed magnitude. She could feel its heat escaping through those hypnotic eyes. She stirred in bed, pulling the sheet over her breasts as a shield against the intense, compressed energy of that man. She wondered if he was always so untouched by ordinary human emotions, or if his feelings were merely buried out of sight of others. He was so much bigger than life, the kind of man she read about in her mother's books, it was difficult to imagine him doing the ordinary things other men did. Still, it was this unapproachability that made his kindness all the more unexpected and inexplicable. She wondered if he really would pay that awful bill, but immediately felt ashamed of herself. She *knew* he would. Cord Stedman would never go back on his word.

She tried to imagine what he was really like, but her experience of men was so limited she was forced to fall back on the fictional heroes in her books. Bit by bit she began to weave a fantastic and exotic past centered around his hooded eyes and hard mouth. She fabricated tales of daring adventure and improbable peril—to her astonishment she found herself the heroine of each episode—and imagined him vanquishing opposition and scattering foes with the ease of a giant among pygmies. Enmeshed in these pleasurable fantasies she drifted off to sleep, a tiny smile on her lips and her dimpled cheek resting on clasped hands.

Ira left for town next morning after breakfast. He promised to fix the roof if he got the chance, but Eliza was to see to the floor before he got back. She cleared away the breakfast things, fed the stock and turned them out, and then directed her full attention to making the cabin fit to live in; she didn't hear the bellows of her milk cow until they became a cry of distress.

Following the mournful sound to a hollow that ran behind the cabin, Eliza found the cow mired up to her shoulders in a small lake of muddy water. A shallow basin, lying directly in the path of the runoff from last night's downpour, had filled up during the night and turned the sand-mud mixture into a sticky bog. The poor creature was exhausted by her struggles and could only bellow helplessly.

Eliza had no idea how to free such a large animal from a quagmire, but she knew the cow would drown if something were not done soon. She kicked off her shoes, hitched up her skirt, and waded into the icy water, but she was speedily persuaded the ooze would imprison *her* just as firmly as it had her cow if she dared go any farther. She fetched her uncle's extra length of rope from the wagon, but fifteen minutes later she still hadn't succeeded in tossing the lasso over the creature's head.

"You deserve to drown, you stupid beast," she scolded in angry frustration. "Why did you have to go in so far?"

The sound of horses hooves caused Eliza to turn around in alarm, but her flight was arrested by the sight of a tall, proud man astride a black gelding. Without knowing where she got the courage, Eliza ran toward the road calling and waving her arms to attract the attention of the owner of the Matador.

Cord had no way of knowing Eliza's uncle had settled into the abandoned cabin along his route into town—he would have dismissed it as immaterial if he did know—but there was an element of youthful impulsiveness in his response to her call. Sturgis and Royce were left behind when he kicked his steed into a gallop, and with a flurry of lashing reins and raking spurs, they rushed to catch up, realizing only when it was too late to draw back that they were being summoned by the same female they'd tried to run off Bear Creek. Royce nearly swallowed his tongue; Sturgis wished he'd thought to complain of a bellyache after breakfast.

"My cow will drown if you don't get her out," Eliza called, too excited to realize her words didn't make sense.

"Where is she?" Cord asked, dismounting with unhurried movements.

"Behind the house. The rain must have flooded it during the night. It wasn't there yesterday." Cord never once asked what *it* was.

"How long has she been stuck?"

"I don't know. I was inside and didn't hear her. I tried to get her out, but it's too soft to wade in, and I couldn't get a rope over her head."

"I expect the boys will have to dig her out."

"But the water's freezing."

"I know. We have to dig our cows out all the time. They're never satisfied unless they're up to their knees in water."

If the boys had had any attention to spare they would have been surprised at Cord's talkativeness, but they were too numb to notice anything more subtle than a thunderclap. Each had put on his best clothes—Sturgis had astonished his friends by washing his neck and face—only to be told they had to wade chest-high into an outsized mud hole. After yesterday's misadventure, this was a nearly mortal blow to their youthful vanity.

"Don't be so slow getting started," Cord said quietly, and the boys started taking off boots, spurs, chaps, vests, anything they could remove in Eliza's presence and remain decent. Sturgis refused to remove his hat, which he had painstakingly decorated with a red bandanna, and he waded into the water with it still pulled down over his eyes. When he started to swim, Eliza was put in mind of a large turtle, and she had to fight to hold back a gurgle of mirth.

The exhausting work of diving under the water to dig out

each hoof fell to Royce. The frigid water quickly depleted his strength, and as he had nowhere to rest and replenish his oxygen, Sturgis would hold his gasping and sputtering friend atop the cow until he had recovered enough to dive once again. Suddenly the wretched bovine set up a pathetic mooing, a signal she had given herself up for lost. She refused to make any effort to free herself, and even after her feet were released from the mud and she began to float, she merely lay there rolling her eyes, flopped over on her side like a hot-air balloon. Sturgis tried to stir her interest by twisting her tail.

"Pull, for God's sake," yelled Royce, holding the cow's head out of the water, but the uncooperative beast spun completely around, and the boys had to push instead. A tiny choke escaped Eliza.

"I'll put a rope on her," Cord called. He measured out a couple of lengths and after a few practiced twirls, sent it sailing through the air to settle easily over the unresisting animal's head. Sturgis tightened the noose around her horns, and at Cord's signal, his gelding began to pull the water-logged animal to shore. She lay perfectly still, resigned to a fate that no longer awaited her, until she felt herself scrape bottom; then she recovered her will to live with a vengeance. As Sturgis and Royce approached the shore in her wake, she gauged the distance to an inch and chased them both back into the water as far as the rope would allow.

"I don't think she likes your red handkerchief," Cord hollered to Sturgis with the barest hint of a smile. That must have been the case, for the cow kept her baleful eye so firmly fixed on Sturgis, Royce was able to deploy around and wade to shore. "Do you hobble her?" Cord asked, mounting his horse.

"N-no," Eliza answered with shaking voice. "S-she g-grazes where she c-can." Cord took her a few hundred yards away and joggled the rope off her horns. Free again, the ungrateful beast trotted away, shaking her head at the men who had rescued her.

"You'll never be able to go into town looking like that," Cord said when he got a look at the bedraggled pair.

"I can wash out your clothes," Eliza offered. "You can wait in the house until they're dry."

Sturgis and Royce vacillated, torn between common sense

and a desire to put as much distance as possible between themselves and this disastrous female.

"Thanks for the offer, Miss Smallwood," Cord said, amusement dancing in his eyes, "but it seems they have a mind to walk back." However, it was impossible to trudge twelve miles in their boots, dripping mud and water the whole way, so the boys moved off toward the cabin, dejection showing in every line of their bodies.

Eliza burst out laughing the minute the cabin door closed behind them. "It was the one who twisted her tail like a windup toy, like she would moo and give milk."

"She wasn't much help, Cord commented, his eyes crinkling in merriment.

"Then she floated like she was already dead," Eliza wailed helplessly.

A handful of muddy clothes sailed through a narrowly opened door and landed on the porch with a wet plop; suddenly Eliza became aware of Cord's nearness, and a tightening in her chest put an end to her laughter.

"You really don't have to wash those clothes."

"It's the least I can do after my cow behaved so badly. They did look so nice." She felt the need to be doing something, and she hurried to gather up the muddy garments.

Minutes later Eliza had the clothes in hot soapy water, but her sense of ease had vanished. She had washed her uncle's clothes for years, but she no sooner pulled a pair of underwear out of the tub than she was badly jolted by the reality of the boys' physical presence. Theirs was not an impersonal male body she had known since birth, they were strangers, young and virile, and they were in her cabin *stark naked!* The clothes seemed to burn her fingers, and she hurried to hang them up, hoping Cord wouldn't notice her shaking hands.

Eliza wasn't fearful of Cord, but she was conscious of him in a way that was wholly different from her awareness of any man before, and she found this far more unsettling than ordinary fear. She could understand her uneasiness around the boys, but she couldn't even begin to unravel the inchoate mass of feelings about Cord that was turning her brain to mush. It was as though she was being lured onward by something that shocked and fascinated her at the same time. Never before had she been so vitally aware of a man s physical presence, nor could she remember feeling this tug of physical attraction. Now the sheer power of it literally took her breath away. She felt helplessly caught in the toils of something she didn't understand but which exercised an irresistible attraction over her.

Cord eased the situation by carrying water to the house for the boys' bath, but once the clothes were hung up and the last of the dirty water dumped into the ditch, Eliza couldn't avoid his nearness.

"You know, I still don't know your name."

"It's Elizabeth Smallwood," she replied blushing, "but I'm never called anything but Eliza."

Eliza timorously raised her eyes from the ground. He certainly was handsome. She didn't know that she'd thought about it before, but there was no doubt in her mind Cord was her ideal. He was big and powerful, and she felt sure he could protect a girl if he wanted to, yet there was something about him that was vulnerable, something that made her feel he was not quite unapproachable. He was looking rather stern just now, but somehow that drew her to him rather than scared her away.

"Miss Smallwood, those clothes will take some time to dry," he said with slightly stiff formality, "and I've got business in town. Will you tell the boys to join me when they're dressed."

"No!" Eliza cried, plummeting from of her daydream with the suddenness of a child tumbling down a haystack. "They can't stay . . . I mean, not by themselves . . . my uncle would be so angry," she sputtered in a welter of half sentences.

"They won't bother you again," he assured her, puzzled by the alarm in her voice.

"You can't leave them here."

"But they're only boys."

"I couldn't take . . . I mean, how will they get . . . they're *naked*," she finally managed to say, gesturing helplessly toward the clothes on the line. Cord smiled.

"I have a better idea. Why don't you come with me and meet your uncle in town."

"That would be even worse!" Now he really didn't understand.

"Then we'll wait under this tree," he said, and led Eliza to a bench built around the trunk of a large cottonwood. Settling himself on the ground, he picked up a piece of wood and took out his knife. "What made your uncle decide to come to Wyoming?"

She spoke haltingly at first, but as the minutes passed and Cord continued to whittle quietly, asking just enough questions to keep her talking, she lost her nervousness and began to speak more easily. Her face lost some of its tautness when, laughing at some of her own stories, she told him of the years when her aunt was alive; he understood some of her uncle's dislike of cowboys when he learned his wife and son had died of scarlet fever brought to Kansas by Texas drovers. It was some minutes before she was calm enough to continue, but Cord whittled silently, allowing her plenty of time to compose herself.

"After that Uncle was too unsettled to stay in one place."

"You must be a great comfort to him."

"Uncle Ira doesn't place much value on girls," she said without rancor. "Some days I don't think he even knows I'm here."

"How could anyone not notice you?"

"He'd notice soon enough if his dinner was late," she said in a funny, sad way. Cord stood up, sending a shower of thin shavings to the ground; in his hand he held a carved head of Eliza's milk cow.

"Oh!" she exclaimed. "It's beautiful. How could you do it so quickly?"

"It's just something I do."

"But I was chattering all the while. Why didn't you tell me to be quiet?"

"I like to listen to you," he said simply.

"That witless cow doesn't deserve to have her likeness made," she said, unable to believe anyone would want to hear her talk.

"She's your cow so you take it," Cord said, holding the carving out to her. Eliza looked at him, then at the carving, and then back at Cord.

"Do you mean it?"

"Of course."

"Are you sure you don't want it for yourself?"

"I've got too many. Go ahead. Take it." When she still hesitated, he took her hands and closed her fingers about the smooth wood.

"It's beautiful," she sighed, looking up at Cord with a rapturous gaze that caused his pulses to beat a little faster. Could she possibly be the lovely, unspoiled girl she seemed?

"I wonder if the boys' clothes are dry," he said, turning his mind from a line of thought that was at once disturbing and intriguing. "They must be tired of being shut up in that cabin."

Eliza didn't hear him because Ira was galloping furiously toward them.

"It's only your uncle," Cord assured her, startled by the fear in her eyes.

"He'll be so angry." The color was gone from her face. "You've got to leave at once."

"But the boys—"

"There's no telling what he'll do."

"It'll be all right once he knows why we're here."

"You don't understand. He *hates* cowboys."

"He can't be too mad, even if he is still angry about yesterday."

"It's not just that. Uncle gets unreasonable if anyone even *mentions* cowboys."

This was hard for Cord to understand, but he soon found Eliza hadn't overstated the case.

As the horse thundered toward them, Ira slid to the ground and headed for Cord like a cow after its calf.

"What the hell are you doing here?" he demanded furiously. "Isn't Bear Creek enough for you, or do you want all of Johnson County?" He pulled Eliza behind him without taking his blazing eyes off Cord.

"I only stopped to pull your cow out of the lake."

"You're lying, cowboy. There's no lake here."

"The rain made one, Uncle," Eliza said, trying to explain as she stepped from behind her uncle, but Ira pushed her back again. "I couldn't have gotten her out by myself."

"She was close to drowning when we happened by," said Cord.

"What do you mean *we?*" Ira demanded, ignoring the muddy lake he couldn't deny existed. "You trying to gull me that you aren't alone with my niece?"

"The other two got covered with mud and I had to wash

their clothes. They're in the cabin." Eliza pointed to the shirts, pants, and undergarments drying in the sun.

"Do you mean there are naked men in my house? You Jezebel!" Ira grabbed Eliza by the shoulders and shook her so hard she stumbled and struck her cheek against the bench. A second later Ira was lying on the ground with blood running from his mouth.

"Your niece has been in full view of the road the whole time we've been here," Cord informed the dazed man. Then he gently removed Eliza's hand from her face to inspect the ugly bruise, and his eyes blazed with an anger that would have caused his own men to quake. However, Smallwood was beyond heeding danger signals, and he leapt to his feet and ran toward the house. There was a momentary confusion of voices, then a shot rang out and the door almost exploded off its hinges. Royce and Sturgis, naked as the day they were born, hurtled out of the cabin. With a horrified gasp Eliza clamped both hands over her eyes.

Cord reached the house as Smallwood aimed his shotgun at their fleeing buttocks. Catapulting through the air, he encountered Ira just as the rifle went off, and they hit the ground with such bone-jarring force Ira was knocked almost senseless. Cord shook him like a dog with a rag doll, but his pungent curses bounced off Ira's armor of fury. Realizing Ira couldn't be reached with words, Cord picked him up, carried him over to the lake, and pitched him in headfirst. The shock of the ice-cold water cooled Ira's rage with painful rapidity, and he rose to his feet, shaking his head to clear it.

Royce and Sturgis had only one thought in mind when they fled the cabin, to get out of the range of Ira's shotgun, but once the threat of instant death was removed, they were horrified to find themselves almost on top of Eliza. Even though her hands were tightly pressed over her eyes, they scrambled for their still-damp clothes, scattering clothespins far and wide in their attempts to jump into their pants as they ran.

"Get back to the cabin," Cord ordered. "I'll keep him here until you're dressed." They looked like they'd rather enter the gates of Hell, but they had no choice unless they wanted to dress in full view of the road. Since they would have spent the rest of the day in the lake rather than be unclad when Eliza opened her eyes, they bolted back to the cabin.

"Are they gone?" Eliza asked in a quavering voice. Cord's gravity deserted him, and he broke into a shout of laughter. Eliza didn't know that fewer than a dozen people had ever heard Cord laugh, but she was too dazed to care; her uncle, muddy and humiliated, felt no amusement either.

"Get off my land," Ira snarled, wiping the mud from his eyes, "and take those fools with you."

"We'll be off as soon as we can." Cord glanced at Eliza, but didn't speak to her. Her situation was difficult enough without his adding to it. "I'd see about putting a fence around that sink if you're meaning to settle here. We get heavy rains right often."

"I don't give a damn what happens to that cow!" Ira bellowed. Cord shrugged indifferently, and fortunately for Eliza, who was looking ready to faint, the boys emerged from the cabin and made straight for their horses.

"Thank you for helping me," she said, defying her uncle's wrath. The boys mumbled their response without looking back.

"Good day, Miss Smallwood," Cord said. He glanced uncertainly at her uncle before riding after the boys.

"I go to town to see about making a decent living, and what do I find when I get back?" stormed Ira. "You have one cowboy acting like he's courting you and two more naked in the house. You couldn't blame folks if they took you for a hussy."

"I couldn't let them go off wet and muddy," Eliza protested, "not after they rescued my cow."

"You should have let the damned cow drown, you stupid girl," he hollered, pushing her before him toward the house. "You quiver and shake every time I mention helping out in the saloon, yet you sit here talking to Mr. Big Britches just as bold as you please."

Eliza tried to explain once more, but her uncle wouldn't listen.

"Maybe if you pretend the customers are Stedman and his hands, you can curl up in their laps. That ought bring the cowboys from miles around. Now get inside and get my dinner ready."

Cautiously fingering the spot on her cheek where a bruise

43

showed quite plainly now, Eliza remembered the feel of Cord's hand on her cheek and a dreamy look settled over her face; it didn't seem to hurt so much anymore. Her uncle's sullen features slowly faded as she withdrew into a world where a man would rather suffer torture than hurt a female.

Chapter 5

"What ails you, child?" Eliza shook so badly Lucy could hardly button up her dress. "There ain't nobody out there but cowhands, and you're so pretty they won't care if you sing like a crow."

In the flickering lamplight, Eliza's deep-red gown shone like velvet. The arms, neckline, and hem were trimmed in a red-black net that made the ruby color of the dress look even richer, but the most striking contrast was created by the milk white of Eliza's flawless complexion.

"I've never seen anything like it," Lucy marveled, "and I've been dressing gals for more than thirty years."

"Nobody's supposed to have skin like that," Lavinia said enviously. "If it was my hide, I'd be queen of St. Louis, not this squalid little cow town."

But Eliza's appeal didn't rest solely on her dress or her skin. Her raven-black hair, piled high upon her head to expose the nape of her neck, ignited the fire in her eyes; thick brows, long lashes of the same color, and vermilion lips were drawn with bold strokes, while deep mortification lived as a perpetual blush in her downy cheeks. Earrings and bracelets dangled from her person, their imitation stones flashing in the light, and a single red stone hung from a narrow black band around her throat. The ensemble was completed by a large feather fan which Lucy had tried, without success, to teach Eliza to use provocatively. Eliza was about to sing for the first time, and she was petrified.

"Now you listen to me, child," Lucy said. "You're prettier than a litter of kittens. All you have to do is sing your best and their tongues will be hanging out. Now what's there to be scared of in that?"

"I don't know, but I'm petrified. And to have to wear a dress like *this!*" Eliza didn't quite know what to think of the woman she saw in the mirror. It shocked and horrified her, but she was also thrilled; the woman in the mirror was beautiful, and Eliza desperately wanted to be beautiful.

"They'll be so stunned they won't be able to move. And when they hear you sing, oh, glory, they'll be quiet as lambs."

Lucy's assurances made Eliza feel a little better, but her fears returned as Ira accompanied her on the short walk to the saloon.

"Wait here," he said, taking her in the back door to a small office. When she was alone in the cold, dingy room, Eliza's courage fled. How could she have ever have believed she could go through with it?

"They're ready," Ira announced with suppressed excitement when he returned.

"Please, Uncle Ira, I can't . . . ." she began.

"I've had enough of your complaining," he declared angrily. "Anybody ought to be able to go out there and sing. Now take that thing off and let me see what you look like."

Ira's whole future was riding on the next few minutes and he was almost as nervous as Eliza, but when she had reluctantly removed her cloak, a wide grin of satisfaction spread over his whole face until his dark, sullen eyes shone bright with triumph.

"There isn't a place this side of the Mississippi that wouldn't pay a fortune to get you," he crowed, almost dancing with joy. "I'm going to be rich. Now stay outside the door until I announce you. Then give them your friendliest smile and walk straight to the piano. You can be a little standoffish if you like, but not enough to make them think you're too good for them. Remember, it's just ordinary cowpokes out there, not fancy ranchers."

What if Cord Stedman was out front?

The question hit Eliza with dizzying impact, and she felt a small dollop of reckless pride stiffen her flagging spirits. Would Cord like her singing? She *could* sing. Uncle Ira often said it was her only accomplishment, but Eliza knew she sang well and that knowledge gave her something to stiffen her courage. Suddenly it mattered very much how she did tonight. It wasn't enough that she just survive; she had to do her best.

Her new sense of purpose wasn't sufficient to banish all her fears, but it was enough to keep her from casting her pride into the dust and running out into the night; it was enough to enable her to marshal her wits and follow her uncle down the narrow hall even though her heart was pounding so hard she felt dizzy.

The noise and the smell of smoke and whiskey hit her full in the face, but she didn't have time to worry about how she was going to breathe or find her way through the blue-gray cloud that filled the room. Ira was already introducing her.

". . . young lady kind Fortune had brought to Buffalo. Her face is the equal of Europe's famed beauties, her voice that of an angel."

"If she's so damned good-looking, how did you get her past Lavinia?" one drunk asked to raucous laughter.

"In a tow sack," someone replied.

"She's a *lady*," Ira declared loftily. Unfazed by Ira's buildup, the audience joked among themselves and shouted for Ira to "sit down and let the little lady talk for herself."

"Sing," corrected his companion.

". . . welcome the lovely *Belle Sage*." Behind the door, a puzzled Eliza looked around for a second performer; in the throes of inspiration, Ira had neglected to tell Eliza he'd given her a stage name.

"I don't see nobody," said one cowboy, beginning to feel like maybe he was being made fun of. Others showed signs of becoming rowdy, and Ira quickly backed through the door.

"Are you trying to get us killed?" he whispered fiercely.

"Who is *Belle Sage*?" asked Eliza.

"*You're* Belle Sage, you little fool. It's a stage name. Now get out there before they tear the place apart," Ira hissed, and shoved Eliza through the doorway.

No one had paid much attention to Ira's introduction, and consequently they were struck dumb when they found Eliza exceeded his extravagant praise. Even Croley could hardly believe this gorgeous creature was the stammering, fearful girl he'd seen just a few nights earlier. The transformation was nothing short of magical, and a hush fell over the room.

"Sing!" Ira whispered imperatively, and somehow Eliza

47

was able to reach the piano. From years of habit the bedazzled piano player's fingers began to move over the keys, and out of Eliza's mouth came the loveliest silver thread of a soprano voice he ever heard. After the initial shock of seeing her, some of the men had started to whisper among themselves, but hers was a restful, easy sound, the kind a man could listen to for hours, and they listened with rapt attention.

The quiet bolstered Eliza's confidence, and when silence greeted the end of her song she felt even better. She gave the pianist the name of a second song and a lilting tune filled the room.

"Sing something lively," Ira prompted, and Eliza launched into a spirited polka her aunt had taught her. This time the room erupted with shouts of approval, and bewildered by the sudden burst of noise and activity, Eliza fled. The loud cheers followed her down the hall, and she didn't stop until she reached the sanctuary of the small office. Ira was close on her heels.

"They're crazy about you!" he shouted, elation overriding irritation. "Get back out there."

"I can't," she hiccupped, on the verge of tears. Ira's dreams of riches threatened to turn into fear of being chased out of town, and his anger mushroomed. Only Croley's arrival, his face wreathed in smiles, forestalled an explosion of wrath.

"The boys are wild. Every one of them is stamping his feet wanting to know when she'll be back."

"She's coming back right now," Ira said fiercely, preparing to drag Eliza through the door if he had to.

"Let her alone. I told them she'd be back in an hour."

"Why?" Ira demanded.

"Because they'll have to wait for the second performance, and most of them will spend the time drinking. Some have already left."

"I *knew* she shouldn't have stopped."

"They've gone to tell their buddies about her. Before the hour's up, we'll be turning them away. Little lady, I never thought to see anything like it, but when you opened your mouth that was a stunner. How did you learn to sing like that?"

"I've always been able to sing," Eliza told him.

48

"Well, you can sit back and relax. Have something to eat, a little champagne maybe, anything you want as long as you do it all over again in an hour."

The last rays of sunlight were fast sinking behind the green hills, enveloping the horizon with a blanket of purple twilight, as nature streaked the sky with one final slash of orange and blue before putting away her pallet. Cord rode leisurely across this living canvas, oblivious to the familiar beauty of the sunset or the vastness of the quiet that settled around him; he was headed for town, and he wasn't sure why.

His outfit had come in from spring roundup a few days before, and his was the only ranch to come through the winter with virtually no losses. Cord knew the ever-increasing thievery was due to rustlers, but to say so only stirred up bitter feelings. He also knew the big owners who lived in Cheyenne and farther east were fed up with rustlers operating without hindrance or fear of reprisal. The winter's losses had them talking about taking the law into their own hands, and why not? The ranchers in Montana had done it, and now they enjoyed complete freedom from the predators who were threatening to drive cattlemen out of northern Wyoming.

Cord didn't hold with their idea of range justice, but they hadn't asked for his opinion. He was an ex-cowhand himself, and they looked on him with suspicion; some even said his rise had been too rapid to be honest.

Cord didn't bother to defend himself. There were those who knew how he bought steers in the spring, fattened them and shipped them out in the fall, then re-invested every penny in his own breeding stock. But not everyone cared to learn the facts, and he would be branded suspect if he raised his voice against them. If he didn't, he would still be suspect, so he held his peace. He never attended the Association's meetings because he had nothing to say to men who looked upon Wyoming and cattle as nothing more than a source of income. To him it was a way of life, and one he wouldn't trade for the finest mansion on Cheyenne's Walnut Avenue.

Yet however much these thoughts disturbed his peace, they wouldn't have caused him to head into Buffalo when he had a week's work to do and the town was full of cowboys working off the excesses of roundup. He had heard talk of a new singer at the Sweetwater Saloon, a beauty who was drawing the men for miles around, but it was a chance conversation between Sturgis and Royce that had fully engaged his attention.

"It's that gal we ran off Bear Creek during the winter."

"You're crazy. That female is scared of her own shadow."

"I swear it's the same one. The boys at the Crazy Z can't stop talking about her. Seems they've been sneaking off to town every night."

"Doesn't the foreman catch them?"

"He's there ahead of them." They had laughed, and after making plans to go into Buffalo when it came their turn for a night off, they had talked of other things.

Cord had tried to put it out of his mind too, but his figures wouldn't add up and he kept forgetting his sums in the middle of the column. He couldn't forget Eliza and her huge black eyes, and the only way he was going to get any work done was to see for himself. Then maybe he could figure out why he couldn't get this girl out of his mind. After Eugenia, that shouldn't have been hard.

Cord had arrived at the Matador one blazing hot summer in the spring of his maturity, handsome, virile, and anxious to prove his manhood. One glance at Cord's powerful chest and forearms, bare and glistening from a brisk wash under the bunkhouse pump, and Eugenia Orr was only too willing to help. That hooded gaze and firmly set mouth were an irresistible challenge and she set about his conquest; Cord fell without a struggle.

He first tasted the heady delights of her warm and yielding flesh in a quiet, dusty glade, and fell hopelessly in love. Certain Eugenia cared as passionately for him, he had asked her to marry him. A single peal of laughter, cruel and taunting, shattered his dream and destroyed his innocence.

For the next six months, through the worst winter to ravage the West in a hundred years, Cord had worked to drive Eugenia out of his mind. Unending blizzards decimated the Matador herds, and Pierce Orr, already deeply in debt from building the enormous house, was forced to sell his ranch. No one would pay Orr for lands he didn't own, herds that no longer existed, or a huge house in the middle of a desolate plain, and the only buyer who offered the cash he needed was Cord Stedman. Even then Cord's inheritance hadn't covered the whole purchase price, and he'd had to borrow the rest.

Eugenia had come to him in the bunkhouse, now empty of the roistering cowboys whose jobs had disappeared, and offered him what he had so ardently desired just a few short months before, but the moment his lips met hers, he knew he never wanted to touch her again and he stalked from the bunkhouse. She was gone when he returned.

Eliza had brought back the memory of that summer, and Cord wondered if he might not be making the same mistake all over again. But then he would remember her wide-eyed gaze and the trembling innocence that were so unlike Eugenia's sultry self-confidence. This was no pampered, over-indulged siren toying with his heart for a summer's amusement, but a young girl too afraid of life to have yet discovered the power of her attraction.

He remembered every syllable she had ever spoken to him, and the simplicity of her words and the honesty of her gaze were beyond doubting. If he feared falling in love again, if he was reluctant to open his heart to the possibility of deception, the fear was for himself alone. Timid, antelope-eyed Eliza would never betray anyone she loved.

Cord doubted she could be the girl who was singing for rough cowboys in the smoke-filled saloon, but he remembered her unnatural fear of her uncle's wrath, and his protective instincts stirred, sending prickles of worry and anger up his spine. What if Eliza was being forced to do what she found frightening and distasteful? Instinctively Cord's legs tightened around the girth of his gelding, sending him into a canter.

Don't be in such a hurry to make a fool of yourself, he admonished. Maybe you're imagining things. Maybe it isn't Eliza Smallwood after all. And if it is, maybe she doesn't object to singing. His mind told him to slow up, and his feelings warned him to calm down, but his heart urged his gelding to still greater speed.

Chapter 6

The weeks had passed in a blur. Each day Eliza moved through the familiar routine of cooking, cleaning, and tending her animals, but every evening she would sing at the Sweetwater. She didn't lose her dread of performing before strangers, but the crowds were small and she gradually lost the worst of her fear. Then the roundup crews returned, wild and randy, and not even a real angel could have kept them respectful for long.

"How about a little leg, sweetie?"

"Come closer. I can't hear you."

"I'd love to see all that hair down on your shoulders." Panic seized Eliza, and she ran from the room.

"Are you crazy? You can't walk out on those men just when they're getting warmed up," Ira yelled when he finally caught up with her.

"One of them grabbed at me," Eliza told him, quaking from head to toe.

"They're just trying to be friendly. It wouldn't hurt you to be a little friendly back."

"He *grabbed* at me."

"I heard you. He grabbed at you," Ira mimicked.

"I can't go back in that room."

"Get this through your head. You're going back in there if I have to drag you."

"They don't mean any harm, Miss Smallwood," Croley said, closing the office door Ira had left open. "They'll settle down real quick once they hear you." Croley was just as anxious as Ira to have Eliza go back, but he realized Ira was getting her so wrought up she might not be able to sing for days.

"Why don't you go sit with Lucy for a bit. That ought to make you feel better," Croley suggested, draping the cloak over her shoulders. "Let her alone!" he whispered furiously to Ira. "Can't you see she's near to fainting?"

Ira accompanied his niece in frigid silence, his tightly contained anger unmistakable. "I'll be back in an hour," he growled when he left her at the door, "and you'd better be ready."

"Land sakes, girl, what happened?" Lucy asked, gently guiding Eliza to her own room. "You gotta stop this crying, or you're gonna look like a windowpane in a rain storm." A hiccup of laughter elbowed its way through Eliza's sobs, and the tears quickly ceased to flow. "Now tell me what's got you so upset."

"It's my own fault," Eliza admitted. "The men started *saying* things and then one of them touched me." She shuddered at the remembrance of the large hairy hand that had brushed her bare arm.

"They're just looking for a little fun."

"I won't have them mauling me," Eliza sniffed.

"Then tell them! Look down your nose until they're afraid to touch you."

"I can't. Just thinking about it makes me start to shake."

"You gotta get over that real quick, honey. Men don't pay attention to timid females. You want your husband to walk all over you?"

"I'm never going to get married."

"Nonsense. A gal as pretty as you could have a dozen husbands." A picture of Cord flashed through Eliza's mind and she blushed involuntarily. "Aha!" observed Lucy sharply. "You're already sweet on someone."

"No!" Eliza stammered, blushing fiery red. "I never thought of it."

"Well, never mind that right now. There'll be plenty of time for figuring out what you *do* feel after you get used to the boys out front."

"I'll never get used to it."

"Yes, you will. It'd be a crime for you to stay hidden away in that old cabin where nobody can see you. There's nothing wrong with a farm, but get yourself a husband, and maybe

53

all this hiding yourself away will have some purpose." Lucy's raised eyebrow caught Eliza between embarrassment and laughter.

"I'm not used to thinking of men that way."

"Then start. They're sure thinking about you that way, and you'll never get anywhere talking at cross-purposes."

"But I can't talk to men. I just stare at the ground."

"You won't stand tongue-tied when it's the right one."

Eliza thought of the quiet interlude under the tree with Cord. She hadn't felt scared then. He was such a big man, so fiercely capable and determined, yet she saw nothing threatening in his powerful, six-foot-three frame. In fact, she couldn't imagine how any man who owned his own ranch and tended his own cows would look any different; being at ease with him was just as natural as breathing.

"But first you gotta tend to those cowboys at the saloon." Eliza's daydream vanished, and the harsh reality of rude, lusting men thrust itself upon her again. "You're going back with your chin up and dare anybody to come near you."

"I don't think I can."

"You've got to. You know your uncle is never going to let you stop singing. You might as well make up your mind to it right now, or you'll never be able to sing in a real theater."

"I could never be good enough for a place like that."

"Yes, you will, but you gotta get over these silly fears first. Nothing else stands in your way." The door opened without a warning knock and her uncle stood in the opening, scowling morosely.

"You ready?" he barked. Eliza looked imploringly at Lucy.

"Remember, dare them to touch you," Lucy whispered, and gave her an encouraging smile. Eliza couldn't hope to do as much as that, but desperate courage stiffened her will. She had given up any hope Cord would come listen to her sing, but even if he wasn't present to see her perish in this miserable place — she felt like she was being thrown into a pit full of wild beasts — she refused to die a coward.

The room seemed smaller and more crowded than ever. Keeping her eyes straight ahead, Eliza walked over to the piano with what she desperately hoped was regal disdain.

The room grew quieter. There were a few whispered comments, but no voice stood out and she was betrayed into a nervous smile. There was never anything disdainful about Eliza's smile; it was friendly, open, and a terrible mistake.

"That's a pretty smile, lady."

"You got pretty teeth too." A ripple of amusement cracked the tenuous restraint. The noise abated during her ballad, the talkers being noisily hushed by their neighbors, but when she finished there were immediate demands for a lively tune. Eliza obliged with a folk dance, and before the first verse was over two cowboys had started to dance with each other.

"Don't waste your steps on Clem when there's a gal right in front of you," prompted one onlooker.

"Otis doesn't know how to dance with a girl. He ain't seen nothing but cows since he was thirteen."

"Give her a whirl. I bet she'll show a prime leg."

Eliza's voice faltered, and the piano player glanced at Ira out of the corner of his eye, but she didn't stop.

"Don't be bashful. Go on, dance with her."

"He's afraid."

Otis turned to Eliza with a wordless invitation; she kept on singing.

"Ask her. She can't say yes unless you do."

"How about it, Miss Sage?" Otis begged, almost as self-conscious as Eliza. She shook her head and glanced imploringly in her uncle's direction, but he looked away. Two more men got up, each asking her to dance and being refused. One tried to take her hand, but she snatched it away. There was no escaping from the room; every inch of space was filled by a milling mass of men who looked to be all mouths asking her to dance, all arms trying to pull her on to the floor, all bodies keeping her hemmed in. Still she kept on singing.

Suddenly a man emerged from the whirling mass and pulled her roughly toward him. Her desperate protests were lost in the crescendo of merriment, and he whirled her about, sending her spinning into the arms of another man, who spun her around until she became dizzy. The music seemed to pick up speed, only a little at first, and then so rapidly she couldn't keep up. Faces began to lose their focus and she felt like she couldn't get her breath; the room started to spin so fast she was sure her legs would buckle under her any minute.

Then the grip on her fell away, there was a distinct thud, and the music stopped. The noise ceased just as abruptly. When Eliza's vision cleared the men in the room were locked into place like so many wax images, a maelstrom stopped in mid-stride. Two men lay sprawled on the floor, and miraculously, Cord Stedman stood before her.

"Are you all right, Miss Sage?"

Astonishment held her speechless; she couldn't even nod her head "Somebody throw these two out," Cord ordered, and moments later the two bodies were sent tumbling into the street. "Now, if the rest of you will be seated, maybe Miss Sage will finish her song."

"What the hell do you mean busting in here like you owned the place?" Ira exploded, oblivious to Eliza' s effort to resume her song. "This is not Bear Creek."

Cord stared at him with smoldering anger. "Is this your niece?" he demanded.

"That's got nothing to do with it. This is *my* saloon and—"

"I wouldn't be surprised to find out you're not related to her at all. A *real* uncle wouldn't toss his own flesh and blood into a dog pit. Even dumb animals care for their young." The audience was not misled by Cord's appearance of calm; he never interfered, but when he did, he meant for things to go *his* way.

"You can't tell me how to take care of my kin."

"Somebody ought to. Seems like you can't get the hang of it yourself." Cord's bushy brows almost met in the center of his head, and his eyes sank further behind their barrier, the lids lowered, his look hooded and speculative.

"He looks like a cougar about to pounce," one man whispered.

"You don't deserve a niece as beautiful and talented as Miss Sage," Cord went on. "Protecting and providing for her should be an honor no man would lay down as long as there was breath in him. And you boys are a disgrace to the calling that gives you your name," he said, turning to face the bemused cowboys. "Bother her again and you'll explain it to me. Touch her and you'd better be south of Douglas before sunrise." Cord's left hand was balled into a tight fist, a fact missed by very few.

Eliza knew she had to be dreaming. No one had ever said such things about her. The idea of protecting her, of providing for her, of being proud of her was almost too much to comprehend. Such things only happened in books, yet in less than three minutes this strange, enigmatic man had turned her whole world upside down, dumped her miserable existence into the dust, and handed her a new, exciting self, but one so much like a princess she could hardly believe it was real.

"I hear tell you usually sing three songs, Miss Sage. If our manners haven't given you a disgust of us, I'd be mighty grateful if you would oblige with another."

Eliza managed to nod her head this time.

He didn't move from his command post. The musical introduction began and Eliza struggled to gather her paralyzed wits and remember the words.

She sang from habit alone. Cord's presence, the rigid attention of the listeners, the atmosphere of forced courtesy made everything seem unreal. She didn't know if she was doing her best; she was still reeling with shock, and all she wanted to do was disappear until she could have time to think.

No one moved until the last note had died away.

Once the applause stopped, Eliza didn't know whether to thank Cord for his intervention, ignore the whole episode, or sing another song. Instead, after a slight hesitation, she left the room.

"Now that you remember how to behave around a lady, see that you do," Cord admonished the crowd, then nonchalantly walked from the saloon.

Usually Eliza hurried to Lucy to change her clothes and go home, but she was so dazed by what had happened she retreated to Croley's office, sank into a chair, and succumbed to the most wonderful feeling of her life. A man had protected *her*. A nobody! He had knocked two men down and even threatened to knock down more. The feeling was unbelievably delicious and she wanted to savor every minute of it.

"That interfering bastard," Ira roared, bursting into the room in a boiling rage. "What did you two do under that tree?"

Eliza sat up a little straighter. Unconsciously, Cord's protection, combined with Lucy's support and her newfound popularity, had come together in one evening to give her a different perception of herself. It would have been too much to say she had gained a realization of her own worth, but she had grasped the tenuous idea that she had value she could give or withhold to her advantage. Even her uncle sensed the change in her.

"It's high time somebody took that man down a peg," he finished a little lamely.

"But it's so much nicer to have them listen quietly. You said from the first that's how you wanted it to be. And now Mr. Stedman has seen to it they won't bother me again."

"Damn the man! This is my saloon," Ira burst out. "I decide whether or not the men dance with you, and I think it's a great idea. We can start a lottery. We'll draw numbers with a different man getting one dance every night."

"No!" shouted Eliza.

"Can't you see what a money-maker this will be? You're a lady who can sing like a canary instead of screech like a bobcat. I might even charge for the dances. No, I'll make it an extra. I'll raise the price of whiskey instead."

"I won't be auctioned off," Eliza declared rebelliously.

"I've got to talk to Croley about redoing this whole place," Ira continued as if Eliza hadn't spoken. "If we're going to charge higher prices, we've got to have a fancier decor. I wonder if it'd be a good idea to get some more girls—maybe give free chances on them too? No, I don't think so, not with you as a centerpiece. But I'll have to talk to Croley."

"I won't do it," Eliza announced so vehemently her words finally pierced Ira's armor of self-absorption. "I'll quit."

"What?" thundered her incredulous uncle.

"I said I'd quit. Then I could become a teacher." Eliza's newfound courage wavered, but it held.

"Who put such a crazy idea in your head?"

"I've always wanted a school," Eliza replied eagerly, emboldened by her first taste of defiance. "And Mrs. Baylis says they haven't had a teacher for almost a year now.

"I told you to stay away from that woman."

"I sometimes go there while I wait for the second performance."

"Then stop it right now. And put this idea of a school out of your head."

"No."

"What did you say?" Ira sputtered, thunderstruck.

"I said I won't stop going to see Mrs. Baylis, and I won't give up the idea of a school. Please, I can keep fixing your dinner and singing."

"You won't do anything of the kind."

"Then I won't sing anymore." Eliza was as surprised as her uncle to hear the words come out of her mouth, but having said them she clung to them tenaciously.

"Of course you'll sing," he growled, too shocked at Eliza's ultimatum to rage at her. "Now let's have no more talk about this. You've had too much excitement and it's gone to your head. You'll feel more like yourself tomorrow."

"I'm not going to change my mind tomorrow or the next day."

"And just what do you propose to do?"

"Mrs. Baylis has asked me to come live with her. She says I work too hard. She also says I shouldn't be singing in a saloon and wearing dresses no God-fearing female would be caught dead in."

"You tell Ella Baylis to mind her own business. You'll do as I say, or I'll lay a broom handle across your backside."

"I'll tell Mr. Stedman." The words, out before she knew it, caused her uncle to regard her with an ugly expression.

"You would dare to trust a cowboy before your own uncle?"

"He said he wouldn't let anyone touch me."

Ira was nonplussed. He'd never encountered opposition from Eliza. That she would claim the protection of a stranger was the crowning blow.

"I swear I'll sing every night," Eliza promised. "And school is only for the summer. Please, Uncle, it's the only thing I've ever asked you to do for me."

"And if I don't?" he challenged.

"I won't sing." The tiny thread of determination was gathering strength, and Eliza spoke her words with stiffening resolve.

"Only if it doesn't affect your singing," Ira said, sufficiently staggered by the thought of losing the money Eliza brought in to own himself beaten.

"Thank you, Uncle," Eliza said, giving him an impulsive kiss on the cheek. "I promise you won't regret it. She gathered up her cape and hurried from the room, leaving Ira to wonder what had brought about this change in his niece.

"Miss Smallwood?"

Eliza nearly jumped out of her skin. She spun about to find herself looking up into Cord Stedman's smiling face, and she was suddenly so addle-brained she could only stare at him in confusion. Each detail of his appearance was burned into her brain, yet every time she saw him, his physical magnetism stunned and bewildered her as completely as it had that first day by the creek. She didn't know why she should be so breathless — she had only covered half the distance from the saloon to the Baylises' store — but she felt like she needed to sit down.

"I wanted to thank you for the other night," she muttered absently. The warmth in his eyes caused her heart to flutter so badly she was in danger of losing her train of thought. "I don't know what would have happened if you hadn't been there."

"Nothing much, but they won't bother you again."

"No," she said lowering her eyes. "Not after what you did."

"They're just boys," Cord told her, as though it explained everything. "They don't know how to treat a lady."

"Maybe they don't think a woman who sings in a saloon is a lady. I know Lavinia's not."

"You shouldn't know anything about women like that," Cord said, a dark expression settling over his face.

"I don't really, but I can't help but guess some things."

"What are you doing going to her place?" Cord demanded with a spurt of anger.

"Lucy helps me dress. I don't know anybody else except Mrs. Baylis."

"There has to be some way to keep you out of that place. Lucy may be a good soul, but the less said about Lavinia the better."

Cord lapsed into thought and Eliza gazed up at him in beatific bewilderment. It was so difficult to believe anyone would take an interest in her, she'd nearly talked herself into believing she'd imagined the other night, but here he was worrying about her again. No girl could have ever been as happy as she was just now.

"You have a mighty pretty voice, but you shouldn't be singing in a saloon either." Eliza flushed with pleasure.

"I have to. At last Uncle Ira has a chance to make a go of something, and I can't let him fail because of me."

"He'll make money without you."

"But not as much, and he has set his heart on having the biggest saloon in Buffalo. This is the first time he's asked me to do anything except keep house. I owe him something for taking care of me all these years."

"You're mighty loyal."

"I promised Aunt Sarah I'd take care of him. Besides, I don't have any other family."

"Don't you have any men friends?" She was too busy blushing to notice the increased gravity in his expression.

"Men don't like plain girls, and it's hard to look pretty in a faded dress with dirt on your nose and perspiration on your forehead."

"You look pretty to me," Cord said softly. "I thought so before I ever saw you in that red dress."

"I don't like to wear it," she confessed, "but Uncle and Lavinia said I must."

"It suits the occasion, but you're made for sunlight and open air." Eliza thought she would burst with pleasure.

"Maybe, but I'll probably go on singing until there's no one in all of Wyoming who ever wants to hear me again."

"Is that what you want?"

"No, but Uncle hasn't been able to settle down to anything since Aunt Sarah and Grant died. Maybe if the saloon is a success, he'll be happier."

"Isn't there something you want for yourself, not to please your uncle or make money?" Eliza didn't answer immediately, but Cord could tell from the guarded look in her eyes he'd touched a soft spot. "There is, isn't there? Won't you tell me?"

"You'll laugh," she said reluctantly. "Uncle says I'm a great fool to even think of it."

"You know I never agree with your uncle."

Eliza was betrayed into a smile. "Okay, but only if you

61

promise not to laugh."

"I promise."

"I want to be a teacher." She paused, expecting some sign of disapproval, but when he just stood there waiting, she had the courage to continue.

"I've always wanted to be a teacher. Mama was a teacher before she married Papa, and so was Aunt Sarah. She taught Grant and me."

"Have you taught before?"

"No," she confessed, "and I imagine it will be quite a shock at first, but I'm sure the children will learn to mind and I'll soon know what to do." Cord doubted children could be made to mind so readily, but he didn't say so.

"Buffalo doesn't have a teacher, and they don't have a schoolhouse either," she told him. "The children want to learn. They just need someone to teach them."

"Have you talked to anyone about this?"

"No, but I'm determined to . . ." Eliza suddenly ducked into an open door leaving Cord alone in the street. "It's Uncle," she whispered urgently from the doorway. "He's coming this way."

"But surely—"

"He must not see us together. Please keep walking."

"I shouldn't—"

"Please!" she begged, and Cord reluctantly resumed walking toward the little man Eliza was so anxious to avoid. But he swore to himself one day Eliza would walk at his side without fear.

Chapter 7

Ella Baylis was not entirely pleased to find Cord Stedman on her front porch. He had acted pretty highhanded on more than one occasion, and some people were reluctant to stop and chat with him.

"What are you doing here?" she asked bluntly. "If you want Ed, he's still at the store."

Cord grinned and Ella understood why women rarely spoke unfavorably of him. "I'd like to come in if you'd let me."

"Come on. I'm not afraid of you."

"I didn't expect you would be, but you'd have no cause to be afraid of me anyway."

"Sit down. I'll get a crick in my neck if I keep looking up at you. What's on your mind?"

"Building a schoolhouse."

Ella was not usually caught off balance, but that was such an unexpected response she half turned around before settling into her own chair. "You got a passel of misbegotten brats you want taught to read?"

Cord's eyebrows moved close together and the eyes began to retreat behind their barrier.

"Now don't start glaring at me like a hawk at a prairie chicken. That was meant to be a joke, but I'll apologize for it nonetheless."

Cord's smile reappeared. "Miss Smallwood, the young lady who sings at the Sweetwater—"

"I know who she is," Ella said, interrupting.

"—wants to teach, but she says Buffalo doesn't have a schoolhouse."

"Since when did you get interested in educating children?"

"I'm not."

"In the teacher maybe?"

"Well, it's got to be that, doesn't it?"

"You believe in straight talking, don't you?"

"It saves trouble."

"I say you're *asking* for trouble. Her uncle has been talking, and it seems you figure large in his conversation, but not high in his opinion."

"I'm not one to go looking for trouble, but I don't run from it either."

"I didn't imagine you would, or go around it when you want something either," Ella replied thoughtfully, "but that doesn't explain what you're doing here. I don't run this town and I can't build a schoolhouse."

"You know who can. It shouldn't be too difficult to get some men to put up the building if you get the county to provide the money."

"As well as permission to do it in the town's name?"

"That too, but I don't plan to wait on the town. My boys can put up a school on my land easier than asking people here to help, but that won't answer as well as one built with town backing."

"What about opposition?"

"I hadn't figured on anything more than a little foot-dragging. That's what I wanted to talk to you about."

"About lifting those feet and making them move faster?"

"Yes, ma'am. You might say that."

Ella enjoyed a rumbling laugh. "I like you," she stated unexpectedly. "I don't know why I wouldn't, what with those broad shoulders and smoldering eyes the girls talk so silly about, but you get right to the heart of things without any shilly-shallying and oiling up to people."

Cord shifted uneasily under the burden of praise. "People generally know when you're lying."

"Maybe, but that doesn't stop them. Which brings me to ask how you propose to enlist everyone's help."

"I was hoping you could do that for me, ma'am. Being on the outside here, I'm not the one to go asking for favors, especially if it means having to come up with money."

"True, though it shouldn't be hard. The women are desperate to find a teacher. If they knew there was one already here, they'd have their husbands here before sundown."

"And the town council? I don't like to push everything off on you, but—"

"Gentlemanly of you, but I'll get Ed to do that. I'll stick with the wives. Despite all their talking and posturing, there's not a man who won't move the faster for a little prodding."

Cord's open and friendly eyes made him look amazingly attractive, and Ella wondered how Eliza felt about this surprising young man.

"Now that brings us back to you." she said.

"Just what do you mean by that?"

"What do you expect to get out of this? You needn't try sweet-talking me into thinking you're out to build good relations with the homesteaders and merchants. I'm not a fool. And whatever reason you have to think Eliza Smallwood will welcome this intervention, her uncle is liable to refuse to allow her to have anything to do with it if he thinks you're behind it."

"I was hoping you could front this whole thing so he wouldn't have to know I had anything to do with it."

"And Eliza?"

"She's not one to make trouble."

"Nor know how to handle it once it's stirred up. You can bet your last maverick Ira Smallwood will make her life miserable if he discovers your hand in this."

"Begging your pardon, ma'am, but I don't think he will."

"Why not? He's completely selfish."

"I had a little talk with him," Cord said with a deprecating smile, "and explained he ought to take better care of his niece if he didn't want someone else to do the job for him."

Ella stared; you never could tell about these quiet ones. Here was a great big lump of a man never showing the slightest interest in any of the women only too anxious to throw themselves at him. But let a shy, schoolteacher type show up, and he not only takes the trouble to see to her welfare, he decides it's time Buffalo has a schoolhouse and wastes no time in seeing it gets one. And all the while no one is supposed to know he has anything to do with it. Rather clever, this cowboy, and clearly determined to get what he wants.

"I'll take on your project, but I never knew a good deed

65

that didn't lead to a lot of bother and aggravation. How soon do you want this schoolhouse?"

"Would the end of the week be too soon?"

Ella gaped.

"I don't see any sense in putting off things," he explained.

"No, and the sooner we give Eliza a chance to get started the better," Ella said, faint but recovering. "You leave things to me."

"The boys and I will be willing to help."

"I hope you won't take offense, but it might be best if you didn't. There's a lot of bad feeling toward big ranchers, if not you directly, and I'd just as soon not be a party to causing any ruckus."

"That's okay with me, ma'am, but it's not all I came for."

"You got something else in your craw?" Ella's curiosity was aroused.

"Yes, ma' am, I do."

"Then out with it. I never thought you'd be bashful over anything."

"It isn't that I'm bashful exactly, but I'm afraid you might say I've overstepped my limits. You might even be so displeased you'd withdraw your offer to help with the schoolhouse."

"I can't imagine what you can be thinking of that's so terrible, but as the schoolhouse is a benefit to the town, I'll try and keep an open mind."

"It's about Miss Smallwood going to Lavinia Pruitt's every night." Ella's look of amiability began to frost over. "It's not fitting for a nice girl to know about women like that, much less talk to them and know what goes on in that place."

Ella thawed completely. "I've told Ira Smallwood a dozen times if I've told him once he should be ashamed of himself, but he never listens," she said.

"That's because he doesn't have another choice. Eliza won't stop singing, so that's not the way out either. The only solution I see is for some decent woman to keep her belongings for her." A weaker man than Cord would have begun to study the carpet or the wallpaper, but he heroically engaged Ella's baleful glare.

"Are you saying I should allow Eliza to bring those disgraceful clothes into my house and help her get herself up to look like some Hell-bound harlot?" she demanded, her ample bosom swelling with indignation.

"No. I'm asking if you won't help a young lady who has no place to go but a whorehouse and no one to see after her but a madam."

"Phew! When you go after something, you use your teeth."

"Then you'll help her?"

"How can I refuse when you put it like that?"

"I never thought you would."

"Cord Stedman, you're a conniving devil. I never met a man in my life with more gall, and any female who allows you to lend her a hand, much less talk to you for as long as five minutes, is weak in the head."

"I sure do appreciate all the trouble you're taking," Cord said with a broad smile that made Ella's knees weak.

"Get out of this house before you talk me into something that'll cause trouble between me and Mr. Baylis. I've given my word, so I'll keep it, but don't let that fool you into thinking I'm grateful for your visit, because I'm not. And to think I didn't go see Anna Maude because she's such a complaining female. Let that be a lesson to you, Ella Baylis. The Lord visits plagues on them that seek to evade their Christian duty."

"Is that how you see me, as a plague?"

"That's a nice word compared to what I'm liable to call you unless things works out a sight better than I expect. Now you get out of here and go look after your cows. Come back in a week or two and we'll see what progress I've made."

"I'm coming, I'm coming," Lavinia shouted crossly in answer to the imperious knocking at her front door; the brightly colored robe she threw over her shoulders did little to conceal her straining bosom and deep cleavage. "Of course you girls are too busy to do a small thing like open a door," she remarked caustically to three scantily clad young women lounging in the sitting room, waiting for the first customers of the afternoon.

Lavinia flung open the door with a jerk. "We ain't open—"

"Then cover yourself up. Nobody would ever guess it to look at you." Ella Baylis was at the door, and if one could judge by the fire in her eyes and her flaring nostrils, there was at least one dragon in her pedigree.

"What are you doing here?" gasped Lavinia.

"Let me in and I'll tell you," Ella stated, and marched past Lavinia without waiting for an invitation. "I bet you wouldn't keep a *man* waiting on your stoop." Ella came to a halt about a half-dozen steps into the hall and turned slowly, her widening eyes taking in every detail of the gaudily decorated interior. "I came for Eliza Smallwood's things. It's a disgrace for a respectable girl to know about this place, much less come here every night."

"If you think you can come in here and insult me—"

"I would if I would lower myself to speak to you," Ella stated somewhat illogically. "Give me Eliza's things without a lot of bother, and I'll never set foot in this place again."

"Polly," Lavinia called up the stairs with a shriek that was nearly impossible to identify as human. "Have Lucy bundle up Eliza's things and bring them to the front hall. And step on it."

"Make sure she doesn't forget anything. I don't want to have to come back here again."

"Get everything!" screeched Lavinia, before turning on Ella. "Now get out before I throw you out."

"It'd take more than you to move me from any place I wanted to stay," Ella snorted contemptuously. "I'm not leaving until every piece of that child's clothes has passed through that door ahead of me."

"To hear you talk, you'd think we had the plague."

"*You're* the plague. If Eliza would take my advice, she'd burn anything that came out of this pesthole. Stand aside. Now that I'm here, I might as well see what a cathouse looks like." She started down the hall, looking into one empty parlor after another, Lavinia following helplessly in her wake. "Sodom and Gomorrah can't be anything to this place," Ella said in wonder. But her eyes positively bulged from her head when they came to rest on the three girls.

"Hussies!" she exclaimed, indignation, condemnation, and consternation ringing in her tone. "You should be ashamed to get out of your bathtub without more on your bodies."

"Now see here," said Lavinia, firing up. "You can't come marching in here and insult my girls."

"Jezebels is what they are," Ella exclaimed, snatching up a cover from one of the sofas and throwing it over the girls. "How dare you flaunt your shame." The girls were unafraid of any cowboy living, but they shared an ingrained dread of a righteous woman.

"Leave if you don't like what you see," stormed Lavinia, who was *not* daunted by outraged virtue. "They're the finest young ladies this side of St. Louis."

"Young ladies!" shouted Ella, her eyes growing more enormous by the minute. "Tramps and strumpets is what they are, and it's what they'll remain until they stop painting themselves worse than any Indian." She advanced upon Dorine and took her unresisting face into her hands. "You should be ashamed to call yourself a female," she said contemptuously, and planting her thumb in the middle of Dorine's pouting lips, smeared the heavy red lipstick in a broad line across her cheek and chin.

"Eeek!" shrieked Dorine, jumping to her feet to stare at herself in the mirror just as Ella, her wrath fully stoked, attacked the shrinking Belle.

"Pull your dress up," Ella commanded, giving the thin garment a yank intended to draw it up over Belle's exposed bosom. Instead, the flimsy material came away in Ella's hand, and Belle stood up in her brassiere and panties. No one was more startled than Ella herself, but having begun a job, she was not one to leave it unfinished, and turned to her third victim. The girl wore her hair in thick, black mounds piled high on her head. Ella pulled out the large pin that held the heavy braids in place, and as the terrified girl shrieked and danced about, she gave the hair a vicious twitch. The whole thing came off revealing a head of thin, ordinary brown hair. "Your harlots don't even offer genuine goods," Ella intoned in righteous triumph.

Lavinia had never lacked courage, but the unprecedented events had occurred so quickly she stood with her mouth open and her own ample bosom in danger of escaping its token bondage. "Out!" she screamed, nearly hysterical. "Get out of my house immediately."

"Not before I sweep this place clean," vowed Ella, her blazing eyes lighting upon a large fan. "Get to your rooms and don't come out till you're decent," she ordered, raising the fan over her head. Uttering a volley of shrill screams, the girls scampered out of the room. Lavinia gave a gasp and sat down in the middle of the floor.

Lucy entered the hall to find Ella standing over her mistress like a lioness at a kill.

"Are those Eliza's things?" Ella asked with all the sangfroid of one making an ordinary request. Lucy nodded, speechless. "Then have the goodness to follow me. Do you help Miss Smallwood dress?" Again Lucy nodded. "Good. Bring her to my house in time to get ready for her performance tonight. This *woman* is unable to attend to her any longer." Ella marched from the room, stepping over Lavinia with all the unconcern she would give a mud puddle after a spring rain.

Cord didn't wait two weeks, or even one. Three days later he hailed Ella in the street, and on the following day he was on her porch before she'd finished lunch. When he stepped into her husband's hardware store on the day after that, she boiled over.

"I never met a more impatient, pesky, bothersome man than you, Cord Stedman. You don't give a body a moment's rest."

"Ella, you know better than to talk to a customer like that," Ed Baylis said in mild surprise. "He's liable not to come back."

"And where's he going to get his supplies? Over to Casper? You go on back to your barbed wire and pay no attention to me. Mr. Stedman knows what I'm talking about, and if he doesn't know I don't mean half of what I say, then he ought to." Ed Baylis merely shook his head. He'd been married to Ella over thirty years and he'd never yet made a profit from interfering with her, or suffered a loss from letting her have her head.

"As for you, Mr. Cat-on-a-Skillet, the sooner that blessed school is up the better I'll like it. You've hounded me until I'm worried to death."

"Ma'am, you know I haven't."

"I don't know any such thing, coming into a decent woman's parlor looking too scrumptious for words, talking me senseless until I agreed to I don't know what, and then dogging my heels to see it's done. And don't trouble yourself to deny it, because I don't plan to listen to a word you say. The sooner this mess is over the sooner I can rest easy."

"When will that be, ma am?" Cord asked with enough artful innocence to save him from having his face slapped, but enough saucy amusement to make her wish she'd done it anyway.

"This weekend. The wives jumped on the idea like a hen on a bug. They've bombarded Eliza with so many questions I'm almost afraid she'll back out."

"She won't. You sure I can't help?"

Ella considered a moment. "I don't see why not if you come by yourself. It'll give you a chance to mend a few fences as long as something doesn't happen between now and then."

But something did happen. The next day the body of a small rancher was found hanging from a tree in a gulch some miles from town. He had been taken away from his home eight days earlier by some deputy marshals whose papers were now presumed to be false. The poor man's wife had not recognized anyone, but they were widely assumed to be in the hire of the big ranchers, and feeling was running high against those ranchers allied with the Association against the small ranchers and the homesteaders.

Undeterred by the widespread hostility and hoping to get a chance to talk with Eliza, Cord pulled his hat over his eyes, and his presence wasn't remarked upon until one man looked up to receive a board from his neighbor and found himself staring straight into the cool eyes of the towering cowman.

"What are you doing here?" he demanded, letting the board drop.

"Helping raise the schoolhouse," Cord said, picking up the board and handing it to him again. "Which is more than you'll be doing if you don't hang on to things better." A couple of men nearby paused in their work.

"Don't you know what happened to Nash?" the man asked.

"You're here, and you know."

"But you're a rancher."

"So are Curly and Jesse, and you didn't drop anything they handed you."

"They had nothing to do with Nash's death."

"Why do you suspect me and not the others?" The men looked at each other uneasily.

"You can't deny you're a big rancher."

"I deny I had anything to do with hanging Nash, and I don't belong to the Association."

"Ask the Dalton brothers what he does," came a voice that took care not to be identified.

"I don't allow anyone to help himself to what's mine. I pay for what I get, and I expect others to do the same."

"Nash didn't take anybody's property. You big guys are trying to starve all us little fellas out."

"You call Nash's thousand horses a little outfit?" demanded Ella, making her way into the center of the group. "And which one of you thought to send a side of beef so his kids could eat?" The men, never at their best against a woman, began to mumble. "You've all got children, but none of you would be here if your wife hadn't made you, yet this man's a bachelor and he gives his beef and his time. And if your cowboy friends are so fine and upstanding, why aren't they here this morning?"

Chapter 8

"I'm not afraid of those boys, ma'am," Cord told Ella as he accompanied her to the hardware store and the "boys" went back to work on the schoolhouse.

"A lot of good your bravery will do today. We need work, and you'll do nothing but stir up trouble if you show your face."

"I don't hide behind a lady's skirts."

"I didn't expect you would, but there's a time and a place for everything. Those men could easily do something foolish."

"That may be, but I have to live here, and if anybody gets the idea I back away from danger, particularly a paltry threat like this, I might as well hand over my cattle and be done with it."

"I suppose you're right. The devil! Why did God make men so stupid? Oh, go on if you must stick your head in a noose, but don't say I didn't warn you."

Cord headed back to the schoolhouse, providing her with an excellent view of his strong back, erect carriage, and unhurried walk. She sighed and trouble knitted her brow. He had never cared what went on in Buffalo before, so why did he have to start when things were worse than ever?

Two married ladies greeted Cord with friendly smiles and received a nod and a good morning for their trouble. Since he rarely spoke to anyone, they were pleased with themselves until they saw the change that came over him when Eliza called his name from across the street. His sleepy disinterest vanished, a kind of tightly restrained energy filled his whole body, and his eyes were more open and intense.

"Would you look at that," sniffed one, struggling to hide her envy. "I'm glad he didn't look to me like that. I would have had to be rude."

"I hear she's forever in and out of *that place*." "That place" was how the respectable ladies of Buffalo referred to Lavinia's.

"They say she's quite respectable. Besides, she's going to have the school."

"Hrump! I'm glad I don't have any children old enough to attend any school *she* runs."

Unaware of the dark mutterings, Eliza met Cord with unalloyed pleasure. "Have you seen the schoolhouse? Mrs. Baylis says it will be finished before nightfall. Can you believe it? It's a miracle."

"It is something of a surprise. Seems you only have to make a wish, Miss Sage, and it's gratified."

"Please don't call me by that hateful name," she begged. "I could never bear it if you only thought of me as a saloon singer."

"I'll always think of you as the girl in the brown dress with her cow mired in the mud." A glimmer of merriment chased her frown away.

"Uncle still gets angry whenever he sets eyes on that cow. To hear him tell it, she intentionally got into trouble so you'd have to stop and lend me a hand."

"Do you have any other animals in need of help? A lame horse? A chicken that won't lay eggs?"

"Now you're teasing, and I never understand it when people tease me."

"Then I won't do it again. You have enough trouble without my adding to it."

"Not as much as before. Mrs. Baylis went to Lavinia's two days ago and took all my things to her house. I heard there was an awful scene, but now Lucy comes to *me*. It makes singing not half as bad."

"Mrs. Baylis is a very kind woman."

"There's more to it than that, but no matter how much I plead, she won't tell me. Oh, dear, I'm chattering again."

"I don't mind." Cord's eyes were wide open and friendly, but his gaze was so heated and the tension caused by his closeness so intense, Eliza suddenly felt uncomfortable.

"Let me show you the school house," she said hurriedly. Cord thought it would have been better if the men didn't see Eliza acting quite so friendly, but she was totally unaware of the tension. Leading him around the structure, she explained how each part would offer some advantage on that much anticipated day when it would be filled with the bright faces of dozens of eager children. Her ingenuous enthusiasm garnered a few smiles from the fond pupils' fathers.

"She never showed half that much interest in singing," observed one.

"Why would a pretty gal who can sing better than any I ever heard want to waste her time teaching?"

"Whatever her reason, you oughta be grateful. After what happened with the last teacher, we're not likely to get another one out here for some time. Especially not for the pay this town offers, and school only lasting four months. A body can't survive on that."

"Did you see the way she went slap up to Stedman just like she'd known him all her life? If one of us was to speak to her, she'd run like a doe."

"She's probably just grateful. Since he dropped those cowboys, there hasn't been any more trouble at the saloon."

"Would you touch any girl Stedman had his eye on?"

"Don't be a fool. I wouldn't touch *anything* Cord Stedman said to leave alone, especially his girl."

The Sweetwater had been refurbished and the inside glittered with bright lights, but a new building was already under construction that was three times as large, and when Croley and Ira finished turning the old saloon into a dining hall with rooms upstairs for lodgers, they expected to have a virtual monopoly on the trade.

Ira mingled with the customers, enjoying his new stature as Eliza's uncle and a successful owner. He had started to wear fancy clothes, this evening a burgundy-colored suit with lavish dull-gold trim and off-white hat and boots, and was rather vain about the figure he cut about town. He stopped at a table where a group was discussing Nash's death, now some two months past, and after listening for only a few minutes, he drew up a chair.

"Stedman's behind it," he said, "but he's too clever to be seen in it himself."

Two men familiar with Ira's prejudice winked at each other, but the third man took him seriously. "Cord isn't connected with the Association. They put him on the blacklist for buying mavericks at roundup for ten dollars a head. They don't like sharing that kind of deal with an ex-cowboy."

"You've been gulled," insisted Ira belligerently. "Stedman's hand in glove with the barons."

"I don't know where you get your information, friend, but you've been handed a load of bad dice. I used to work for an outfit near Sybelle Creek, one of the inside group, and they were hard set against all cowboys who turned their hand to ranching. Cord is the most successful ex-cowboy in Wyoming, and what he's done, others hope to do. The big ranchers don't want that."

Realizing Cord's reputation had actually benefitted from his talk with this loud-mouthed stranger, Ira left the table swearing, but Eliza's appearance caused him to swallow his curses. Watching these rough, unsentimental men sit hypnotized by her singing was balm to his wounded pride; it also meant money in his pocket. By the time her performance had ended in a storm of applause, his good mood was restored, and he went through the remainder of the evening without thinking about Cord again.

Eliza's worried expression deepened as she surveyed her students. It was the third week of school, and more than half the seats were still empty. She had been certain the schoolhouse would barely hold all the children who would show up the first day, but the dire predictions of the disgruntled were proving to be correct. Some parents didn't care enough to see their children made the long journey into town each day, and it was much more enticing to the children to get lost in the shoulder-high grass of the valleys and draws than to spend the day cooped up in the schoolhouse.

"Put your books away, children. It's time for morning recess." Almost before the last words were out of her mouth, several boys were on their feet and headed for the door, leaving their books still open on their desks or tumbled onto the floor in their hurry to be the first outside.

"I'll pick them up, Miss Smallwood." It was nice to have a student as eager as Melissa Burton, but even Eliza found her Goody Two-Shoes attitude, along with her habit of tattling on everyone, extremely wearing.

"That's okay, Melissa. I'll take care of it. You go on out and enjoy the fresh air."

"I'd rather stay in and get ahead on my next lesson."

Eliza gave up and went outside. Melissa was sixteen and already two full levels ahead of anyone else, which meant Eliza would have to spend even more of her precious time preparing lessons especially for her.

Today the children could choose their own games, and they broke up into groups largely determined by age and sex, and soon were busily working off some of the energy they had stored up during their morning's lessons. Watching them play naturally, without restraint and bursting with high spirits, Eliza forgot her concern over the truants and marveled at the energy, excitement, and animation in the bright, hopeful faces. They alone seemed to be untouched by the fear and hatred that wrapped its tendrils around Johnson County a little more tightly each day.

"You look like the old woman in the shoe." Eliza's face broke into a smile at the sound of Cord's voice, and her heart immediately began to beat double-time. Fortunately she did not blush, but her face felt hot and her brain was in a fever of excitement.

"Did you come to see if I survived?"

"I knew you would. I was wondering how your students were getting along."

The cloud descended on her face again. "The ones who come are making good progress, but there are so many who aren't here."

"How many?"

"I can't be sure. Maybe a third more."

"Where do these come from?" he asked, indicating the children in the yard.

"Town mostly."

"It seems enough to me." Looking at the mass of running, shrieking children, Cord felt there were too many for any one spot.

77

"Every child in the county needs to learn to read," Eliza stated earnestly. "It will be doubly hard for them when they grow up. Aunt Sarah taught Uncle Ira, and she said teaching a grown person was the hardest thing she'd ever done." She smiled ruefully. "It's not easy for the children to concentrate on their work either when they know their friends are out in the hills having a delightful time."

"Miss Smallwood, Otis is pulling Sarah Jane's pigtails."

Eliza felt trapped and rather irritated. It was hard enough to keep her wits about her in Cord's presence without Melissa dropping trouble in her lap.

"Tell him to stop, or I shall give him an extra page to copy out."

"I already did."

Eliza hesitated. She was too kindhearted to punish Otis in front of the others, but she couldn't let his behavior go uncorrected.

No such reluctance troubled Cord. "Otis Redding, if you touch Sarah Jane's hair once more, I'll tan your backside right here in the middle of the school yard." The offender, in the process of possessing himself of the second pigtail of the shrieking Sarah Jane, stopped as if shot. He released his quarry, who ran away with shrill jeers and a promise to "sic my brother on your dirty hide." The children resumed their activity, but at a subdued level.

"You may go back and play, Melissa."

"I shall begin my reading."

Eliza wondered whether it was harder to endure Melissa's help or Otis's pranks.

"You seem to have your hands full."

"They're no problem really. They just kick up a fuss when they have free play. If Melissa could just learn to mind her own business . . ."

Cord's eyes seemed to laugh. "Content yourself with keeping Otis from cutting off Sarah Jane's pigtails before the end of the summer."

"Do you think he would?"

"Certainly. Think of what a trophy that would make."

"You're teasing me again," she said, feeling unaccountably shy. "I know I've got a lot to learn, but they are good children and they work so hard."

78

"Are you enjoying it?"

"Yes, and no," she confessed after a pause. "I love to see their faces when they learn something they didn't know before and are so proud of themselves, but it's an awful lot of work. I hardly have enough time to get everything done for the next day. And if all the students came who should, I never would catch up."

"Those missing students really disturb you, don't they?"

"Of course. Now that we're a state, things are going to change quickly, and they'll have to be properly educated or spend the rest of their lives regretting it."

"Don't let them wear you down," he said, moving toward his horse. "After all, you're doing them a favor." Eliza walked with him.

"I'm being paid," she said proudly. "Didn't you know?"

"No, but if you're paid as much as a cowhand, I'd be surprised."

"I'm paid thirty-five dollars a month."

"Do you remember those two boys who stopped you at the creek, the ones who have trouble getting out of their own way? I pay them forty-five dollars a month, twelve months a year, not just four or five months in the summer. Go back and demand a raise." He swung easily into the saddle. "Now I have to get back to *my* charges before some of them disappear."

Eliza was disappointed at his coolness and the briefness of his visit, but when she turned back to her students, she found several of them staring at her with open curiosity.

"Was that Mr. Stedman?" asked one girl, agog with excitement.

"Of course," said one of her classmates. "Who else rides that big gelding and acts like he owns everything this side of Powder River?"

"My dad says he's a terrible fierce customer, and shoots people for the fun of it."

"That's a lie. He just breaks their legs."

"You should not gossip," Eliza admonished, horrified at the conception the children had of Cord. "Now it's time to go inside and begin your reading lesson."

"Will you tell us about Mr. Stedman, ma'am?"

"I can't. I hardly know him." Eliza had intended her words

to forestall any further questions, but once they were uttered she realized she had spoken the truth. She *didn't* know much about Cord except that he was tremendously kind to her, and seemed to be around whenever she needed him.

One thing she did know: He had the power to affect her as no other person ever had before. One word, or a single glance, and her body and mind ceased to function in their usually dependable style. Yet even though his nearness might throw her into utter chaos, she was already looking forward to seeing him again.

A week later Eliza looked out over the bowed heads of her students and wondered for the tenth time where she was going to find enough books for them. She had already used the last desk. The next student to come was going to have to stand.

The new students had started to arrive in a trickle, two the day after Cord's visit, three more the next day, five the day after, and five the day after that. Now there was nowhere to put the desks and chairs even if they could be found.

A serious shortage of books forced Eliza to have the better students share with the slower students, and help them at the same time. All except Melissa. No one wanted her help. She had a sharp tongue, a condescending attitude safely encased in a leather hide no barb could puncture, and a determination to demonstrate to her fellow pupils just how superior she was. Eliza didn't know what to say the day she announced she wanted to become a teacher—"just like you, Miss Smallwood"—but she put Melissa's newfound dedication to use by assigning her to help the youngest students.

But something had to be done about the shortage of books and desks, or the students would soon disappear back into the wide open spaces from which they had so mysteriously emerged.

Chapter 9

"So I came to you, ma'am, because somebody has to do something about getting books for the children." Eliza sat uneasily in the parlor of Jessica Burton, Melissa's mother, and the wife of Sanford Burton, the town banker.

"And you thought I would know how to make people open their pockets?" she inquired with a vague hint of distaste.

"Melissa is so good with her studies and you are such a champion of education, I decided you would be the most logical person to ask. Since your husband is on the town council, he must know everybody." Eliza hated to resort to flattery, but since it was for the school, she overcame her qualms. "Everyone knows you're the leader of Buffalo society. If you decide something has to be done, people will support you."

Mrs. Burton could not repress a smile of self-satisfaction, but she seemed less than gratified at this particular request. "I agree with you, of course, and shall try find a way to get the money, but this trouble between the cowmen will make it difficult. It's hard to raise money unless the ranchers give it, and right now they're not particularly anxious to help the children of the men they see as their enemies."

"I wasn't thinking of asking anyone to give the money," Eliza said diffidently. "I was hoping we could raise it."

"How?" Mrs. Burton's manner was not encouraging.

"You've probably thought of several ways already," Eliza said, not stinting the flattery, "but I thought we might have a social, a dance maybe, and charge something for everybody to attend. Maybe we could have the ladies fix dinner and charge the men to eat."

"Really!" Mrs. Burton said disdainfully.

"The ladies could each fix a picnic basket, and the honor of dining with them could be auctioned off to the highest bidder. Of course their husbands would bid for them," Eliza added hastily when Mrs. Burton's aspect began to turn positively frigid, "but even if they only bid a dollar or fifty cents, we would get some money, and we're desperate, Mrs. Burton. I don't have books for half the children or desks for them to sit in. And the little ones can't work standing up or with their books in their laps. I'm afraid if something isn't done soon, they'll lose their enthusiasm and go away again. And it's so soon after the last ones came."

"Yes. I've been told Mr. Stedman's campaign was most successful."

"What?" Eliza was so surprised, her question sounded more like a squawk.

"Didn't you know?"

"How could I?"

"I assumed the children would have told you. It's been the talk of Buffalo. Apparently he set himself the task of visiting every ranch and homestead in the county, and that in itself has raised his reputation considerably. There are people who wouldn't mind if Cord Stedman didn't return from one of those long rides. It must have taken great courage to ride up to some cabins knowing a rifle was aimed at his heart the whole time."

Eliza wasn't sure how she escaped from Mrs. Burton, but somehow she found herself outside. Even with the cool, early evening breeze lightly brushing her heated skin, she had to lean against a hitching post to steady her nerves and calm her wildly pounding heart.

Mrs. Burton must think her a complete fool. Maybe she felt so surprised because she was the only one who *didn't* know why the children had come to school, but after the number of times he'd come to her rescue, she shouldn't have been.

She was suddenly conscious of a great desire to speak to him, and for a moment she actually considered riding out to the Matador, but she reluctantly decided she would have to wait until chance brought them together again.

"Stand still and stop craning your neck," Lucy ordered. "I never saw your like for looking in the mirror." Lucy and Ella were helping Eliza into the blue dress with white lace she was to wear at Jessica Burton's supper-and-dance social. The project had been announced with great fanfare, and Jessica had mobilized her influence to see that every woman turned out, husband on one arm and picnic basket on the other. She had done her best with the outlying families, but admitted her influence rarely extended beyond the town.

Ella had been more successful there, telling people she'd have Ed send them a bill for what they owed if they didn't contribute something to the school fund. Since every farmer or rancher got paid at harvest or roundup and lived on credit in between, that threat had the effect of emptying the surrounding hills, and Mrs. Burton was able to bask in the belief that only she could have produced such a turnout.

The festivities were to begin at the schoolhouse, where the children would recite, read poems, give speeches, and take part in a spelling bee. Then, while the children went home to cold suppers, their parents would settle down to dinner—word had gone out that husbands were expected to bid on their wives' picnic baskets—followed by a dance in the schoolhouse yard. It promised to bring half the cowboys in off the range looking for a chance to square up with some farmer's daughter. It was the biggest event to take place in Buffalo in years, and for one night at least, the feelings of mutual distrust were put aside.

"Don't worry. There won't be a female present tonight as beautiful as you," Ella assured Eliza.

"I know I'm not beautiful," protested Eliza, free at last to inspect herself in the mirror. "I'm just trying to make sure I'm pretty."

"Stuff," Ella said with a snort. "There's no use pretending you're not beautiful anymore than there is pretending it's not Cord Stedman you're thinking of." Eliza tried to demur, but neither woman would listen to a word.

"I've been around young gals most of my life, and I can read them like a book," Lucy said with a huge smile. "You've been nutty on Mr. Stedman from the night he knocked down those men."

"All week you've been acting like a girl about to come down

83

with the ague," observed Ella. "I never saw such carrying-on, blushing red one minute, milk white and tongue-tied the next, wanting to leave the room and dying to know who was at the door. If I didn't know you better, I'd say you had made plans to meet him at the dance."

"I do want to see him," stammered Eliza, flustered, "but it's not what you think. Truly, it isn't," she persisted when she saw skepticism on their faces. "I was never more astonished in my life when Mrs. Burton told me he was responsible for the children coming to school. Why should he do something like that?"

"Why should he care about building a schoolhouse?" Ella said, watching Eliza carefully.

"You did that," Eliza said with a smile.

"Who do you think gave me the idea? It wasn't Ed. Who else could sweet-talk me into spending my mornings chasing down mothers and convincing them to corral their menfolks into giving up their spare time?"

"Why? When? How?" Eliza stammered, completely overcome.

"He came by one morning chuck full of plans, but he had enough sense to know he wasn't the one to push them through, and I let him flatter me into doing the job for him." Ella laughed at the remembrance. "He sat himself down in my parlor, big handsome fella that he is, and I think he could have talked himself into half of the store if he'd tried. I don't know how he's managed to stay unmarried so long."

"It's not so hard if you never get close to a female who's not wearing horns," said Lucy.

"I know a dozen females willing to be carried off over his saddle the minute he cocks an eye. I had two in the store the other day just about fainting with the thought he might bid on their basket. If that man escapes this party alive, I'll own myself surprised. You ought to let him buy your basket so you can bring him off safe."

"My basket!" Eliza squeaked. "He wouldn't. I mean, why should he? He probably won't even be there." Eliza wouldn't admit to anyone she had taken extra care with her basket in the hope Cord *might* be present and *might* make a bid for her company.

"I'll bet you two new dresses he'll be there," said Ella.

"And *I'll* you bet a new hat he'll buy your basket," added Lucy. "You did fix one, didn't you?"

"Of course, but Uncle Ira is going to buy it. He said it would be bad for the saloon if I was seen to be favoring one man above another."

"You'd be better served if he thought more of you and less of that saloon," Ella remarked acidly. "Especially when you're the one who made it into something besides a smelly pit."

"You take my advice and tell your uncle to *stay* in the saloon," said Lucy.

"It's closing. Mrs. Burton told all the merchants it was their duty to support the schoolhouse."

"Well, God bless a nanny goat! Ever since you came to Buffalo I never know what's going to happen next," Ella marveled. "Jessica must have threatened Sanford with the kitchen knife. That man loves a dollar better than he loves his wife!"

"You take yourself over to Mr. Stedman, Miss Eliza," recommended Lucy, "and see if he doesn't bid for you."

"I can't do that. It wouldn't be proper."

"Wouldn't it be more proper for him to have supper with a sweet, beautiful gal who loves him than to get caught in the clutches of some hussy after his money?"

Eliza turned fiery red. "I'm not in love with him. I am grateful for his help, but I never thought of anything more."

"Then think of it now," Ella commanded. "It stands to reason he won't remain a bachelor for the rest of his life. He's got to marry and raise a son to leave all those cows to. Wouldn't it be better if he married you, who loves him whether you know it or not, instead of some heartless little minx like Jessica's Melissa?"

"But Melissa is only sixteen."

"She's nearly seventeen, and in two years she'll be almost nineteen, prime marrying age out here. Cord's not a day over thirty, so in two years they'll be just about right."

"But Mrs. Burton wouldn't let her marry an ordinary cowboy."

"Cord's not ordinary, and he's got a good business head on his shoulders. Who better could Sanford Burton find to run that bank when he dies?"

"But he's never mentioned marriage."

"Lord, child, hasn't he built you a school, emptied the hills of every brat he could find, and dared the whole of Johnson County to lay a hand on you?"

"Y-yes."

"What more do you want?" Ella concluded dramatically. "He never paid that kind of attention to any female around here, and I can promise you plenty have tried to catch his eye."

"You should hear what Lavinia's girls say about him," Lucy said with a giggle.

"I don't want to hear a word about those painted Jezebels," Ella said crushingly. "Now you make up your mind what you're going to do, Eliza, or tell him to go throw his rope over some other heifer."

"I couldn't do that!" Eliza gasped, truly horrified.

"You've got to. It isn't fair to keep a fella on tenterhooks without giving him some idea which way you mean to jump. If you don't want him, you've got to tell him so's he doesn't go and make a fool of himself. You finish getting yourself prettied up," Ella said, abruptly changing the subject. "Lucy and I have to finish up our baskets."

Eliza's brain was whirling so fast she was hardly aware of their departure. She was stunned by the notion Cord might be in love with her. She kept remembering the times Cord had come to her rescue, from the day at Bear Creek until he had given her the school and students to fill it. "The only thing he hasn't done for you, you stupid girl, was talk Mrs. Burton into the picnic," she said aloud. "And I wouldn't be the least bit surprised to find he had a hand in that too."

She sat down, dazed by the possibilities this new light shed on his intervention. No wonder the ladies of Buffalo regarded her with reproachful glances. She blushed. Nobody would believe that it had never occurred to her — she wasn't sure she wanted anyone to know she was quite so naive — but her uncle was no better. If he had even suspected Cord wanted to marry her, he would probably have gone after him with a gun.

Her heart constricted painfully at the thought of Cord lying dead in some gulch or hanging from a tree, and she knew then she was already in love him; it had probably started that day at the creek. Oh, Lord, how could she fall in love and not know it? Why hadn't she realized he was the *only* man besides her uncle she'd ever been completely comfortable with? Now she knew why she'd been in such a state that day he came by the school, and why she had thought of him every day since.

Suddenly her heart skidded to a halt with a sickening lurch. Suppose he didn't feel the same way about her? What if he really *was* just trying to be polite? The doubt was like a knife thrust to her heart, but she had to face the possibility. After all, he'd never actually *said* anything. What if someone had told him everyone in town was expecting them to announce their engagement any minute? She couldn't, she *wouldn't*, allow him to be tied to her if he didn't love her just as much as she loved him.

She would clear the air tonight. She would tell him she could never have gotten the school started without him, but people were beginning to talk and it might be better if they weren't seen together so often. That ought to set him free without throwing cold water in his face. She didn't want to discourage him if he *did* want to see her, but she wasn't going to have him feeling under obligation to her.

Hot metal bands seemed to be tightening themselves about her heart, squeezing it until she thought she would die. What if he was relieved to discover she hadn't interpreted his kindness as anything more than a desire to help a young lady? It would be too much to discover she was in love with him only to learn he regarded her as nothing more than a friend.

It was a good thing she wasn't singing tonight. She suddenly felt an overwhelming desire to burst into tears. There's no use in crying before there's any need, she told herself. Besides, Lucy will never forgive you if you get tear stains all over your face.

She would keep dry eyes if it killed her, but oh, please, let him like her just a little bit.

Chapter 10

Upwards of two hundred people were crowded into the schoolhouse yard when Eliza arrived, their wagons and buggies forming a backdrop against the limitless Wyoming horizon. Eliza was nearly the last to appear because Ira didn't want her to go at all.

"But I've *got* to be there. How would it look if I stayed home after asking all those people to give money to the school?"

"I don't give a damn about those people or their school. You're a fool to waste your time on a pack of ungrateful brats."

"I still have to be there," Eliza said firmly.

"Then we won't leave until late. Having a lot of cowboys hanging about getting ideas won't do the saloon any good. You're wonderfully popular with everybody, and I want to keep it that way."

"Then you ought to thank Mr. Stedman." Eliza hadn't meant to say anything so certain to enrage her uncle, it just popped out before she realized what she was saying, but when Ira exploded with a tirade of harmless curses, it struck her with numbing impact that she had the power to say something her uncle didn't like and not fear him. It was a small thing perhaps, but so important her mind leapt with excitement. It was like chains falling away; for the first time in her life she tasted freedom, and it buoyed her spirits so she didn't care if they were late.

There were no unmarried girls in sight when they reached the schoolhouse, but the porch was nearly covered with baskets. "At last," sighed Mrs. Burton, relief and reproof in her voice. "I had begun to fear you did not mean to attend."

"I'm sorry to be late," Eliza mumbled, and put her basket

down with all the others.

"You're here, and that's what counts," Mr. Burton said as he motioned the crowd to get quiet so he could begin the raffle. "We can't rightly get started until everybody's been paired up," he said with forced heartiness, "so we'll start with the wives and husbands." It was obvious from the widespread grumbling that some in the crowd had hoped to be spared a few hours of domestic togetherness, but Mrs. Burton's mouth was folded and pressed into an expression no one could misunderstand.

"And just so you won't think you can get away with bidding a quarter, I'm going to start with ten dollars for Mrs. Burton's basket," Sanford announced as his wife held up a prettily decorated basket large enough to hold food for a dozen people. "Now how much will you bid for your wife's fried chicken, Fred?" he called to one of the town merchants as Jessica held up a second basket smaller than her own. The man responded with five dollars, a bit more than he had intended to pay, but Mr. Burton refused to let him go until the poor man, embarrassed by the public nature of the event, also bid ten dollars. The message was unmistakable, and the bidding progressed rapidly, but not as quickly as the feeling of gaiety fled. Even two dollars was a sacrifice for some of the homesteaders.

"Now we come to the fun part, bidding for the unattached ladies. You married men step back so the single fellas can come up to the front row. I don't want anybody bidding nickels when a better view would encourage them to come up with dollars. Bring out the little dears, Mrs. Burton."

Maintaining her stony front, Mrs. Burton beckoned to the cracked door and the girls, penned up against their wishes, poured out, their eyes quickly adjusting to the afternoon sun as they tried to pick out the young men they hoped would bid for their company. Melissa Burton immediately planted herself at her father's elbow, almost forcing him to auction her basket first. She waited with an air of self satisfaction while her father raised a basket fully as large as her mother's and commanded the crowd to "loosen up your wallets. Who'll start the bidding at five dollars? Come on, Joe," he called to the son of the livery stable owner. "You've got five dollars."

"Not anymore," the boy whispered angrily. In this manner

89

the bidding was relentlessly pushed forward until the luckless Joe, forced to bid fifteen dollars by a glare that threatened his father's credit at the bank, committed himself to Melissa for the afternoon.

But Melissa didn't seem any more pleased than her escort. She had discovered Cord Stedman at the back of the crowd and her young woman's fancy had shed any lingering interest in boys. When a discreet whisper from a friend informed her he was rich as well as notorious, her infatuation was complete.

"Now where's the little lady who's responsible for our school?" Eliza was pushed forward.

"That's Belle Sage," exclaimed one cowboy who didn't know of Eliza's double identity. Quite a few others must not have known either, for at the mention of her name, the circle became thronged with eager faces crowding closer to the porch. Mr. Burton had never heard Eliza sing, but he seized on the chance to exploit her reputation.

"Ain't she the prettiest little songbird you've ever seen?"

"And she can cook and keep house," Ella whispered loud enough for Cord to hear. He had steadily elbowed his way to the front but didn't show any sign he had heard Ella. Several around him did, though, and the excitement continued to grow.

"Who will open the bidding at five dollars?" An overeager cowboy opened at ten, but before the ripple of laughter had faded the bid had reached twenty-five dollars with no sign of stopping. It paused at fifty, but Mr. Burton was cut short in the midst of a flowery tribute by an arctic glare from his wife.

"Who'll give me sixty?" coaxed Mr. Burton. "We can't let a pretty girl go for such a paltry sum."

"Sixty dollars ain't paltry," shouted one incensed cowboy. "That's nearly two months' wages."

"Sixty dollars." Cord's entry into the bidding caused a ripple of excitement. He'd never been known to seek the company of any female, or to spend a nickel on anything except his ranch, yet here he was breaking both rules at once.

"Sixty-one," yelled Ira, enraged Cord would dare seize on a civic occasion such as this to appropriate Eliza's company.

"Sixty-five," responded Cord without hesitation.

"Sixty-six," Ira countered defiantly.

"Seventy."

"Seventy-one."

"Seventy-five."

"Eighty."

"Eighty-one."

"Eighty-five."

"Ninety."

"Ninety-one," Ira answered growing hot under the collar.

"One hundred dollars," responded Cord, holding Ira's eye with an unflinching gaze. The bids had come too fast for Mr. Burton, and the crowd fell silent. The protagonists watched each other, one with ironic coolness and the other poised between anger and stinginess.

"One hundred and one," Ira bid, but the words nearly stuck in his throat.

"A hundred and five," Cord countered immediately.

Every eye turned to Ira; every ear waited for his next bid. He had turned this into a personal duel and now he was being forced to continue or back down publicly. Several times he made up his mind to bid, but the rational part of his brain balked at what it saw as a waste of money.

"Come on, Mr. Smallwood," coaxed Burton. "You don't want to see your niece carried off by a rancher. Think of what the cowboys and homesteaders will say. Come on, just a little more." Ira glanced up at Eliza standing ramrod still and then at the crowd.

"One hundred and six," he shouted, but the words came out in a strangled whisper.

"One hundred and ten dollars. Cord enunciated each word carefully, and the slump of Ira's body told the crowd he could bid no more.

"If there're no more bids, the pleasure of Miss Smallwood's company goes to Mr. Cord Stedman," Burton stated, not expecting anyone to top such an absurd figure. "You can pay the town treasurer." Before the crowd's open-mouthed gaze, Cord unbuttoned his shirt pocket and took the necessary bills from a thick fold as casually as if they had been ten dollars instead of a hundred and ten. Then he took the picnic basket handed to him by Mrs. Burton and turned to Eliza.

Eliza had dreaded the possibility her basket would be bought by a total stranger, and had been relieved when Cord made his first offer, but she was mortified by the angry desperation with which her uncle had pursued the bidding. It was bad enough to be at the center of attention because she was the school teacher, but to have her participation turned into food for gossip was dreadful. As the bids had risen and she'd seen the crowd's excitement building, she'd shrunk from the ordeal of publicly sharing her dinner with Cord.

One of the girls, momentarily falling victim to her demon of jealousy, gave Eliza a little push when Cord held out his hand, and Eliza reached out to keep from falling. To the crowd, it must have looked as if she was so anxious she'd run toward him, and Eliza turned crimson with shame and anger. She knew there was no hope of passing it off lightly. As one woman sapiently observed, "No woman can blush like that and have a clean conscience."

Cord led Eliza to a position a little behind the ring of active bidders, and they stood without exchanging a word while the remaining baskets were auctioned off. Though there were a couple of spirited contests, only one of them exceeded twenty dollars. There was nothing to compare to the contest over Eliza.

"Where would you like to eat?" Cord asked, taking advantage of the general confusion to shield her answer from the ears of the curious. Eliza shook her head, unable to reply.

"Maybe the Baylises would allow us to join them," Cord suggested, pointing to where Ella was busily setting up a small table. Eliza cast him a look of profound thankfulness and tried hard not to run to Ella's comforting presence.

"I don't blame you for not wanting to sit on the dirt, even if you did bring a blanket," Ella said, giving them an understanding welcome. "I wonder more people didn't think to bring a table." Mrs. Burton had, but as no one else seemed to have possessed as much foresight, the hillside was soon covered with blankets or families eating standing up at the back of a wagon or buckboard.

"You sure set everyone in a bustle, Cord Stedman," chuckled Ella, getting to the heart of things right away.

"No need. I was just buying my supper like everybody else."

"Don't play the simpleton with me, young man," admonished Ella. "I'm up to your tricks."

"Not all of them, I hope."

"Respectable women don't concern themselves with *all* the

shenanigans a man gets up to," Ella informed him with devastating directness, "but I know enough. Now don't you worry about a thing, dear," she said to Eliza. "It caused a stir at the time, but before dinner's over everybody'll be too interested in their own partners to pay you any mind. By tomorrow they'll have forgotten all about it."

Ella's prediction proved only partly true. As soon as the picnickers had time to settle into the business of eating, the stares became fewer and the whispering and nudging almost stopped. Seeing Eliza and Cord sharing their supper with one of the town's most respected couples divested the incident of much of its excitement.

Eliza expected she would soon relax, but every time she looked at Cord she sensed the presence of a submerged heat, volcanic in its power, and it left her tense and shaken. To all outward appearances, Cord seemed to be talking quietly with Mr. Baylis and paying no more than the usual attention to Eliza, but a blazingly intense energy escaped through eyes more hooded and withdrawn than usual, and she felt the temperature of the afternoon climb. By the time they were through eating, she felt terribly hot even though the cool evening air was making her shiver; the presence of others was no protection from the broiling emotional heat that enveloped her, and the ease she had always enjoyed with Cord had vanished.

"Why don't you two take a walk and get the kinks out of your legs. I'll clean up. And I don't need any help," Ella said before Eliza could offer. "Cord hasn't left me much to clear away."

Eliza felt so weak she wasn't sure she could get to her feet.

"You can show me how you plan to use the money you raised," Cord said, extending his hand to help her rise. Eliza expected to be scalded by his touch, but his grip was firm and cool, and it enabled her to command her own reluctant muscles.

"Since you gave so much of it, I feel I owe you an explanation."

"You don't owe me anything. I wasn't thinking of the school when I bid that money."

How was it possible for eyes to gaze at her with such blistering intensity and not turn her to smoldering ash?

"What were you thinking of?" Eliza's heart was pounding so hard she feared she might not hear his answer.

"You," he answered, and the afternoon became even hotter.

"Me? But that's absurd. No supper is worth that much."

"I didn't say food, I said *you*."

"Mrs. Baylis tells me I have something else to thank you for," Eliza stammered. She headed toward the schoolhouse wondering if it would be safer ground.

"Oh?" He didn't sound interested.

"The schoolhouse itself."

"Why?"

"Because you talked her into getting the town to build it. That is true, isn't it?"

"We did talk over a few ideas," he admitted evasively, his thoughts seemingly elsewhere.

"In other words, you did talk her into it. It seems you're always coming to my rescue." Cord closed the door behind them. She raised her hand to protest.

"The glare," he said, smiling in such a way she didn't care about his lame excuse. "Show me what you do here."

"You won't think it's very exciting."

"I promise not to say so."

"I know you wouldn't. You've always been tremendously kind to me," she said, smiling, thinking the door should probably be open. "We don't have enough desks, so some of the children have to sit on the floor. And these are all the books we have." She showed him a rough-hewn bookcase half full of tattered and dog-eared volumes. "There aren't enough to go around, and some are missing so many pages they aren't much use."

"Do you use only schoolbooks, or do you use the regular kind? The kind everybody reads," he clarified.

"We use regular schoolbooks for spelling and sums, but we can use any kind of book for reading, even a novel."

"Then why not have the children take one day and go to every house in town and collect old books they don't use any more. You'll get a lot of trash, but you ought to end up with some good books too."

"Now there's something else I have to be grateful to you for."

"All this gratitude can be wearing. Have you ever considered paying your debts?"

"How can I?"

"I know a way." He was now so close she could feel the heat of his body.

"What?" She was almost afraid of the answer.

"This." His arms encircled her and he kissed her gently.

"Was that for saving my books?" she asked mindlessly. Everything about her felt disembodied. Only her lips, burning with his kiss, retained any feeling.

"If you like," he said with a smile which imperfectly masked the building intensity. "And this is for the cow." He kissed her again.

"And the saloon and getting Ella to let me dress at her house?" asked Eliza. He kissed her twice more, and it felt so wonderful she kept trying to think of reasons for him to continue.

"The schoolhouse and the books," he said with a husky croak, "and another one for just being you."

Eliza didn't know how it happened that her arms were around his neck, but she was so weak she had to cling to him or fall. But that's foolish, her disordered wits reasoned. It would be impossible to slip from the hold he had around her waist.

The sound of footsteps on the porch and voices outside the door penetrated the fog surrounding Eliza, but she was unable to summon the energy to break Cord's fierce embrace. She knew any moment Melissa and Joe, for it was their voices she heard, would enter the schoolhouse, but she still couldn't move. She was in the arms of the man she realized in one thundering crash she loved, and she didn't ever want to let go again. She looked up at Cord, totally breathless and unable to hide the truth that she loved him as much as he must love her. The expression on her face caused him to crush her in another embrace.

But the noise of someone trying to open the door forced her to wrench her mind at least partly away from Cord's kisses. Why wouldn't the door open? She hadn't locked it. She pushed him away and pointed to the door, which was now clattering loudly from the energetic pushes against it.

Cord motioned for her to remain silent and pointed to the floor. A battered book was firmly wedged underneath the door.

"It's stuck. Careful, or you'll break it," she called out. Cord tried to keep her in his arms. "I can't," she whispered, breaking away. She crossed the room quickly and wrenched the book from the door, throwing it quickly to Cord, who had the good sense to catch it. He was in the process of restoring it to its place on the shelf when Melissa and Joe entered.

Melissa was angry and more than a little suspicious. She looked around, but found nothing unusual. Cord showed not the slightest trace of embarrassment, and Miss Smallwood was no more upset than she ever was around strangers.

"I can't imagine why it stuck. It never does."

"Maybe it's wet."

"But it didn't stick for you," Melissa insisted with the tenacity of a small mind bogged down in unimportant detail.

"It's unstuck now, so don't worry about it anymore. Are you having a nice time?" Eliza asked, trying to turn Melissa's thoughts in another direction.

"It's all right," she said, eying Cord, "but it's such an unsophisticated party." Cord glanced up, and a more perceptive girl would have been abashed by his look, but Melissa smiled archly at him, quite in the manner of a young girl trying to act ten years older.

"But the *children* will have the books they need. Do you read a lot, Mr. Stedman? Not these books, of course." She laughed artificially.

"I don't have time," he answered shortly. He replaced the book on the shelf and crossed the room with his long, swinging stride. "Don't stay too long. Your mother might get worried." Melissa swelled with lacerated pride, but Cord was utterly unconcerned with her feelings as he escorted Eliza outside.

"The fiddles are about to strike up," Ella informed them when they returned. "Don't wander off or you'll miss the first square dance."

"Oh, dear, do I have to dance?" asked Eliza. "I don't know if I can."

"What? You can't dance? Don't be silly. Of course you can."

"But I've never been to a dance."

"Neither have I," added Cord.

"And you two having to lead the set. Well, I'll be a pig's uncle. This ought to be a sight, both of you stumbling over

96

each other without knowing which foot to put where. Charlie, you'd better scrape something slow and easy. The schoolmarm and her fella have never set foot on a dance floor." Eliza cringed at Ella's calling Cord her fella, but the crowd was so delighted at the expected fun they hardly noticed.

"Bring her out here and we'll show you how," Charlie encouraged Cord.

"Always lead with your right," called one helpful assistant from the sidelines.

"But not if you're the lady."

"Just stay away from his boots, miss, or you'll never walk again."

"Everybody knows cowboys have trouble walking. Let a farmer show you how it's done."

Eliza felt like running away, but Cord took the kidding in good part and led Eliza into the middle of the open space marked off for dancing.

"Get somebody to show us what to do, and we'll follow as best we can," Cord directed the onlookers. The rowdy element set up a hoot, and several comments were bandied about that were not generally complimentary to cowboys, but a young farmer took up the challenge.

"Now play it real slow, Charlie, or he's liable to do her a mischief with those boots," said another wag. The mood of the picnic was rapidly being reduced to one of hilarity, and the first awkward steps taken by Cord and Eliza did nothing to dampen the mood.

"We need more examples," Cord called, and several more couples moved onto the dance area. Caught in the middle of the swinging, twisting mass of bodies and moving about in what was unkindly referred to as a goose waddle, Cord and Eliza tried to copy the steps of some of the slower-moving dancers. When the dance ended, everyone applauded the couple and gaily offered suggestions for the next dance, but when the music started again they quickly forgot Cord and Eliza in their own enjoyment of the evening.

Chapter 11

The sun went down, and the school yard glowed in the light of lanterns hung from the porch, from poles on buckboards, and from poles sunk in the ground for just that purpose. The lanterns cast plenty of light into the circle of dancers and on the groups gathered around talking and playing cards, but the space immediately beyond was plunged into utter darkness and several couples wandered quietly into those discreet shadows.

Cord led Eliza into this nebulous region, and as the night closed around them like a cloak, she was able to imagine they were alone, the only two people on the vast, primeval plain. The evening air was crisp with expectation and Eliza had never felt more vitally alive. She was on the verge of something unimaginably wonderful, something to do with the man who guided her willing steps.

"I want you to come out to the Matador. I want to show you the whole ranch." Eliza could hear the pride in his voice, and she trembled with happiness that he would want to share the work of his life with her.

"I can't, not with school during the day and singing at night. I barely have time to do my housework."

"When is school over?"

"Not for another three months." Eliza could not hide her disappointment. "But we have a holiday next week," she added, brightening suddenly.

"Can you come then? I've only collected the first installment on your debt." She felt his arms close about her again. She knew she shouldn't let him hold her, and she was sure

Melissa would suddenly appear to point an accusing finger at them, but she couldn't stop herself. His touch vanquished her resistance, and all she wanted to do was melt into his arms and stay there forever. She had no idea why it felt so natural and so wonderful, and she didn't waste time in needless inquiry. She felt better than wonderful, and that was all that mattered.

"Do all cowboys collect their debts in installments?" she murmured mindlessly.

"The smart ones do." Cord kissed her gently, but it quickly turned into an impassioned embrace. She felt his body against hers and she no longer cared about Melissa. It was warm and comforting; she leaned against him and let her arms wind around his neck. A groan escaped him and she felt his body tense and begin to tremble. She wanted to ask him the cause, but his mouth was kissing her eyes and ears, and then, in a searing explosion of feeling she would never forget, his heated lips touched her neck, and her body grew limp. It was as though her bones had turned to jelly and only his arms prevented her from sliding to the ground.

"Will you come?" he asked without pausing. His hand caressed the back of her neck while his lips teased her eyelids.

"When?" His lips tortured her ear and she felt a strange warmth begin to travel all along her body. His body, strangely stiff and unyielding, pressed against her and she could feel the heat through her dress. She knew she should draw away, but she was caught in a viselike embrace that allowed for no exit.

"Next week, on Sunday. You'll come early?" She became aware of her breasts pushed firmly into his chest and his raging heat flowing into her body.

"I'll pick you up at daybreak," he said. She gradually became aware of a hardness, a place of intense heat, pressed against her. Her brain was bombarded with questions, but she was too disconcerted by his seeking, plundering, demanding lips to have thoughts for anything else.

"Eliza!" It was her uncle's voice, loud and angry.

"Damn and blast!" muttered Cord, reining back hard on his rampaging emotions.

"Where are you? It's time to go." Eliza fought against the pull of reality. She didn't want to leave the warm circle of

Cord's embrace, she wouldn't have objected if her uncle had gone off and left her, but Ira's voice was insistent. Eliza nervously straightened her clothes while Cord tried to calm his racing blood so his aroused condition wouldn't be quite so noticeable.

"Uncle mustn't find us here," she said.

"Then let's run." Cord took her hand, and they ran around the wagons, staying beyond the reach of the lights until they reached the far side. Eliza was out of breath and laughing helplessly when they stopped.

"Sunday, early," Cord said softly, looking at her with a long, lingering gaze that drank in every part of her.

"Sunday, early," she repeated after him as her laughter gave way to a look of wonder and longing. Cord kissed her lightly and led her back to the circle of light.

Eliza sat sipping a cup of coffee in Ella's parlor, wondering how to begin. When she formed the question in her mind, it seemed all she had to do was open her mouth and the words would come right out, but even Ella Baylis's benign countenance appeared forbidding when the question was actually perched on her lips.

"And Peggy Withers is so pleased with what you've done for her Cam she was praising you to the skies just yesterday. If you knew half the things she said about the last teacher, you'd know that's a near miracle. And you haven't been listening to a word I've said."

"I'm sorry," Eliza said, recovering with a start. "I'm afraid I was woolgathering."

"You've been distracted ever since you got here. Are you worrying about Cord?" Eliza was betrayed by an incriminating flush. "I thought as much. What's he done now?"

"Nothing," Eliza assured her earnestly. "I'm sure no woman has ever been treated with more kindness and respect."

"I never thought Cord would be such a stuffed shirt."

Eliza stared blankly at Ella.

"Never mind my silly jokes. Tell me what's wrong."

"Nothing, at least not in the way you mean," said Eliza, squirming uneasily. "It's just I haven't had much experience with men, or people really, and I don't know how to tell what

100

a person means. When somebody talks to you in a store, you know exactly what he means, but when he talks to you at a picnic, or when you're alone, he might not mean exactly the same thing, even though he uses the same words. Do you know what I'm trying to say?"

"I *think* so," Ella said with a smile. "You want to know if Cord Stedman likes you as much as you like him." Ella's paralyzing way of reducing her meandering thoughts to a single, blunt sentence jolted Eliza badly.

"No," she protested, flushing still.

"Then what is it?" Ella asked kindly.

"I want to know how to tell if *I'm* in love," Eliza managed to say all in a rush. "I've never felt like this before. It's nothing like my feelings for Mama and Papa or Aunt Sarah. Every time I think I've got things all sorted out, they get confused again."

"And you want me to help you get things straight?"

"If you would."

Ella laughed heartily. "Tell me all about your young man."

"It's not Cord. It's me."

Ella had never experienced any such agonizing doubts herself, but she was wise in the ways of others. "If Cord Stedman hadn't walked into your life, would you be here now asking me questions?"

"N-no."

"I thought so. Now, tell me about Cord."

Eliza looked quite unable to comply, but Ella waited patiently, allowing Eliza time to gather her thoughts. "He's the kindest man I know," she began with a smile that told Ella all she needed to know. "He seems to always show up when I need him, and he's never asked one thing of me. I can't tell you how much better it is at the saloon now. There are some nights when I really don't mind it at all. Then there's the schoolhouse and buying everything new for us. I'd have to think he was something special even if he was as ugly as a buffalo."

"Do you think he's ugly?"

"He's more handsome than any hero in a book," Eliza said rapturously. "Whenever I'm in a mood to get carried away, I tell myself he's really not perfect. I point out every fault I can find, but whenever I *see* him, I don't care if he has dozens of

101

flaws."

"That sounds pretty conclusive to me."

"If he's near me I can't think of anything else," Eliza continued, warming to her subject. "When he held me in his arms, at the dance," she added quickly, "I wanted to stay there forever and not worry about Uncle, the school, or anything else ever again. I wanted to cook his dinner, wash his clothes, and be at the door every time he came home."

"Calm down, for goodness sakes," Ella said with a chuckle. "You're so worked up you're liable to run out and propose to *him*. He hasn't asked you to marry him, has he?" she asked suddenly.

"Goodness, no," replied Eliza, embarrassed by her excess of enthusiasm. "I hardly know anything about him."

"Out here we don't need to know much about a man except the color of his courage and the value of his word, and nobody doubts Cord's courage *or* his word. What he says, he does. What he wants, he takes."

"But does that make a good husband?"

Ella's eyes were instantly alert. "I didn't know we were talking about husbands."

"I just wanted to know," Eliza said, avoiding Ella's eyes. "I've never known a man like Cord, and his way of life frightens me a little. With all this talk of rustlers and home-steaders, small and large ranchers, the Association and mav-ericks, I sometimes feel I don't understand *anything* about Wyoming. Why can't he do something safe like run a store? I don't even know if I love him yet, and I worry every time he goes out he won't come back."

"You love him," Ella stated emphatically. "No girl talks about a man like this unless she's positively nutty on him."

"Are you sure? I don't remember Mama much, but she never seemed to act like this, and I know she was nutty about Papa. Aunt Sarah never told me what it feels like to be in love."

"What could she say to a girl of ten? She thought she had years to watch you grow into a beautiful woman before she lost you to some handsome young man."

Eliza's eyes grew misty.

"You think back on some of the things your Mama *did* for your Papa, or your Aunt Sarah for Ira, and I'm sure you'll find they're the same things you're so anxious to do for Cord."

"Yes, they are," Eliza answered softly. Memories she had almost forgotten provided an understanding she had never had of her mother, and suddenly she felt much closer to her than she had ever been in life.

"All men in Wyoming live dangerously, even if they run a store. Ten years ago this was Indian territory, and five years ago it was still unsafe to ride out alone. If you're not ready and able to fight for what you have, somebody will take it from you."

"But that's a horrible way to live."

"Either you do what you have to, or you move back East. And no matter what Cord may tell you, he'll despise anybody who's a weakling or a coward. He came up tougher than most, and if you want him, you're going to have to take him the way he is!"

"If he wanted me, I could do anything for him."

"Good, because the first battle is going to be with your uncle."

"Please don't tell him I've been here. I probably shouldn't have said anything to you at all. Mr. Stedman may not feel at all the way I do."

"If Cord Stedman doesn't ask you to marry him within the month, he's not the man I think he is, and I'll tell him so."

During the next few days, Eliza barely thought of anything except Cord. The feeling of his arms around her waist and his lips on hers had been a revelation, but the feeling of his lean, hard body against hers had given birth to new and insistent cravings. She knew little of physical love; she only knew his nearness gave her such a delicious weakness in her bones she could hardly wait to experience it again.

But after suffering through sudden flashes of heat or cold, abrupt swings of appetite and mood, and a restlessness that kept sleep at bay, Eliza decided there was more to this than just a yearning for closeness. Even the children noticed her irritability, and Friday afternoon she spoke so sharply to Otis she was startled quite as much as he. She was tempted to talk to Ella Baylis again, but she didn't want to admit Cord had kissed her and that she longed for him to do it again. What if

Ella told her it was wrong? Eliza doubted she could make herself stop. She knew she didn't want to.

Saturday night came at last, but she was too excited to sleep and she rose long before dawn. Ira continued to sleep undisturbed even after she stumbled into a chair, but Eliza was so unnerved she hurried outside before she could stumble over something else. By the time she finished feeding the animals, milking the cow, and gathering eggs she had herself under control again.

She put on her best dress and bonnet, but her reflection in the mirror provoked a frown of dissatisfaction. She tossed the bonnet aside and unearthed a small parasol from her trunk. It had been her mother's and was trimmed with bows and ribbons that streamed from the handle. She opened it, put it over her shoulder, and looked critically at her reflection. Pleased, she brushed her black hair until it glistened like sable. No traces remained of the rouge Lucy had used the night before, but her cheeks flamed prettily just thinking about Cord. Then, afraid she had spent too much time at her mirror, she grabbed up her parasol and ran outside. She dared not contemplate what would happen if Cord came to the door.

The first streaks of dawn had turned to cool morning sunshine when she reached the seat beneath the tree. She was sure Ira would wake any minute and demand to know what she was doing, but Cord appeared before her courage could fail, and his presence filled her with such complete happiness she forgot her fears and rode off eagerly looking forward to a whole day spent by his side.

The morning flew past. It was soon apparent the ranch was vitally important to him and she tried to remember everything Cord told her, but her concentration was badly shaken by his nearness. Their bodies continually brushed against one another as they lurched over the uneven ground, and the feel of his powerful frame against her own left her feeling branded.

Cord took Eliza to every part of his ranch they could reach in the buckboard. He showed her the endless range covered by lush grass and the canyons, gulches, and arroyos that scarred the plains. He showed her the creeks and explained why every rancher had to secure water no matter what the cost. And he showed her his hay meadows. "Winter feeding is the best way to avoid winter losses, and it keeps the cowboys on the range. A herd of two hundred and fifty was run off one of the spreads in the Bighorn basin last winter, and nobody knew about it until the rustlers sold the steers in Montana."

Eliza understood less clearly when he tried to explain the Cheyenne Cattleman's Association and their conflict with the homesteaders and small ranchers, but she did understand they were in a life-and-death struggle with rustlers to determine who would control the grazing lands of northern Wyoming.

By the time they stopped for lunch, her head was so full of irrigation, open-range policy, maverick laws, and the stupidity of the Association's policy toward everybody, she doubted she would remember a word of it. It did, however, give her a very different idea of the life of a rancher. She realized her uncle had greatly underestimated the hard work, courage, dedication, and tough business sense that lay behind every successful cowman. It was the ranches backed by Eastern money, more particularly those backed by European capital, that made the local people so bitter. They came in with their huge herds, crowded everyone else off the best range, overgrazed the grasslands, and treated their employees with an arrogance that offended their American sense of independence.

"I never thought of bringing anything to eat," Eliza said with barely a thought to spare for Ira, home alone with no one to prepare his midday meal. "I was sure I'd be back before now."

"We're at least three hours away from your cabin, but I brought along a little something." Cord pointed to an enormous basket resting under the seat.

"Did you fix it yourself?"

"You wouldn't be able to eat it if I had. Ginny Church fixed it. She's has been trying to get me married off for years, and she packed enough food for us to stay gone for a week. Maybe she thinks I can weaken your resistance if I feed you."

Eliza hardly knew how to respond. His reference to marriage was made in fun, but by now she knew that marriage was what she wanted.

"There's a willow-and-cottonwood thicket on the creek not

far from here," Cord said. The sun had grown quite hot, but Eliza had been in such a continual fever of excitement she hadn't noticed. Cord stopped the wagon next to the trees and helped Eliza down. He chose a shady spot in the lush grass and spread out one blanket after another until he had a mat thick enough to take the hardness out of the ground. "If you'll set out the lunch, I'll unharness the horse."

The enormous basket contained chicken, potato salad, deviled eggs, cold ham, several kinds of preserves, a pot of creamy butter, and some biscuits tightly wrapped in a napkin and still retaining some of the heat from the oven that baked them early that morning. There was also honey, an apple and raisin pie, and a bottle of wine.

"Give me the butter and wine, and I'll put them in the creek." Cord's voice behind her made her jump. "We can put the bread and meat on a rock to warm it up."

"Shouldn't we go ahead and eat? The ants will get it if we leave it too long."

"I want to show you something first." He led her to a rise a few hundred feet beyond the edge of the thicket and, facing her to the east, swung his arm in an arc that encompassed land stretching for miles in all directions. "Everything as far as you can see is mine," he said with the simple pride of ownership.

"Do you mean you *own* all this?"

"I've had to bend a few rules and it's taken every bit of cash I could lay my hands on, but most of it is mine. I do my best to control all the rest."

"How about the place where we camped that first day?"

"No, and unfortunately it's right in the center of my range. I'd have no end of trouble if a homesteader settled there."

"Can anyone homestead it?"

"Anyone willing to build on it."

"And then sell it to you?"

"That's how I got most of my land," he confessed with a grin, "having my boys stake claims and then sell to me."

"Then I could claim it and sell it to you?"

Cord looked at her strangely. "You would do that for me, against your uncle's wishes?

I would do anything in the world if you would just keep looking at me like that, she thought. Aloud she said, "He wouldn't have to know."

"I'm afraid he would."

"It doesn't really matter," she answered, unsure of what she did mean but badly disconcerted by the way he was looking at her.

Suddenly he smiled and kissed her lightly on the lips. "Let's eat. You might feel less foolhardy if you weren't starving to death." Cord's face gave no clue to his thoughts, but Eliza vowed she would stake a claim to that land just as soon as she learned how to do it.

Lunch was leisurely and wonderful.

"Do you always eat this much?" Cord asked with a laugh as she bit into her third piece of chicken.

"I didn't have any breakfast," she said with her mouth full. "It must be past noon."

"Later," Cord said, pouring out some more wine. Eliza looked doubtfully at the pale liquid. It bubbled excitedly, but after just one glass everything around her had assumed a much friendlier hue. Her uncle's scowling disapproval had long since dwindled into insignificance.

"What *is* this stuff?" she asked, taking a sip from the glass. "It tastes awfully funny."

"It's champagne. It seems the Orrs left a few bottles behind, so Ginny put them away for a suitable occasion. Apparently, she thinks this is one."

"It makes me feel delightfully woozy. I don't think I can stand up."

"That's because you've eaten so much you weigh twenty pounds more." Cord laughed. "You haven't had enough to get intoxicated."

"Is this how the men feel in the saloon?"

"Not exactly, but something like it."

"Hmmm. Do you think I would like beer or whiskey?"

"No, I *don't*," Cord stated decisively.

"I didn't think so, but why do I like this?"

"Wine is different from strong spirits. Still, I think you've had enough. Lie back a little while until the dizziness goes off."

"I think I will," she said, feeling relieved not to have to make any more conversation.

"Go to sleep if you like," he said with a tender smile.

"No, I just want to lean back." But her eyelids began to sink. "I got up so early," she mumbled, and before long she was sound asleep.

Chapter 12

Eliza opened her eyes to find a canopy of trees overhead.

"Do you feel better now?" Cord's voice startled her, and she sat up so quickly his image spun madly before her eyes.

"I fell asleep. How awful."

"You barely dozed." He smiled at her in a way that made her pulse race tumultuously.

"But you must have so many other things to do."

"They can wait. Do you have any idea how beautiful you are when you sleep?"

"Please don't. You know I never understand it when people tease me."

"I'm not teasing. Do you think I would do anything to hurt you?"

"Not intentionally, but you can't understand what it's like to want so much to be beautiful. Uncle made sure I never thought I was more than passable."

"And you believed him? What about all those men at the saloon? And I'm sure Croley Blaine hasn't missed a chance to flatter you."

"That's just it. They're all flattering me."

"Not Lavinia's girls. They dislike you intensely, and there's no more sure sign of beauty than the envy of another woman."

"Do you *really* think I'm beautiful?" she asked, hoping to be convinced. Cord took her face in his hands.

"I've never seen any woman who was half as beautiful as you. Ever since that day on the creek I haven't been able to get you out of my mind. I tried during the roundup, but I came back to find a shy, entrancing darling cringing before a room full of drunks, and all hope of keeping my distance was gone. It was all I could do to keep from sweeping you into my arms that night."

"I was never happier to see anyone," she said with becoming honesty, her eyes sparkling happily. "I almost wished there were a few more for you to knock down."

"Do I have to knock somebody down before I can do this?" Cord kissed her. It was a long, lingering kiss and it left Eliza weak and breathless.

"No, not if you really want to." Cord kissed her again, ruthlessly this time.

"Now do you believe I want to?" he asked softly.

"Yes," she replied unevenly. "Oh, yes!" She threw her arms around his neck in a passionate embrace. Cord let his fingers trail over the planes of her face, caressing each part with a lingering wonder. As his fingers trailed over her chin and down her neck Eliza shivered convulsively, completely lost in a welter of sensations.

She could barely believe Cord found her beautiful and desirable, but the feeling was so wonderful, so exhilarating, she would have been willing to die rather than give it up. After a lifetime of avoiding men, her anxiety equally divided between dread of what they might do and fear they wouldn't find her attractive enough to want to do anything, it was sheer bliss to bask in the warmth of Cord's adoration. Her entire body tingled with anticipation as waves of happiness wafted over her.

"Lucy says every woman in Buffalo is after you."

"It wouldn't matter if every woman in the *world* were after me. You are the only one I want."

"Why?" She found it difficult to believe he *really* meant what he said. Years of being ignored had nearly destroyed her sense of worth, but in the short time she had been in Buffalo she had begun to be appreciated and her spirits had soared, nourished like a thirsty desert plant that grows doubly fast when the fickle rains come. But in Cord's love she had more than admiration; she had someone who had sought her out, had worked to earn her approval, and had done it all without asking for a reward.

"I'm not sure I can give you a reason for it. Certainly not a listing of qualities I like. I loved you from the moment I saw

110

you."

"But you've got to have a reason to love somebody."

"Why? Do you?"

Eliza was nonplussed. "I don't know. I suppose I do, but I've never thought about it like that."

Cord laughed softly.

"I didn't know until the picnic I even liked you particularly. It upset me so dreadfully I couldn't think sensibly for days."

"Do you have to think about it?"

"Aunt Sarah always said I should never do anything without a good reason. She said people make their most serious mistakes when they act without considering beforehand."

"Does your uncle follow that advice?"

"No, and I suppose I couldn't want a better reason to heed Aunt Sarah's warning."

"Okay. If you *must* know, I'll tell you, but you'll think it's pretty silly." Eliza found it impossible to believe Cord could be silly.

"You're so lovely it would be hard not to love you. You sing like an angel and bake pie a man would walk a mile for."

Eliza felt disappointed. She expected him to mention milking the cow next.

"But I don't think I love you for any of those reasons. I love you because you're so worried about the children's education and are too soft-hearted to tell Otis Redding you'll switch him if he touches another pigtail. I love you because you need someone to protect you from your own innocence and because there's something about the look you give me that makes me feel so big and powerful and completely wonderful I damn near burst my britches with pride."

Eliza stared at him misty-eyed. How could she, insignificant soul that she was, make this huge, powerful man who owned thousands of cows and hundreds of thousands of acres, and who dared any man to touch what was his—how could she affect him so?

"I know that can't really be true," she said, barely able to say the words, "but it was so very nice of you to say it."

"*Nice* be damned," Cord said explosively. "I think my cows are *nice* and my land is *nice*, but I never felt as if losing them would tear the insides out of me. I think about them constantly because they are part of the work I do, but they're not

111

part of *me*. They don't keep me awake wondering if they're comfortable, if they're happy, or if they might permit me to spend a little more time with them."

"And I do all those things?"

"You're the most wonderful thing that has come into my life. When will you believe I'll never be happy until I spend the rest of my life loving you?"

"Not until you tell me at least once every day."

"Neither once a day nor once an hour will be enough until you *believe* I love you, until you *know* it so thoroughly I won't ever have to tell you again." He took her in his arms and kissed her roughly, bruising her mouth and bending her head back until she thought her neck would break. "I want you to know, beyond any doubt, I don't look for any higher honor on this earth than for you to become my wife."

Eliza almost stopped breathing. Not even she could doubt his intentions now. "I don't know anything about being a rancher's wife. I'm nervous around horses and the only cow I know anything about is a milk cow. It'll be just like taking on a new hand, only one much greener than Royce and Sturgis."

"I'll chance it if you will. I don't know anything about being a husband, but I'm willing to dedicate the rest of my life to making you the happiest woman in Wyoming."

"Please love me," she begged, her desperate cry echoing from the empty well of ten loveless years. "Love me until I scream and try to drive you away. Hold me tight and never let me go."

Cord's arms closed around her so tightly for a moment Eliza thought he *would* crush her to death and she would die in his arms, but not only did she continue to live, she felt more alive than ever. Her head fell back, and she shivered with pleasure as his lips trailed down the white, fluted arch of her throat. She held him tightly, returning with full value the intensity of his caress. His rough cheek, newly shaved and smelling refreshingly clean, tore at the satin texture of her cheeks and neck, but she invited him to kiss her again and again. His lips had ignited a fire within her that burned away all the years of doubt and misery.

She felt engulfed by his embrace; in contrast, her arms around his neck felt like the merest thread of restraint. He was like a living, breathing dynamo in her arms, one that

112

could explode at any minute and shatter her whole fragile existence. Yet this awe-inspiring strength enclosed her in a protective circle that made her feel wonderfully safe.

But that was as nothing when compared to the erupting rockets of sweet anguish that rippled through her when Cord unbuttoned the top of her dress and slipped a warm hand under her breast. Her eyes flew open in startled inquiry and her body became rigid. It was on her lips to deny him, to halt this invasion by his impudent hands, but the pleasurable yearning that rapidly spread through her body deprived her of the ability to think or act. Delicious, aching, paralyzing desire traced a fiery path to the nerve centers of her body like sparks from a dynamite fuse. Then Cord's lips touched the heated flesh of her rosy-tipped breast and her whole being was racked by an explosion of ecstasy. It was as though her body had been reduced to one fiery spot seared by his scalding lips. Nothing else mattered, there *was* nothing else but the plunging desire to rush toward this exquisite torture. Under the torrid onslaught of his hands and lips Eliza's body twisted and arched against him.

"By God, you're beautiful," Cord muttered, hoarse with desire, "more beautiful than I ever imagined." His eyes devoured her inch by inch while his fingertips luxuriated in the softness of her skin and his lips tasted the sweetness of her flesh.

Eliza hardly heard him. Her whole body had become a symphony of unfamiliar desires while urgent need welled up from somewhere deep within and washed over every part of her being in ever more turbulent waves. She couldn't think, she didn't *want* to think, only immerse herself in the sensations that were propelling her toward a state of utter bliss; she yielded herself wholeheartedly to the fiery confluence of emotions she barely understood and needs she had not even suspected.

Eliza's whole consciousness was so absorbed in this sensual uproar she was unaware Cord had unbuttoned her skirt until one hand zigzagged its way up her bare thigh. With the power and suddenness of a bolt of lightning, a feeling of panic sprang up that utterly vanquished the desire striving to reduce her will to a pool of nothing. Quite abruptly, the searing heat turned to ice-cold terror and her body, so will-

113

ingly entwined with Cord's, became rigid with fright. Her lips ceased to plead for his caresses, and her arms fell from his neck; she lay in his embrace like something inanimate.

Cord was deep under the sway of powerful desire, but he stopped at once. "Did I hurt you?"

Eliza was unable to speak. Her head shake was barely perceptible, but when he moved his hand tentatively along her thigh her eyes stared at him like a terrified animal.

"I've frightened you," he said, and sat up without waiting for an answer.

"It was just that it was a surprise to me," she said softly.

"Odd, isn't it," Cord muttered, angry at himself. "I'm the one who insisted everyone treat you like a lady, yet I go grabbing at you like a bull in heat."

Eliza wanted desperately to explain, to save him from this self-flagellation, but she didn't know what to say. Her mind and body were in such chaotic disorder she didn't know what anything meant. She longed to go back to when Cord held her tightly and covered her face with passionate kisses, but the magic of the afternoon was shattered beyond repair, and she didn't protest when Cord gathered up the picnic things and helped her into the buckboard. As much as she longed to stay with him, she desperately needed time to think and to absorb what had heretofore been a mystery to her. It wasn't that her feelings for Cord had changed. Rather, she had discovered being in love involved more than she imagined, and she needed time to see how it all fit together.

Eliza hardly remembered the trip home. Cord talked and she responded, but all the while her mind was frantically searching for answers despite the fact Cord's nearness kept her wits in a constant tangle. Only after he had left her at the cabin could she begin to make sense of her thoughts. She put off going inside even though she knew it was time to start supper.

Why hadn't she ever been told about love between a man and a woman? Shock had caused her to withdraw from him; that and pure terror. She still trembled so it was hard to think. To be loved and admired, to be wanted and pursued, was enough to learn in one day. To discover that Cord intended to claim her body, as well as her soul, was too much.

114

But what was she afraid of? Certainly not Cord. Even now she would have given anything to be at his side, to know she would never have to leave him again. She trusted him as she had never trusted anyone since her Aunt Sarah died. A shocking idea occurred to her. She trusted him *more* than she ever trusted her aunt! That shouldn't be possible, yet somehow it was. She had trusted him after the first few minutes and had yielded up her mind and soul to him long before she realized it. He had never violated this trust and had continued to build on it without any promise of reward.

And now he had asked her to marry him; he was offering himself and everything he had worked so hard to acquire to her. Wasn't she ready to offer him her all?

And that's what it was, Eliza realized with sudden clarity; it was a commitment to Cord that would neither waver nor alter throughout the span of her life. Yielding up her soul *was* different from yielding up her body, but weren't they part of the same? Was it possible to do one without the other? Could she say she truly loved him and continue to withhold part of herself from him? Still, it was one thing to admit to being in love, even desperately, hopelessly, wildly in love, and quite another to confirm it by yielding up the most private parts of her body. It was a commitment Eliza knew she wanted to make, but it was one she wasn't sure she was ready to make now.

What if her uncle found out? He might not throw her out, but he would subject her to abuse worse than abandonment! Yet somehow that didn't frighten her anymore. Whether or not she lived with him would affect her inner comfort, but only Cord had the power to affect her inner being, and Eliza felt certain he would never abandon her. Noticing the sun had begun to set, Eliza pushed her thoughts aside and hurried toward the cabin.

"Where have you been?" Ira demanded when the door opened to admit his niece. "Don't you realize it's nearly dark and you haven't even started dinner?"

"It won't take long." Eliza moved quickly past her uncle to take a leftover stew from the larder. He had been drinking, and that always made him cross.

"Forget the food," Ira ordered illogically. "Tell me where you've been all afternoon?"

"I was restless, so I went for a walk," Eliza stated, keeping her back to him. "I guess I stayed longer than I realized." Ira regarded her suspiciously.

"But what have you been doing this whole time? I couldn't find you anywhere."

Eliza's brain whirled, frantically trying to guess where her uncle would have searched for her. "I'm sorry if you had to saddle up the horse just to look for me."

"That's no answer. *Where* did you go?"

"I went over the ridge, past the Hodgess' place, and along the creek."

"I didn't see you."

"I must have been in the grove."

"Why didn't you answer me? I nearly yelled my head off."

"I guess I didn't hear you. I wasn't paying much attention."

"If you were in those trees, you'd have heard me."

"I don't know why I didn't hear you," Eliza said desperately. "I just didn't." She hoped the smell of the warming stew would make her uncle forget his curiosity, but Ira was like a dog with a bone.

"I don't supposed you cared that I might want to know where you'd gone?"

"You were asleep."

"You could have left a note."

"I didn't mean to be gone so long." He continued to watch her, suspicions forming in his mind. Eliza dared not raise her eyes; she was no good at dissembling.

"I need some eggs for the cornbread," she said.

"I'll get them. You keep on with dinner."

Eliza hoped he would have grown tired of the subject by the time he returned, but he was more agitated than ever.

"You weren't at the creek," Ira announced, setting the eggs down so hard Eliza wasn't surprised to find two were cracked. "And you weren't in those trees either." Eliza broke the eggs into the bowl. "Where were you?"

"I told you, I didn't pay much attention to where I went."

"I think you paid extra special attention to where you went and who you saw."

"It's Sunday. Nobody's about."

"You went to meet someone, didn't you?"

"Who would I meet?"

Ira paused a moment, then his face went black with rage. "You met Stedman, didn't you, even though the bastard tried to kill us?"

"That's not true." Eliza was shaking, a strained look in her eyes. "He just ran us off the creek."

"You admit it! You ran off to meet that whore's son."

"You've no right to call him names," Eliza declared, roused to wrath by the attack on Cord.

"Now you're defending him."

"I am not," she said, attempting to sound disinterested, "but you're making a fool of yourself going on about him every time you get a chance. People are beginning to snicker behind your back, even Croley."

The truth of these accusations only served to fan Ira's temper. "You needn't think to hide anything from me, Elizabeth Smallwood. There's not a person within thirty miles of Buffalo who doesn't know he's after you."

"They're not as blinded by hate as you," Eliza said caustically as she placed the plates on the table with a clatter. "But they do know they'll have to answer to him if they lay a hand on me." She slammed the stew down in front of her uncle's plate, but Ira, too angry to notice his dinner, grabbed Eliza's arm and forced her to look him in the face.

"Do you know what it would do to the saloon if everybody knew you were sneaking off to see Stedman?"

"Don't I mean more to you than a bunch of cowboys laying down their pay for a drink and a few songs?" she asked miserably.

"That's no answer. *Where did you go this afternoon?*" Ira demanded, his wrath unabated.

"I told you I just wandered around," Eliza repeated, saddened by her uncle's complete indifference to her question.

"That's not true," he raged, shaking her like a sapling in a storm. "Tell me where you went!"

"I've told you, but you won't believe me."

"You haven't told me the truth."

Eliza knew that no matter what she said, he wasn't going to believe her. "If you can't believe anything else, maybe you can believe that wherever I went, I've done nothing I'm ashamed of."

"Damned, bloodsucking cowboys!" he roared. "They're

determined to take everything from me." Striking out blindly in his rage, Ira hit Eliza in the mouth and she slumped into a chair, unable to hold back a whimper of pain. Ira was frightened by what he had done, and he tried to cover his shock by helping Eliza roughly to her feet. "It was an accident," he mumbled. "I lost my temper."

"If you lose it again I won't be able to sing for a month." Eliza knew no matter how furious he might be with her for seeing Cord, Ira hadn't intended to hit her.

"Get dinner on the table," Ira directed, still conscience-stricken but turning angry at Eliza for putting him in the wrong.

"I already have," she said through a rapidly swelling lip. They sat without speaking.

"You're not eating," he finally said.

"I'm not hungry."

"You need to keep up your strength." She didn't respond. The look of sadness deepened, but gradually a hard look remolded her countenance, a setting of features that had never before appeared on Eliza's face.

Ira's disposition gradually recovered its equilibrium, and by the time the meal was over he had forgotten he had ever been repentant. "Hurry up with the dishes. You don't have much time to get dressed."

Eliza lifted her eyes from her plate and looked squarely at her uncle. "I'm not going to sing tonight," she said.

Anger and hurt made Eliza say the words; a desire to be treated as something more than a workhorse gave her the courage to stand behind them.

"The swelling is hardly noticeable. It'll be gone in a couple of hours."

"I will not be seen with a swollen lip and bruised cheek." There was a moment of stunned silence, and then Ira's features settled into a look of angry displeasure.

"Do you want Mr. Stedman to see me and start asking questions?" Eliza paused. "Even if he's not there, someone's bound to tell him."

"You mean you'd tell him I hit you?"

"I will if I have to," Eliza promised, willing to make use of any leverage she could. "I'll tell him and Mrs. Baylis and Mr. Burton and everybody else."

"You'd set all them against me?" Ira asked furiously.

"Only if you force me." Eliza's confidence grew with each passing minute.

They remained perfectly still, two people frozen in time, each gauging the other, each realizing they no longer knew the person they faced.

"You know I wouldn't hit you intentionally," Ira acknowledged, knowing he had already lost.

"I know, and I'll continue to sing, but I won't go back until the bruises are gone."

"That could take several days," Ira hollered, flaring up again.

"You should have thought of that before you hit me."

The decision hung in the balance; Eliza wondered if her courage would hold out, but she remembered Cord's arms around her, and the flutter in her stomach disappeared. She was fighting for more than just a bruise; she was fighting her own fears and her habit of running away. She was fighting to be worthy of a man who could stand up to a town, an entire county, the whole *state* without fear.

Ira couldn't read Eliza's thoughts, but he knew she meant what she said, and there was nothing he could do about it. If it ever got out he had struck her, even accidentally, Ella Baylis would see to it everybody heard of it in a matter of hours and that could ruin him. Ira ground his teeth in anger, determined not to give in to any further demands, but he remembered what Cord had done in the saloon and was uneasy. Croley wouldn't protect him, and the customers would enjoy a fight, if you could call murder a fight.

"Be there by Wednesday."

"If the bruises disappear."

"I'll tell everyone you're sick. Until then, you're not to leave this cabin."

"I won't see Mr. Stedman if that's what you mean, but I will go to school. And to the store."

"You can't be seen looking like this."

"But I need supplies."

"I'll get them. One look at you and Ella will have it all over town."

"Okay, you go to the store, but I have to go to school. The children won't care. I can tell them I ran into the bedpost.

119

It'll be a great joke."

"You're not to leave the place for anything or anybody," Ira exploded.

Eliza's knees started to knock, but she found her resolution had stiffened. "You can't keep me locked up like a prisoner and then expect me to sing for you," she argued. "I've got to be able to come and go like any other grown woman."

"Not so you can sneak off with that scum."

Cord doesn't need you to defend him, Eliza told herself. Just keep your mind on your own self for now. "I'm not running off to meet anyone."

"What about this afternoon?"

"I told you, I went walking and lost track of the time."

Ira didn't believe her, but she had clung to her story so tenaciously he was beginning to wonder if she might not be telling the truth after all. "Only to school," he said, giving in reluctantly. "Mind you, I'll be keeping my eye on you."

"Of course." Eliza lowered her eyes, afraid Ira might see her look of triumph. She busied herself with cleaning up.

"Women are ignorant fools," he muttered as he stalked angrily out into the night, but if he could have seen Eliza after he closed the door he might have had second thoughts.

She stood perfectly still until the sound of his horse's hooves died away, then she let out a whoop and danced wildly around the room until her head was spinning so madly she couldn't keep her balance and she collapsed into a chair.

"Life is so beautiful," she said, laughing with happiness. "I'll never be afraid of it again."

Chapter 13

A week later Eliza drew the buckboard the town had provided for her use to a stop before a cabin nearly as run-down as the one she and her uncle occupied. She was about to make her first call on the parents of a student, and she wasn't at all sure what she was going to say, but she had insisted on having this school, and it was up to her to make it work.

Bear Creek ran close by the cabin and the crops near its banks flourished, but the ground that rose from the creek level was very rocky, and the hills behind the cabin looked to be full of blind canyons and hidden draws. Not the sort of land for a homestead.

Susan Haughton was very surprised to open her door and find the new schoolteacher on the steps, but she invited Eliza in, offered her coffee, and made her comfortable.

"Though no lady can be comfortable in a place like this," she said bitterly, gesturing at the poor but spotlessly maintained cabin. "It's worse than a cow barn."

"I wanted to talk with you about Billy," Eliza began, so disconcerted by Mrs. Haughton's apologizing for her home she plunged straight to the object of her visit.

"Has he been late to school? I make sure he is dressed and out of here early every morning."

"He hasn't come to school at all the last three days."

"What?" his mother asked, suddenly still and tense.

"Billy is a nice boy, very quiet and obedient, but he got into a fight last week and I haven't seen him since."

Susan twisted the corners of her apron, and then abruptly

sank into the chair opposite Eliza. "It's Sam and me." She encountered Eliza's blank look. "We fight all the time. Sometimes it goes on for days."

"Why?" It was impertinent, but she didn't know what else to say.

"Because I hate Wyoming and I hate cows, but most of all I hate the unending grind to eke out a miserable living here." In her agitation, Susan started resetting all her hairpins. "I know it's my fault we're here without anything to go back to, but I can't stop blaming Sam. No man could bear it, but he puts up with it as long as he can and then he explodes. Now I'm pregnant again." Eliza's rush of joy was rudely dashed down. "I don't want my baby to be born in this place," Susan said fiercely.

"We had a small farm in Missouri," she went on, "not much, but enough to make a living. Sam liked to go to the saloons. He got drunk occasionally, but mainly he told stories and sang songs a female would be ashamed to hear. The men loved it so much the saloon owners started to pay him a little something whenever he would come in, but I was afraid the company would ruin him and I kept after him to stay home. Well, you might as well ask Sam to give up and die as pass a saloon and not go in, so I talked him into coming out here. I made sure we were a long way from town. I also made him promise he wouldn't go into town without me. He's stuck to his promise, but it's taken the life out of him."

"Maybe you should go back to Missouri."

"It took most of the money we had to set up here. It took the rest to keep going. Now, with the baby coming, I don't know what to do."

"What does Billy think about Wyoming?"

"He really doesn't care where he is, but he's a sensitive child, and I hate to see him bullied by other children."

"Doesn't he know how to fight?"

"No, but his Pa insists he stand up and defend himself. I supposed he's in the right of it, but I don't like it. They pick at him because we're farmers, especially the boys whose pa's run a few head of cattle or steal even more."

"You know who rustles cattle?" Eliza asked, astonished.

"Everybody knows. They don't keep it a secret. The way they see it, if you don't steal, something must be wrong with

122

you. That's what the fight was about. Didn't you know that?"

"No," Eliza said, faltering, her face drained of color.

"The other boys taunted him, said his pa was a fool to starve with Matador steers around for the taking."

"But the Matador belongs to Mr. Stedman," Eliza exclaimed involuntarily.

"And he never lets us forget it," Susan said bitterly. "I suppose the only reason he hasn't forced us out is because he knows we'll have to leave on our own before long. Though God knows where we'll go, or how we'll find the money to get there."

"But Mr. Stedman's not like that."

"Maybe not, but he's made it abundantly plain he doesn't want us here."

"Won't he pay you for the land?"

"Yes, but Sam refuses to sell to him. And of course nobody else is fool enough to buy this place, so we're caught between Sam's pride and my foolishness." The cabin door opened and Billy Haughton entered with his father.

"Sam, what happened?" shrieked Susan. Billy was wet and muddy, tears stained his cheeks, and his right hand massaged his tender buttocks.

"Go on," his father commanded, "tell your mother what you did."

"I tried to run away from Pa and fell into the creek. He gave me a licking."

"Sam Haughton, how could you, after all that boy's been through?"

"Being soft and dreamy is one thing. Running from me is another."

Eliza's inclination was to escape as quickly as she could, but she had to stay. It was her duty as a teacher; it was her desire because of Cord.

"He's no coward," Susan declared in angry defense of her child. "You know he got into that fight because of you." It was obvious how much it pained Sam Haughton to know his failure to provide for his family was the reason for his son's trouble.

"Billy doesn't like the rough games the other boys favor, but he's not cowardly," Eliza said, surprised to find the words coming, unbidden, out of her mouth. "They don't understand him, but he has earned a grudging respect." All three Haughtons stared at her. "He's very proud of both of you, but he doesn't understand what's happening. Why not sit down and explain everything to him. It won't change things, but it will help him understand the problems you face. You may also learn something of the difficulties he encounters every day.

"Now I must be getting back," Eliza said, getting to her feet. "My uncle will think I've forgotten his dinner." She hurried out to her buckboard despite Susan's offers to join them for supper. Sam Haughton followed.

"Thanks for taking an interest in Billy," he said a little awkwardly. "His ma and I don't see eye to eye on how to raise him, but he's a good boy." Eliza allowed Sam to help her into her seat. "Would you come again?"

"I'm sure Billy will be all right once you've talked things over with him."

"Not for Billy. For Susan."

"Your wife?"

"She doesn't get much company. We live too far from town for the ladies to visit, and we're too poor for them to want to. It would mean the world to her if she could have someone to talk to now and then."

"Surely one of the farmers' wives . . ."

"I could tell she took a liking to you."

"All right," Eliza agreed with a smile. "I can't get away often, but I'll do the best I can. I know what it's like to be so lonely you make up people to talk to."

"Susan does that!" exclaimed Sam, surprised to find anyone else indulged in the habit he found so peculiar. "I thought it meant she was going crazy."

Eliza peered in at the window of the land office and was relieved to find it empty. She had come by three times that morning only to discover someone talking with the agent each time. She plucked up her courage and went in. The room was quite small, and under the stress of the unrelenting heat the agent appeared to be cross and out of temper.

"What can I do for you?" he asked disagreeably without raising his eyes from his work.

"I would like to claim some land."

The agent looked up at the sound of a female voice and his eyes nearly started from his head. "Where's your husband?" he managed to ask, swallowing hard.

"I don't have one."

"Ought to if you want to claim land."

"Can't I claim it myself?"

"I suppose so, but you ought to have a husband," he repeated idiotically.

"Well, I don't."

"Say, aren't you that singer at the saloon?"

"Yes, I am," Eliza replied, glad he didn't connect her with the school.

"What's someone like you wanting with a homestead?"

"You can't expect me to go on singing in saloons for the rest of my life, can you?" she said, thinking fast. "I need a piece of land to settle on some day."

"Ought to have a husband."

"I don't intend to get a husband just to claim some land," she snapped, her temper beginning to rise.

"I guess not," the agent replied, deciding her objection seemed reasonable enough. "Where is it?"

"Where is what?"

"The land."

"On Bear Creek, at that big willow thicket." The agent's eyes flew open.

"Do you realize where that is?"

"Yes. It's right next to Mr. Stedman's land."

"It's in the *middle* of Matador land."

"What's wrong with that? Mr. Stedman seems to be quite a nice gentleman." The agent suddenly remembered something he had heard about Stedman taking a interest in the singer. Well, that might explain it, but he couldn't believe Cord Stedman would allow anyone to homestead that land. Still, it was none of his business, and he had no intention of getting in the middle of anything like that. He pulled out his maps.

"What are the boundaries of your piece?"

"What?" Eliza tried hard to keep her dismay out of her voice.

"Where does your claim stop and start?"

She had no idea what to say . "Do I have to tell you that?"

"Of course. I have to know the exact limits so no one else can claim the same land." He waited for Eliza's reply with patient resignation.

"I want as much land next to the creek as I can get," she said remembering what Cord had said about control of the water.

"There isn't all that much left."

"Can I get all the Matador doesn't have?"

"That'll put your claim on both sides of the creek."

"I know."

"It floods in the spring, sometimes right bad."

"Oh, that doesn't matter."

Women, thought the agent, flipping his maps around with a jerk. "You're going to have to give me some boundaries," he said irritably. "You just can't say you want land on the creek."

"Could I see the map?" He spun it around again.

"Here is the piece you're talking about," he said pointing out a particularly twisting part of the creek.

"Does all that other land belong to Mr. Stedman."

"Every acre."

"Then give me that whole piece right there."

"You still have to have boundaries."

"Could you set them for me?" she asked smiling helplessly.

"I suppose. You could meet me there and show me what you want."

Eliza began to fidget. "I'd rather nobody knew about this. You see, I want this to be a surprise to Mr. Stedman and if you and I were seen walking about with measuring rods, or whatever you use, that would spoil everything."

I *bet* it would, the agent thought privately.

"Can't you just put something down?"

"No, I can't," the little man said, raising his voice in exasperation. "I have to have exact measurements or landmarks. The United States government doesn't deal in approximations."

"But I can't give you any measurement or landmarks. All I want to do is claim that land. Isn't there some way you can give me all I'm supposed to have without me going out there?"

The agent couldn't resist the appeal of those huge brown

126

eyes. "I *could* record the claim and do the measurements later. It's not like the land is going to disappear." He laughed at his own joke.

"I would appreciate it so much," said Eliza, distracted by the sound of footsteps on the walk outside the land office. "I'm certain I can trust you to see it's done properly." The steps passed on and Eliza drew a long, slow breath, but her courage was gone.

"Stop," the agent called out as she turned to leave. "You've got to sign the deeds."

"Can't I sign them some other time?"

"Would tomorrow suit?"

"No. How about early Saturday morning?"

"Nine o'clock?"

"Eight. And remember, not a word to anyone." Eliza stuck her head out the door and looked up and down the sidewalk as she stepped out, but she saw no one she knew. She settled her bonnet low over her face, tilted her parasol over her eyes, and walked quickly toward the saloon.

"Billy hasn't been fighting again, has he?" Susan asked anxiously as Eliza climbed down from the buckboard a week later.

"No. I just came to see how you were getting on, and to bring you some of Mrs. Baylis's peach preserves. She has more than she can use, but no one could convince her to let the fruit drop."

The two ladies were soon enjoying a cozy chat. Susan toasted some slices of the bread she'd made for supper and spread some of the peach preserves over it.

"Just look at me, and after telling Billy time and time again he couldn't have anything to eat because it would ruin his dinner."

"Surely he won't hold it against you. Not just this once."

"You have a lot to learn about children, Miss Smallwood, if you think they'll allow adults even one mistake."

"Please, call me Eliza."

Susan looked rather teary-eyed. "Only if you'll call me Susan. Every time someone calls me Mrs. Haughton, I feel like I'm about to be punished."

127

Eliza smiled as a reflex, but her mind was wrestling with how to bring the conversation around to the reason for her visit "Have you and your husband come to any solution about leaving Wyoming?"

"We can't. Not now with me expecting a baby. I don't travel well."

"What are your plans for the winter?"

"To tell you the truth, I'm afraid to ask. Sam grows more silent every day. There are times when I wish he *would* go to a saloon."

"Do you really mean that?" Eliza asked eagerly, relieved to have the difficult subject broached for her.

"I certainly do. As much as I missed having him with me of evenings, I know it was a mistake to make him stay home. Besides, it gave him a chance to be with people, and that's something he needs. It's something *I* need as well, but I never realized it until you came last week."

"There must be other women. . . ."

"Plenty of them, but they're too busy with their own families to be paying social calls."

"Most people come into town on Sunday. They often stay around and visit for a while, even have dinner. Maybe you and Sam would like to come."

"I'll think about it," Susan promised, knowing they barely had the money to feed themselves as it was.

"I had wanted to talk to Sam."

"What about?"

"You know my uncle owns a saloon, and he's been looking for someone to help me." Eliza blushed. "I sing there each night."

"I know. Billy couldn't wait to tell me his schoolteacher was the *Sage* lady."

Eliza smiled reluctantly. "Well, I can't sing very much—the school takes up an awful lot of time—and I was hoping Sam would agree to help out some, tell some of his stories and sing a few songs. You have no idea how hard it is to find anyone who can hold those cowboys' interest for more than a few minutes. Do you think he would agree to give it a try? It would mean a lot to my uncle."

"Give it a try!" squealed Susan. "He'll probably be at the door before you get back. Can I tell him now? He's out back splitting wood." She paused, her happiness rigidly held in check. "Will he get paid for it?"

"Naturally. Of course he'll be on trial at first—I couldn't get my uncle to hire him without seeing if the men liked him—but he'll get two dollars every night."

"Two dollars a night!"

"I know it should to be more."

"That's more than enough," Susan assured her, rushing to the door to call her husband. "You're a good friend, Eliza."

"The peach preserves were friendship," Eliza told her, blushing furiously. "This is business. If Sam's successful, I won't have to sing so often."

"Do you really dislike it? I should think it would be wonderful."

"I don't dislike it as much as I used to, but it still makes me very nervous."

"But to have all those people applauding. It must be the most wonderful feeling in the world to make so many people happy."

"I never looked at it like that," Eliza confessed. "I always thought my teaching was the only worthwhile thing I did."

"I don't know what it was like in Kansas, but Wyoming is the biggest empty space in the world. It's just like coming to the edge of the world and falling off into nowhere. Don't let anyone talk you out of singing for those men. That's as much a community service as teaching the young'uns." Eliza didn't know quite what to say, but when Susan broke the news to her husband, she didn't have time to think of anything except getting out of the cabin before she was overwhelmed by their gratitude.

"If you want me to start tonight," Sam said, "give me a few minutes to wash up and I'll come with you."

"Eat your dinner," Eliza said smiling. "Uncle wants you late."

"I'll be there, and I promise, Miss Smallwood, you won't be sorry you did this."

"I'm sure I won't. Now don't forget to help Billy with his lessons for tomorrow. His work is better, but his handwriting is still difficult to read."

"You mean impossible," sighed his mother. "I've had him copying out his letters every night and his father goes over his

129

sums."

"That's more than enough. He can't help but improve." She waved goodbye and sent her horse back toward Buffalo at a quick trot.

Chapter 14

The hot afternoon sun beat down upon Cord, making it hard to stay awake. He was near the cabin of that stiff-necked, stubborn squatter Sam Haughton, and usually just thinking about a block of land in the middle of his range that didn't belong to him would have been enough to rivet Cord's attention, but today he could barely keep his eyes open. Too many nights in the saddle, he thought rather vaguely. He badly needed rest, but he hadn't worked like a slave for five years to relax his guard just when the reward for his labors was in sight.

Beef prices had finally risen again and his first calf crop would go to market this year. For the first time he would be selling steers he hadn't had to buy as yearlings or as two- or three-year-olds, and his margin of profit would be twenty to thirty times greater. Homesteads in the middle of his grazing lands were a threat to the safety of his herds, and he couldn't rest easy as long as the land was not in his control. Not that Haughton's claim was worth much. Only a greenhorn would have picked it for a homestead.

A vision of Eliza rose to Cord's mind and cut short his ruminating. He tried to make his mind return to Haughton, but it was no use. At least a dozen times a day he relived the moment when fear replaced the look of trust in Eliza's eyes and his insides shriveled into a painful knot all over again. All the emotional energy had been wrung out of him days ago—could it really have been just over a week?—but still it continued to rob him of his sleep and destroy his peace of mind.

He cursed himself for thinking of nothing but his own

needs. Hadn't it been her innocence that had appealed to him in the first place? Hadn't he known she was shy as a hummingbird around men? God only knew by what providence she had always been at ease with him, and he had so stupidly, selfishly, blindly ruined it all. She had trusted him to keep her safe, not expecting anything for herself, just accepting his love with a sense of wonder and a feeling of unworthiness. Now he didn't know if she would ever feel comfortable around him again.

He hadn't worked up the courage to face her. More than once he'd stopped himself in the act of getting ready to go to town; he was loathe to approach her again so soon because there was so much at stake. She was everything he ever wanted in a woman, and he couldn't afford to make another wrong move. He couldn't ask anybody for help either. He had to do this on his own, and he had to do it right.

Eliza allowed her horse to wend its way back toward town at a slow trot, her mind full of the Haughtons' misfortunes. Not that there was as much to worry about now that Sam had a job at the Sweetwater, but it did help keep her mind off Cord.

She still didn't have answers to all her questions, but she knew the final answer to every question was Cord himself. No matter what she decided on her own, it would all come down to him in the end. She had hoped he would come to see her before now, but even though he was the solution to her problems, he was still at the center of her difficulties and she didn't know what she wanted to say.

The sight of Cord's huge black gelding topping a nearby rise caused her to involuntarily pull back sharply on the reins. Her horse reared in protest, and that brought Cord to her side at a gallop.

"Are you meaning to rescue me again?" she asked. It felt so natural. She wasn't nervous at all.

"Your horse could have bolted."

"I'm afraid I'm not a very good driver."

"All you need is someone to show you what to do." He paused. "I'd be pleased to teach you, if you'd let me." She was smiling like she used to, and Cord pressed ahead. "Maybe we could begin this Saturday?"

"I can't," Eliza said, regretfully. "School started late this year and we're using Saturday as a makeup day."

But Cord met Eliza in town two days later, and was surprised to learn she had developed a sore throat.

"I'm taking a few days off from teaching," she informed him. "Uncle Ira hired the postmaster's wife to take over until I'm better." Cord looked surprised. "I couldn't believe it either, but he would have gone all the way to Cheyenne for a replacement when the doctor told him I might not be able to sing for weeks unless I had some rest." So without offering much resistance, Eliza let Cord talk her into going for a drive two days later.

The day was hot and the sunshine blinding. Cord was coaching Eliza as she carefully guided the buckboard down a steep and rocky incline. "Pull up next to that thicket, and don't let off on the brake or you'll run over your horse." He had spent the last two hours teaching her how to handle a buckboard, but it was time to eat, and the deep shade of the cottonwood thicket was a welcome sight. He unharnessed the horse so it could it graze, and then spread several blankets on the hard ground. Next he unloaded the wagon, and while Eliza set out the food, he headed down to the creek for some fresh water. For some reason he was feeling unusually warm.

The creek was high with the runoff from melting snow and summer rains, and its inviting, sparkling clearness made Cord think he would feel better if he splashed some water on his face. Then thinking better of that, he took a deep breath and plunged his whole head under water.

Cord had been so preoccupied with his own thoughts he had paid no attention to the tracks in the soft earth leading into the coolness of a canebrake, and he didn't know he had disturbed a bull resting in the tall rushes. The animal thrust its head and shoulders out of the cane far enough to see Cord kneeling only a few yards away. He pawed the earth furiously, and when the human did not respond, he lowered his head and charged.

Eliza had paused in the midst of laying out the food, her whole nervous system keyed up by the stimulus of Cord's presence. Somehow, she had to find the words to let him know she still loved and trusted him and that nothing he could ever do would destroy that. She allowed her gaze to wander down to the stream in search of Cord; otherwise, she would never have seen the bull when it emerged from the thicket.

She was numb with fear, but she jumped to her feet the instant the animal begin to paw the earth. "Cord!" she screamed with all her might, and without a thought for danger, started down the hill at such a rapid pace only sheer good luck kept her from falling. She hadn't taken into account the steepness of the descent, and she was soon traveling faster than her feet could run. A sense of panic seized her. She took a few bouncing strides in a desperate attempt to keep her feet under her, then with a shriek, she lost her balance and dove into the water, colliding with Cord and knocking him into the middle of the stream and out of the path of the charging bull.

Cord had raised his head out of the water just in time to see the bull charge, and as he dived into the water, Eliza hit him broadside and the bull's attack was met by a discouraging gush of water full in the face. The heavily muscled beast bellowed in fury at his quarry, now out of reach in the deep water, pawed the creek edge angrily, and then turned and trotted off.

The swirling waters soaked through Eliza's clothes before she could regain her feet, and their enormous weight immediately pulled her under. Cord plunged through the water to her side and hauled her up. She was gasping for air and from the shock of the cold water that was rapidly drawing the heat from her body. Eliza wiped the streaming water from her eyes in time to see the bull lumbering over the rise, and her body slumped in relief.

"What on earth made you pitch headlong down the hill like that?" demanded Cord, relief that she was safe easing the tension in his body.

"I saw the bull," Eliza gasped, still breathless. "You had your head in the water."

"So you came skittering down the slope intending to save me from the indignity of being soundly butted from behind."

"Yes, I mean no," Eliza stammered. "I was afraid he would

134

gore you. You could have been killed."

"Did it ever enter your mind, my fair savior, that *you* could be lying dead on the bank this very minute?"

"He didn't see me."

"Or did you think that by throwing yourself into the water with a horrific splash, you could *scare* him into running away with his tail between his legs?"

"I don't suppose I thought about it at all," Eliza admitted, "but he did run away."

"Look at yourself. You're sopping wet." Eliza looked down and was horrified to see her dress clinging to her body like a second skin.

"Let's get out of this water before you catch your death of cold."

"I can't move," Eliza exclaimed in surprise. "I feel like I'm anchored to the bottom."

"I'll carry you," Cord offered, and swept her up in his powerful arms. Eliza had never been picked up by a man, but she found she liked it very much and snuggled down quite happily even though her teeth chattered uncontrollably.

"You're dripping wet too," she said.

"I'm used to being wet, cold, or covered with snow."

"We didn't have mountain streams in Kansas, because we didn't have any mountains, but I've been wet and cold many times before," Eliza said a trifle defiantly.

"Are you trying to say you don't need me to take care of you?"

"Well, not exactly."

"How about this? After risking your neck to chase the bull away, I could have the decency to be the tiniest bit grateful."

"Well, you could," Eliza said with a tiny smile. "I could have just stayed by the buckboard." Suddenly she chuckled, tried to hide it, and then burst out in a laugh.

"What's so funny?"

"You should have seen yourself."

"I couldn't now, could I, not with my head in the water."

"Your rear end was stuck up in the air like you were digging your way into a prairie-dog hole head first."

"You didn't look so clever yourself," replied Cord, "hurtling down the hillside like a clump of tumbleweed in a high wind."

"I was just trying to get to you in a hurry. I screamed at

135

you, but you didn't hear me."

A hiccup of laughter shook Cord.

"You ungrateful man. If I had a mirror I'd let you see yourself."

"No, you wouldn't. You'd be afraid I'd show you what you look like with your hair in your face and your bonnet floating away."

Eliza looked around to see the straw-and-flower confection rapidly disappearing downstream. "My hat!" she cried. "I've got to get it back."

"You couldn't possibly wear it after that soaking. Can you imagine what Mrs. Burton would say if she were to see you now, especially with that soggy flowered thing drooping over your face?" Cord stood Eliza on her feet, and she clasped her hands to her sides in an effort to control the shivers that shook her from end to end.

"No more than she'd say about you," Eliza said with an unexpected shudder of desire. The swell of Cord's manhood, always disconcerting, was positively riveting in its prominence.

"Then it's a good thing she's not here. I've never had to revive a fainting female and I don't want to have to learn on her."

Eliza sank down on a rock.

"Now don't go getting settled. I don't suppose you thought to bring a change of clothes."

"Of course not. How was I to know I would end up soaking wet? I'll probably get pneumonia now."

"Seems I'm always rescuing you from some fix or other."

"You ungrateful man. I'm determined that for once *you* shall be indebted to *me*."

"Okay then, you figure out how we're going to dry off."

Eliza looked nonplussed. "We can sit here until the sun dries us out. It's really quite warm."

"It'll be dark before then, and the nights are usually very cool. You've got to take off those clothes. They'll dry a lot faster if you spread them in the sun."

"You can't be serious," Eliza exclaimed. "What if somebody comes along?"

"Except for the Haughtons, this is all my land, and the boys are several miles to the east. Besides, it's impossible for anyone to see us through all that cane."

"I just couldn't."

Cord took his rope, tied one end to the buckboard, and looped it around two trees. Then he took several more blankets out of the wagon and hung them over the rope, effectively screening them on all except the creek side.

"How many blankets do you have?"

"Enough." Cord's smile made her feel weak. "Come sit here."

Eliza left her seat on the rock and settled down on the blankets. "Are you *sure* no one can see us? I'd never be able to explain how I came to be sitting here with both of us dripping wet."

"I'm sure. What I need now is a bootjack," he said as he dropped down beside her and began to wrestle with his boot.

"Here, let me help." Eliza hugged the boot to her chest while Cord struggled to extract a foot wedged tightly inside by socks swollen with water. By the time the second boot was off, Eliza felt her brains were rattling around loose in her head.

"That's the last time I ever offer to take off a boot." She laughed as he pealed off his socks and spread them over the rock to dry.

"They'll have to be oiled tonight, or the leather will crack," explained Cord as he unbuttoned his shirt and spread it on the ground. Eliza wasn't paying much attention to his words. Cord didn't wear anything under his shirt, and his bare chest with its masses of short, curly dark hair and well-muscled shoulders filled her gaze.

"Same with harnesses. And if they break, nine times out of ten the horse will run away with you."

Eliza felt horses were already running away with her. Cord was making unmistakable preparations to remove his pants.

"Don't!" she managed to say in a hoarse whisper. By sheer force of will, she dragged her eyes from him, but her nerves were subjected to a second deadly battering when he settled back down beside her.

"You're cold," he said softly, his lips near her ear. "You really should get out of those clothes."

"No," she answered breathlessly.

"Then at least take off your outer garments. That way your

dress can dry and you can preserve your modesty." Eliza was unable to move, but Cord's nimble fingers, dancing like hot coals across her body, rapidly undid the buttons of her jacket and shirt. She felt helpless to resist as he took both those garments from her body; her soaked skirt seemed to disappear of its own accord. Cord stood up to spread her clothes out in the sun and Eliza closed her eyes. It was one thing to stare at him in fascination while she was safely dressed, but it was quite another to do so when her own body was perilously close to being stripped of its protective covering.

"You're still wearing your shoes."

Eliza nodded miserably.

"Hand over your foot."

Steeling herself, Eliza offered him her right foot. Her body went rigid as his fingers traveled up her leg, past her knee, to the roll in the top of her stockings halfway up her thigh. Her whole body seemed to consist of that one leg; every nerve was concentrated there.

"Now the other." Cord's removal of the second stocking merely substituted one limb for the other. When he had finally finished, Eliza felt limp, wrung out, too weak to even attempt to follow him with her eyes. Her whole being was on fire, her mind inflamed. Her nerves actually hurt with the intensity of their feeling.

"That's much better," Cord said, settling down beside her again. "It ought not take your things more than an hour to dry."

"An hour? What are we going to do for an hour?" Even if she could not have read the answer in Cord's eyes, her own body was screaming at her mind, forcing her to acknowledge that only the soggy petticoat remained as a bar to what filled her consciousness to the exclusion of everything else.

"You could sit close to me so I could keep you warm."

Eliza didn't tell him her blood was already boiling.

Cord moved closer and gathered her in his embrace. He kissed her tenderly, then with fierce, possessive energy, and all the tension between them dissolved. Eliza melted into his arms, not questioning why she was there, only glad that she was. She returned his kisses eagerly, her whole being longing to be as one with him. Any lingering doubt was gone. She knew then that whatever the future held for her, she must

138

give all she had and was into his safekeeping. That was the way she wanted it! That was the way it *had* to be.

"You are so beautiful I can hardly stand it," Cord murmured, burying his face in her fragrant hair. "After the other Sunday, I was afraid you might never want to see me again."

"Nothing could make me not want to see you again," she said solemnly.

"I've been going around all week wondering what to say and afraid of what would happen when I saw you again."

"It's all right," she whispered, looking into his passion-shrouded eyes. "I won't be afraid this time." For an instant Cord was motionless, his gaze plumbing hers to make sure he had heard her correctly, then he clasped her in an embrace that threatened to crush the life out of her body and covered her lips and eyes with an abundance of hot kisses.

Cord didn't need a second invitation. Before she had recovered her breath, his hands had unbuttoned her shift and his hungry lips captured her breasts as his hands roamed over her soft skin, seeking out sensitive points and driving them into a frenzy of pleasure. Spasms of aching need radiated to every part of her body, awakening a chorus of desire that overwhelmed her by its full-throated cry.

It was all going too fast, but neither of them could stop it. It was as if their bodies had been held in some kind of suspended state for the last several days, waiting to finish what they had already begun. There was no surprise, no resistance or feeling of embarrassment when he lifted the shift over her head and she lay naked before him; there was only the sense of final resolution. Cord's whole being was held motionless as he gazed in wonder on her unblemished loveliness.

"Is something wrong with me?" Eliza asked, confused by his sudden immobility.

"No," Cord answered, his breath escaping in a long sigh. "Everything about you is absolutely perfect." His fingers reached out to caress her skin, his hands to cup her breasts, his arms to draw her near. Slowly and deliberately his hands moved across her belly, down her side, and over her thigh. He felt her tense under his caress, her breath coming in short gasps, but she did not withdraw from him. Even more slowly his hand moved between her thighs and over her quivering

139

mound. Eliza's breathing stopped completely, only to begin again twice as fast when his fingers started to seek her out.

His hot lips sank to her aching breasts and he tortured first one and then the other with his restless tongue. All the while the probing, caressing, massaging fingers were doing the unthinkable, and a new kind of aching need began to well up from between her thighs. Eliza was caught between the desire to hold them at bay and the need to invite them to do more. In that instant Cord's fingers entered her and her body arched rigidly, her eyes open wide. She trembled violently until she felt exhausted, drained of all power to resist. Slowly she relaxed, helpless against him, helpless against herself, her open thighs inviting him to do as he would.

Cord shed his pants, but even the surprise of finding herself in the arms of a naked man had no power to restrain Eliza now. It was as though every question, every doubt, every longing had been answered, and nothing could keep her from reaching her goal. Here, in the person of one man, was all she wanted, and she rushed toward her fate with the inevitability of a river to the sea. She was not dismayed to find him suddenly above her, his body between her thighs and something firm and hot pressing into her innermost self. As wave after wave of delicious desire coursed through her, she invited him to become one with her, to enter into a union of body and spirit.

Eliza flinched at the sharp, unexpected pain of Cord's entry and her body tensed involuntarily, but her runaway need compelled her to draw him deeper inside her. His mumbled apology went unheeded as she wrapped her arms around his neck and drew his lips down to her. The passionate kisses became an exchange of volcanic lava as Cord penetrated deep with her. Eliza sucked in her breath, and let it out in an outpouring of longing. She clung to him, his lips, his body, trying to merge herself with him. The accelerating of Cord's movement within her served only to make her efforts more determined. Waves of desire flooding over her with increasing speed and power separated her from her earthly surroundings and she felt as though the two of them existed separately from anything else in creation.

Deliberately Cord brought her to a pitch where all her senses were simultaneously screaming for release. Even then

140

he did not heed her pleas, but drove her on to such exquisite agony she thought she would not be able to stand it. She clung to him, inviting, demanding, longing; she pounded on his back, drawing him into her, determined to *make* him satisfy her tormented body. At last, his own raging senses driving him toward the limits of his control, he could withhold himself no longer, and he plunged deep within her. With a moan of sheer ecstacy she rose to meet him and in a mounting frenzy they achieved release from a passion that had reached to the very core of their beings.

Chapter 15

For a long while they lay in each other's arms without speaking. Eliza was certain there were no words that could express the feeling of awe and wonder that filled her heart. Never in her wildest dreams had she thought she would find someone as wonderful as Cord. It seemed impossible he was next to her, his warmth spreading over her like an enveloping blanket. The heady wine of love filled her cup to overflowing, and it was all the more sweet for having been despaired of so long.

Cord stirred. Powerful muscles rippled along his limbs as he raised himself to his elbow. His eyes gazed at Eliza and a slow smile of contentment spread across his face.

"Did I please you?" she asked.

"I would have to be the most ungrateful man ever created not to be pleased." He drew her to him and planted kisses on her eyelids.

Eliza's heart overflowed with happiness, and she eagerly returned his embrace. It felt so natural to be next to him, his arms holding her tight, his naked body teasing her senses, she could not imagine why she had ever been afraid.

"You're offering me so much, and I have so little to give in return," Eliza said, but Cord put his fingers to her lips.

"All I want is you just the way you are. That's more than I ever hoped to find."

"For years I worried I would never find anyone who could make me feel as safe and wanted as you do. I still wake up some mornings and can't believe you're real."

"I'm very real, and I'll never stop wanting and needing you. I love you, and I'll never stop as long as I draw breath."

Eliza's throat constricted, damming up her words of love, but her tear-filled eyes were all the invitation Cord needed to smother her in his embrace. She welcomed the renewal of his passion and urged him to take her body into blessed captivity.

His big hands cupped her breasts and agile thumbs stroked her throbbing nipples. Abruptly Cord's lips took over the teasing of one breast, and Eliza's body arched as a free hand found its way between her thighs, massaging, probing, titillating until she felt fire beginning to spread through her body, engulfing her mind and senses in a haze of desire. Her hands reached out, encountered his chest, and slowly wandered down his body, over the rippling muscles of the flat abdomen pulled suddenly taut, until they reached the undeniable proof of Cord's desire for her.

Dimly, for the fire kindled by Cord's lips and hands was gradually dazzling her, she wondered that anything could be so soft and hard at the same time. She wondered how anything so enormous could fit inside her, but realized she was pulling him toward her, that she wanted him to become part of her.

"Please," she whispered, "now." Gently Cord eased within her, and with a shudder of relief Eliza relaxed and opened to accept him. Cord plunged ever deeper until Eliza thought she could burst with him. Then, gently he began to work within her, withdrawing slowly, and thrusting deep, then withdrawing once again. All the while his lips and hands caressed her body, finding the places where her sensitivity was the most acute, and tapping them to add fuel to the raging fires that consumed her body. Eliza thrust herself against Cord, demanding and insistent, willing him to proceed more quickly, to end the torture that was driving her out of her mind with ecstasy. But Cord kept the rhythm teasingly slow, just fast enough to spin out the crescendo of need in ever-widening wispy spirals. She began to squirm, her arms trying to draw him nearer, pull him deeper within her, make him move more quickly, but he remained impervious to her wants.

Eliza's breath came in deep gasps. She heard herself cry out, telling of her need, of the agony she was suffering, and still the maddening rhythm continued. She tried to capture

143

his body with her slim legs, tried to hold him with her lips. Only when her teeth sank into his shoulder did he give her relief.

With the grunt of a savage animal taking what was its own, he threw himself at her, driving, pumping with rapid, powerful strokes, surging deep within her until the fires of passion exploded all around her.

But Cord did not expend his seed, did not cease the torrid pace that quickly picked Eliza up and hurtled her into another spiral of pleasure until it burst around her, causing her whole body to twist and writhe. Still he rode her, driving her to another explosive release.

Eliza felt herself slipping away as wave after way burst over her. Then, through the dimness, she felt Cord's body tense, and the rhythm slow and become unsteady. Cord's breath sounded rough and labored. He grew more rigid and the pace slowed even further. Eliza felt him expand within her, become so hot she felt like she housed a volcano. For an instant Cord almost ceased to move, then with a guttural shout that tore from his body in one long moan, he plunged deep within and released himself in a series of driving thrusts. The swift change enveloped Eliza in one final burst of pleasure, and then they both subsided, completely drained of all energy, content to lie still and hold each other close.

Eliza sat listening to Melissa Burton's graduation speech, but her thoughts were miles away from the seventeen-year-old girl. As the minutes ticked by, events from the summer crowded in on her thoughts until she was no longer aware of the sound of Melissa's voice.

It had been a glorious three months. She had continued to see Cord, though not very often, and there was no doubt in her mind now that she loved him totally. Their time together was all the more precious because it was so short and stolen with such difficulty. It hadn't been easy to keep their meetings a secret, but her uncle's hatred of Cord was as great as ever, and she hadn't been able to think of anything to reverse it. As of yet, Cord hadn't put any pressure on her to announce their engagement, but she knew he wouldn't wait forever and she dreaded the prospect of her uncle publicly rejecting her fiancé. She couldn't bear the thought of the whole town discussing her private affairs.

In addition—and probably more important in the long run, unless she could reconcile her uncle to Cord—it would mean a permanent split with her uncle and she couldn't accept that. Every time she even considered the possibility of leaving Ira, she would remember her vow to Aunt Sarah and realize she could not go back on her promise.

Besides, she couldn't stop singing now that the saloon depended on her, and she knew Ira would be so furious if she married Cord he probably wouldn't let her in the front door. She couldn't leave him without someone to take care of him and doom the saloon to failure at the same time. That wouldn't be merely going back on her vow, it would be stabbing him in the back as well, and Eliza couldn't bring herself to do that.

She had tried to explain to Cord why it was necessary that they keep their meetings secret until she could somehow talk her uncle into accepting him as her husband, but Eliza doubted he understood or agreed with her. Right now he was so preoccupied with the ranch he let her have her way, but she was sure that come winter, after the fall roundup, he would be less patient with Ira's persistent dislike.

Meanwhile, Eliza continued to bask in the joy of Cord's love. It had taken a long time to accustom herself to being loved so wondrously, to be certain at each sunrise his adoration was not a fabrication of the night, but gradually she had become secure in his devotion and had began to go though each day with a feeling of confidence, a sense of serenity, a palpable happiness. She hoped to be able to give him as much as he had given her, but it was hard to give to a man who seemed to be sufficient within himself.

". . . and the challenge of the future is one that can only be met by the mastering of our world, and ourselves. These laudable ambitions can only be attained through acquiring the knowledge which will make the world our servant, not our master. In that light I am doubly proud to be the first graduate of Buffalo Normal School, and I wish to express my appreciation to Miss Smallwood for making this possible."

Melissa led the assemblage in a generous round of applause, which caused Eliza to blush fiercely. This lead to a series of tributes from both of Melissa's parents, several leading citizens, and even a few students. Eliza was so embarrassed she could hardly lift her eyes from the ground, but Ella Baylis and Susan Haughton happily nodded their agreement with every word spoken. Cord, arriving late, listened with no visible emotion, but Eliza's uncle was distrustful of anything that might take her mind off singing at the Sweetwater, and he seemed to grow more unhappy with every word uttered in her praise. Abruptly, she snatched her mind from the random thoughts; Mrs. Burton was calling upon her to take the podium.

Eliza had never been required to stand up in front of such an assembly or to make a speech, and she had no idea what to say. The applause mounted as she rose to her feet and mechanically walked the distance from her chair to the speaker's stand. The palms of her hands were sweaty and her mouth felt dry. She looked out at all the happy and smiling faces and knew she had to say something, but what? Then she saw Ella's beaming face and she knew.

"Thank you for your kind words. It *has* been a good year for the school and for the community, and I'm sure next year will be even better." Applause. "There are a few people other than myself whose work has made this year possible, and I would like to publicly express my appreciation for their contributions. We must thank Mrs. Burton for her chairmanship of the fund-raising campaign. We finally have enough desks and books so that no child has to stand up or share a book." Polite applause. "Then there is Ella Baylis, who, even though she has no children, gained permission from the council to start the school and organized the men to put up the building." Enthusiastic applause. "But there is another person who, maybe more than any other, is responsible for our gathering here today." Ella shook her head vigorously, but Eliza wasn't looking at Ella. Mr. Burton looked around to see if anyone thought Eliza could be talking about him, but everyone was just as mystified as he.

"It was Mr. Stedman's idea to rebuild the schoolhouse, and when attendance was slow, it was his encouragement that convinced the outlying families to send their children to school." There was only a smattering of applause, and that

146

rendered out of grudging recognition of a disagreeable truth.

Eliza was stunned; Ella dropped her head. Cord showed no response, but Mr. and Mrs. Burton looked as if they'd rather have been almost anywhere else. Suddenly she felt she had to leave, that she had to get away from all these people and their cold, cruel faces.

"I hope every pupil will be back next year, and that you won't have forgotten all your lessons in the meantime." To the accompaniment of polite giggling among the students, Eliza walked quickly to her seat and sat down, her eyes on the ground and a feeling of deep disappointment destroying all her pleasure. Despite the townspeople's unfeigned acceptance and generous praise, she had never felt more like an outsider than she did now.

Two days later Eliza returned to the schoolhouse to give it a final going-over before closing it up for the winter. She was going to miss it; for the first time in her life she felt she was making an important contribution. It also provided her with a place of her own in the community, one that didn't depend upon her uncle or singing in the saloon. She was *somebody*, and that somebody was a person she wanted to be.

She was busy fastening one of the heavy wooden shutters when she heard footsteps mount the porch. She was surprised to see Cord watching her from the door when she looked up.

"I was just closing up for the winter."

"Will you be sorry to leave?" he asked, stepping into the semi-darkness of the interior.

"Not as much as a few days ago." There was a vein of still-warm resentment in her voice.

"I wish you hadn't said anything about my helping with the school."

"I don't see why it's okay to thank Ella and Mrs. Burton but not to thank you."

"You'll find out soon enough," Cord commented dryly, "but that's not what I came for. I wanted to tell you I'll be going on roundup in a couple of days."

"Do you have to go?" The words were out before she could stop them. "I mean, I thought you had already gone on roundup this year."

"The spring roundup was for branding new calves. Now we have to cull the steers for market. It won't take half as long."

Eliza's face brightened.

"Then they go to market, and with all the trouble people are having with impounded herds, I mean to take them myself."

"Why would anyone impound your steers?"

"They haven't yet, but they might. My success has made me very unpopular with the Association, and tying up the money I get for the sale of my herd would be one way to keep me under control."

"When will you get back?"

"Six weeks, maybe longer."

Eliza tried to keep from showing the disappointment that swept over her, but she failed completely. Cord had never left her before and the feeling of loss was a shock.

"What are you going to do?"

Cord looked puzzled.

"I mean, why does it take so long?" She didn't really care what he did, only how long it would keep him away.

"We have to go over the whole range again, keeping an eye out for any unbranded calves while rounding up the steers old enough to sell. Then we drive them to the railhead in Montana. Once we get to Chicago, I'll try to find the best possible price. Even a dollar a head can make a big difference. It's important to the boys too. They have steers of their own going to market along with mine."

"Do all the owners take their own cows to market?"

"Most of them send their foremen, or even sell them to jobbers at the railhead," he said, taking her in his arms, "but I can't afford to pay anyone for work I can do myself. This herd is the most important I'll ever sell. If I get the kind of price I think I can, I'll be able to pay off the last of my debt. Then the Matador and every head of cattle on it will be mine, free and clear."

"Is there anything else in your life as important as those cows?"

"You." Cord put his hand under her chin and tilted her face up until he could look into her eyes. A pair of teardrops

148

had streaked her soft cheeks with their glistening moisture. Cord gently wiped them away and kissed her lingeringly. "You do believe that, don't you?"

"It's hard sometimes." She looked into his eyes with such heartfelt earnestness Cord almost considered sending Franklin to Chicago. "It's just that I don't see you very often. Sometimes, when I'm in the schoolhouse or the saloon, I find it hard to believe this part of my life is real. I realize it's not your fault — I'm the one who insisted on keeping everything a secret — but sometimes, when I'm feeling particularly lonely, I wonder if I haven't made you up just to pretend there's someone who cares for me."

Cord folded her in a crushing embrace. "You don't ever have to doubt me or my love," he assured her. "This is not the time to stir up a lot of trouble, especially when I won't be here to stand the heat with you, but we've got to get things settled with your uncle. I can't wait much longer."

"Miss Smallwood, are you in there?" It was Melissa's voice. Eliza sprang away from Cord, hurried over to the only window remaining open, and began to fasten the shutters.

"Damn and blast!" exclaimed Cord as Melissa, afraid to enter the nearly dark schoolhouse, stood in the doorway, peering intently into the shadows.

"I'm here, Melissa," Eliza answered. "Mr. Stedman is showing me how to fasten the shutters so they wouldn't come undone before next spring."

"You'd better make sure they're good and tight, or some vagrant cowboy is likely to burn it down again," Melissa said. "They're a real nuisance, turning up all over town and pestering decent people to give them jobs." Eliza could feel Cord stiffen with fury, and she reached out to take his hand to forestall the caustic words that rose to his lips.

"They don't have much choice when the ranchers turn them off every winter and then refuse them jobs if they try to run a few cows for themselves," Cord said in low barbed tones as he stepped out into the bright sunshine.

"Mr. Stedman, what a pleasure to see you," Melissa simpered, batting her lashes in such an obvious way Cord's anger turned to amusement. "How did you ever find the time to help close up the schoolhouse?"

"I was in town getting some supplies for the roundup, and

offered Miss Smallwood a hand. Now I must be going. Remember what I said about your uncle," he said to Eliza. He bid a perfunctory goodbye to Melissa and went on his way.

"He is such a handsome man," Melissa sighed. "Don't you think so, Miss Smallwood?"

"Well, yes, I suppose he is," Eliza said, faltering, not sure how to respond.

"I think he's the most handsome man I've ever seen," Melissa gushed, "and I'm going to ask Mother to invite him to the Christmas party." Eliza couldn't think of a response, and wisely decided not to say anything at all. But her silence was hardly noticed. Melissa continued to sing Cord's praises all the way back to the center of town.

"Do you think he will come if we invite him?" she asked Eliza just before they parted ways.

"I'm not sure," she stammered. "I can't say what he will or won't do."

"You and he seemed to be such friends, I thought you might know."

Eliza could feel her face turning red. "You mustn't let his helping me mislead you. I'm new to Wyoming and unfamiliar with its ways. Mr. Stedman has been kind enough to lend me assistance and offer advice several times when I needed it."

"That just proves what I told Mother."

"What did you tell your mother?" asked Eliza, terrified of what Melissa might have said.

"That Mr. Stedman should be considered one of our leading citizens. His helping you just proves it."

Melissa waved goodbye to Eliza and headed toward home while Eliza turned her steps toward the saloon. She hoped Melissa would not use Cord's helping her as an excuse to importune her mother for an invitation to her Christmas party. Eliza had heard nothing about it, but she was sure only the most substantial citizens would be invited to the inner sanctum of Green Street. Certainly not the school-teacher, and especially not when the schoolteacher sang in a saloon.

Chapter 16

"There's really nothing we can do as long as the range is crawling with his hands," Les said to Croley. "Besides, he's selling his best steers, and they don't pay us enough for those old cows to make it worthwhile."

"Nobody pays enough to get me to go after anything of Stedman's," reiterated Harker. "I told you before, if you start messing with him, you can count me out."

"You don't have to worry you'll end up with a broken leg," Croley said scornfully. "I've worked out a plan. Besides, we'll be taking unbranded calves so there won't be any way he can prove they're his."

"I still don't like it," said Les. "We've had pretty good luck running off a few beeves at a time and selling them to the mining crews. They pay good and we don't have to keep the beef on our hands waiting for someone to come along and prove they ain't ours."

"You're running from Stedman like he was God."

"On his land, he might as well be. There ain't nobody gets past him, and every damned cowboy on the place rides the range from daybreak to sundown poking his nose in canyons and asking questions just like those steers was his."

"You leave the worrying to me. I told you I had it worked out. We won't hold the calves ourselves and there'll be no way anybody can tie them to us."

"And how do you plan to do that? You might as well tell me you plan to take them across the Bighorns as think there's a single acre of his land Stedman and his boys don't cover."

"I'll tell you when the time comes. No point in too many people knowing about it. Besides, I plan to set up a decoy in

151

case anything does go wrong."

"Where're you going to find anybody that dumb?"

"Ira Smallwood."

"That sodbuster! He barely knows enough about horses to stay on one."

"But he hates Cord Stedman enough to do just about anything, even something as stupid as getting himself caught with his rope on one of Stedman's calves. With him as cover, any number of men could get away."

"Does he know anything about it yet?"

"No. I'm letting him stew, and Stedman's interest in his niece is making it certain he'll be in the right mood to join us. She mentioned Stedman at the graduation last week and the old man is still raving about it. I figure a few judicious words dropped here and there, and Ira will be ready to pull the trigger himself."

"I ain't getting mixed up in no killings," exclaimed Harker. "I told you right from the beginning I was off to Montana the first time anybody pulled a trigger. There ain't no steer worth swinging from a rope."

"Nobody's ever convicted around here."

"Not for rustling, but killing is different."

"I think you boys are getting soft."

"Then you try riding after some ornery, cussed steer in the middle of a pitch-black night and see how much you like it. We got a good system going for us, and I don't see any reason to change it now."

"Money."

"Anybody'd think you had enough, what with the money this place brings in and half of what me and the boys take. You must be rich."

"Maybe I am, but neither of you is getting any younger. In a few more years you won't be able to ride a hundred miles a night. You're going to need enough money to buy yourself a piece of land and some cows."

"I ain't running no cows when I quit," stated Harker. "I want a saloon, just like the one you got here, where I can sit back, look at the pretty girls, sleep in a soft bed, and watch the money roll in."

"You're too much of a fool to put together an operation like this." Croley spat. "You'll always be for hire by someone with more brains and vision. Now get out of here and come back when you're ready to work." The two men left, disgruntled.

"One of these days I'm going to punch him right in the mouth," Harker promised.

"Aw shut up," said his companion. "You ain't never going to do nothing and you know it."

"Why didn't they applaud for Cord like they did for Ella and Mrs. Burton?" Eliza asked Susan Haughton. "He deserves more credit than either one of them."

"People don't trust him, and some don't like him. Sam and I don't."

"But why? He's been the one person I could always depend upon."

"Cord Stedman may have befriended you, but you're not trying to homestead any land he's after."

"We did once." Susan looked up sharply. "Well, not actually, but he thought we were."

"And what did he do?"

"His men tried to burn our wagon."

"That's exactly it."

"But he replaced everything they ruined."

"Are you sure we're talking about the same Cord Stedman?"

"Didn't he come see you about sending Billy to school?"

"Yes, but—"

"He was also the one who gave Ella the idea of building a new schoolhouse."

"Who told you that?"

"Ella."

Susan appeared to take some time to digest this. "He does appear to have been remarkably busy, especially for a man who's not even married. Maybe that's why they don't trust him. I mean, why should he be interested in a school?"

"People shouldn't have to like him to thank him for something he did."

"This county is deeply divided between the small owners and homesteaders and the large ranchers who're trying to drive them both out. Do you remember I said the schoolteacher before you left when two people were killed?"

"Yes."

"Those people were ordered killed by the Association, those same big ranchers, because they were supposed to be rustlers. Only nobody around here believes they were guilty. Nothing was ever done to the killers even though every one of them was known by name. There were four witnesses, but when it came time for the trial, none of them could be found."

"Do you mean somebody murdered them?"

"Maybe. At least that's what people think."

"But what has that got to do with Cord?"

"He used to be one of us, but he's been so successful he doesn't belong anymore. No one really believes he's gone over to the Association, but they wouldn't be surprised if he had. Right now they'd rather not be forced to make up their minds, and I don't think it's a good idea for you to try to force them. He's been known to defend his property against several of them, and that has left some pretty hard feelings. I know it must seem strange to you that people should dislike Cord for trying to protect his own herds, but the rustlers are their neighbors, or relatives, and they won't turn against them no matter what they do."

Later, she talked to Ira. He said much the same thing, but Croley intervened in her behalf. "Let the girl alone. I don't like her being associated with Stedman anymore than you do, but it hasn't done us any harm. And you have to admit his interest has heightened her appeal to the customers."

Eliza flushed.

"I won't have her patting him on the back in public," said Ira. "It's bound to give people the wrong idea. You should have seen how the Burtons looked."

"I wasn't trying to praise him," said Eliza. "I was just trying to give him credit for helping with the school, just like I did Ella and Mrs. Burton. Nobody complained when I mentioned their names."

"That's because everybody likes Ella, and they're afraid Sanford Burton might call in their loans," Ira snapped.

"But that's not fair."

"I don't give a damn about fair or the Burtons or Ella Baylis or Stedman for that matter," Croley said, interrupting. "As long as she keeps bringing in the customers, she can

154

thank anybody she wants. The more people who hear about her, the more will want to see her. These cowboys worship women, especially the pure ones. They'll come all the way from Sheridan just to have a look at her.

"Not that there's going to be many to listen to you for a while," Croley added, and a sour look settled over his features. "With everybody on roundup, it's going to be mighty slim pickings."

"Which reminds me," said Ira, "you can go back to singing two times a night now school is out. It's time you learned some new songs too. I'm sick of the old ones and I'm sure everybody else is."

"You don't need me to sing that often, not with Sam here practically every night."

"Sam's doing fine, but it's not the same as a girl."

"I been thinking," said Croley, watching his partner out of the corner of his eye. "It's about time we got ourselves a dancer."

"Don't be a fool. Why pay a second set of wages when we don't need to?"

"I think we do." Croley's voice hardened. "Nobody is more appreciative of what Eliza has done than I am—"

"So why waste money hiring some ordinary dancer when they can see them at a dozen places within a hundred yards?"

"I wasn't thinking of anyone ordinary. Your niece's class has set us apart from everybody else, and I don't think we ought to change it. I even told Sam to go easy on the dirty songs."

"So why are you looking for someone else?" Ira could see his importance at the saloon, and consequently his leverage in its management, shrinking. He had never accepted Sam's success happily, even though he had gotten credit for finding him, and now there'd soon be someone else to cut into his influence.

"I was looking for someone who could get close to the customers," Croley revealed. "Someone who could dance with them once in a while."

"See what you've done?" Ira barked, turning on Eliza. "I tried to get you to dance, but no, you were too scared to let anybody touch you."

"And she shouldn't," Croley agreed. "She should stay just

155

as she is. Don't you think it's a good idea to get another performer, to broaden our appeal?" Croley asked Eliza.

Eliza didn't know enough about what cowboys liked to be able to answer that question, but she saw it as a way to take the pressure off herself. "I really don't understand much about saloons," she confessed, "but it sounds like a good idea to me."

"Great. And that will give you all the more time to work up your new songs. See if you can be ready by the time they get back from the roundup."

Ira proceeded to argue further, but Eliza slipped away. They had recently moved into rooms over the new saloon, and that made it difficult to have any time to herself. Since she was no longer teaching, she had to spend long hours in her uncle's company, and she was finding it increasingly difficult. He shared none of her interests and constantly complained of one thing or another, mostly Cord.

Eliza had begun to wonder if she was ever going to get Ira to accept Cord, but now that he was gone on roundup it was especially hard for her to keep quiet when Ira talked about him. She was feeling his absence acutely, and had to struggle not to let her dejection show.

She had never seen Cord every day. In fact, sometimes a whole week would pass without her even hearing a word about him, but she knew he was close by, that if she had any need of him he would be there. Now he was gone beyond her reach, and she felt unaccountably alone. Unaccountably because, since she had acquired several new friends, Susan Haughton being foremost among them, there was more to do. As she became more involved in the town and got to know its citizens better, she had less unoccupied time on her hands, but this increase in activity did not fill the void created by the departure of one tall, confident, perhaps even arrogant, cowboy.

Not since her aunt's death had she been so aware of anyone's absence. It was as though a part of her was missing. She knew if Cord didn't return, she would never feel whole again. She had given him a part of her self, and he had absorbed it into his being.

Maybe this was the love Ella had tried to tell her about, the feeling that you were part of someone else and that you would always be incomplete without him. If it was, she wasn't at all sure she liked it. Being with Cord was so wonderful she couldn't find words to express her happiness, but being without him was equally awful. If love could lift you to the pinnacle of happiness, then it was equally capable of plunging you into the depths of despair.

"They busted in on Lem and Bucky without any warning and started shooting."

"Are they dead?"

"Naw. They ain't even hit."

"How come? The gun musta been near 'bout on the end of Lem's nose."

"Them fellas were too cocksure. They had to shoot off their mouths about what they were going to do. Lem yawned and had himself a big stretch, just as cool as you please, and reached out for his six-shooter hanging from the bedpost. They forgot he's left-handed."

"What happened then?"

"They got off the first shots, one bullet coming so close to Lem's cheek it gave him powder burns, but the other buried in the mattress next to him."

"Don't tell me Lem sat there just looking at his gun."

"Naw. They turned and ran, but he thinks he got one of them in the stomach."

The saloon was usually empty after lunch, no cowboy being around to invade the cool quiet of its interior, and Croley and Ira had taken advantage of this slowdown to move out of their small, stuffy office at the back of the building. Their conference had been interrupted by the two men who'd burst into the saloon to tell them of the attack on Lem Poteet and Bucky Lloyd. Since they had stopped to spread the news to every person they met on their way into town, the saloon soon began to fill up with people angry over the open, unprovoked attack on men they considered their friends. Croley opened the bar, and it wasn't long before they passed from discussing the facts to surmises as to who had lead the attack and why.

"Everybody's sure it was the Association's hired guns. They've been after Lem for more than a year now."

"Why do you to have to go all the way to Cheyenne for who's responsible when we've got members of the Association right here in Johnson County?" Ira declared heatedly. "Not to mention one who's made a habit of taking the law into his own hands."

"What makes you think it was Stedman's men?"

"It was Stedman himself. You won't find him letting his men do anything without him."

"You don't find him failing once he sets his mind on something either," pointed out another. "Sounds like those men made a fair mess of it."

"Lem is a first-rate shot. He probably rattled them."

"Neither you nor anybody else has ever seen Cord Stedman rattled. And if you think Lem is the best hand with a gun in these parts, you haven't seen Stedman."

They broke off. Eliza and Perkin Messmore, the piano player, had entered the main room. For the last few weeks they had been practicing her new songs when the saloon was empty, and Eliza was brought up short by the presence of a large knot of men.

"Come on in," Croley called to her. "We won't bother you."

"I can wait until later," she said, and turned to leave.

"It's not likely anybody will be paying attention to you," Ira said. "We've got *important* matters to discuss."

Eliza was doubtful, but decided it would be better to go ahead. They were at the opposite end of the long room, and maybe if she sang a song or two, they wouldn't notice when she stopped.

The men waited for Eliza to begin. She sang as softly as she could, and before she had finished the first song they had started to whisper. Eliza turned her back, and by the end of the second song they were so involved with their discussion they didn't notice when she stopped. But Ira did, and Eliza chose a third song.

Before long neither group was aware of the other. Singing always enabled Eliza to get away from her trouble, and she finished the song and mechanically turned the page to the next one.

". . . can't make me believe that Cord Stedman didn't have something to do with it. Not when Lem's shack is no more than twenty miles from his place."

Eliza's attention was riveted by the mention of Cord's name, and she forgot all about the next song, even when Perkin began the musical introduction.

"What can we do about it?"

"We can tell the sheriff."

"We don't have any proof."

"We could go after him ourselves," Ira suggested.

"With every cowboy on the Matador ready to back him up?"

"I don't like it when something like this happens, but I ain't taking the law into my own hands. We'd be lucky to get out of there with a whole skin, and I got a family to think of."

"You might not live long enough to take care of them if Cord Stedman is allowed to go around shooting anybody he wants."

"Stedman ain't never done anything to me, and I for one ain't so danged sure he did this either, but it don't matter. I'll say my piece any time you like, but I ain't picking up no gun and going looking for trouble."

"You're a coward, Pete Bosley."

"Maybe, but I ain't a dead coward. Are you going to take care of my kids if I bite it?"

"Nobody's talking about shooting anybody," interjected Croley smoothly. "That's what we're objecting to."

"There'll be plenty of shooting if you go out to the Matador accusing Cord Stedman of attacking Lem, you mark my words."

"Mr. Stedman had nothing to do with that attack." Eliza's soft voice reduced the rather loud, argumentative group to a stupefied silence.

Chapter 17

"Go back to your singing, girl," Ira shouted angrily. "You don't know anything about this."

"Not until you stop accusing Mr. Stedman of something he didn't do."

"Cord Stedman is a cold-blooded, calculating bastard who doesn't give a damn for anything but his own success."

"He's done more than anybody here to see the children of this town get an education."

"It's a fact he came by my place and talked my wife into sending the young'uns," stated one dubious farmer. "He got to talking about the future of Wyoming depending on the education of our children, and she got so excited them kids would have been in school if I'd had to carry them myself."

"And he gave the Haughtons a beef to help them through the winter. I know because I helped cut it up," volunteered another.

"It's all a trick to keep you from knowing him for the cold-blooded killer he is," fumed Ira.

"That's not true."

"Don't you argue with me, girl," Ira shouted, startling the men who had been brought up to revere women, especially one as pretty and gentle as Eliza.

"I'm not arguing. I'm just stating a fact. Mr. Stedman couldn't have done it because he's not back yet."

"That just shows how much you know. The roundup was over last week. The men are taking the cattle to the railhead at Sheridan right now. Stedman's been home for five days."

"He is taking his steers to Chicago and won't be back for at least two more weeks."

"Come to think of it, I do think I heard some of the boys say Stedman was thinking about selling his own herd."

"How do you know this?" Ira's glare condemned his niece.

"He told Mrs. Baylis when he was in buying supplies for the trip," she said, not wanting everyone to know Cord had sought her out in the schoolhouse. "He said he wanted the top price so he could pay off the last of his debt."

"That's right," Pete Bosley corroborated. "Mr. Burton was telling my boss Cord Stedman was going to be the richest man in the county in a couple of years."

"Then he couldn't have done it?" Ira asked, deflated.

"You should never accuse people without evidence," Eliza said, angry over the men's irresponsible charges. "You have let mere prejudice lead you to a false conclusion. In a more careless condition"—she eyed the pitchers of beer—"you might have decided on some course of action which could not only have resulted in injury to innocent people, but might have stirred up bad feelings and possibly had dire results."

The men looked abashed.

"I guess the little lady has set us right," Croley said quietly, smiling at Eliza in a way that made her skin creep. "Let this be a lesson to you."

Eliza was bored now that she and Ira were living above the new saloon. At first she was delighted to have a room of her own with space for all her clothes and a large copper bath, but she soon found she had nothing to do. Ira had sold all their animals. There was no cow to milk, no rooms to clean, and no meals to cook. After a life of hard work, she felt at loose ends with no more to do than study her music, be fitted for a new dress, or read and do needlework.

They had turned the old saloon into a dining room, and Croley had discovered he needed someone who could do more with food than his Mexican cook. Eliza told him about Lucy, and much to Lavinia's fury, Croley had hired her away with orders to do better than the competition or find herself out in the street. Lucy told him she was ready to take herself off that very minute if he didn't change his tune, then had proceeded to turn out the best food in Buffalo. Some of the cowboys complained it wasn't what they were used to—Lucy was from New York and didn't cook things long enough or in enough grease for their tastes—but they kept coming back. Even the town merchants began to find their way to the dining room at lunchtime.

Eliza and Ira's meals were served in their rooms, but Ira preferred to eat downstairs with the guests, and Eliza dined alone most evenings. She invited Ella as often as she dared, and even coaxed Mrs. Burton and Melissa into being her guests for one memorable dinner, but day after day she was alone until it was time to go downstairs and sing.

Today her uncle had deserted her after breakfast, going out with the slightly mysterious injunction "Don't look for me until late. Croley and I have business to see to."

About mid-morning a knock sounded at the door, and Eliza jumped up eagerly, willing to welcome almost anybody just to have company.

"Cord!" she exclaimed, unable to hide her happiness at seeing him.

"May I come in?" His arms were full of packages wrapped in brown paper, and only his face showed above the stack.

"Of course," she bubbled, trying to hide her excitement. "When did you get back?"

"Last night. We got into Sheridan on the evening train, but I couldn't wait until morning. Anyway, the boys are used to riding these hills at night." A ghost of a wry smile danced in his eyes, reminding Eliza of the rustling that kept an undercurrent of uneasiness forever simmering near the surface.

"Where can I put these?" he asked, indicating the packages.

"Anywhere. On the table, I guess. Who are they for?"

"You. Whom did you expect?"

"Me!" she squeaked in a mixture of astonishment and delight. "Whatever did you do that for?"

"Well, you couldn't get to Chicago, and I saw so many things I thought you would like. I couldn't buy them all, but the boys thought I tried." He chuckled.

"You shouldn't have done it. How am I going to explain it to Uncle Ira?"

"Tell him I gave them to you. Where is he anyway?"

"He's gone off. He didn't say where—and you know I can't

tell him that."

"Then don't tell him. Keep it a secret."

"I really shouldn't accept them, and I wouldn't if you could take them back."

"But I can't," he said, smiling.

"No, not even Uncle could expect you to travel all the way back to Chicago. Oh, dear, what can I do?"

"If you don't take them, I guess I'll have to give them to Lavinia."

"You wouldn't dare!"

"Well, *I* can't use the stuff, and if I was to give it to Ella Baylis, Ed would probably come after me with a shotgun."

Eliza giggled in spite of herself.

"Lavinia's girls never get anything this nice," he said.

"Are you trying to force me into accepting these presents by threatening to give them to that terrible woman?"

"I was getting desperate," he drawled, taking on the accent and demeanor of one straight out of the hills. "I was willing to try just about anything to get you to take a peek. You don't have to keep anything if you don't like it, mind you. Just look at it so you'll know what it was. That's to keep from hurting my feelings too bad. I suppose I could give them to Ginny, or Sam's wife if I was very careful to explain first, but I'd rather you took them."

"All right," agreed Eliza, not immune to Cord's wiles or the pleasure of having a towering stack of presents all her own. She'd always gotten a couple of small gifts at Christmas, maybe one on her birthday, but never anything like this.

"Let me show you what I found," Cord offered, nearly as excited as Eliza. "I didn't know anything about women's things, so I had to ask the lady in the store to show me what I ought to get. I think she took me for a great booby from the territories." Eliza looked at Cord's well-formed shoulders and handsome, sunburned features, and doubted any woman would much care where he came from.

Cord opened one of the smaller boxes to reveal a selection of Pear's Soaps, each cake molded in a different shape and smelling delightfully of it's own exotic fragrance. "She assured me every lady ought to have a whole box, as well as these little bottles. Apparently, Eastern women set great store by smelling pretty." The second box contained several bottles

163

of bath oil.

"I hope you like this," Cord said, opening still another box and lifting out a muff of rich, dark-brown fur. "I told that gal I could get you one of bear, wolf, or coyote just for the asking, but she seemed to think you wouldn't have it unless it came off the back of these mink critters."

"It's beautiful," sighed Eliza.

"I have to admit it is a mite prettier than coyote. And this thing is supposed to go with it," Cord said, extracting a mink tippet. "Though I can't see why you would want to wear a chain of critters holding on to each other by their tails."

"It's gorgeous," Eliza cried, wondering if she'd ever get the courage to wear them.

"Well, as long as you like it," Cord noted doubtfully, already digging into another box. There was much more: rich velvet for a new gown, yards of exquisite lace, a hat that would be the envy of any woman who saw it, and high-heeled boots of glossy black leather. "The saleslady tried to sell me a corset, but I told her there was nothing about you that needing squeezing or hiding. She didn't seem to believe me, but if the fat women I saw in that store are the kind they grow in Chicago, I can see why. Squeezing is not going to turn them anything but purple."

"What am I going to do with all of this?" exclaimed Eliza, overcome.

"Wear it, I hope. After hauling it a thousand miles, I'd hate to think it was going to sit in a box under your bed. There's still one or two more here somewhere," Cord said, rooting around in the litter of open boxes and scattered tissue paper. "Here, I knew I'd find it." He held up a very small glass bottle filled with amber liquid.

"What's that?" inquired Eliza.

"Perfume. The gal said no lady would be without at least one bottle. When she told me the price, I could see why you had to do with just one. Seems to me after all that soap and bath oil, you'd smell ripe as a skunk in season. You just take a tiny dab and put it behind your ear."

Eliza moistened the tip of her finger, but even before the droplet touched her skin, she inhaled its heavenly odor and tremors of pleasure danced all over her body.

"This is the last one, unless I lost something in this pile."

"No," Eliza protested. "I couldn't possibly accept another thing. You've given me far too much already."

"You've got to take it. There's nobody else I can give it to."

"No."

"It's just a little thing," he coaxed.

"Well . . ."

"I asked what was proper to give a lady friend in the way of jewels, and she seemed to think it wasn't proper to give her anything. Seems they don't trust their womenfolk much in Chicago, but she finally agreed some little thing wouldn't be too awful. I took a fancy to these, and she allowed that *maybe* I could buy them for you if I knew you awfully well. I told her I did, and that must have embarrassed her because she blushed." Cord abruptly abandoned his role of the genial yokel. "I know I shouldn't, but I couldn't help myself." Eliza went pale when he showed her a pair of delicate, pearl-drop earrings.

"I could never wear them," she exclaimed, almost snatching them from Cord's hands and rushing to the mirror to put them on. Cord wisely forbore to ask *why* she couldn't wear something which obviously gave her so much pleasure.

"How could you afford all this?" she asked turning to face him. "You must have sold your steers for millions."

"Not that much," Cord said, taking her in his arms, "but I did get a good price. Most of the money won't be mine for long, but right now I feel as rich as a king."

"You'd have to be to spend so much on me."

"This is nothing compared to what I'm going to give you when we're married. Have you ever seen Chicago?" Eliza shook her head. "Well, I hadn't paid much attention to it before, but it's got hundreds of stores full of the most amazing things. You could spend weeks and not go into the same place twice." Eliza found it hard to imagine an Eden such as that could exist.

"I'll take you there one day. We'll go into every store, and you can have anything you want."

"Silly, you'd find yourself out of money in no time. I don't know much about fancy shopping, but if these are the kinds of things they have for sale, I wouldn't ever want to stop!"

Abruptly, Cord swept her into a crushing embrace, and Eliza surrendered utterly to the delight of being in his strong arms once again.

"I've missed you these past weeks," he murmured in her ear. "Every time I bought a present for you, it was a reminder of our separation."

"I missed you too. I feel safe when you're here. With you in Chicago I felt all alone, and even a little scared."

"Is anything wrong?" he asked anxiously.

"It's not that," she assured him with a weak smile. "I guess I've just gotten used to knowing you were here." As he buried her in another embrace, Lucy came in to set the table.

"Oh, it's you," Eliza gasped, pale with shock.

"You should be glad it's not your uncle," Lucy declared.

"You won't tell him?" Eliza asked anxiously.

"Of course not," Lucy replied indignantly. "I don't like his fits and starts any more than you do."

"What are you doing here?" Cord demanded, all the amiability fading from his face. "I didn't know anybody got up before noon at Lavinia's."

"I live here now. I'm the cook," Lucy informed him proudly.

"And I suppose the specialty of the day is tarts and tenderloins?"

"I helped the girls dress," Lucy stated indignantly. "I didn't accompany them downstairs."

"Mr. Stedman won't mention it again," Eliza interrupted, trying to placate the two, who were beginning to circle like tomcats. "I'm perfectly sure you weren't affected by anything that happened in that place."

"I give thanks every day you took me out of there. My poor Joe would bawl himself sick if he knew the miseries I've had to bear." Lucy showed every sign of doing a bit of crying herself.

"I trust it wasn't *poor* Joe who taught you to walk into rooms without knocking," Cord said. That remark caused Lucy to forget any idea she had of shedding tears, and she turned her glittering black eyes on Cord, fixing him with an angry glare.

"It's okay for me to come and go," she said, pounding herself on her ample chest. "But for you to be in a lady's rooms when she is alone is disgraceful."

"We do things differently out here in Wyoming," Cord

pointed out.

"Do you make babies any different?"

Eliza flamed scarlet.

"No, I don't suppose we do," Cord admitted in a shaking voice, "but we're not doing that."

"No one ever is, at first," Lucy said, shaking her finger at him. "But things start to get hot when young people are left alone, and before you know it the girl's stomach is out to here and the father is after the boy with a shotgun."

"I promise you I won't do anything to hurt Miss Smallwood."

"Words," snorted Lucy. "They come easy."

"Please, Lucy," Eliza pleaded.

"But you have no mamma or papa to take care of you. As for your uncle—a steer would be of more use to you than he is."

"Miss Smallwood's honor is in no danger."

"I know it's not, you Wyoming wolf, because I will see to it. You know what you should do?" she said, abruptly descending from her high plane. "You should marry Miss Eliza. She's pretty, and she can cook as good as me. Where are you going to find another one like this?"

"I don't know," said Cord with a glint in his eye. "She's getting a little old, and—"

"Old!" squeaked Eliza.

"—then there's the question of a dowry. I was thinking about someone like Melissa Burton."

Lucy spat out one of the words she had learned at Lavinia's. "That one is a fool for all her learning. And as for the mother . . ." Words failed her.

"Stop it right this minute, both of you," Eliza cried, mortified. "Don't pay him any attention, Lucy. He's only teasing you."

"Lucy's right," Cord said, shamelessly taking Eliza into his firm embrace. "There's not another woman in the whole world to compare with you." Eliza blushed again, but Lucy positively melted.

"You should get married right away. Then . . ." Lucy winked wickedly at Cord.

"Lucy!" exclaimed Eliza, breaking out of Cord's embrace.

"*Then* your uncle would have nothing to say. He seems like

a nice man," she said, gesturing to Cord. "So good-looking with his big muscles and dark, brooding eyes." Eliza flushed again. "In New York the girls would eat him up."

"Do you think you could leave me to broach the subject in my own time?" Cord asked, amused in spite of himself.

"You're too slow," Lucy informed him candidly. "If you don't make up your mind soon, Miss Eliza will be an old maid. Now I'll get lunch." She bustled out leaving a mortified Eliza alone with Cord.

"If you dare say one word," Eliza managed to say while keeping her eyes firmly fixed on the carpet, "I shall go to my room and not come out until you're gone." Cord sighed. This was definitely not the time to ask Eliza to set the date.

"I promise to discuss nothing more important than Mrs. Burton's Christmas party. Now lift your eyes from the carpet. It's not polite to eat lunch without even looking at your companion."

"You're staying?"

"I think Lucy invited me, unless you mean to rescind the invitation."

"No."

"Good. I would take it unkindly if I had to ride all the way to the Matador on an empty stomach."

Chapter 18

Eliza was too upset to eat. The noise coming from the saloon had been growing all morning, and her feeling of uneasiness along with it. A homesteader who lived some distance from Buffalo had been found dead the day before, his wagon hidden in a gully and his horses shot, and the town was in an ugly mood. Even worse in everyone's mind, the wagon was loaded with Christmas presents for his children, including a little dog that was whining pitifully when the wagon was discovered. Lucy told her the body had been found on a road running just beyond the westernmost edge of Cord's range, and some of the men were making nasty accusations.

"And your uncle is the loudest among them, blast his wicked hide," said Ella Baylis, who came to visit just as Lucy was clearing away the dishes. "That man has fed on his dislike of Cord until it has grown into a sickness."

"Do the other men believe him?" asked Eliza apprehensively.

"I can't tell. What do you think, Lucy?"

"I didn't hang about, but it seems to me they're acting like a bunch of dogs growling over a bone for the pleasure of it." She stacked the last dish on her tray and left.

"She's probably right," said Ella. "There's not much going on this time of year, and with everyone in town since Thanksgiving, it's only to be expected they would worry any bit of excitement to death."

"It still bothers me," Eliza said. "Every time something happens, they try to blame it on Cord."

"Most of them would prefer to blame it on the Association — it's big and impersonal and they can damn it with a free conscience — but it's your uncle who keeps shoving Cord down their throats."

"I've tried to talk to him, but he won't listen. Croley laughs and says he isn't hurting anything, to let him alone and he'll finally calm down, but he hasn't. He's actually gotten worse. And I think Croley encourages him, though I can't understand why."

"Does he know about you and Cord?"

"There's really nothing to know." Eliza blushed fiercely. She had kept her engagement a secret from Ella for so long she was afraid to tell her now.

"You're still seeing him, aren't you?"

"Yes."

"Then there's plenty to know. If your uncle thought you were about to marry Cord, he'd go after him with a shotgun."

"That's why I begged you to keep his presents over at your house."

"You'd better come get them soon," said Ella with a sudden laugh. "If I look at that mink one more time, I'm going to wear it myself."

"Please do," Eliza said, but her words lacked any ring of truth.

"Don't be absurd, child. That little thing might fit around you, but it would be more likely to choke me. It's those pearl earrings that are in real danger."

"Wear them. I can't."

"Why not? Nobody would notice a little thing like that."

"Uncle would. If he doesn't remember buying it, he demands to know where I got it."

"Forget about your uncle. Who knows, maybe you won't be living here much longer."

Eliza lowered her eyes in embarrassment. She could never get used to Ella's bluntly stated hopes that she and Cord would soon get married. "Uncle would dislike it so much."

"When are you going to forget about your uncle? Ira isn't going to like it no matter when you tell him. You wouldn't let him keep you from marrying Cord, would you?" Ella demanded sternly.

"No."

The noise from below increased suddenly, and Ella had to

raise her voice. "You wait until I see that boy. It's about time someone asked him if he means to wait until you're too old to do anything but hold hands."

"You wouldn't."

"I certainly would. No point in waiting for a man to come to the point when a little push will do the trick."

"Why should he be afraid?"

"They say once burned is twice shy."

"What do you mean by that?"

"Only that Cord was badly burned by Eugenia Orr, and maybe he needs a little shove to realize he's dealing with a different kind of cat this time." The noise from downstairs wasn't so loud now, but it seemed to be broader, like a subterranean buzzing.

"How can you refer to a woman as a cat?" Eliza giggled. She knew all about Eugenia.

"All women are cats. Some are wildcats, some lap cats, others ordinary tabbies. Then, of course, there's Lavinia's alley cats. There's nothing wrong with being a cat as long as you're the right kind."

"And what kind am I?"

"A pussycat. You let everybody run over you."

"What are men?" Eliza asked, curious.

"Dogs, with wolves and coyotes thrown in for good measure."

"I guess that's why the two sexes have so much trouble getting along."

"They'd get along fine if they could just agree on what's important. Men are always worried about how they look in other men's eyes. That's what that crowd's doing downstairs. Everything's got to be their way, or they're ready to fight. Women would never be so silly. Maybe we'd pull a little hair, but we'd work out a compromise and get on with the business of living. We don't believe in killing, especially not over something as senseless as cows."

"Do you think Cord's like that?"

"He's worse than any of them. He's so stuffed full of courage and honor he's bound to get himself shot in the back if some gal doesn't talk some sense into him. Melissa would only encourage him to buy more cows and take over more land. You owe it to him to save him from himself."

"You make him sound defenseless."

"All men are, especially against a conniving woman. They can't see half what a woman can with her eyes closed. Why, any one of us could have told you what Eugenia Orr was going to do. That girl was rotten to the core, but Cord would have killed the first man who dared say a word against her. Women aren't so stupid. We know our men aren't perfect, but we accept them as we find them. Men get all caught up in their ideals, and they get fighting mad when anything threatens to blow it up in their faces."

Lucy came hurrying into the room. "They've found another man dead, somewhere on the road that runs along the south edge of Mr. Stedman's range, and the whole crowd is about to go crazy."

"Who was it?" demanded Ella.

"The young Frater boy."

"Oh, Lord, that's Simon, and him about to be married."

"They say his brother is over at the sheriff's office calling for somebody's blood."

Abruptly, the noise from below grew louder, with shouts punctuating the din, and then it subsided once more.

"There's bound to be trouble now," said Ella, genuinely worried. "They're still talking about the attack on Lem and Bucky, and that was nearly two months ago. Now there's two more killed." She shook her head. "I should have known it wouldn't stop with those killings over at Newcastle. Sooner or later it had to end up here. I don't know where it's going to stop."

Ira burst into the room, stopped abruptly when he came face to face with the three women, then turned to Eliza, his face warped by anger.

"You're damned cowboy friend has gotten himself in a mess he can't get out of this time."

"Stop talking foolishness," Ella commanded impatiently. "If you know something, tell us. And don't give me any of your wild imaginings."

"It's no use defending him now. This time it's too obvious for anyone to ignore."

"What's too obvious?" Ella snapped testily.

"Both the men were shot in the back, and both were killed on his land."

"Lucy said Simon was found on Red Creek Road. It runs to the South of the Matador."

"It's just over the ridge, so close Stedman could have picked him off without ever leaving his own land. It's as clear as daylight it's Stedman. Everybody knows he's the best shot around here."

"You've got no proof," Eliza said, badly frightened. "Just because Mr. Stedman can shoot doesn't mean he did it."

"I know he can do no wrong in *your* eyes, but for once what you think doesn't matter."

"I happen to think rather highly of Cord Stedman myself," Ella stated majestically, "and I *dare* you, Ira Smallwood, to tell me that what I think doesn't matter."

Ira was considerably worked up, but not enough to brave Ella's wrath. "Even the sheriff thinks it looks suspicious."

"And I've no doubt Croley Blaine agrees with him."

"Croley's not for rushing into things, but he thinks we ought to see what's been going on at the Matador."

"Nothing has been going on," Eliza insisted, "and you won't find anything either."

"I've no doubt his cowhands would lie to cover for their boss, but he's gone too far this time." Ira headed toward his room.

"What are you going to do?"

"I'm going to get my guns so I'll be ready when they decide to go after him."

"Don't be a fool," Ella said. "You can't take the law into your own hands, not even if you have proof." But Ira disappeared into his room, and moments later the women could hear him going through his drawers and closets in search of guns and ammunition.

"What are we going to do?" Eliza asked.

"Nothing," Ella stated flatly. "There's nothing we can do. I'll own myself surprised if the sheriff lets these hotheads get out of town, but if he does, there's nothing you or I can do to stop them."

"But what about Cord? Somebody has to warn him."

"Don't you worry about Cord. He can take care of himself. Ira's right about one thing. It would take the whole army regiment from the fort to get past his cowboys."

"Don't wait dinner," Ira said to Lucy as he reentered the

room, his hat on his head and a gun belt around his waist. "Maybe none of us will be back before tomorrow. You're to sing just like nothing has happened," he told Eliza and was gone before she could protest.

"I'm going to see what's going on," Ella said, heaving herself out of a deep chair. "And don't you leave this room, Eliza Smallwood, especially not to go down to that saloon. There probably won't be any trouble to speak of, but with the boys getting this riled up, there's bound to be a lot of drinking, too much for some people. Then they get into fights and start shooting up things. It won't do for you to be seen."

"But I can't just sit here and do nothing."

"Lucy, you keep an eye on this foolish girl. More people have gotten hurt because some silly female, with no idea in the world of how a cowboy's mind works, thought she could settle a dispute if she could just get them to talk about it. The sooner you learn that out here men are most apt to talk with guns first and tongues second, the sooner you'll stay inside and leave well enough alone. They're mostly blowing off steam, but it won't do to put a match to it." Ella put on her coat for it was early December and a bitter wind was blowing. "I'll let you know what I find out."

Eliza sank back into her chair, her stricken countenance ashen, her eyes wide and staring. Lucy watched her out of the corner of her eyes, wishing there were something she could say to comfort her. Angry men seldom took thought for the consequences of their actions; it was left to the women to wait and weep.

Lucy hadn't been gone ten minutes to check on dinner when Eliza stuck her head out of the door; seeing no one, she walked quickly down the narrow hall leading to the back of the saloon, tiptoed down the stairs, eased out the back door, and hurried to the stable where her uncle rented horses. A surly lad of fifteen opened the stable door.

"Afternoon, Miss Sage. What you doing out today?" Eliza stiffened. She always disliked it when people called her by her stage name.

"I've been cooped up all morning, and I want to go for a ride."

The young man didn't move. "This is not a good day to be driving about. People are all upset about the killings."

"Well they're not upset at me," retorted Eliza, irritated he had made no move to harness a horse to the buggy.

"Does your uncle know you're leaving?"

"Please harness my horse at once," Eliza responded, quite angry now. "I intend to go visit a friend."

The boy got up to fetch out Eliza's horse. With maddening deliberation, he settled the harness over the placid animal and methodically attached it to the buggy, making sure that every trace was secure and every harness strap properly buckled.

Eliza was barely able to contain her impatience, but she knew she must not do anything to arouse the boy's curiosity. It was imperative that her uncle and the others not guess she was going to warn Cord.

"Don't be back too late," the boy informed Eliza as she climbed into the seat and took the reins. "The boss don't like it when the carriage horses are kept out after dark."

Eliza drove away at a smart trot without giving him an answer.

She had intentionally chosen a bonnet with a large brim in hopes no one would recognize her, and she got out of town, recognized or not, without anyone stopping her.

Eliza pulled the buggy to a halt in front of the gate. She had never been to the house before, and she didn't know where to look for Cord, but she was nearly rendered speechless when a woman stood up, practically from under her feet, where she had been working in the garden. It had never occurred to Eliza there might be a woman at the ranch.

"How do you do." The woman's greeting was open and cheerful. She was pretty in a buxom sort of way, and obviously not one to mind hard work. She wore a bonnet with an even larger brim than Eliza's, and her gloves were soiled from working in the dirt.

"Forgive my appearance, but if I don't get the last of these roses properly buried, the cold will kill them. I keep telling Mr. Stedman it's a shame to let his garden go to ruin, but he can't see the value of anything cows won't eat. They would eat the whole garden if I let them, the nasty beasts, but everything here'd be no more than a few mouthfuls for one of them. I told him some day he's going to get tired of living on the back of a horse, and then he'll be sorry he let his yard go."

Eliza gaped at the garrulous young woman who seemed as much at ease as if she were in her own home. But she *is* at home, thought Eliza; I'm the outsider.

"You'll have to forgive my running on like this. It's so seldom I see a female my tongue starts spinning like a windmill in a wind storm. I'm Ginny Church, the foreman's wife. I don't believe I know you."

"I'm Elizabeth Smallwood."

"So *you're* the schoolteacher." She pulled off her gloves as she stared quite openly. "They told me you were pretty, but they never said you were beautiful. Come on inside. We can't talk with the wind freezing our wits. I suppose you've come to see why I haven't been sending my boy to school." She opened the gate surrounding the little garden and indicated for Eliza to precede her. "I mean to send him next year, along with Myra Landis's boy, but he's just turned six and that's too young to go such a distance by himself." She looked at Eliza a little guiltily. "Besides, I wanted to keep him with me a little longer."

"It's not that at all," Eliza assured her. "I came to see Mr. Stedman on a matter of some urgency. I very stupidly assumed he would be at home. I should have known this was probably the last place I'd find him."

"He's in," Ginny said. "I'll have my husband see if he can round him up for you!" She ushered Eliza inside. "This house used to be just about as empty as the plains, but Mr. Stedman brought back a whole houseful of furniture. I don't know when I've been more surprised by anything."

Eliza was led into a room that would have done justice to any parlor in Cheyenne. Instinctively she took off her bonnet.

"Ain't it pretty?"

"It's beautiful, but I must see Mr. Stedman. It's rather urgent." Eliza realized she sounded rude, but she couldn't stand around talking about furniture when Cord's life might be in danger.

"Make yourself comfortable. I'll see if I can find Frank."

But she didn't get a chance to leave the room. The sound of boot heels on the polished hall floor was quickly succeeded by the appearance of her husband.

"Frank, this is Miss Smallwood. She's come to see Mr. Stedman."

"We've already met," Frank said; Eliza frowned in an effort to remember. "In town."

"Now I remember." She didn't. She felt dull and stupid, and she couldn't think of anything else to say.

"Do you know where to find Cord?" asked Ginny. "It'd be a pity if she came all this way and he was halfway to Casper."

"He's here somewhere, miss. I'll find him. I need to see you a minute, Ginny."

"Frank," she chided, speaking like she would to a small boy, "you know I can't leave Miss Smallwood alone."

"It won't take long." Still his wife hesitated. "It's important."

"Excuse me, miss. I won't be but a minute."

"You needn't hurry."

"Now what's so important?" Ginny asked her husband as soon as they were out of the room.

"Do you know who she is?"

"Sure. She's the schoolteacher."

"But do you know who else she is?"

"Quit with your games, Frank. She can't be more than one person at a time."

"*She* can. That's Miss Belle Sage, the singer at the saloon."

"Oh, go on. She's only the schoolteacher. Though I must say she's pretty enough to do just about anything she wants."

"They're one in the same, and unless I miss my guess, she's the reason for all this fancy furniture."

Chapter 19

Ginny's eyes suddenly glowed with excitement. "Find Cord and get him in here as quick as you can. Then you take every cowboy on the place and get them away from here. I don't want one of those bumpkins stumbling in complaining about some cow just when he's about to pop the question. Where is Cord anyway?"

"He should be coming through the back door any minute," her spouse informed her.

"Lord have mercy, and you letting me stand here just as useless as yourself. Get out the front door, and don't show your face until Miss Smallwood's gone." Frank dutifully let himself out while his wife hurried to a closet under the stairs where she extracted a heavy coat and driving gloves. Then, alternately tapping her foot impatiently and pacing the broad hall, she waited until she heard the back door open. She quickly erased the smile from her face, replaced it with a look of mild concern, and pounced on Cord the instant he stepped into the hall.

"There you are, and not a minute too soon. I've been fretting over whether to go and leave you to guess where I'd gone." Ginny hurried on before Cord could open his mouth. "My sister has fallen and hurt herself, or something like that, her Jim wasn't explaining things too clear, and there's someone to see you in the parlor."

"Who is it?" Cord asked when she paused for breath.

"The schoolteacher, I think, but I was too distracted to pay much attention." She hurried out of the house intending to keep him from asking any more questions, but Cord had forgotten Ginny before her sentence was finished; he hurried into the parlor where he was greeted by Eliza turning apprehensively toward the doorway.

"Eliza," he said in a husky voice, and crossed the room in five strides. Eliza rose to her feet in time to be swept into his arms and ruthlessly kissed.

"There's something I've got to tell you," she protested, trying to avoid his ravaging lips.

"It can wait." He pressed his hot mouth to the pulsating column of her throat.

"No it can't," she insisted, pushing him away. "Two men have been found dead, and everybody thinks you did it. They may be coming out here this very minute."

Cord stopped abruptly. "Who were they? When did it happen?"

"Simon Frater and someone named Keller."

"Harry?"

"I think so. They found one of them last night and the other this morning. Both were shot in the back."

"But why do they think I did it?"

"One was found on the road that runs west of your land. The other somewhere to the south."

"So if they were killed close by, I must have shot them?"

"I guess so, but it doesn't matter. There are a lot men at the saloon drinking and talking about how something's got to be done to protect the little people."

"They're going to have to look for someone else to blame this time," he said with a deep frown. "I can prove I didn't do it."

"But they won't believe you or your men. They say they'd all lie to protect you."

"Probably not every one of them." Cord smiled so brilliantly Eliza's heart skipped a beat. "But this time they won't have to. I was in Cheyenne with two perfect strangers who can swear to my whereabouts for the last week."

"Are you sure they will listen to you? They are mighty upset, and some of them swear you must be behind it."

"I'm sure."

"And if they come out here?"

"They won't. The sheriff and Sanford Burton both know where I've been."

179

"Then you're really safe?"

"Yes, I'm really safe."

"You can't believe how worried I've been. And all the time you weren't even here." The sense of relief was so great she felt light-headed. "What were you doing in Cheyenne?"

"I was winding up the details of my loan and buying enough furniture to fill this house. You, Miss Smallwood, are looking at the proud and sole owner of the Matador. Every stick of wood on the place and everything on four hooves is *mine.*"

Freed of the need to worry about Cord, Eliza broke into a broad smile. "You've paid off the whole debt?"

"Every penny of it. I'm not a rich man, but I've got enough for now. In five years I'll be rich enough for you to throw everything out and buy whatever you like."

"But this is your house," stammered Eliza. "I would never tell you what to put in it."

"I'm inviting you to make it *our* home, my little love," Cord stated, compelling her eyes to look into his. "I want to get married, *now.* Would Christmas be too soon?"

"C-C-Christmas?" Eliza stammered, tightening her grip to support her weak knees.

"Yes, Christmas, with a preacher, a church, a white dress, and anything else you want." Eliza looked completely stunned. "You do still want to marry me, don't you?" Cord asked intently.

"Of course. I've been in love with you for months, but what am I going to do about Uncle Ira?"

"I really don't care whether he likes me or not. I'm not going to ask him to live with us."

"But I can't abandon him. I promised Aunt Sarah *on her deathbed* I would never leave him, and I can't go back on that vow now. I just can't."

"You're going to have to face the possibility he may never change his mind, and if he doesn't, you'll have to choose between us."

Eliza began to feel as though she was being assaulted from both sides. There seemed to be no way out that would be acceptable to both men. "Maybe when he sees how badly he's misjudged you this time, he'll realize he's been misjudging you all along," she said hopefully.

Cord doubted Ira would see anything he didn't want to see, but he didn't say so.

"Will you wait until I've had a chance to talk to him again?"

"Okay, but only if you set the date somewhere between Christmas and New Year's. I have a feeling 1892 is going to be my lucky year, and I want to start it as a married man."

"I feel the same way," agreed Eliza, torn between her desire to marry Cord as soon as possible and fear of what would happen when she confronted her uncle. "I just don't know what to do about Uncle."

"I'm not interested in Ira right now. You haven't answered me yet. Will you marry before the end of the month?"

"If you're really sure, I would like it very much."

"I'm really sure," Cord said, and smothered her in his embrace. But this time both his hands and his lips showed a tendency to stray. Eliza felt her body respond to the heat of his presence, and allowed Cord to unbutton the sacque she wore, and then the lacy blouse underneath. His lips trailed kisses while his hands found her breasts and massaged them until they rose against the restraints of her chemise.

"Someone could come in," she managed to whisper, not wanting to say the words.

"I'm the only one who stays in the house," he said, his lips never losing contact with her velvety skin. "And Ginny's gone to visit her sister." Cord's entire concentration was on Eliza and the nearness of a body that nearly drove him crazy.

Eliza felt her resistance fade quickly. "I guess I could stay for a little while."

Cord sat up in the bed. "Did you know you're the most beautiful woman in the whole world?"

Eliza smiled happily, but he could read disbelief in her eyes.

"I mean it, absolutely the most beautiful woman in the entire world."

"And how do you know that?" she teased, tickling his nose with her index finger.

"I checked out every one of them myself." He let his fingers trail between her breasts down to her bare belly. "I traveled to the far corners of the earth until I found you."

"And all the while your twin brother was spending twenty hours a day riding this range."

He grinned. "I may not have actually *seen* every girl in the world, but I know none of them can come close to you. I thought I was in love once before, but now I know how wrong I was."

"I didn't know what I was missing. I thought I was *supposed* to spend the rest of my life cooking and cleaning, and running at the sight of any man."

"I still want you to run at the sight of me, but always toward me. When will you talk to your uncle?"

Some of the happiness faded from Eliza's eyes and she sat up, pulling the sheet over her nakedness. "I don't know."

"Suppose I go into town with you and we get it over tonight."

"No!" It was a cry of panic.

"You're not afraid of him, are you?"

Maybe, Eliza thought, remembering the bruised cheek. "What is he going to do if I stop singing?"

"Sam's been packing them in lately, and Ella told me Croley had hired a dancer. It won't be the same without you, but they'll do all right."

"It's not just that. Uncle Ira doesn't like you. He hates all cowboys."

"Are you going to let that stop you from marrying me?"

"No, but I'd rather tell him myself, in my own way. He's going to be awfully mad, but it would make things worse if you were there. He wouldn't listen to a thing I said."

"When will you tell him?" He pulled back the sheet and dipped his head to let his tongue caress a ruby nipple that immediately began to throb with warm desire. "I warn you, I'm not a patient man." He stroked the other nipple with his fingertips.

"I'll tell him tomorrow, as soon as I can," she said, finding it difficult to concentrate on her words. Tendrils of desire radiating out from her breasts to every part of her body caused her flesh to quiver with expectation. The ever-widening

182

nature of Cord's onslaught turned her thoughts to mush and her senses into an uproar. The driving insistence of her aching would not allow her to passively acquiesce to his lovemaking, but forced her to reach out to discover him as he had discovered her. Her fingers lost themselves in the mat of hair on his chest, and she pulled him down until their lips locked, their tongues probing, searching, driving their bodies toward a tumultuous fulfillment.

"Touch me," he said, his voice harsh with tightly leashed desire. "I want to feel you hold me." A shudder shook Eliza's entire body, but she forced her hands to reach down until they encountered the white-hot rod of his passion. Slowly her fingers closed around it, feeling its throbbing length, cradling its molten stiffness. A groan escaped from between Cord's compressed lips, and his tongue ravaged her mouth.

"Now guide me to you," he said. Tentatively Eliza obeyed, thrilled by the realization that her touch was pleasing him so. She opened her body to accept him and he entered ever so slowly. Eliza gripped her lower lip in her teeth to keep from crying out as he sank ever deeper into her warm, inviting flesh with maddening slowness, tempting, teasing, driving her into a tempest of longing. Her legs closed around him trying to force him to probe deep within her to reach and satisfy the longing that was turning her inside out, but still he inched his way in, pausing, withdrawing a short way, and then resuming his entry.

"Please," she begged in a ragged voice, and Cord drove deep within her with one knifing stroke. With a cry of joy Eliza rose to meet him, forcing him ever deeper, then withdrawing to thrust again. She was unable to wait for him to lead her, to determine the course of their pleasure. Her body demanded satisfaction and it demanded it now. She threw her head back and wrapped both her arms tightly about Cord, holding him close to her, forcing him to plunge still deeper to reach her raging need. The spiral of longing and pleasure wound ever higher until it caused her whole body to shudder with ecstasy.

But Cord drove her on, and soon a second spiral, quickly followed by a third, enveloped her in its ever-widening circles, and she began to feel as though her entire body was tormented by the need to absorb Cord into herself. Wave after wave of disabling sensuality rolled over her, building to a crescendo that became so overwhelming that Cord became a victim to its engulfing, spreading rings. His breath came fast and hot, and his body drove insistently into the very depth of her, until, with a shattering explosion, he too reached that pinnacle of pleasure.

"Another minute, and I'd a had the place locked up," the boy stated impudently as Eliza drew the buggy to a stop in front of the livery stable. "Then you'd a had to go disturbing Mr. Hadley at his dinner, and that would a caused a ruckus."

"I'm glad you didn't have to wait."

"Look, lady, I don't wait for nobody, not even a fancy saloon singer."

"Take good care of my horse, please. He's had a long drive," Eliza instructed the boy, and abruptly turned her back on him. He made an unpleasant face as he spat out a stream of tobacco juice, then led the horse and buggy inside.

"Ain't nobody else gonna keep me from my dinner," he muttered. He locked the door behind him before beginning to strip the harness off the exhausted horse.

Outside, Eliza hurried along the street toward the back door of the saloon. She cracked the door and listened attentively, but she heard no unusual sounds so she slipped in and tiptoed down the hall to the stairs. She could hear voices coming from the kitchen, but no one stepped out into the hall to see who had come in. She paused again upon reaching the upper floor, but there was no one in the long passageway and she hurried toward her rooms. She put her ear to the door, straining to hear the slightest sound; the silence didn't mean her uncle wasn't inside. Taking a deep breath, she schooled her features into a look of casual disinterest and opened the door.

The room was empty. She let out her breath in a great rush, then hurried to her own room, closed the door, and sank on the bed, relief flooding all through her body. She lay there for several minutes until her pulse returned to normal, her mind lingering on the time spent in Cord's embrace.

Her daydreams were soon interrupted by sounds from the parlor, indicating Lucy's preparations for dinner. Realizing she had no idea what had happened during the long hours she'd been away, Eliza made herself presentable and went into the sitting room.

"So there you are. I wondered where you'd got to."

"I was tired of being cooped up, so I went visiting."

"Just as well, with all the fuss and bother."

"Is Uncle still angry?" Eliza asked.

"Yes, but not about the same thing," Lucy answered, and surprised Eliza by breaking into a chuckle.

"What do you mean?"

"You know how he was trying to talk everybody into going out to Mr. Stedman's place for a shootout? Well, the sheriff showed up and told him to stop making a fool of himself, that Mr. Stedman had gone to Cheyenne a week ago and was still there for all he knew. Now they're back to thinking it was one of the Association's hired guns or maybe an informer."

"What did Uncle do?"

"What could he do? He shut his mouth. Now nobody will listen to anything he has to say, and that's made him even madder. It's about time for your dinner, so you'd better get dressed. There's lots of men in town because of the shootings, and the place is bound to be as full as it can hold. Your uncle is still boiling mad, so there's no point in giving him an excuse to take it out on you."

"Do you think I should try out the new songs tonight?"

"You're going to need something different if you're going to take their minds off the killings. There's nothing like a dead body to set people's tongue to clacking. If I didn't know better, I'd swear they *liked* it. At least it gives them something to talk about besides cows and that infernal Association. What is this Association anyhow?"

"It's nothing really. Just a lot of rich men who get together to talk about keeping ranching to themselves."

"You wouldn't think that would be anything to get excited about. Sounds downright boring to me."

"Me too, but every time anybody mentions it, people get upset and angry. Uncle even talked about buying a newspaper so he could campaign against it."

"If you ask me, it's a waste of time to fight something that doesn't exist."

"It exists. It's just not something you can see."

"If you can't see it, it don't exist," Lucy stated positively. "Unless it's a ghost, and I don't believe in ghosts. Now you sit down to your dinner and stop talking nonsense. The menfolks will do plenty of that for you."

Chapter 20

Ira swallowed his breakfast in sullen silence. He usually slept late, but he was still smarting from yesterday's humiliation. Eliza knew it would be better to choose another time to tell him she was going marry Cord, but he wasn't going to like it no matter when she told him, and she hoped that maybe he had used up so much of his energy already he'd be too tired to get terribly angry at her.

"What did you do yesterday afternoon?" Ira asked, nearly causing Eliza to choke on a mouthful of ham.

"I stayed in for most of the day, then went for a ride."

"Singing a couple times a day isn't enough to keep you busy. You should work in the saloon," he said, eyeing her speculatively.

"You said all I had to do was sing."

"Yeah, but it's not good for you to be so idle."

"I will have plenty to do when school starts again. Besides, it was your idea to move here from the cabin."

"Don't tell me you miss living in that tumbled-down shack."

"No, but I do miss the animals and being up and around. I'm used to it."

"You need some babies to look after," he announced, nearly causing Eliza's chair to rock from under her. "A husband and a house too, of course." Eliza knew Cord was not the husband he had in mind, but she wasn't going to get a better chance to break the news of her engagement.

"I have been wanting to talk to you about that. I've received an offer of marriage."

"Not from another cowboy, I hope. They get carried away

with your face and start talking a whole lot of foolishness, but you can't live on a cowboy's wages, not even if you worked as a schoolteacher all year round."

"He's not a cowboy. He's a rancher."

"What rancher do you know?" he asked, looking up. The question remained in his eye for only a moment and then realization hit. "You mean Cord Stedman! Don't tell me that bastard asked you to marry him?"

"Yes, he did."

"When?"

"Yesterday. I met him when I was out riding."

"And what did you tell him?" Ira's whole body was tense.

"I said I had to talk to you first." Eliza could see Ira relax slightly and she knew a moment's desire to turn and run. Instead she looked her uncle square in the eyes. "But I told him I would marry him."

"You'll do no such thing," Ira exploded, rising from his chair so quickly he spilled his coffee and sent half the silverware clattering to the floor. "I'd rather see you dead than married to that traitor."

"I know you don't like Cord—" Eliza began, but her words were buried under the volcanic blast of Ira's ungovernable rage.

"He's a traitor and a murderer!"

"You know he didn't kill those men."

"How do you know?"

"Lucy said the sheriff told you he was in Cheyenne."

"The sheriff didn't know he was back yesterday afternoon. Maybe there's a few more things he doesn't know."

"He was in Cheyenne. He told me so himself."

"That doesn't prove anything."

"Why do you hate him so? You can't still be mad at being run off Bear Creek."

"Nobody runs me off any place and gets away with it," Ira said wrathfully. "I swore I'd get even with him, and I won't let you marry him."

"He knows that, but he asked me anyway."

"I'll have no argument on this. I know you're wanting a husband, but just be patient a little while, and I'll come up with one."

"But I'm not arguing." Much to Eliza's surprise, she was not shaking but was actually almost calm. "I intend to marry Cord with or without your permission."

"Are you defying me?" Ira demanded, his entire body quivering with rage.

"I will if I have to."

"You're not old enough to get married without my permission."

"Then I'll wait. It's only four months until my birthday."

"I'll never let you marry Stedman," Ira swore, his face rigid with rage. "I'll lock you up in your room if I have to."

"You know you can't do that," Eliza said unruffled, her uneasiness subsiding now that she was faced with a concrete problem. "Lucy would let me out. Besides, I can't sing locked in my room."

"I'd let you out at night."

"Do you really think I would sing and then calmly let you lock me up again?" Eliza asked, incredulous.

"You can't stop singing," Ira said, tremors of uneasiness and iron determination sounding in his voice.

"You don't really need me anymore. Sam is very popular with the customers, and Mr. Blaine has already hired a dancer. You won't even miss me."

"I won't allow you to marry that sneaking double-crosser."

"When are you going to stop trying to blacken his name? Nobody listens to you anymore. They just laugh behind your back."

"Nobody laughs at me!" Ira thundered.

"Then you'd better stop talking about Cord."

"So now it's *Cord*? You're sounding mighty familiar all of a sudden."

"I'd have to know him rather well to want to marry him."

"He's a traitor and a murderer," Ira repeated, momentarily stymied but undaunted.

"Mrs. Baylis likes him too. She's been encouraging me to marry him for weeks."

"How can you even think of marrying a *cowboy*. Don't you remember what they did to your Aunt Sarah? And your cousin!"

"Uncle, can't you see what you're doing to yourself? For

189

ten years you've blamed every cowboy you've met for Aunt Sarah and Grant's death, and it's eating the heart out of you. For your own sake, you've got to stop. They're dead and nothing is going to bring them back."

"It was cowboys who brought the tick that killed our stock, and it was cowboys who brought the fever that killed my Sarah and poor little Grant."

"But it's not fair to blame Cord for what happened years ago and hundreds of miles away."

"Don't you have any shame?" Ira raved. "You don't care about anything as long as you get that smirking cowboy for yourself. Have you been seeing him on the sly?"

"It was the only way," Eliza admitted, rising from her chair. "Would you have let him come here?"

"No!" Ira virtually screamed in her face. "And I'll not have him here now. I'll kill him if he sets one foot in my house."

"This is my home too, and considering it's my singing that paid for it, you ought to give some consideration to what I want."

Ira stared at Eliza incredulously. She had been standing up to him more often lately, but she had never dared to throw in his face the fact that *she* was making the money which enabled him to live in comfort.

"You never used to talk to me like this," he reproached her, genuinely puzzled. "What's gotten into you?"

"I never used to think I was worth anything, that I could do anything important or had any opinions that mattered, but things are different now. I don't enjoy singing in the saloon, but it has taught me I can do something no one else can. I'm a success. People come just to hear me. Teaching school proved I could do something on my own."

"And where does your strutting cowboy come in?"

"He thinks I'm the most wonderful person in the world," Eliza told him almost rapturously. "Do you know what that means? After nearly ten years of slaving without a word of thanks, someone wants to do things for *me*. Not because I can sing, or make money, or do anything else useful, just because I'm me. It's the most marvelous feeling in the whole world."

"I'll kill the bastard," Ira screamed.

"You won't raise a hand against him," Eliza returned fiercely. "In fact you're going to stop saying anything against him, anything at all."

"You can't order me around. I'm not one of your students."

"I don't mean to sound like I'm giving orders, but Cord is going to be my husband, and I'll not have my own uncle talking against him."

"I'll say what I want to anyone I like."

"If you don't stop, I'll walk out that door and never come near this saloon again."

"And where will you go?" demanded Ira, shaken but struggling desperately to keep control of Eliza.

"I'll go back to the cabin if I have to, but I won't stay here. Can't you understand that I love Cord just like you loved Aunt Sarah?"

"How dare you profane your aunt's memory," Ira moaned, suddenly transformed from a petty tyrant to the tortured, sad little man he really was. "She was the most wonderful person in the world. She was much too good for me."

"That's how I feel about Cord, even if you can't see it. Whenever you doubt it or get angry, just remember how you felt about Aunt Sarah. Then you'll know what Cord means to me."

They were interrupted by a knock at the door.

"It's open," Ira shouted. It was Croley who opened the door, but he was preceded into the room by a pretty brunette of impressive physical endowments and an easy, confident air.

"I wanted you to meet Miss O'Sullivan, our new dancer and singer. She just got in on the morning stage."

"Looks a little long in the tooth to me," Ira observed ill-naturedly. "I thought you were getting somebody young."

"I couldn't find anyone else with Miss O'Sullivan's talents."

"I'm Elizabeth Smallwood, Miss O'Sullivan," Eliza said, deeply embarrassed by her uncle's comment. "I hope your trip went smoothly. You must have had to get up awfully early."

"I never went to bed, but I did doze on the train. My name's Iris."

191

"I hope you'll call me Eliza. Everyone does."

"She's Belle Sage around here," stated Ira, his dislike obvious. "You could do with a stage name yourself."

"Iris has always suited me just fine."

"We'll decide that, miss."

Iris's slate blue eyes grew hard. "It's *Mrs.* O'Sullivan, and I'll thank you to remember that."

"You hired a married woman? Are you crazy?"

"She's a widow," Croley said. "And she's got a kid."

"A little girl," said Iris. "Someone named Lucy lured her into the kitchen with a promise of hot chocolate."

"That's nearly as bad," Ira fumed. "The boys don't want a mother."

"And they won't get one," snapped Iris. "But they won't get a sister or a saint either. No offense, Miss Smallwood, but I don't have your looks, and from what Mr. Blaine says about your voice, I can't sing like you either, so it wouldn't make any sense for me to try to ape you."

"Don't let Ira upset you," Croley said soothingly. "His niece has had all the attention up until now, and he's not happy about her having to share it."

"I wouldn't mind sharing," said Ira. "It's a helluva lot better than giving it up altogether. Yeah, you ought to stare. You don't know what the foolish girl has done."

"Uncle Ira—"

"Don't you *Uncle* me, not after getting yourself engaged to Stedman."

"What!" exclaimed Croley. "Do you mean he asked you to marry him?"

"What else would I be talking about? Of all the people, she had to go and pick that murderer."

Iris looked from one person to another in bewilderment.

"Nothing's been proved against him," said Croley, badly jolted, "so I don't think it's exactly fair to go accusing him, especially when the sheriff swears he was in Cheyenne."

"The sheriff is blind, or willing to look the other way."

"Uncle Ira! How can you possibly accuse the sheriff of covering up for Cord?"

"Nothing is beyond Stedman. It seems he can do anything he wants and get away with it. I promise you, I'll bring him to his knees if it's the last thing I do."

Ira's behavior had embarrassed Eliza badly, but at those words all thoughts of apologizing vanished. For the first time in her life, Eliza was coldly angry.

"Mr. Blaine, I have explained to my uncle that I intend to marry Mr. Stedman and that I will not have him slandered. If he doesn't stop, I'll leave the Sweetwater and sing for every other saloon in town if I have to, but I will not have my husband called a murderer."

"I forbid it," shouted Ira.

"And I'll hold a drawing every night to see who gets to dance with me."

"You might as well close up this place now," declared Iris. "And I'd better see about catching the first stage back to Douglas. I'm not about to tie myself up to a ship that's going to sink and take me with it."

"Nobody needs to catch any stages," said Croley, forcing a smile on his lips and making his voice sound relaxed and easy. "If Miss Smallwood wants to marry Cord Stedman, then we must respect her wishes."

"I'll be damned if I will," said Ira.

"We *must*," reiterated Croley, with so much meaning in the glance he threw Ira that he swallowed the hot response hovering on his lips. "I realize there're a few difficulties, but they can be ironed out when everyone is calmer. I brought Miss O'Sullivan up hoping Eliza would offer her some breakfast."

"I haven't had time for a bite," Iris explained, apologetically, "and I'm about to starve."

"She can have mine," Ira rasped, and stormed out of the room.

"I'd be happy to have you join me," said Eliza, again embarrassed for her uncle. "If Mr. Blaine will tell Lucy—"

"I already have," Croley said, some of the tightness gone from his voice.

"Would you mind talking to Uncle?" Eliza asked. "I'm afraid of what he might do."

"I'll go after him. Trouble for you is trouble for the saloon. Now you two get acquainted. You're going to be working together a lot in the next few days."

Iris picked up her coffee and followed Eliza into the sitting room. "So when my husband died, I decided to go back on the road. Mr. Blaine's offer was the best one I got. I always did want to see the West."

"You've certainly had an exciting life," Eliza said. "I've never even seen a circus."

"Believe me, it's much more fun to watch one than live in it. I was always after my husband to give it up. But tell me something about yourself. You must be all excited about getting married."

"It makes it very hard to be happy when your uncle loathes the man you're going to marry."

"Fathers and uncles always want us to marry someone else. My father wasn't too pleased about my choice either, but he came around."

"I'm afraid Uncle Ira won't."

"Surely you're marrying a nice, upstanding young man. He's bound to grow to like him when he sees how happy you are."

"I hope so. Cord really is wonderful."

"Is he a cowboy?"

"That's what he calls himself, but he owns his own ranch and is going to be very important in Buffalo some day. Maybe even the whole state. He's very smart, and works very hard."

"Is he rich? I mean, having a ranch makes him sound rich to me."

"I don't really know, but he probably is."

Iris set down her cup and stood up. "I'm sure you'll be very happy, have loads of children, and your uncle will become dotingly fond of all of you." She smiled a little mechanically. "Now I have to get settled into my room. Mr. Blaine insisted I stay here for now. It's certainly convenient, but I hope to get a place of my own before long. Oh, I'm told there's a Sam somebody who works here too."

"Sam Haughton. He sings and tells stories. I don't think they're very *nice*, but the men seem to like them."

"Something else I can't do," Iris said philosophically. "Mr.

Blaine has told me you've made this a classy joint. I'm supposed to give the customers a little more spice, but I'm still to take my lead from you."

Eliza blushed slightly. "I'm sure you'll be very successful. You're very pretty, and much more *robust* than I am."

Iris broke into a shout of laughter. "Yeah, I'm a big girl. The boys always did seem to like me, but I'd trade it all to look like you. Listen to me, dearie. You're exactly what every man, cowboy or rancher, wants and never thinks to find. Your Cord will take you and your cranky uncle and think himself lucky."

Chapter 21

"Eliza, wake up. They've put your uncle in jail for stealing Mr. Cord's cows." Lucy shook Eliza again, but the girl only stared at her with vacant eyes. "Oh, do wake up. Mr. Blaine is nowhere to be found, your uncle is calling the sheriff every terrible name he can think of, and Cord just stands there looking like a great stone carving."

"Cord?" Eliza repeated sleepily, sitting up in bed. "What about Cord?"

"He's hauled your uncle to jail for rustling."

"What!" Eliza gasped, wide awake now.

"I *said* Mr. Cord has caught your uncle trying to take one of his cows, and he's had the sheriff lock him up."

"B-but that's impossible," stammered Eliza, certain she was still dreaming. "There must be some mistake."

"Maybe," said Lucy, handing Eliza her robe, "but your uncle *is* in jail and you're going to have to get up and go down there. Nobody can make head or tail out of anything he says."

Eliza's mind refused to accept Lucy's words. It couldn't be happening. Her uncle wasn't a thief! She threw on her clothes as quickly as she could, convinced everything would be straightened out by the time she reached the jail.

Iris stumbled in wearing a night cap and a voluminous flannel nightgown under a thick housecoat. "What on earth is going on? Why are you getting dressed at three in the morning?"

"Mr. Stedman has had her uncle locked up for stealing one of his cows. The man's raving like a lunatic, and Miss Eliza's got to go down there and make some sense out of all that gibberish." Lucy's story was beginning to grow with each telling.

"Give me a minute and I'll come with you."

"Maybe you'd better not," Eliza said apologetically. "Uncle says some pretty terrible things when he's mad. When he calms down, he's angry at everyone who heard him."

"I never got out of bed," said Iris with a crooked grin. "Be sure to let me know if I can do anything to help."

"Where is Mr. Blaine? Can't he talk to Uncle?"

"Nobody has seen him," Lucy related. "Though I'd like to know what *he's* doing out of his bed in the middle of the night."

"Don't worry about that now. Just send him to the sheriff's office the minute you find him. I'm sure it's all a ridiculous misunderstanding, but I need Mr. Blaine. Uncle Ira never listens to anything I say."

The scene that greeted Eliza's eyes outstripped even her worse fears. The Buffalo city jail had to serve the whole of Johnson County, but it was a rudimentary affair with no separate area for the cells, and Ira was locked up only a few feet from the sheriff's desk. He had an unobstructed view of his hated protagonist and was screaming profanities at Cord and ignoring the sheriff's orders to be quiet so he could get down what Mr. Stedman was saying. Cord, accompanied by Royce and Sturgis, was answering the sheriff's questions with a steely calm that immediately made Eliza uneasy.

Still followed by Lucy, Eliza came to a halt in the middle of the room, uncertain of whom to turn to first, the sheriff, Ira, or her beloved Cord.

"Sorry to get you out of bed like this, Miss Smallwood," Sheriff Joe Hooker said, rising from his chair, "but I'm mighty glad you came." He was a likeable young man, only on the job a little over six months, but he was too young and inexperienced to understand the crosscurrents threatening the peace of Johnson County.

"Why has my uncle been arrested?" Eliza asked, turning to Cord. Sheriff Hooker hurriedly set out a chair which Eliza ignored.

"Mr. Stedman and his boys say they caught your uncle trying to make off with one of his steers. Your uncle says it isn't so, but I can't make head or tail of what he says he *was* intending to do with that beef."

"If he says he's innocent then why is he locked up?"

"Mainly 'cause I can't keep him from jumping Mr. Stedman any other way."

"Is that any reason to put an innocent man in jail?" demanded Eliza.

"Yes, miss, it is. It's my responsibility to protect the citizens as well as their property, and your uncle is not willing to leave Mr. Stedman alone."

"My uncle would never steal from anybody," Eliza insisted, turning quickly filling eyes to Cord's hard gaze. "There must be some other explanation."

"He may not steal from anybody else, ma'am, but he sure had his rope on Matador meat this time," Sturgis stated, nettled.

"I saw him myself, Eliza. There was no mistaking what he was doing." There was an implacable quality in Cord's voice Eliza had never heard before. She stared at him, unable to understand the change.

"There *must* be another answer," Eliza maintained. "Please, Uncle Ira, tell them what you were really doing."

"I'm not saying a word to that sneaking son of a bitch," her uncle blared. "And the sheriff is nothing but his pawn."

"I've told you that kind of talk will do you no good, Mr. Smallwood."

"And I've told you I've got nothing to say until my partner shows up. He's more interested in my welfare than my own flesh and blood."

"That's not true," said Eliza

"Does that mean you're not going to marry that villain?"

"No, but—"

"Then you're wasting your breath talking to me. You might as well desecrate your Aunt Sarah's grave as marry that devil." Ira turned his back on Eliza and sat down on the bunk in the cell area.

"He's still angry about our engagement," Eliza said to Cord. "He'll get over it if you just give him some more time."

"I'll give him all the time in the world to learn to tolerate me"—Cord was still cold and unbending—"but that doesn't include letting him help himself to my cattle."

"But he wasn't stealing your cattle."

"Then maybe you can tell me why he had his rope on a steer and was leading him off my land?"

"I don't know, but I know he wasn't trying to steal it. He's never taken anything in his whole life that wasn't his."

"All I'm asking for is an explanation. I asked for one when I caught him and the sheriff's been after the same thing for the last hour, but he won't talk."

"I'll never talk to you, you Judas."

"Uncle, don't," begged Eliza. "Please," she said, turning once more to Cord, "let him go, for my sake. He won't bother your herds again. I promise."

"Don't you go making promises in my name because you can't deliver them," said Ira.

But Eliza's attention was on Cord, tensely awaiting his answer. This wasn't the same man who had held her in his arms, igniting fires of love in her mind and body, loving her until she felt disembodied. Something had happened to Cord; she didn't know this man.

"I can't drop the charges until I have an explanation I can believe," Cord said with wintry severity. "To let him go now would be an open invitation to every rustler in the county to help himself."

"We should have given him a warning instead of wasting time coming here," muttered Royce, who found the whole proceeding tedious and unproductive.

"Shut up, you fool," Sturgis hissed in his ear. "You can't expect a man to beat his fiancé's uncle senseless and then show up in her parlor asking her to marry him." Since neither boy knew how to talk in a voice quiet enough to be considered a whisper anywhere except on the open prairie, their exchange was heard by everyone in the room with widely different reactions: Cord with icy stiffness, Ira with a hot rage, Eliza with shocked indignation, and Sheriff Hooker with plain curiosity.

"Miss Smallwood, am I to understand that you and Mr. Stedman are engaged to be married?" Sheriff Hooker asked.

"No, they're not," Ira bellowed from his cell.

199

"Miss Smallwood has agreed to become my wife," Cord said very formally, "but knowing her uncle's opposition, we decided to withhold the announcement until she had had a chance to talk with him."

"I forbid it," shouted Ira. "I'll stop it even if I have to take her to St. Louis."

A welcome interruption occurred with the entrance of Croley Blaine. Cord wasn't the only one to notice Blaine's clothes were more than ordinarily dusty and that he was breathing too hard to have come from anyplace in town.

"What's going on here, Joe? Iris tells me you've arrested Ira."

"Mr. Stedman and his boys brought him in about an hour ago and swore out a complaint. His niece insists he's innocent, but Ira just sits there calling Mr. Stedman names and being as uncooperative as a grizzled lobo."

"If Ira was caught with a rope on one of Cord's steers, he did it to get back at Mr. Stedman," Croley said, crossing over to the cell and looking at Ira rather than the others. "He didn't take the news of his niece's engagement very well."

"That won't wash," Sturgis stated in a flat denial. "I don't know how he felt about Miss Smallwood's engagement, but there's been some shady business going on on our range lately and he was there as a cover."

"Are you accusing my uncle of being involved with a gang?" asked Eliza, incredulous.

"I don't know what he's involved with, Miss Smallwood, but he wasn't out there taking one steer in a fit of anger. We've got cows wandering around bawling for their lost calves, and it ain't wolves that took them this time."

"Cord, are you going to let that man talk about my uncle like this?"

"Something *is* going on, and at least this time your uncle acted as a front. When we caught up with him, he started shouting and shooting his gun—"

"I was shooting at you, you coyote."

"—and did his best to delay us. He didn't even try to escape."

"Of course he didn't," Croley said, "because he was angry.

I've been Ira's partner for nearly six months now, Joe, as long as you've been sheriff, and I can vouch for it he has a hasty temper. He has a particular grudge against Mr. Stedman for throwing him off a piece of property on Bear Creek and for showing an interest in his niece."

"That's true." Eliza turned from Cord to the sheriff. "Anyone who comes to the saloon can tell you that."

"Let him go, Sheriff, and I'll stand surety he won't bother Mr. Stedman's herd again."

"I intend to let him go, but I can't stop his trial unless Mr. Stedman drops the charges."

"You will drop the charges, won't you?" Eliza said, turning hopefully toward Cord. "He wasn't really trying to steal anything. Tell him you weren't, Uncle Ira," Eliza pleaded, whipping around to face her uncle.

For a moment it looked as though Ira was going to have another outburst, but under the steely gaze of his partner, his eyes dropped to the floor. "Yeah, I was only doing it to aggravate you." He lifted his head, his eyes blazing, and pointed a shaking finger at Cord. "But I'll never let you marry Eliza."

"See, I told you. Now will you drop the charges?" Eliza implored.

Cord stood facing Eliza, his eyes staring at something beyond her.

"Cord," Eliza entreated, unable to believe he would not immediately free her uncle, "tell the sheriff you'll drop the charges."

His gaze refocused on Eliza. "But I'm not going to." He said the words in a quiet voice Eliza had never heard before, but one his men had experienced often enough to know Cord's mind was made up.

Eliza staggered as though struck a physical blow. "But you heard him say he was only doing it to get back at you. You can't mean to bring him to trial in front of the whole town."

"That's exactly what I intend to do. He's lying and we caught him red-handed. This is the best chance I've had to get a conviction in three years.

"Don't you love me enough to forgive him for my sake?"

"It's not a question of my love. I can't back down now, as

201

much for the other ranchers as for myself. There's a ring of rustlers operating out there, a gang intent upon stealing whole herds instead of single steers, and if the only way to get to the heart of it is by cutting off the arms one at a time, that's what I'll do."

"Then you really mean to humiliate him in front of the whole town?" Eliza inquired, stunned. "It's my uncle your trying to convict. Have you stopped to consider what this will do to me?" Eliza demanded, growing angry.

"I still say we should have busted him up. Then there wouldn't have been any of this trial business," Royce whispered. Sturgis stomped on his toe, hard, with the heel of his boot.

"You know I wouldn't do this if I could help it," said Cord. "The last thing I want is to hurt you."

"Then have my uncle released," Eliza snapped.

"I can't. The sheriff has already set the day for his hearing."

"Isn't that awfully fast, Joe?" Croley asked.

"It can't be helped. The judge will be in town next week, and if he doesn't stand his trial now, it'll be another six months before he gets his chance. You don't want this hanging over his head all that time, do you?"

"No I don't," Eliza stated emphatically. "I want him tried as soon as possible so his innocence can be proved once and for all."

"He ain't innocent, lady," Royce protested, unable to keep quiet during what in his eyes was a miscarriage of justice. "He had his rope around that calf's neck."

Eliza's indignant gaze didn't flicker for one instant from Cord's face. "I never thought you'd let a foolish misunderstanding blind you to all fairness. I've spent months trying to get Uncle to stop talking against you. Mr. Blaine even promised to do what he could, but you won't do the same with your hirelings."

"I don't hide behind my boys," Cord responded, his eyes hooded and his face impassive. "I lodged this complaint."

"Then why won't you withdraw it?" asked Eliza, deeply hurt and completely bewildered. "I even threatened to sing for the competition if he didn't stop talking against you.

Can't you do as much for me?"

"That has nothing to do with you or me. It's about gangs and rustling."

"But nobody believes Uncle Ira was trying to rustle your cows, by himself or as part of a gang."

"I do. If you can have so much faith in your uncle, why can't you have a little in me?"

Eliza's heart lurched at the bleakness of his voice and her anger faded. "Whatever Uncle may have been doing, I *know* he wasn't trying to steal. I never thought you would accuse him unfairly, only that there was some sort of misunderstanding."

"And if I still say I'm not wrong?"

"You *must* be," Eliza insisted, feeling Cord slipping away from her. Why was everything going wrong? Why didn't someone do something to stop it?

Cord stared at Eliza, the rigid cast of his features preventing his face from reflecting the struggle going on inside. The room waited for him to speak, but still he stared at her, his gaze unwavering and inscrutable.

"I can't have the man I'm going to marry calling my uncle a rustler," Eliza said finally, unable to stand the almost eerie silence. "You've got to drop the charges."

"And if I don't?"

Eliza searched Cord's face for any sign of acquiescence, but his expression was more austere than ever. Would he force her to choose between them? Would he require her to make a decision that could ruin her life forever? The alternatives were cruelly clear: If she chose Cord, she must desert her uncle and break her death bed vow to her aunt; if she chose her uncle, she could not marry Cord and would condemn herself to a life of unutterable misery. The choice was so harrowing, her mind and tongue were reluctant to put it into words. "How can I continue my engagement?" she said at last, each word produced by strenuous effort. "I can't desert my uncle."

"You mean to desert me instead?"

"You know I'll never stop loving you," Eliza said, a terrifying feeling of loss knifing deep into her heart with the swiftness and pain of steel. "I couldn't if I wanted to, but how can I publicly choose you over my uncle when it would mean his utter humiliation? Can't you see this is nothing but a pitiful attempt to strike back at you?"

"Can't *you* see it's much more than ill-tempered spite? It's part of an organized attempt to hit at the very heart of what I've labored through twenty-hour days in the saddle to achieve. It's not one man stealing one calf, it's a dozen attempting to steal hundreds, to cripple me just when the Matador has become mine."

"That can't be true!" Eliza cried, thrusting aside the unwelcome picture Cord was painting. "You make him out to be a cold-blooded thief rather than the pathetically sad little man he is."

"Pathetic! Sad!" erupted Ira, purple with rage.

But Eliza took no heed of him. "I can't let him be portrayed as a *criminal*. You've got to see you're wrong."

"I'm not."

"You won't accept my word?"

Cord shook his head.

"You intend to press charges?"

Cord nodded.

"But how can I choose between you?"

"That's something you'll have to decide for yourself."

Unreasoning anger and heartrending pain united to destroy the last remnants of Eliza's control, and it was all she could do to hold back the impending flood of bitter tears. "Come on, Lucy, there's no reason for us to stay. Mr. Blaine will see that Uncle is released."

She turned on her heel and swept out of the jail into the moonless night. She was unaware of the cold that turned her breath into steamy billows or the mud that soiled her dress and slippers. What did either of them matter when everything that made her life worth living had just been wrenched from her grasp? What did *anything* matter now?

Lucy glanced back at Cord, and the look of misery in his unguarded expression was so great she felt an almost overpowering desire to comfort him. Instead, she hurried after Eliza, already turning over in her mind how to bring them back together.

"Tell everyone to lie low," Croley growled furiously to Les. "That damned fool Ira nearly spoiled everything."

"Did he tell on us?" asked Harker, quaking at the thought of Cord Stedman on his heels.

"No. At least he had the good sense to keep his mouth shut. I hope I turned them off with that yarn about his being so angry at his niece's engagement he tried to steal the steer for spite."

"Say, that was clever," Harker said admiringly.

"It'll have to be to rescue this operation. Stedman knows something's going on, and he won't stop until he finds out what it is."

"We'll have to call off the whole thing," said Les. "I never did like it."

"No, we won't," Croley said mulishly. "The holidays are coming up, and not even Stedman's men will stay on the range the whole time."

Chapter 22

"But you can't go on refusing to even speak to him," Lucy said to Eliza. "The man has been here every day for the last week, and it's nearly breaking my heart to have to look him in the face and say you aren't here. Anyway, he knows it's a lie."

Since the evening in the jail, Eliza had experienced misery of a depth and kind she had previously thought impossible. It had been her words that had set Cord apart from her, and even though she felt she couldn't go back on them, even though she nearly gave in at least three times an hour, the agony was no less severe. She moved though her days, eating, sleeping, and rehearsing with Iris without using more than a fraction of her mind. Often she had to be spoken to two or three times just to get her attention, and even then her answers might be totally meaningless.

"You know you love him and he loves you, so what does all the rest matter?" argued Lucy. "So your uncle gets angry and tries to steal a steer. You're still speaking to him. But all Cord does is try to protect his own property, and you turn your back on him like he's the one who did the stealing."

"I wouldn't have minded if he'd knocked Uncle down or even put him in jail for a short while, but not bring him to trial."

"Mr. Cord is very jealous of his cows. He never lets anybody touch them."

"People are more important than cows. If that's how he treats my uncle before we are married, what can I expect him to do to me *after* we're married? Will he arrest me, knock me down, or break my legs? There won't be anybody

206

to protect me then."

"This is foolish talk and you know it," scolded Lucy impatiently. "Mr. Cord loves you. He'd never hurt a hair on your head."

"There's more that needs protecting than the hair on my head. I practically *begged* him to let Uncle go, but he wouldn't. He can't love me nearly as much as I thought if one steer is more important to him than my happiness."

"I don't think you understand Mr. Cord very well. That steer stands for everything he's worked for, and he means to defend it against anyone who tries to take it from him."

"But it *is* just a cow. Surely he can learn to see that."

"I don't think so. It's something that comes from way down inside, and I doubt he can change it. All you see is one cow, but he sees everything he has worked for being threatened. To him, it represents what he is, what he has to offer you."

"But I would love him just as much if he were nothing but a plain cowboy or dirt farmer."

"No, you wouldn't. If he had been content to remain a cowboy, he wouldn't be the man he is now. And he wouldn't be the man you fell in love with."

"You're not making any sense," Eliza protested.

"You're surrounded by cowboys, but did any of them bother to build you a schoolhouse or fill it with students? Who paid a fortune for the privilege of eating dinner with you, and talked Ella Baylis into virtually letting you live at her place?"

"What difference does that make?"

"You like Sam, don't you?"

"Sure."

"Do you love him?"

"Of course not!"

"Only because he's married?"

"I wouldn't love Sam no matter what he was."

"How about all those cowboys?"

"None of them either."

"Just Cord?"

"Yes."

"Then there must be something special about him, and

whatever it is that made him special enough for you to fall in love with made him rise from being a cowboy to a rancher, made him determined to hold on to his own and see it increased. You can't take a man apart, keep the pieces you like, and toss the rest away. Men come with the good and the not so good, just like women, but it all comes together."

"How do I know you haven't been blinded by Cord's smoldering eyes and muscled shoulders just like every other female in town?"

"I've lived in almost every city from New York to San Francisco, and I've seen every kind of man there is. I've seen handsome creeps who would sweep you off your feet, use you, and discard you all in the same night. I've seen honest Joes with hearts of gold, but no backbone and no ambition, and I've seen all the kinds in between. Mr. Cord belongs to the group at the top. Only in his case, he's the best of the cream. He got where he is by being tough, and he's going to be tough on you. This is only the first of many times, and probably not the hardest. He's a man worth having, worth fighting for, but he's going to cost you a lot."

"He's already cost me too much," said Eliza, struggling to hold back tears that swam in her eyes.

"Give him a little time," Lucy urged, giving Eliza a hug. "You'll find a strong man is a mighty nice thing to have around."

The trial was a mockery, and Cord would have been the first to admit he was a fool to have bothered with it at all.

"He got off with a warning," Royce muttered in disgust. "We could have done that without bringing him in."

"What are you going to do now, boss?" Sturgis asked. "You can't leave things like this."

"I've got to. I knew I was handing him over to the judge when I had him arrested. I have no other choice now but to abide by his decision."

"But you've got to do something."

"We will. I intend to keep a twenty-four-hour watch on every foot of my land until we catch whoever is stealing those calves."

"And this time we don't waste time with the courts?"

"I'm not sure what I'll do, but no, I won't waste time with the courts."

"I want a word with you, Cord Stedman." Ella Baylis's sharp voice cut through the crowd. "And I want it away from the sharp ears of your hired guns." She glared at Sturgis and Royce, who held back, unsure of how to deal with a woman as forceful as Ella. "Come back to the store with me. Everybody'll be at the saloon getting drunk, and we'll have the place to ourselves." Ella marched off without waiting to see if Cord followed.

"There's that Liza Hanks, made up like one of Lavinia's hussies, giving you the eye," she said as they walked.

"I can't say I remember her," Cord responded, nodding to a woman obviously trying to attract his attention.

"She's shameless, and her with a husband and children. There goes Ellis Gaddy, drunk as a skunk and the trial not over thirty minutes. I don't know when I've set eyes on a more worthless weasel."

"You don't seem to like much of anybody today."

"I've never had any opinion of fools," Ella stated flatly. "And don't get off with the idea I think a whole lot more of your intelligence," she said the moment she closed the door behind them. "You couldn't have done anything more useless if you'd set down and thought about it."

"It doesn't give me any pleasure to agree with you, ma'am."

"You knew locking up Eliza's uncle was bound to set her against you."

"I guess I was so mad I wasn't thinking clearly."

"The way I see it, you weren't thinking at all."

"If you'd spent as many nights in the saddle as we have, you'd understand why it goes against the grain to let anybody off," he explained. "You'd think with three of us swearing to his having a rope on that steer, and him not denying it, they couldn't do anything but find him guilty."

"Have you been to any of the rustling trials before?"

"No, ma'am. I haven't had the time."

"If you'd taken the time, you'd have known better. Last fall, Preston Spears thought he had some scoundrel dead to rights. Caught him in the act just like you did, but the scalawag got his friends to stand up in court and swear—under oath, mind you—it wasn't unusual for an unweaned calf to leave its mamma and lock itself up in a barn. Swore they'd seen it happen many a time, and the judge let him go. Now if they'd do something like that, how do you think you're going to get a conviction? There's not a person in Buffalo who believes Ira was taking that steer for anything but spite. And there isn't anybody who knows him that thinks he would have done anything with it except let it go once he cooled down."

"Ira is part of a gang. They may just be using him, but there were others on the plain that night. His carrying on warned them off, but I know they were there."

"And you thought you'd get to them through Ira?"

"Yes, ma am, I did."

"I used to think you had some sense, but now I'm beginning to wonder. If someone is using Ira, and I don't want you to think I'm swallowing that idea whole by any means, then they won't hesitate to get rid of him the minute he's no good to them. You're wasting your time with him."

"So it would seem."

"And then there's Eliza."

Cord's body stiffened. "I'm not talking about Eliza."

"You don't have to. I'll talk enough for both of us. How many calves have you lost?"

"I don't know."

"Guess."

"Two dozen, maybe more."

"How many calves is Eliza worth?"

"I'd give the whole damned ranch for that woman." Cord's words exploded from him with such intensity even phlegmatic Ella was astounded.

"Then why in the name of all that's good and holy did you go and lose her over one measly steer?"

"I never expected her to break our engagement."

"Good God, man. Did you think to have the girl's uncle locked up, accused of rustling, and forced to go through a public trial, and have her thank you for the pleasure? Where're your brains?"

"I never thought she would react this way. Not with her uncle never denying it."

"Didn't she tell you exactly what would happen if you insisted on going through with it? Didn't she beg you not to do it for her sake?"

"Yes, but—"

"Then why didn't you listen to her? Have you ever known Eliza not to mean what she says?"

"No," he admitted miserably.

"Of course you haven't. She's full of the most rigid principles of anybody you've ever met. If she says she'll do a thing, she'll do it no matter what."

"What should I do?"

"Don't go near her. You're both so upset you're bound to say something you don't mean. I'll let you know when it's safe to talk to her again. The girl's crazy about you and about to die of the misery. Otherwise I wouldn't get myself involved in a silly mess like this."

"I'm not going back on what I did, or apologizing for it."

"I know. That's why it would be fatal for you two to meet now. You just go look after your cows. Seems that's the only kind of female you know anything about."

"You can't go to bed now," Ira objected peevishly to Eliza. "Croley and Iris are coming up in a few minutes. We're going to have a celebration."

"What for?" Eliza asked suspiciously.

"My being judged innocent."

"I hardly call it *innocent*," Eliza replied derisively, "when your defense was that you were guilty of the deed but you only did it because you were angry."

"You sound unhappy that I got off."

"I'm unhappy your temper forced us into this disgrace in the first place."

"It was your lover's arrogance and stubbornness that was responsible for it all."

"You know he's no longer my fiancé, or anything else," Eliza said, nearly choking on the words, "but you also know if you had done what I asked, this wouldn't have happened."

"It was worth it to get rid of Stedman. Now we can go back to being comfortable again."

Eliza was absolutely certain she was the most miserable person alive, and would remain so for the rest of her life, but Croley and Iris came in just then, and she was spared having to try to communicate to her uncle an idea that was completely foreign to him.

"I brought an extra bottle of champagne," Croley announced jubilantly. "The Sweetwater now has another attraction. In addition to Eliza, Iris, and Sam, we have Ira Smallwood, hero of every little man in the district. And they can't wait to buy him a drink."

"I would think you would dislike such notoriety," Eliza said, half angry.

"I don't dislike anything that brings in business, and ever since Ira got himself arrested, the place has been about to burst its seams every night." Eliza angrily retreated to a corner, but Croley didn't seem to care. He was euphoric over the receipts of the last two weeks.

"Don't talk yourself dry before you open the bottle," Iris prompted.

"You're my kind of woman," Croley said, pinching Iris on the bottom. He was rewarded with a sharp slap.

"My only job in this place is to sing and dance," she said, her eyes as hard and unrelenting as Croley's. "I'll do what you ask in the way of work, but I'm a decent woman and I mean to stay that way. If that's not what you bargained for, I'll get out now."

"Don't get your nose out of joint," Croley replied with a forced smile. "You can be as snooty as you please as long as the customers keep coming in. Eliza's done very well by it."

"Miss Highbrow is her act, not mine," Iris said with a spurt of annoyance, "but I intend to keep my reputation just the same."

"Have some champagne," Croley said, pouring out a glass and handing it to Iris. "We've all had a tense time with Ira's trial and your first weeks on the job, but it's over now so let's celebrate."

"I'm celebrating being spared Stedman as a nephew," said Ira, "even though Eliza can't seem to get him out of her

212

mind."

"No girl can get a man she loved out of her system that fast," Iris said sympathetically. "Even if she knows she's made a mistake, it takes a long time for the hurt to heal. Only a hussy can turn her back on a man and forget him in the same instant. You wouldn't want people accusing her of being a heartless temptress, would you?" Iris asked Ira.

Ira was not pleased at having to swallow his words, and he favored Iris with a scowl. "Eliza's reputation in this town is spotless."

"Nevertheless, quite a few people know she was engaged to Stedman, and before long everyone will know she's broken it off. That will add to her attraction in the saloon, but having it appear that she doesn't care won't."

"You're a smart gal, Iris," Croley conceded. "I hadn't thought of that, but of course it will appeal to those romantic cowboys. I might even bill her as the heartbroken songstress."

"No, you won't," decreed Ira. "I won't have it broadcast about my niece was bowled over by that upstart and is still wearing the willow for him."

Eliza was too thankful for Ira's support to care what motivated it. Just the mention of Cord's name twisted a knife in her belly, and she couldn't have borne to enter the saloon if Croley had dared to advertise her misery.

Even now she lived in fear she would look up and see Cord watching her, as he had every night since she had broken their engagement, staring at her with pain and a hopelessness that tore at her heart, almost demanding that she give in to him out of sheer human decency. She was sure her singing hadn't been' very good and was grateful no one had mentioned it to her, but it took all her willpower just to remain on stage when Cord was in the audience.

"Thanks for defending me," Eliza said to Iris later when Croley and Ira, immersed in the pleasure of their recent success, had no further thoughts for the two girls.

"Forget it. You'd have done the same. Men don't understand a woman's feelings, and you have to remind them ever so often we don't operate the way they do. You gotta make them remember you're not about to be stomped on."

213

"I never used to be able to do that," Eliza confessed. "I'm much better now, and occasionally I do things that surprise me, but generally I can't stand up to anybody about anything."

"Does that include Cord?"

"W-what do you mean?"

"Are you still determined not to marry him, even if he were to come in here this very minute and plead with you?"

"Uncle wouldn't let him in," Eliza answered rather desperately. "And if he did, I wouldn't see him."

"Are you sure? You looked badly bitten to me."

"I'm quite sure, and if I look *badly bitten*, as you put it, it's because of my disappointment rather than languishing for a man who is quite obviously not the kind of person I believed him to be." Eliza's words sounded hollow even to herself, and she asked abruptly, "Why do you want to know?"

"I thought you'd come down off your high horse the minute you thought someone was after your precious cowboy," said Iris.

"I beg your pardon," said Eliza offended.

"Save the grand-lady act for the patrons," Iris advised her brusquely. "It doesn't impress me."

"I'm not *acting*!" warned Eliza, rapidly becoming angry *and* jealous. The feelings were aggressive and unfamiliar but they were a relief from the pent-up emotions of the last few weeks.

"Forget it. I just wanted to know if you were done with Cord."

"Yes." The single syllable was torn from Eliza.

"Because I intend to go after him."

"You!"

"Don't act so surprised. It's not flattering."

"I didn't mean it like that. Only it's so unexpected."

"Cord's a good catch. I don't like being a widow or working for people like Croley Blaine and having to fight off his pinches. I want a husband and a home of my own, and Cord Stedman would be just perfect. I've never seen a better-looking man, and my competition out here isn't what it was back East. I know I'm not a looker like you, but I'm decent, not bad looking, and I know how to make a man

214

happy."

"I no longer have any claim on Mr. Stedman's affections," Eliza stated. "What you, or he, does is none of my business."

"I just wanted you to know," Iris said, preparing to depart. "I'm not the shy type, or overly conscientious when it comes to a man, but I draw the line at trying to take away another gal's fella."

"He's not my fella," Eliza said, then burst into tears and ran from the room.

Chapter 23

"I don't care what anybody thinks, Sanford. I will not invite Ira Smallwood."

"But it's rude to invite Eliza and not her uncle."

"Next I suppose you'll tell me it's just as rude to invite one partner without the other."

"Well, it is, especially since both of them are clients of my bank."

"Then give a party at your bank. You can fill the place with squatters and claim-jumpers for all I care."

"Would you serve as hostess?"

"I most certainly would *not*. I took on the schoolhouse because there was no one else who *could* do it, but my charity goes no further. I will not invite people into my home whom I consider unfit company for my daughter."

"She's my daughter too," her husband pointed out.

"Then I'm surprised you don't take a greater interest in her future."

"I offered to send her to any Eastern school she liked, but she refused every one of them," Sanford said somewhat pettishly. "What more can I do?"

"Find her a husband."

"A husband!" Sanford echoed as though the idea had never occurred to him before.

"And one who can support her suitably. Not some merchant who'll expect her to work in his dusty store."

"Then she should have gone East. She'll never meet that kind of man here."

"There is one suitable man here, one that Melissa already feels a certain partiality toward."

"And who in the hell is that?"

"Sanford, I will not be *cursed!*" his spouse warned him awfully.

"Sorry, but who *are* you talking about?"

"Cord Stedman. Who else could I possibly mean?"

"Stedman?" repeated her dumbfounded husband. "But he's close to ten years older than Melissa. Besides, he's involved with the schoolteacher."

"Ella Baylis says she's broken their engagement."

"And what are you expecting me to do? Walk up to him and ask him to marry my daughter."

"No, but you can speak to him more often, seek his friendship, even include him in a few of your business deals." The greedy look grew in her husband's eyes. "I know you can't bear to part with a cent, but think of it as an investment in your daughter's future. You're going to have to leave your bank to Melissa's husband some day, and I can't think of a better businessman than Cord Stedman. When you consider what he's done with that ranch—"

"And the size of the check he deposited with me just last month."

"—and it's all free and clear."

"I'll think about it."

"Do, but put inviting Ira Smallwood out of your mind. I may invite Mrs. O'Sullivan, but I will go no further."

"But I don't want to go. I'll be miserable."

"You and Iris are the only ones the old dragon *did* invite. Iris has to work, so you've got to go."

Eliza knew her primary reason for not wanting to go to the party was a fear of meeting Cord, but upon reflection she decided it was unlikely Mrs. Burton would invite anyone she considered a cowboy, even so well-to-do a cowboy as Cord. Eliza wasn't sure why she had received an invitation, but she decided it must have been Ella Baylis's doing and since Ella was going, it would be okay.

So while Eliza relaxed in a luxurious bath, heavily scented with the bath oils Cord had given her, Lucy pulled out a dress made from some of the material Cord had given her, one she'd never had a chance to wear until now. It was a deep ruby-red velvet lavishly trimmed with Cord's creamy lace, and cut low enough to raise a few eyebrows, even with Cord's tippet of minks thrown around her shoulders.

"My, my," said Lucy when she finished piling Eliza's raven locks on top of her head and securing them with a red velvet band and an imitation diamond pin. "You are going to turn heads tonight."

"If I've got to go to this dreadful party, I might as well look my best. There probably won't be a man present under fifty, so it won't matter what I wear."

"Whoever told you old men didn't notice pretty girls must have been a gelding," said Lucy. "I don't doubt they're not quite as ready to paw you and jump straight into the hay, but it's what they've got in mind, no matter how long it takes to get around to it."

"You know you shouldn't talk like that," protested Eliza, pretending to be scandalized, though she was gradually getting used to Lucy's forthright conversation.

"It's time *somebody* talked to you, for sticking your head in the sand never taught anybody anything. Now go look at yourself in the mirror and thank the Good Lord he didn't see fit to make you look like me."

Eliza felt a thrill of excitement when she saw her reflection in the mirror, and her first thought was to wonder if Cord would think she was pretty. The question was even more portentous because she was wearing so many of his gifts. She doubted if she would have had the courage to take them out of their boxes, but Lucy had practically made her wear them. In the end, she had only given in because she was certain Cord would not be at the party. It was true she didn't have anything else half as becoming, but if he were to see her covered with his presents, he might think she was no longer so determined to keep him at a distance, and she didn't think she could stand the strain of denying him again.

She had thought about him nearly every minute for the last three weeks, but thinking had neither changed her mind nor healed her heart, so she forced herself to try to put him out of her thoughts.

Her milk-white skin and near-black hair were a perfect complement in color and texture to the rich lushness of the red velvet. Cord's pearl earrings hung from the lobes of her ears, and a choker made of ruby-red stones, the only piece of jewelry Eliza inherited from her mother, was fitted around her slim throat. There was just enough color in her cheeks to prevent her face from looking pale, and for the first time she had allowed Lucy to lightly tint her lips with a red color borrowed from Iris.

"You might as well use it," Iris had said with good-natured generosity. "But if I thought there was any way I could get away before midnight, I'd burn it first. You'll look stunning, and nobody will notice me unless I go naked."

Iris was right. Eliza did look stunning, and when Lucy threw the minks over her shoulders, she felt like a princess about to step out of a storybook.

"You're wasted in this town," Lucy wailed. "With your voice and sweet disposition, you could have Chicago and New York at your feet. Men would shower you with jewels and fight duels just to sit next to you."

"Then it's just as well I'm here in Buffalo," Eliza observed, reluctantly turning away from the agreeable picture of herself.

Croley's senses, if not his heart, were almost as powerfully affected. He came into the room just before Lucy drew the heavy cloak over Eliza's shoulders, and even though he had become accustomed to her looks, the sight of her nearly made him speechless.

"You're breathtaking," he said, gasping in surprise.

"She certainly is, but don't you go getting any ideas about showing her off downstairs. I was in a riot once, and I can tell you it wasn't a pretty thing." Lucy tied the cloak under Eliza's chin and fitted the capacious hood over her head. "She's sneaking out the back door and being delivered in a rented carriage. Ain't nobody going to see her who isn't at that party."

But Croley had an idea, one that was as new and unexpected as it was pleasant to contemplate, and as Lucy shepherded Eliza out the back door, a broad smile spread over his face.

"It was your decision to go, so stop dragging your feet and get dressed," Ginny said, prodding Cord. "It's rude to put off getting dressed until you're late."

Cord rose from the table and headed toward his room without comment. Attending this party was definitely not the kind of thing he usually did, any more than it was usual for him to receive such an invitation, but he had accepted it hoping for a chance to talk to Eliza.

She hadn't spoken to him since breaking their engagement after Ira's trial. Cord was not one to let unfavorable conditions influence his actions, but half the population of Johnson County had been at the courthouse that afternoon and not one of them had had a good word to say for the Matador outfit. He was willing to fight any man, even with the odds against him, but not for one minute had he considered trying to convince Eliza of his continuing love in front of such a hostile audience. That would have required him to admit strangers into the knowledge of his most deeply felt emotions, and on that level Cord was as vulnerable as any other man.

Cord stripped off his shirt to reveal a muscular torso with a thick, walnut-colored fur covering his chest and upper arms. With swift clean strokes, he removed his pants and underclothes, standing naked before stepping into his bath. He was totally unconscious of a body that would have caused nine out of ten women to swoon, and one Eliza could describe in minute detail without stopping to think. Endless hours spent in the saddle and wrestling steers to the ground had kept his muscles supple and rippling, while his abdomen was taut and the hips firm and well rounded. Gripping the sides of countless horses had given him powerful thighs and firm calves. The glory of his physique had never been more than barely masked by the tight, functional clothes he wore, but freed of their restraining cover, his was a body that could cause women to risk much for a chance to be in his arms. His manhood, denied its pleasure and sensitive to the slightest touch or change in pressure, hung stiffly between his legs, half aroused with longing, half deflated with neglect.

Cord stepped into the tub and allowed the steaming water to come up to his chin. The heat felt good. The room was cold and his body tense from work and worry. Slowly his knotted muscles relaxed and he spread out his full length, luxuriating in the hot water, and letting his mind break free of the around-the-clock watchfulness he had imposed upon himself. As usual, when there was the slightest break in his concentration, and many times when there wasn't, thoughts of Eliza filled his mind.

He hadn't anticipated Eliza's reaction to her uncle's arrest. He had come to think of her interests as inseparable from his own, and had assumed she would side with him if forced to choose; he had been stunned when she hadn't. He couldn't understand how she could be willing to marry him in the teeth of her uncle's opposition, then turn around and break their engagement to stand by Ira when he was clearly guilty.

But it was inconceivable to him that he should back down from his stand, even though Ella Baylis never missed an opportunity to tell him what a fool he was. His property, his very existence, was being threatened, and he had to fight back. He had prevented the boys from administering their usual beating because he knew someone was behind Ira and he had hoped Ira would expose them, but the little man had demonstrated more courage than Cord had expected, and had maintained such an attitude of righteous indignation throughout the trial you would have thought Cord was the one guilty of a crime.

Eliza had appeared at her uncle's side when he entered the courthouse looking stoically unemotional, but Cord was watching when Ira admitted that he *had* tried to steal the steer, and her hard-won control buckled in the face of that brazen admission. Cord knew then that Ira had let Eliza go on believing in his innocence, knowing all the while he would have to admit his guilt in court. He felt sorry for her, but he was proud of the way she had held her head up throughout the trial.

Cord could only guess at what she had been forced to endure in private because after that night at the jail, she had been careful not to come near him. He had understood Eugenia's motives when she threw him over, but not even Ella's efforts to explain Eliza's behavior helped.

He was certain Eliza was still the same honest, loving woman he had learned to adore and that she still loved him just as much as before, so he couldn't understand why she would break their engagement and refuse to see him just because her uncle had been caught trying to do what hun-

221

dreds of others were doing all over Wyoming.

Cord stood up in the bath, like Neptune rising from the sea, and toweled himself briskly until he was dry and his skin tingled. Then he washed his hair with a scented soap, dried it in the same ruthless manner, and brushed it until his whole head was covered in a thick mat of wavy hair that glistened in the lamplight like Eliza's minks. Then, completely unconscious of his nakedness, he shaved.

He ached so severely for Eliza it was beginning to affect his work. Not even Franklin dared mention it, but he hadn't missed the looks of surprise when he missed what they said to him or was slow to move out of the way of a steer. That was dangerous, and something Cord had never done before.

He pulled on his underpants, unconsciously smoothing them over the still-sensitive groin, and chose a stiff, white shirt from Ginny's carefully ironed pile. He wondered what Eliza would be wearing. Would she wear any of his gifts? He stepped into his form-fitting black pants and buttoned them up, being careful to tuck the shirt in so it wouldn't wrinkle the rigid front. He remembered the scent of her hair, the feel of her skin, and wondered what they felt and smelled like tonight. Had she used the perfume, the one he'd bought by the quarter ounce?

Cord struggled with his tie. He had seldom worn dress clothes, and while he didn't feel uneasy in them, he had trouble getting the recalcitrant tie to do his bidding. At last it was tied to his satisfaction, and he reached for the swallow-tailed coat. He had purchased this suit in Chicago, and he'd never seen himself in it before. He turned in front of the mirror, plainly unsure of what he saw. What he *did* see tempted him to change into his trusty black suit, but Jessica Burton's invitation had plainly stated dress would be formal, and the salesman had assured him this was the only formal attire for a man of his standing. He gave his glistening hair a few final brushes and then reached into a large box and extracted a hat, which he set gingerly on his head.

Eugenia would be shocked to see him now, he thought with a smile. All he needed was a cane and an eyeglass and he'd look just like those slick dudes she used to admire.

Thoughts of Eugenia no longer had the power to disturb him, but they inevitably led to Eliza. He took the hat from his head, found his overcoat, and went downstairs. If he didn't get a chance to speak to her soon, he was going to do something desperate.

"Look what a haircut and a bath have done to this dust-covered cowboy," Franklin said when his boss came into the front hall.

"It took more than a bathtub," said Cord with a grimace.

"You look good enough to eat," Ginny said, giggling. Cord's love for Eliza was an open secret at the Matador, but neither Ginny or Franklin dared hint that Cord had gone to all this trouble for Eliza. Ginny was incensed that Eliza would turn her back on Cord, but she was careful not to let Cord see her resentment.

"Don't wait up. I expect I'll be rather late."

"Besides which you're taking Sturgis with you," Ginny added with dancing eyes.

"You're both very good to worry so much about me," Cord said. "I'm very fortunate to have you."

"Oh, go on," said Ginny, blushing. "Have a good time and remember every detail. I'll never get invited to a party like that, and I'm counting on you to tell me what it's like."

"I'll do my best, but you know how I am."

"Hopeless, unless you want to be," Ginny said, teasing him.

"Good luck," Franklin called after him. They both knew what he meant.

Chapter 24

Eliza was enjoying the party; she actually smiled at a pleasantry made by one of the town's substantial citizens who was making a foolishly gallant attempt to entertain her. His wife regarded her husband's effort with accepting tolerance. After all, Eliza had an unblemished reputation, and what could he do right under Ella Baylis's nose?

"Wiley, get us something to drink and make sure it's cold," Ella commanded. "I'm about to burn up. I'll never understand why Jessica can't keep her invitations to a reasonable number."

"I thought her list was very exclusive," observed Eliza as her admirer went in search of the required refreshments.

"The first one is, but by the time Melissa and Sanford are through making additions, and Jessica *condescends* to invite a few more souls, the party is twice the size it ought to be and everyone is squeezed tight as sardines. After a few waltzes they start to smell about as bad."

"Then I promise not to dance."

"You have to. You and Melissa are the only young gals present. And if you think old men want to dance with old women, you don't know old men." Ella's eyes searched the room. "Where's your young man?"

"I've told you, I don't have a young man," Eliza said, her mood plummeting at the thought of Cord. "I neither know nor care where he is."

"If you're going to start telling lies, you've got to learn to do it better. Land sakes, girl, a baby could tell the mere mention of his name sends you into the dismals. If he were to walk through that door, you'd faint."

224

"But he can't. I mean, I wouldn't. I'm sure he wasn't invited."

"He was, for Melissa, but apparently he decided not to come. That's put Jessica a bit out of temper."

"Why for Melissa?"

"Don't be a fool. Jessica has a daughter to establish, and everyone knows Cord is the most eligible man within a hundred miles. Now that you've made it unnecessarily clear you'll have nothing more to do with him, the hopefuls are closing in."

"Iris has already told me she's going after him."

"He'd be better off with her than Melissa. She's no fool, for all she doesn't have fancy grades and school prizes to prove she's smart."

"Do you think Cord would marry her?"

"He's got to marry somebody, and Iris isn't such a bad choice." Just then Wiley Quinn came back with their refreshments. "Don't bore her with your tired stories," Ella instructed him, "and don't try to keep her to yourself all evening either." She then drifted away, and was not on hand to witness Eliza's reaction when Cord entered with Iris.

"We'd given you up," Sanford said, greeting them.

"It took a while to get into these clothes," Cord said. "It's quite a change from Levi's and a flannel shirt."

"I had to sing before I left," Iris added. "If Cord hadn't offered me a ride, I'd probably still be fighting off drunks."

"Come with me, Mrs. O'Sullivan. I'll show you where everything is, then introduce you to my other guests. It's disgraceful that decent women can't feel safe to leave their homes after dark," Jessica said with deep disapproval." I've been trying to get Sanford to help me close those dreadful places, but money is more important to the men of Buffalo than the safety of their wives and daughters." She bore Iris away, leaving Cord to her husband.

"Glad you could make it," Sanford said again, looking acutely uncomfortable. "It's always nice to have a few young men at these things. It gives the young ladies something to do." He smiled nervously, and his task was not made any easier by seeing that Cord's eyes had already searched out and were dwelling on Eliza.

"I haven't had a chance to talk with you since you got back

225

from Chicago, but you seem to have done quite well for yourself."

"The place is mine, if that's what you mean," Cord said without taking his eyes off Eliza. Sanford looked a little less miserable at not having to ferret out that bit of information.

"Then you must be looking to settle down. You've got to be getting close to thirty."

"Twenty-eight this past September." Cord was obviously not going to help him.

"It's a good idea to get married before you get too set in your ways. Of course, it's not always an easy thing to choose a proper wife, especially out here where the selection is limited."

"Nope."

Damn, thought Sanford. The man might at least look at him. "A man might be encouraged to take the first thing he sees for fear something else might not come along."

"Yep."

Sanford swallowed hard. "It's always a good idea to marry to your advantage."

"That's the only way."

"After all, many a woman has made a man rich through her inheritance. If he's willing to wait for it."

"It happens."

Sanford put his finger in his collar to loosen it. "Of course, a father can't be too careful in choosing a husband for his daughter either."

"Especially if she's pretty and an heiress."

"Exactly," agreed Sanford, relieved Cord finally appeared to be following his thoughts. "Her father would want to leave his money in the hands of a man who could be trusted not to waste it or neglect his wife and children."

"There's a lot of careful men in these parts."

"But not many of marriageable age, reasonably good-looking, and who have proved themselves successful businessmen."

"No, I guess there's only one who fits that description."

Cord's eyes were now on Sanford, and he found himself wishing they'd return to Eliza. "A fellow businessman might be willing to join with such a man in various financial undertakings. There are lots of ways to make money, not just cows, and a father might be willing to share some of his secrets with a man soon to become his son-in-law. You might say it would be an investment in his daughter's future."

Cord's gaze grew more intense and vague hints of a smile seemed to tremble on his lips. "A *man* might be awfully grateful for an offer like that if he hadn't already set his mind on another young lady."

"But she's not even speaking to you," Sanford burst out without thinking.

"But I'm going to speak to *her*," Cord said, and the promise of a smile was brilliantly fulfilled. "I think I'll get me something to drink," he said, leaving Sanford gaping.

"Damn, if that's not the first time anybody's refused help from me," he said. "I'm not sure whether I like him for it or not."

But Cord did not reach his objective. Melissa, materializing, as it seemed, from the ground underneath his feet, cornered him with demands to know all about Chicago, his trip to Cheyenne, and the wagon loads of furniture she heard he had bought.

"Naturally I don't remember the Matador ranch house terribly well because I haven't been there since the Orrs left, but I remember it was such a huge house and furnished so nicely."

"It's too big," Cord said forthrightly. "It needs enough furniture to fill three sensible houses."

"You're teasing," said Melissa with a not entirely successful effort at a trill of laughter. "Think of the marvelous parties you could give and the guests who could be invited."

"And the food they would eat up," Cord added most unromantically. "A rich man could be ruined by such a place."

"Not one like you," Melissa said, looking at Cord with adoration so obviously adolescent he was hard pressed to keep from smiling.

"Not everybody likes big houses and large parties, and I guess I'm one of them. My work is hard and the hours long. I don't want a house to drain my purse, and when I do come home I don't want to find the place filled with lots of people hankering after a good time."

"Not ever?" asked Melissa, stunned to think that anyone could dislike parties.

"This is the first party I've been to in five years, and it'll probably be twice that long before I go to another. I see your ma motioning to you, so I'll move on," Cord said, and left the girl as opened-mouthed as her father.

This time Cord was not to be denied, and he didn't stop until he stood before Eliza, who felt cornered and betrayed.

"You're looking mighty pretty tonight," he said softly. "Red suits you."

"Thank you," Eliza replied, nearly choked by the emotional turmoil within her. "You look nice too. I never expected to see you in such a suit."

"Neither did I," he said, with a rueful grin, "but I let that clerk talk me into believing this was the only way to dress fancy, so when Mrs. Burton's invitation said formal I decided to bite the bullet."

There was a moment of awkward silence.

"I see you're wearing my presents."

Eliza felt her pale skin turn crimson. "I . . . they're so pretty . . . Lucy made me," she finished, the words wrung from her.

"I see." Cord looked a little downcast. "I was hoping you'd worn them because I gave them to you."

Eliza would have given anything to be able to vanish into thin air. How could she tell him she had retrieved his presents from Ella's and was wearing them tonight because they were all she had left of him? "It seemed a shame to leave them in their boxes. And I did need something to wear."

"I bought them to give you pleasure, not to keep you from going naked." The anguish in Cord's voice cut Eliza to the quick. "But that's ungrateful of me," he said with a weak smile. "I should be pleased you're wearing them at all. You do look magnificent."

Eliza felt like the greatest criminal unhung.

"You look good enough to eat," Ella Baylis announced in a hearty voice from behind Eliza. "If you don't dance with Eliza, I'm going to take a chunk out of you."

"Please, no," mumbled Eliza, "I really would rather not."

"If you don't dance with Cord, some old geezer will grab you up," Ella pointed out. "You might as well dance with the best-looking man here."

"I'll be in the prettiest company," said Cord.

"You two can argue that between you, but you do make a mighty pretty couple. Now get going before I give you a push."

Eliza's eyes remained on the floor, but she didn't resist when Cord led her to a corner where a few couples found enough space to dance slowly and rather close together. "I see you came with . . ."

"I was hoping to have the chance . . ." They both had begun at the same time. There was a pause. "Ladies first," said Cord.

Eliza appeared reluctant to say anything and lowered her eyes once more. "I was about to say I see you've met Iris."

"Yeah. Saw her coming out of the saloon and knew she'd dirty her skirts, so I offered her a ride."

"Do you think she's nice?"

"She seems to be. Not half as pretty as you, though."

Eliza didn't raise her eyes, but she felt herself flush. "She's popular with the cowboys."

"Hmmm," replied Cord, uninterested in the cowboys' likes or dislikes. "You ready to start speaking to me again? It's been nearly three weeks now." He felt Eliza stiffen.

"I am *speaking* to you," Eliza replied in a tight voice. "But I meant it when I said I couldn't be engaged to a man who would have my uncle arrested for a stupid prank."

"You admit he was guilty now?"

"Guilty of poor judgment and treating you unfairly, but he's not a thief, and to say he is in league with a gang of rustlers is absurd." She had worked herself up to the nearest thing to anger Cord had ever seen.

"Then I don't suppose you're ready to forgive me and announce our engagement?"

"Of course not," she said indignantly. "Every time I think of you I remember what you did to my uncle."

"Then you do still think of me?" Cord asked, greatly heartened.

"I meant," Eliza said, correcting herself and trying to shift the basis of a discussion in which her position was being weakened by every sentence, "I could not marry a man who believes my uncle is a thief."

"You'll soon forget that. Everybody out here is a thief of some kind."

229

"I'm not," answered Eliza hotly.

"You stole my heart," he said with simple directness, and Eliza thought she would burst into tears. "You haven't given it back either."

A stifled sob was forced from her. "I would if I could."

"I don't want it. I just want you, and us the way we used to be."

"That's impossible."

"It will happen. Until then I aim to wait."

"Please, excuse me," she begged, and fled from the room.

"What did you say to make her run off like that?" demanded Ella, coming up behind him almost immediately. "I thought you had enough sense not to push her too hard."

"I just put some burrs under her saddle cloth so she won't ride too easy."

"She's suffering terribly from divided loyalty. Give her enough time and she'll come around to you."

"I didn't make the Matador mine in five years without having some sense," Cord pointed out. "If I give him enough rope, Ira will hang himself. Then she'll come tumbling into my arms."

"Maybe she will and maybe she won't," Ella warned. "There are ways to do things, and if you'll take my advice, you'll do nothing. Time is on your side. Girls like Eliza think funny sometimes, and if you do the wrong thing you might lose her forever."

"I promise I won't do anything stupid."

But less than thirty minutes later Ella could have brained him with relish. Eliza had returned from the bedroom, a little limp, but still looking magnificent. She was clearly unhappy and her eyes kept wandering to Cord as he moved about the room. They were merely jealous when he talked with other women, tolerant when he was once more corralled by Melissa with the help of her mother, but when a conversation with Iris broke into laughter and showed no sign of ending, they turned to molten coals.

"I've never seen Cord laugh," a matron said loud enough for Eliza to overhear.

"Mrs. O'Sullivan seems to be a charming lady. It's a shame she has to work in a saloon to support her little girl." Ella made a mental note to repay both ladies, but the stormy look in Eliza's face convinced her this was not the moment.

"Do you think he likes Iris?" Eliza asked Ella when the conversation between Cord and Iris had gone on so long her teeth were on edge.

"I don't think he's had a chance to get to know her yet," Ella replied with devastating directness, "but if you persist in keeping him at arms' length, he may find he does."

"I wouldn't think of holding on to a man who might wander at the first inducement."

"A man isn't likely to wander when he has what he wants." Ella's eyes followed in the direction of Eliza's gaze. "Not even for Iris and her *darling* little girl."

Eliza suddenly laughed. "You think Cord would prefer to have his own daughter?"

"I know he'd prefer to have his own sons, and he wants you to be their mother."

"And you don't think he wants Iris?"

"Not unless you hand him to her."

"I'm not that generous," Eliza said with the closest thing to a giggle Ella had ever heard.

"Hallelujah!" Ella almost shouted. "I was ready to think you were going to lie down and let Iris take your man without a fight."

"I don't know what you mean by a fight, but I can't give Cord up, no matter what he said about Uncle Ira. The way he sees it, Cord was right and I turned my back on him. From any point of view, Uncle Ira was wrong, yet I stood by him."

"Why don't you chuck all this right-and-wrong and standing-by-and-forsaking nonsense and just follow your heart. You love him and you're never going to be happy unless you marry him."

"I know. I discovered that when I saw him laughing with Iris and realized I was jealous because he wasn't talking and laughing with me."

"You know why he isn't?"

"You don't have to tell me. I've been a fool, but not anymore. I came too close to losing what I wanted most in the world."

231

Chapter 25

Eliza was awakened from a sound sleep by a loud, insistent banging. She sat up quickly, fear penetrating the heavy fog of sleep; why would anyone be pounding on her door in the middle of the night unless there were some kind of trouble? She pulled on a heavy robe and fur-lined slippers and tiptoed to her uncle's room. His bed hadn't been slept in, yet the clock said ten minutes past four. Where could he be?

"Who is it?" she called out, apprehensive of who might be on the outside and reluctant to open the door to anyone until she was dressed.

"It's Cord. Let me in."

Eliza's heart began to pound erratically. She had left Cord at the Burtons' party only hours earlier. What could he possibly want now? "You shouldn't be here."

"I've got to see you."

"No."

"Open this door, or I'll break it down."

"Hush! You'll have Mr. Blaine up here any minute."

"He's not here. Neither is your uncle. Now open up."

Eliza's hand shook as she took the key off its hook; she had no doubt but what Cord would be as good as his word.

"What do you want?" Eliza demanded angrily. But Cord's expression turned her displeasure to apprehension. He was still in the clothes he had worn to the party, but his face was a mask of tightly contained fury.

"Do you know where your uncle is?" he demanded in a voice that brutally swept aside any concern for Eliza's embarrassment at being dragged out of bed in a disheveled condition to face an old love still dressed handsomely enough to make any female swoon.

"He hadn't come home when I went to bed," she muttered, trying to pull her distracted thoughts together. Cord's unbending, unrelenting gaze banished the last traces of sleep, and a cold, unidentified fear gripped Eliza's heart. "Do you know where he is? Is he hurt?"

"At this very minute, he, Croley Blaine, and a gang of rustlers are herding freshly weaned Matador calves into a boxed canyon on Sam Haughton's land."

"I don't believe it," Eliza gasped, anger rising quickly in her voice as she moved away from him. "Why would he do such a thing?"

"The same reason as before."

"But why would Mr. Blaine be involved? He doesn't hate you."

"Croley is greedy. He'll never have enough money."

Eliza's mind reeled from the double shock of Cord's renewed accusations and fear her uncle might be guilty, *again!*

"It's a lie!" Eliza was even more stunned than Cord to hear the words come out of her mouth. It hurt to know he thought more of his ranch than he did of her, and she was furious he would attempt to accuse her uncle again, but she had never before doubted he was telling the truth as he saw it. Did she disbelieve him now? Could this mean she no longer loved him? Surely she couldn't love a man she didn't trust.

The idea no sooner occurred than it was banished. Through the fog of confusion and anger her heart shouted its message in loud, unmistakable words: she was hopelessly in love with Cord Stedman and nothing he could do or say would ever change that.

"It's not a lie," Cord assured her, his eyes open and brilliantly intense.

But something inside of her pushed reason aside and would not let Eliza accept his words. "I loved you, Cord Stedman, more than I ever thought possible. I would have done almost anything for you, but for some reason plain love isn't enough. You had to try to drive my uncle from me." Cord tried to make an objection, but Eliza ignored him. "I thought you could ignore his foolish hatred, but now I see you harbor the same kind of senseless need for revenge that has eaten away at him all these years. I've lived with that and I've seen what it does to people. I couldn't marry a man like that no matter how much I loved him."

"If you're through talking foolishness, I'd like to say a few words." Cord's eyes were hard, but there was no anger in his voice. "I don't give a damn what your uncle thinks or says. Others say worse and I still sleep at night. I've got too much to do to waste time making up lies and trying to get people in trouble, but I won't allow anybody to rob me of a single calf, no matter what the reason. I was within my rights when I had Ira arrested, and I thought you were honest enough to see that. My boys were itching to break his legs, but I wouldn't let them because I wouldn't intentionally do anything to hurt you." The fire blazing in Cord's eyes softened momentarily, but almost immediately it flamed forth again, setting Eliza at a distance once more.

"I love you so much it hurts sometimes, but your stubborn, blind loyalty to a man who has done nothing but exploit you has turned just about everybody against me. It almost cost me my best calves as well. I've been so worked up since the trial I haven'tbeen able to think. It was my boys who found these thieves, not me."

"Don't try to make me feel guilty for honoring my vow," Eliza said fiercely, her swimming eyes staring up at Cord. "You know nothing about love. Ever since I agreed to marry you, you've attacked my uncle and embarrassed me. All you ever think of is that everlasting ranch. You never think of me first or pay attention to anything I say."

"You're just about all I do think about," Cord said, gripping her by the arms in spite of her efforts to escape him.

"Let me go," she said, struggling helplessly against his powerful grip. "I'm not one of your cows to be wrestled to the ground and branded as your property." But Cord was so intoxicated by the feel of Eliza in his arms he barely heard her words; he could only think of the need that had been tearing at his insides for weeks, a need that only she could satisfy.

"I've ached to hold you in my arms."

"I don't want you to hold me."

But Cord pulled her closer to him. His lips were only inches away from hers and the feel of his body all along the length of hers was maddening. Eliza's struggles grew weaker as his lips found hers and his tongue invaded her mouth; they stopped altogether when his hands pushed her robe off her shoulders, revealing her white, satiny shoulders to his hot gaze. His lips trailed kisses along her neck, his teeth nibbled at her ear, and his hands found her breasts. A moan escaped him, and he suddenly picked her up and started toward the bedroom.

"Stop!" she protested. "Put me down, or I'll scream."

"Just thinking about making love to you causes me to break out in a cold sweat," Cord groaned. "Having you so close is killing me." He kicked open the door and carried Eliza over to the bed.

"I won't be loved by a man who accuses my uncle of infamous crimes," she panted, feeling desire for Cord threaten her control.

"I haven't been able to get you out of my mind day or night." He lowered her to the bed and dropped down beside her.

"I'll not be forced!"

Cord's body froze, the mask of desire hardening into one of scorn. "I don't need to force you," he snarled. "I can *buy* what you have to give." Eliza felt as though the wind had been knocked out of her.

"Get out," she spat. "I don't want to ever see you again!"

Cord came to a swift decision. "Get dressed, and put on the warmest clothes you have. You've got a long drive ahead, and it's very cold."

"Drive where?" Eliza demanded.

"We're going to the Matador. I'm going to *show* you what your uncle is doing."

"Don't be absurd," Eliza said backing away. "I'm not going anywhere with you."

"Put your clothes on, or I'll do it for you," Cord commanded in a voice that caused Eliza's resistance to evaporate. "I'll give you five minutes." He stalked past her door and slammed it behind him.

Eliza felt like she'd been knocked down and trampled on. That Cord, the only man who'd ever valued her for herself and who had beguiled her into giving him her love, could betray her so easily, could pursue her public humiliation so remorselessly, shattered her illusions of the perfection of love. It was a black hell filled with unsolved conflict, unquenched need, and unfulfilled longing. It was chaos, a chilling betrayal that was much more devastating than loneliness could ever be; it was a brutally swift ending to her fledgling flight of happiness, and Eliza felt empty of all that had given her hope and new life. She blindly and mechanically picked out her clothes and put them on.

How could you die and not feel the pain? Did it come later when you had time to assess your loss, or was this what death really was, a feeling of nothingness? Did dreams always come crashing down in a stupefying void of utter silence? Could illusions be banished without one final piercing shriek of protest?

Eliza's brain was too numb to think, but she *would* have answers. Six months ago she would have meekly accepted her fate, but since then she had glimpsed the Elysian Fields where love dwelled, and she could never again settle for anything less than paradise.

"I think you should know I don't intend to believe anything you show me," Eliza stated defiantly as she settled into the buggy next to Cord, acutely aware of his harsh, uncompromising posture. Why was she saying these hateful words? Why must she lash out at the one person she needed and desired above all others? Was she too afflicted with an insane craving for revenge?

"Do you have a brand?" The cold night air cut into Eliza's soft skin as Cord drove his horses forward at a dangerous gallop.

"Of course not. What would I want with a brand when I don't even own a milk cow?"

"There's a brand in your name, or rather in the name of Belle Sage. It was registered this past month."

"But I didn't do it. You've got to believe me."

"I do. You're still underage." A fleeting warmth vanished. It wasn't faith, just cold facts, that made Cord believe her.

"But you will admit it's an odd occurrence for a woman who owns no land and runs no cows to have a brand. And there's something else strange about that brand. It's remarkably similar to the Matador brand. In fact, if you put your brand over mine, mine disappears altogether."

"Do you mean someone could put my brand on your calves and no one could tell?"

"That's about it." Eliza could not doubt his words.

"Why?"

"To make stealing easier. I've known for some time rustlers were systematically working this part of Wyoming. They either skin the beef and sell the meat to miners and construction crews, or they rebrand them and sell them to other ranchers. They haven't come up with a way to get around me and the boys yet, but they've been after my herds from the first."

"But why you?"

"Some would try it for the thrill of proving I'm not invincible. They damned near succeeded too."

"But how?" asked Eliza, forgetting her uncle in her growing outrage against the rustlers.

"They're using a hidden canyon on Sam Haughton's land. That was a stroke of genius. My land completely surrounds it. I never would have thought to look there. Knowing I was at the Burtons' party and everyone else would be too tied up with Christmas to be watching carefully, they decided to brand them tonight and drive them out at dawn."

"But how did you find them?"

"It was something Iris said." Eliza stiffened. "She said it had been an easy night with Croley and Ira both gone. I didn't pay any attention to it at first, but then I got to thinking. Croley *never* leaves that saloon, and Ira doesn't stay away for long because he loves the adulation he's been getting since the trial. The boys were just setting out when I got back. I didn't even have time to change my clothes."

Eliza withdrew into silence. For a time Cord tried to draw her out, but after a while he too became quiet.

To Eliza, it seemed that her whole life had turned into a cruel nightmare. If there was such a thing as malevolent destiny, it was bent upon denying every promise it had held out to her without offering anything in exchange. To have Cord so near, yet see him moving inexorably away from her, was a crueler agony than any she had yet endured.

It was a relief when they at last left the road. The uneven ground forced Cord to slow his pace, though not by much. They passed by the rough track that led to the Haughtons' cabin, and Eliza wondered how Susan was doing; it was almost time for her baby. The terrain became even more rock-strewn, and minutes later a wall rose up on either side, cutting off the open prairie from view.

"How could they bring the calves in this way without Susan or Sam seeing them?" Without knowing it, Eliza had accepted the fact that Cord's calves really had been rustled.

"This is only one of several ways in."

Eliza was taken unawares when they rounded a bend and the sounds of men and cattle and horses and the smells of burning hair and flesh burst upon her ears and nostrils with startling suddenness. Cord dropped his horse into a walk.

"The corral is just beyond that rise. It's a perfect spot. Not even a cow would think to come here." Still Eliza did not speak. Cord stopped the buggy. "Get down and be careful to keep under cover."

Eliza stumbled along as Cord dragged her across the rough ground. She tried to pull back, as much in anger at his harsh treatment as in reluctance to find irrefutable proof of her uncle's guilt, but Cord was much too powerful and she was forced to keep up with him.

"What's happening now?" Cord asked Franklin as they moved into position behind the rocks.

"They're still bringing calves in from the range, but they've started to brand them." He nodded to Eliza, but his grim expression didn't alter. "I'm having a difficult time holding the boys back. One of those calves belongs to Rick."

"They don't have to wait any longer. I just wanted Miss Smallwood to see what was happening."

"What are you going to do to them?" Eliza asked uneasily.

"Why do you care? I thought you denied your uncle was here."

"I can't recognize anybody this far away," she said evasively.

"We can get closer. Just stay in the shadows and keep quiet." They moved into an open space between the rocks and Eliza had an unobstructed view of the rustling operation. The men moved quietly and efficiently, cold-branding each calf and putting it into the corral before going after the next one. Croley Blaine stood at the center of the operation, directing the men mostly with signals, and next to him, holding the iron that made a painless brand that would last just long enough to drive the animals to safe territory, was Ira Smallwood. Eliza felt as if she would collapse, but she actually grew tense, furious, and alert.

"Stay down or they'll see you," Cord warned, but before he could stop her, Eliza sprinted toward the group doing the branding.

"Run!" she screamed. "Cord's men are behind those rocks."

The effect on both groups was instantaneous. Firing in the general direction of the rocks and making little effort to avoid hitting Eliza, the rustlers abandoned the evidence of their guilt and ran for their horses.

"Come back, you little fool," Cord shouted, and ran after her. A bullet grazed his thigh as he pulled her to the ground, but he didn't loosen his grip even though she fell on top of him. The Matador crew streamed past in pursuit.

"What were you trying to do?" Cord demanded, sitting up and inspecting the damage to his leg.

"I hope they get away," Eliza flung at him, between sobs.

"You could have been killed."

"I wish I had been." She pulled away from Cord and rose to her feet.

"I wouldn't be sitting here with a grazed leg if you'd stayed still." Cord wrapped a bandanna around his wound.

"I wish it had grazed your *head*," said Eliza, walking away from him. She was at it again, saying things she didn't mean. The thought of Cord lying in his own blood made her feel sick.

"You seem to forget I was the one who was being robbed," Cord said angrily. He struggled awkwardly to his feet and followed her. "*I* was the one who held my men back so your uncle wouldn't be hurt."

"Don't talk to me," Eliza said, almost running in the dark.

"I seem to be talking *at* you," Cord responded, his bitter resentment denying any warm feeling for her. "You're not hearing a word I say."

"Don't come near me. Don't speak to me. Don't even look at me."

"You've got to put up with me for a while yet unless you're prepared to walk back to town. I only have one buggy."

"You can ride your horse."

"He's at the ranch. I took the buggy because I thought it

239

would be more comfortable for you. I never thought you'd be so ungrateful as to throw it in my face."

"You ought to be glad you're saved from marrying such a selfish ingrate."

"I thought you were a kind, sweet, sensible woman, but you're almost as bad as Eugenia. At least she never pretended to be anything but what she was."

"And I thought you were a loving, thoughtful man, not some kind of beast who brutalizes everything about him."

"I thought I'd found the woman I was looking for," Cord snapped, suddenly losing his temper, "but I was mistaken."

"You weren't looking for a woman," Eliza said, choking with sobs. "You were looking for the naive, stupid, credulous female I was when you saw me at the creek. But I grew up, and you didn't like that." She struggled to control her tears. "There's no point in discussing it any more. I want to go home, and I don't ever want to see you again."

"You said that before."

"I mean it this time."

"You'll get your wish. I'm tired of throwing myself at a female too weak to shed worn-out loyalties and too scared to shoulder the responsibility of honesty and fair play."

Eliza felt ready to burst with indignation, but she clamped her hands over her ears and refused to open her mouth.

She sat in determined silence as Cord drove back toward town, but when he turned on to the path that led to the Haughtons' cabin, she was surprised into speech. "Where are we going?"

"I'm going to find out what Sam knows about this."

"I don't want to go to the Haughtons," Eliza said freezingly.

"I don't give a damn what you want. I want some answers, and I mean to have them now."

"But you can't believe Sam had anything to do with this. I promise you, they're honest people."

"You can't really expect me to have any faith in your assurances," Cord said, ruthlessly clubbing her reeling pride. "Less than an hour ago you were swearing your uncle had nothing to do with stealing my cows."

Eliza gripped her seat with both hands to keep the volcano of rage burning within her from erupting, rage at Cord, rage at her uncle, rage at being helplessly caught between them.

"You are a cruel and unforgiving man," she exploded, unable to muzzle all her pain. "I'm not surprised no one likes or trusts you."

Chapter 26

Eliza could have bitten her tongue. The words were mean-spirited and cruel. Even though they weren't true, they were close enough to hurt.

"I know there are many who distrust me," Cord replied after a pause, "but I never associated you with them."

Eliza felt she had been slapped, but maybe she deserved it. Cord had compelled her to accompany him, but he was only forcing her to face the truth; she was trying to erase her shame by injuring him with words, as if *any* words could erase the pain in her heart.

She was so shocked at having her uncle's guilt irrefutably confirmed, she could only react violently against the agent of her disgrace. Her pride was lacerated, she felt disgusted with her uncle and ashamed to be his niece, and all she could think of was to get away from the one man in the whole world before whom her humiliation was unbearable. She had defended her uncle in public and turned her back on Cord, yet he had proved her judgment at fault and her loyalty misplaced. Her championing of her uncle, her refusal to believe anything Cord said, her breaking their engagement and refusal to see or speak to him had all been grave injustices, and she had persisted in them against the weight of Cord's sworn word and the advice of every person whose opinion she respected. How could she expect Cord to believe she still loved him, or feel she was worthy of love?

And until he lost his temper tonight, he had been a perfect gentleman, never saying anything cruel and unkind. All the more reason for Eliza to feel a screaming need to run away.

Cord stared straight ahead, saddened and discouraged. He had been so sure Eliza would return to him once she knew the truth about Ira, that she would see, in his refusal to allow his men to harm her uncle, he was only trying to defend what was his and not to harm her uncle. He simply could not understand why facing the truth should make her run away. It wasn't as though he thought she had anything to do with the rustling scheme. Even if he hadn't loved her, he wouldn't think her dishonest.

He hadn't meant to fall in love with Eliza, or anyone else after Eugenia, but Eliza had seemed so different, so innocent and loving his defenses had collapsed with only token resistance. The weeks before the trial had been the most wonderful of his life, and he had started to take it for granted she would always be at his side. He knew he still wanted her there, but if she couldn't take him the way he was, he was determined to stamp out his love for her.

Maybe being a rancher's wife wasn't glamorous and exciting enough. Maybe she was like the rest of her sex, irrational, unreasoning, and greedy. Yet Cord was forced to admit that even if the worst were true, he still wanted her back.

Miserable, angry, and confused, the two rode in silence until Franklin overtook them.

"Blaine and Smallwood got away, but the rest won't be stealing Matador cattle anytime soon," he announced with grim satisfaction.

"What did you do?" Eliza asked, quivering with revulsion.

"Nothing they won't get over, but you needn't look for them at the saloon for a while."

"I don't know those people," Eliza stated coldly, "and I don't *look* for them anywhere."

Franklin's attitude toward Eliza did not soften. "You can also tell your uncle and Croley their luck has run out. The next time we won't settle for a few broken bones."

Eliza turned to Cord.

"Twice I wouldn't let anybody touch Ira because of you and twice he got away," said Cord. "I won't do it again."

"Do you mean you'd kill him?" Eliza asked terrified.

"No, but I can't watch the men all the time, and it's their job to deal with outlaws any way they can. If I continue to allow Ira to go unpunished, others will think they can do what he does."

Eliza slumped in her seat, truly aware for the first time of the dangerous consequences of her uncle's irrational hate, and horrified that Cord could be the instrument of his punishment.

Franklin was at the Haughtons' before Cord drew the buggy to a stop. He hammered on the door with the stock of his rifle, but got no answer.

"They must have been asleep for hours," Eliza protested.

"That's what I mean to find out," Cord replied.

"Sam couldn't have anything to do with the rustlers. He was at the saloon until it closed," Eliza pointed out.

"Not necessarily," Cord said.

"He had to be," Eliza argued. "If Uncle and Mr. Blaine weren't there and I was at the party, that left only Iris and Sam. You must have seen Sam when you stopped for her."

"There's been many a farmer who's turned a blind eye to rustlers using his land," Franklin volunteered before applying himself to the door with renewed energy. It was finally opened by a very pregnant Susan, who regarded them with a sleepy lack of comprehension.

"Eliza? What are you doing here?" she asked drowsily, her stomach protruding so much it looked like she could be hiding Sam under her nightgown.

"Looking for your husband," Franklin announced as he pushed past into the cabin. Loud snores coming from an unlighted corner of the cabin guided Franklin unerringly to the rumpled bed where Sam lay sound asleep.

"Get up," Franklin called, unceremoniously pulling off the covers.

With her mind full of the murders of less than a month ago, Susan Haughton let out a shriek and placed her ungainly bulk between her husband and his presumed attacker.

"Don't touch my Sam. He hasn't done anything. For the love of God, Eliza, don't let them kill him."

"They aren't going to hurt him," Eliza assured her, moving between Franklin and her friend. "They just want to know if Sam's been in bed ever since he got back from the saloon."

"Of course he has," Susan said emphatically. "He was so

drunk he could hardly find his way home."

"Wake him up," Cord ordered. "I want to talk to him."

"No," Susan said, determined to hold her position between Franklin and her husband, but Franklin picked her up and moved her out of the way.

"This is barbarous," Eliza cried, half angry, half fearful. "Make him stop."

Cord shook his head at Franklin. "He won't hurt her, but I've got to know if Sam is involved with the rustlers."

"We've never had anything to do with rustlers," Susan stated proudly, drawing herself up to her full height of five feet and one inch. "We may be poor, but we're not thieves."

"That's what everybody says," Cord stated cynically.

"It's true," Susan insisted. "We don't have to worry about money anymore now Sam's got a job at the saloon."

"Mama, what's wrong?" Billy stuck his head out of the loft, and his eyes widened with alarm when he saw the two men.

"It's just Mr. Stedman wanting to ask your pa a few questions. You go on back to sleep." But it was impossible for Billy to sleep, and he tumbled out of the loft, too courageous to stay hidden, but so frightened he began to cry when Franklin threw a dipper of water in his father's face.

Rudely jerked awake by the icy water, Sam glowered at the intruders. "What in the hell are you two doing here?"

"What do *you* mean by letting rustlers use your land to steal Matador calves?"

Sam looked at Cord like he was a madman. "What rustlers?" Sam asked, trying to clear his cloudy brain. "I don't know what in blazes you're talking about. Now get out of my cabin before I get my shotgun." Franklin pushed him back down on the bed.

"Why did you let Blaine's gang corral my stock on your place?" Cord's inflexible determination sounded in his voice.

"I don't know what you are talking about. Nobody's been using my land." Sam was angry, but he was also wary; the icy menace in Cord's voice unsettled him.

"Don't waste time denying it. We found the corral and caught the gang cold-branding yearlings. They could have been in Montana before the end of the week without any-

245

body being the wiser."

"You're just making this up so you can get my land," Sam said, his uneasy gaze shifting from Cord to Franklin. "I'm not selling, and you're not running me off."

"This is no bluff." Franklin dragged Sam to his feet and sent him to the floor with a right to the jaw. Susan screamed and Billy threw himself at Franklin, driving his little fists into his stomach.

"Leave my pa alone," he cried, shaking with sobs. "He didn't touch your old cows."

Cord picked up the child and handed him to Eliza. "Keep him out of the way."

Eliza clutched Billy to her, staring at Cord in stunned horror.

"Now I'm going to ask you one more time about that corral," Cord said, turning back to Sam.

"I don't know anything about a corral. Anyone passing by could see if I had one."

"Not here. Up in those canyons."

"I never go up there. There's not enough grass to keep a sheep alive."

"That's what Blaine was counting on. That and everybody being busy because it's Christmas."

Finally Sam understood what Cord had been saying. "But there couldn't be a corral up there and me not know it."

"You've got over a thousand acres."

"How do you know?"

"I make it my business to know, though I could never understand why you wanted those hills."

"Greed," said Sam gloomily, "and the excitement of getting so much land for almost nothing. I didn't have enough sense to realize it wasn't worth the paper the deed was written on."

"Is that why you decided to let Blaine use it?"

"I never let Blaine or anybody else use my land," Sam reiterated, his voice rising with annoyance. "Not now, not ever."

"You'd better be telling the truth." Franklin made a threatening move, but Cord checked him with a tiny shake of his head.

"Stop it!" Eliza cried. "No herd of cows is worth terroriz-

246

ing innocent people." Susan had turned white; Billy's whole body was shaking.

"I'm not sure they are innocent," Cord said. "Now I want some straight answers."

Sam swallowed hard. "I don't know anything about a corral, or any rustlers. We were about to starve when Miss Smallwood talked her uncle into giving me a job at the saloon, but I've never had any truck with rustling. Billy even got into a fight in school because the other kids thought I was a fool not to help myself with your steers practically coming up to the door."

"That's true," Susan said quickly. "Tell him it's true, Eliza." Eliza nodded her head.

"Maybe Blaine wouldn't let you *keep* that precious job unless you agreed to help him?" Cord suggested, still not convinced.

"I wouldn't let thieves use my land to keep a job," Sam burst out. "I want to see that blasted corral. How do I know it exists?"

"Tell him," Cord commanded Eliza sharply. Eliza stared at Cord, horrified he would ask her to humiliate herself still further. "Tell them what you saw if you're so interested in helping."

"There really is a corral," Eliza said, her voice barely above a whisper. "And I saw Mr. Blaine and a lot of other men branding calves." Cord's gaze, implacable and demanding, never once left Eliza's face. "I saw my uncle too," she said, nearly choking on the words.

She raised her eyes, and Cord was staggered at the blazing fury he saw, the kind of unyielding, unforgiving rage that could easily turn to hate. He felt sick inside, and for an instant was tempted to ignore the cows and rustlers and everything else if Eliza would just forget everything and go back to loving him the way she had during the summer. The thought of her tenderness and her beauty nearly swayed his determination, but the long years of struggle had built a powerful habit within him and his resolve hardened. If she couldn't love him like he was, then he could do without her just as he had done without Eugenia. Some voice deep inside warned him it wasn't so, but Cord resolutely closed his mind; on this there could be no compromise.

"I want to see it for myself," Sam insisted.

"Stay with the women," Cord told Franklin. "We won't be long."

Defeat seemed to have destroyed Sam's dislike for Cord and during the short trip he poured out his whole history. The sight of the abandoned corral banished any lingering resistance.

"I can't believe it," he said over and over. Even he could see how impossible it was to detect from the plains below and there was an uncontested route to Montana through land honeycombed with the small holdings of sympathetic ranchers and homesteaders. "They could have gone on using this place for years. And I thought you were just trying to scare us off."

"I always wanted this land, but I've never sunk to terrorizing innocent people. At least, not before tonight," Cord added.

"I see why you didn't believe me, but I'm too easily unnerved to be a crook," Sam said with an effort not to show how greatly relieved he was. "Sooner or later I'd get liquored up and say the wrong thing."

"We won't bother you any more, but I want to pull down that corral and check these hills regularly."

"You can do anything you want as long as you don't upset Susan. She's due soon and she's had a hard time of it."

Cord started back and Sam followed, wondering what was in Cord's mind. He *thought* he was fair-minded, but a man like Cord was extremely dangerous when cornered, and with rustlers and their sympathizers on every side, Sam admitted Cord had reason to be suspicious.

While Sam was reaching a kind of understanding of Cord's position, Eliza was back at the cabin moving even further away. The door hadn't closed behind Cord when she rushed to Susan's side.

"I would appreciate it if you could wait outside," she said to Franklin, who was being eyed by Billy as though he were a combination of Jessie James and the Bogy Man.

"I told Mr. Stedman I'd watch you."

"Where could we go at this time of night?" Eliza snapped

248

surprised at the sharpness of her own voice.

"The boy could run into those hills."

"It's unlikely he could outrun your horse," she said caustically. "And surely you don't mean to accuse this poor woman of stealing your cows?"

Like every cowboy, Franklin was at a disadvantage when faced by a woman, especially a woman like Eliza. Besides, holding pregnant women and little boys hostage was against his nature, and now that his temper had cooled he was a little ashamed of himself.

"Okay," he said, and stepped out into the night. Billy, released from his fear, rushed to his mother.

"What are they going to do to my Sam?" Susan exclaimed, clutching her son to her protruding stomach.

"Nothing," Eliza answered, trying to sound calm and assured. "Cord was just trying to make sure Sam wasn't involved with the rustlers."

"Were there *really* rustlers in the canyon?" Susan's curiosity quickly replaced her fear.

"Yes," Eliza said lowering her gaze. "I saw them myself." Susan was perceptive enough to realize Eliza had suffered as much because of her uncle's guilt as she had from fear, and she did not pursue the subject.

"How long before they'll be back?"

"Twenty minutes. The canyon isn't far."

"I'm going to make some coffee. Would you like some?"

"Very much," Eliza said, sinking into a chair. She was terribly tired, and suddenly the whole nightmarish situation seemed so overwhelming she felt like crying. Odd that as soon as Susan regained her control, she should lose hers. Never in her life had she felt such an overpowering desire to scream and throw things.

"Mr. Stedman is a bad man and I hate him," Billy announced to Eliza. "Why did you let him hurt my pa?"

"You should be ashamed of yourself, Billy Haughton, for talking to Miss Smallwood like that."

"But she didn't make him stop. He's her friend and everybody says he does things for her."

"Hush, boy, you don't know what you're saying."

"Let him alone, Susan. He's partly right. Mr. Stedman

249

was my friend," Eliza said, struggling to keep her voice steady, "but we aren't friends any longer and I can't make him do anything."

"Why?" Billy asked. "I thought everybody liked you." Eliza looked to Susan for help, but Susan was awaiting Eliza's explanation just as anxiously as her son.

"Lots of times people find they don't agree on sóme very important things."

"Like Ma and Pa arguing about the saloon?"

"Yes, but your mother and father have found a way to solve their differences."

"They still fight." Susan blushed while Eliza searched for a way to explain the difference to the small boy.

"People can disagree and still be friends, but sometimes the things you disagree about are too important and you stop being friends."

"Like with Mr. Stedman?"

"Yes, like Mr. Stedman."

"Won't you ever like him again?"

Eliza thought she was going to burst into uncontrollable tears. "Could you love a man who threatened your friends and their children?"

"I never loved Mr. Stedman. I only liked him a little."

"Of course," Eliza replied with a breaking voice. "I meant to say *like*."

"You leave Miss Smallwood alone," Susan said, fearing Eliza might break down any minute. "Go outside and watch for your pa. Be sure to tell Mr. Church you don't mean to run away."

"I ought to throw a rock at his head."

"Don't you dare. Now get out of here." The boy left reluctantly, and Susan got busy with the coffee while Eliza tried to collect herself.

"I'm sorry for Billy's questions," Susan apologized. "He's used to us telling him everything."

"That's all right," Eliza said, sniffing. "It's about time I admitted it was over. You knew I was in love with him, I guess everybody did, but I was such a fool I thought it was a secret."

"Is it really over?"

"Yes."

"I'm so sorry," Susan said, and Eliza burst into tears.

"Will you have any trouble with your uncle when you return?" Cord asked. They had been riding for several minutes without exchanging a word. "I could explain I forced you to go with me."

"No!" Eliza said, jerking bolt upright. "If you so much as come within sight of the saloon something terrible will happen."

"I don't want you to suffer because of me."

Eliza wanted to scream wildly that her uncle's anger was but a drop in the ocean of misery Cord had caused her. An agony so profound she felt as though she wanted to die consumed her, tempting her to plead with him to assure her he was not the same man who had brought her uncle to trial and invaded the Haughtons' home, that some pretender had taken his place so the wonderful, kind, loving Cord she knew would receive the blame. But a single glance at his rigid jaw and unyielding eyes told her she was merely indulging in a daydream. This was the same man to whom she had given her heart and body without reservation. Part of her seemed to die a little.

"It shouldn't be hard for you to convince him I forced you to go with me, not after the way you warned them."

"No, it won't be very hard," she replied. Even though she didn't look his way again, she was acutely aware of his presence, the sheer force of his physical nearness. She clenched her fists, shutting her eyes to free herself of the temptation to look at that mesmerizing profile once again. She could *feel* his hands on her body, his lips on hers, his lean, powerful loins thrusting into her in pursuit of an ecstasy that fulfilled them both. She struggled to blot those memories out of her mind, but nothing could rid her of the awareness of his nearness.

She was also aware of the brute strength, the inflexible, driving will of this man who had brought himself up from cowboy to ranch owner. She had known only the kind, warm, loving side of him, but now she saw the ruthless, unstoppable man Wyoming knew as Cord Stedman. She could *feel* the steel, the sheer grit, the killer instinct that had blazed a trail through Johnson County against enormous odds. The other Cord was the man she had fallen in love with, but this Cord was just as much a part of him.

Chapter 27

Cord moved along the walk with an unhurried stride. It had taken him one sleepless night to repent of everything he had said to Eliza on that cold Christmas morning, but it had taken more than a week before he had ventured into town to see if her feelings had undergone a similar reversal.

The saloon looked empty when he entered, but as his eyes became accustomed to the dimness he noticed Iris going through one of her routines at the far end of the room. She hummed softly to herself, her limbs tightly encased in a skin-tight suit that left no detail of her lush figure to the imagination. He walked forward slowly, making no attempt to remain unseen, but moving with noiseless steps. Iris finished up her number and looked up to find Cord placidly watching in silent appreciation.

"Oh!" she exclaimed, reaching quickly for her robe. "I didn't hear you come in."

"I didn't want to bother you."

"That's okay. I was just practicing some changes in my act. I can think better in the morning." She walked over to the bar. "It's thirsty work. Want a beer?"

"I'd better not. I came to see Miss Smallwood."

Iris took a pull from the mug and gave Cord a measured look over the rim. "You seen her since the Christmas party?"

"Why? Is something wrong?"

"Not exactly, but you'd better sit down." She pulled a chair off one of the tables and motioned Cord to do the same.

"Still mad at me?"

"More than that. She moved Lucy in with her and gave orders to be told the minute you walked on the premises.

She intends to run out the back if you force your way in. Of course, Croley or Ira may shoot you first."

"I think I'll have some whiskey," Cord decided. Iris handed him a bottle and he downed three glasses without pause.

"You believe in laying a thirst good and proper, don't you?" inquired Iris in admiration.

"Do you know why she doesn't want to see me?"

"Eliza doesn't confide in me, but I do know the mere mention of your name causes her to start shaking." Iris watched him closely. "She's told everybody her engagement is off."

"Yeah. She told me too."

"I got the impression she told you a good deal more. I was up when she got in that morning, and she didn't stop crying for hours."

"Did she tell you everything that happened?"

"No, but I heard enough."

"She absolutely won't see me?"

"No."

Cord downed another drink. "So how did you come to be in Wyoming?" he asked abruptly. "From your accent, I would guess you grew up in Indiana."

"Westphalia. How did you know?"

"I come from Sandborn, just down the road."

"Well, I'll be. Do you know the Bradleys?"

"Heard of them."

"They're cousins, my mother's family. Is your family still in Sandborn?"

"Guess so."

"Trouble, huh?" asked Iris, undaunted by Cord's unencouraging replies.

"Not especially. My dad died young. My ma left home a couple of times soon after, then one time she just never came back. My grandfather raised me. I left town the day I buried him."

"Ever been back?"

Cord shook his head.

"Do you hear anything of your mother?"

"She's not one for writing."

"My folks write all the time. I'll ask them about her."

"Don't bother. She wouldn't know me if she met me on the street." He took another drink.

"You'd better go easy on that stuff. It can get to be a habit, and not a good one."

Cord looked at the bottle. "Seems everything I like is bad for me. It's enough to make a man wonder if he's marked for life."

"It's probably not the time to mention it, but there are other fish in the sea," Iris said giving his hand a pat. "And some of us aren't too bad."

"You swimming in that sea?"

"Sure. All women need a husband, and I'm always on the lookout for a good man, especially one who's as rich and good looking as you. It doesn't make sense to take dog food and let prime beef go begging."

"Can't be anything prime about me," Cord said, tossing down another tumbler. "I've been turned down twice."

"Then the third time will be lucky," Iris said, finishing her beer and rising from her chair. "If you feel like talking, or just want some company, you're welcome to drop in."

Cord's eyebrows went up.

"No, not here," she said with a hearty chuckle. "My little girl is staying with the Culpeppers. I visit her every afternoon. Weekends too, if I can."

"It's not often a man gets an invitation like that, even with a kid to make things look proper."

"Don't get your hopes up," Iris said with a provocative laugh. "I won't let you one step past the front porch. A girl can't be too careful of her reputation, especially in a town like this."

"You're an idiot," Ella informed Cord with biting emphasis. "A handsome, hulking fool to have lost Eliza for the sake of a few cows, and little ones at that. Or don't you think she's worth a couple dozen calves?"

"I'd trade my whole ranch for Eliza," Cord stated simply, "but I won't let anybody rob me."

"I always knew men were blind, stupid, and obstinate, but I never met anybody who carried it to the extremes you do.

There must have been a thousand ways to keep Ira from coming near your steers without dragging Eliza out of her bed and forcing her to see with her own eyes that her uncle is a low-down thief and a liar to boot. No girl is going to run into your arms after that, even if her uncle is a worse piece of cow dung than Ira."

Cord started to speak, but Ella cut him off. "And if that wasn't enough, you had to drag her along while you pulled one of your vigilante acts on a man too drunk to defend himself. And you threw in the pregnant wife and child just to make sure she couldn't possibly have any sympathy for you. I'm sure she just loved sitting there while you discussed Ira's crimes in front of her only real friends. I hope you at least had the good sense not to mention him by name."

"Sam wouldn't believe me, and I made Eliza tell him what she saw."

"The man's a lunatic!" Ella raved, throwing her hands in the air to emphasize the point. "You have an absolute genius for doing the one thing out of a thousand guaranteed to drive that girl from you. You'll be lucky if she doesn't shoot you herself. As for marrying you, would you bed down with a rattlesnake after it had bitten you twice?"

"I'm not sure she's the kind of girl I thought she was," Cord said stiffly.

"Hogwash!" Ella said with regal disdain. "Look me in the eye, Cord Stedman, and tell me you don't love her."

Cord looked directly at Ella but said nothing.

"I knew you couldn't do it! You're just as crazy about her as ever. But since you've practically branded the girl a criminal—"

"I *never* said she had anything to do with it."

"You might as well have. When you proved her uncle a scalawag, you tarred her with the same brush."

"I don't understand."

"Frankly, neither do I," Ella admitted, "but it's got something to do with a dratted vow she made to her dead aunt. Myself, I'd tell Ira to get off and good riddance, but I know Eliza. She was real upset when you had her uncle arrested and the trial made her good and mad, but she'd have gotten over that if you hadn't had to go and *show* her that her uncle

256

was a thief. That put the bar on the door for sure. Now she can't look you in the face without coming smack up against her uncle's guilt."

"I never held her responsible for Ira."

"You don't have to. She's done it herself."

"How do you know?"

"She told me, you big oaf. Whose shoulder do you think she's been crying on? It's not that widow woman who sings and dances for her uncle. She's got her eye on you herself. And that doesn't leave much of anybody except Jessica Burton, and not even a sainted martyr could expect any sympathy from her."

"All I wanted to do was prove I wasn't lying."

"And you had to do it within hours after I *told* you not to do anything or you'd wreck things entirely."

"I didn't plan it. It just happened."

"Good generals never *let* things happen. They *make* them happen. And you know that because until you saw Ira with his rope around that steer, you were just about the best general I'd ever seen, with cows, with men, and with Eliza. But you let yourself get unraveled real bad. I don't know if you'll ever get Eliza back now."

Cord stood staring in front of him for a long moment. "Then I guess there's nothing I can do."

"Maybe not, but getting drunk won't help things." Cord looked up inquiringly. "You don't have to tell me you've been drinking. I can smell it. That's a road that will lead to nothing but ruin. Time may heal this thing between you and Eliza or it may not, but if you give yourself over to drink she'll never have you."

Ella felt her heart go out to Cord. She had never been a romantic herself. She and Ed had lived together comfortably for thirty years, always talking through their differences and encountering few problems. Maybe now and then she had wondered what it would have been like to be madly in love, but after seeing what it had done to Cord and Eliza she was just as happy she had been passed over. She might never know the bliss of love that surmounted reason, but at least she would never suffer the agonies that were making two of her favorite people utterly miserable.

257

"You can't wait much longer to get married, or you'll be an old maid," Ira said to Eliza through a mouthful of steak. "You might as well marry Croley."

"Mr. Blaine?" Eliza repeated, her voice jumping an octave. "He never knows I'm around unless I'm singing."

"Croley notices everything you do," Ira said, putting another fork load of food in his mouth. "He talks about you all the time. In fact, he's gotten to be something of a bore."

Eliza hardly knew what to say. She knew her uncle stood in awe of Croley. It would be comfortable for him to have her marry his business partner, but she didn't like Croley, and now that she was certain he was responsible for Ira's involvement with the rustlers, she didn't trust him either.

Neither had mentioned what had happened that night, Eliza because she hated to think of being involved in such a shameful deed, and Ira because Croley, in a savage rage over the failure of his elaborately planned operation, had ordered him to keep his mouth shut.

"I don't want to marry anybody. I think I'll dedicate myself to teaching school."

"You can marry Croley and teach all you want," Ira said, still eating. "Croley is going to be a rich man." Ira wiped his mouth and backed away from the table. "You could find yourself married to much worse."

"No, I couldn't," exploded Eliza. "I will not marry a rustler, even if my uncle is one." At last it was out, she had said it, and she felt as though a great weight was off her heart.

"You watch what you're saying," Ira growled.

"I saw you," Eliza said, her eyes flashing angrily. "I was forced to watch you brand cows with a brand registered in my name."

"Oh, well—"

"Do you know why I hide in this room day after day? It's because I'm ashamed to appear in public knowing my only relative is a common thief. It makes me sick to my stomach just to think about it."

"It didn't make you so sick of Cord Stedman you didn't go

258

with him."

"I will not be accused of duplicity, and especially *not* by you," Eliza said furiously.

"Never mind. I believe you," Ira said, backing down.

Ira had lost control of Eliza. She was so volatile he was afraid the slightest thing would cause her to refuse to sing at all. She'd insisted that someone watch the door, and the only time Cord had appeared she'd fled in the middle of her song and locked herself in her room.

"You still in love with Stedman?"

"You know I haven't seen him since that night."

"I thought you might still be pining over him. You sure do act lovesick."

"I'm acting *mortified*," Eliza practically shouted. "I'm ashamed to have been so mistaken in his character I would consider becoming engaged to him. I'm also chagrined to be the niece of a man of still fewer principles. I imagine people are saying Cord's exactly the kind of husband for a silly, spineless fool like me."

"Then marry Croley and put an end to this foolishness."

"Marry the man who tried to rustle my previous fiancé's cows? That ought to set tongues in Buffalo wagging for a good year. Let him marry Iris."

"He doesn't want her. He wants you."

"Well, he can't have me," Eliza said defiantly. "I didn't give up Cord to marry a rustler." Try as she might Eliza could not keep the tears from her eyes.

"You *are* still in love with him," Ira said triumphantly. "I knew it."

"You don't know anything about me," Eliza accused. "You never have. All you ever think of is how much money I can make. You don't care a button whether I'm happy or miserable as long as the customers keep coming."

"I'm trying to find you a husband."

"Do you really think I could settle for Croley Blaine after Cord?" A sob caught in her throat. "Even Iris ignores Croley, but she can't keep her hands off Cord."

"Let Iris have him, but don't you speak to him again."

"You've forfeited the right to tell me what to do, ever again," Eliza said. "You forced me to deny the only man I've ever loved, and all you can offer in his place is Croley Blaine."

"I'll have the bastard shot, then you won't be able to pine after him," Ira threatened.

"You do and you'll never see me again."

"And where do you think you'll go?"

"If Cord were dead, it wouldn't matter."

Eliza sighed disconsolately and moved to another chair. She tried to concentrate on her needlework, but she kept making mistakes and having to pull it out. Finally she threw the embroidery frame from her and began to pace the room.

"I don't think I can stand this much longer," she said to Lucy, who watched her from across the room. "I feel like I'm suffocating."

"There's nobody keeping you here but yourself. I certainly didn't tell you to lock yourself in tighter than a steamer trunk."

"I'm not being locked in. Cord's being locked out."

"I can't see it makes any difference. You're still the one sitting in this room."

"Well, I'm tired of it. And I'm tired of being scared to death I'll run into Cord or that he'll come barging in here and carry me off again."

"You could go East with me. You wouldn't have to worry about Cord, and you'd be a big star."

"I doubt it. I'm more likely to stay here and be forced to marry someone like Mr. Blaine."

"Then you'd have reason to lock yourself in. What you need is a hero to rescue you."

"My *hero* is the reason I'm in trouble. Please, Lucy, what am I going to do?"

"I keep telling you, but you won't listen. Go sing back East."

"But I don't know anybody *back East.* And I don't know about the theaters, where they are, who to write, or anything else."

"You don't need to know," insisted Lucy. "I still know some theatrical agents. I ought to be able to find one who can fix you up. In no time at all, you'll be rich and famous."

"I don't want to be rich and famous. I just want to get away from here."

"Not want to be rich?" Lucy squeaked as though Eliza had spoken some heresy. "Cut your tongue out. You are young and beautiful. Naturally you'll be rich."

"You can write those agents and tell them to look for a job for me, but make sure to tell them I'm going to keep on doing things just like I am now."

"Such a waste," Lucy said, hauling herself out of the chair. "I will tell them, but they won't be happy."

The contraction gripped Susan's body, forcing her to halt her conversation.

"Aren't you afraid to have your baby by yourself?" Eliza asked when she could gather the courage to speak. She had come to visit Susan and found her beginning her labor.

"Sam will help. I never had the least trouble with Billy," Susan said, panting for breath. The spasm passed as suddenly as it had come, and her strained expression relaxed into a smile.

"You're much braver than I would ever be," said Eliza.

"It's not bravery at all." Susan chuckled. "You can scream all you like, but there's nothing you can do once your labor starts. I hope this one's quick." The contractions had started three hours ago. Eliza couldn't see anything quick about that.

"I hope Sam gets back soon," Eliza said, but when Sam did arrive there wasn't anything he could do.

"Are you sure you don't want me to fetch the doctor?" he asked.

"You know he won't come this far for a baby. And if you think I can ride in a wagon all the way to Buffalo, you don't know what it's like to be in labor."

"I wish I could help you," her husband replied, tucking in her sheets. But her water broke, and by the time they had changed the bed and her clothes, the contractions were stronger and coming closer together until Susan's pain was nearly unbearable.

"Something's wrong," she said with tears in her eyes. "It wasn't like this with Billy. It hurts too much." Another contraction caused her to scream in pain and Sam lifted the sheets covering his wife.

"Oh my God," he said after only a glance. "The baby's arm is showing. It's coming out the wrong way."

Eliza turned deathly white. It was a breach birth. Unless the baby could be turned around, it would die. And Susan could die too.

"Get the wagon ready," Eliza said, coming to her feet. "We're taking her to town. Send Billy ahead to warn the doctor. What do you want to take with you?" Eliza asked as she began gathering sheets and blankets. It had been warm during the day—a chinook wind had melted much of the recent snow—but the temperature would probably drop below freezing before morning.

"Just the baby's clothes," Susan said. "And you'd better tell Sam to bring along something for him and Billy. Otherwise they're liable to smell overripe before we get back."

"I'll take them to the saloon and they can have a bath and borrow all the clothes they need."

"It's good of you to stay with me," Susan said, in a teary voice.

"I wouldn't think of leaving, not that I'm much help."

"You'll be a help to Sam. He's a good man, but he can't stand it when things go wrong."

"You stop worrying about Sam and concentrate on having that baby."

But by the time every mattress and blanket in the house had been loaded into the wagon, Susan was in considerable distress. She turned white with pain when Sam carried her out to the wagon, but she clenched her teeth, determined to endure the agony of the long trip to town.

It was impossible to avoid every rock and gully in the road, and although Sam kept the horse to a walk, Eliza had to sit by helplessly and listen to Susan's piteous groans at the wagon's every wrenching move. Even in the rapidly cooling air, perspiration ran from her forehead.

They hadn't covered a quarter of the distance when they heard a rider approaching rapidly from the direction of town, and an exhausted and terrified Billy burst upon them from out of the gathering dusk.

"The doctor's away. Some man's horse fell on him, and the doctor's gone to set his leg," he reported, gasping for breath.

"What can we do?" asked Sam, beginning to unravel.

"Turn in at the first ranch or homestead you see," Eliza said, forcing her brain to think. "Maybe somebody there will know what to do."

Billy stared at her in bewilderment. "Don't you remember?" he asked. "The Matador is the closest place."

Chapter 28

Eliza's heart began to pound rapidly. For the first time in weeks she had gone several hours without thinking of Cord, but he must have slipped inside her defenses during that time, for coming face to face with the possibility she would see him, would actually have to speak to him, Eliza had to force herself to keep Susan's danger uppermost in her thoughts. Somewhere in the back of her mind there was a splinter of panic, a sliver of determination to seek another farmhouse or let the Haughtons proceed alone, but it was quickly banished by the uprush of joy at the thought of seeing Cord again. Her treacherous heart actually rejoiced because it was her *duty* to accompany her friend to Cord's ranch.

"Are there any women there?" Sam's voice recalled Eliza to the presence. Her own troubles must be set aside in the face of Susan's need. Maybe she wouldn't even have to see Cord. Being at the Matador would be terribly difficult, but she would survive. She *had* to.

"There's the foreman's wife," she said. "Billy, go ask if she knows where we can find a midwife."

"Yes, ma'am." After witnessing one of his mother's harrowing paroxysms, the boy was only too anxious to get away.

"Put that horse into a trot," Eliza directed Sam. "Time is running out."

It was with conflicting emotions that Eliza saw the Matador ranch house materialize out of the night, but she didn't have time to think of her own heartache. Billy's warning had sounded the alarm, and Ginny met them at the door with men ready to carry Susan, mattress and all, up to one of the

264

bedrooms. Ginny's one passion in life was babies.

"Miss Smallwood! What are you doing here?"

Eliza was jolted by the unexpected hostility in her voice. Cord's anger she could understand, but that anyone else would be angry for him was stunning. But before Eliza could reply, Ginny had put aside her anger in the face of the crisis. "What's wrong?"

"Breach," muttered Susan, barely conscious.

"Good God," Ginny exclaimed. "I'll have to turn it around, or we'll lose them both. You see about the boy," Ginny directed Eliza tersely. "Her husband can give me what help I need." She superintended the whole operation, all the while scattering clipped commands with the elan of a seasoned general, and within minutes she firmly closed the bedroom door against the outside world.

At first Eliza occupied herself in an attempt to divert Billy's mind, but one of the cowboys took him off to the bunkhouse for the evening and Eliza was left alone in a house she had once thought would be her own. She would have preferred to face the two miners again.

At first she sat rigidly erect trying not to look at her surroundings, but the minutes rolled by and nothing happened to keep her thoughts from reverting to Cord and the knowledge that he must soon return and find her in his house. What was she going to say? What was she going to *do?*

Suddenly she saw herself in Susan's place, having Cord's baby, and the pain she had tried to push away came crashing down on her once again. Why had Fate held out such promise only to snatch it away once it was within her grasp? If she'd never met Cord, she could have endured a life without love; after all, she had only read about it in her mother's books. But it was a fearful misery to have to give it up after tasting its joys.

"Mr. Stedman says for you to come to dinner," Franklin said, sticking his head in the door.

"What?" squeaked Eliza, starting up from her chair.

"He's waiting for you in the dining room."

"I can't," she began then stopped abruptly. "I'm not hungry. I'll just wait here." Franklin watched her closely, and

265

some understanding of the pain she suffered softened his expression.

"Ginny fixed it. It's pot roast and hot rolls."

Eliza's mouth watered and she realized she was hungry, but she would starve before she faced Cord. "I'd really rather not."

"It's none of my business what's between you and the boss," Franklin said without feeling any of the embarrassment that nearly mortified Eliza, "but I suspect if you don't come to the table, he'll have it served in here."

Eliza checked a reckless impulse to make a dash for the door. She couldn't run away from things for the rest of her life and she might as well make a stand now. Instinct told her she was attempting too much and would probably be overwhelmed in the struggle, but she was cornered with nowhere to go—at least nowhere her pride would allow her to accept. She felt rooted to the floor, but long habit made her feet move her to the door with little outward sign of the emotional turbulence inside her.

"Any word on Susan?"

"It's too soon, but if anybody can help her it's my Ginny."

"Has she turned a baby before?"

"Only once, and after the doctor had near 'bout killed the poor woman." Eliza's worry eased somewhat, only to mushroom again when she saw Cord waiting to hold her chair.

The sight of his heavily muscled profile caused her throat to constrict, but when he turned toward her and she felt the full power of that ruggedly handsome face, saw the sadness in his eyes, was assaulted by the dynamic force of his presence, she feared she was going to swoon. She sat down, and incapable of forming words, responded to his talk with a nod. Gradually her brain began to function, to process sounds and decipher speech.

"...able to get here. Ginny says we're in for a night of it."

"Has there been any news yet?" Hadn't she already asked that question?

"Only that it's going to be slow work." He smiled at her concern and Eliza's pulse began to beat erratically. She looked down at her plate, and then at the empty places around her.

"The men eat in the bunkhouse," Cord explained, "and Franklin is busy helping Ginny." He filled a plate and handed it to her. "I imagine Iris will have her hands full tonight. The saloon's going to be a dull place without you and Sam."

"Oh, my gosh, I forgot," Eliza uttered, starting to her feet. "I've got to get back."

"Sit back down. I've already sent one of the boys to tell your uncle where you are. I'm afraid you'll have to stay the night."

"I can't," Eliza said, feeling panicky. "I have to get back." Could she spend so much time near Cord and not collapse under the weight of her need for him?

"It's too dangerous to travel at night."

"Uncle will worry. In fact, he'll probably come after me."

"Then you can certainly go home. In the meantime, a bed has already been made up for you."

Eliza's eyes flew to his.

"Not mine, though it was a sore temptation."

Eliza turned beet-red. How dare he remind her of the intimacies they had shared in that distant, halcyon past. She felt a certain calm returning, the kind of calm one feels in the middle of a battle when fighting for one's life and seeing little chance of survival, but Eliza had unplumbed reserves of strength and it came flooding to her rescue. She might be outflanked by a surprise attack, but she was not defeated.

"It was kind of you to allow us to invade your home. It must have been disconcerting to come home and find it overrun."

Cord looked at her oddly, but answered with his usual calm. "I was already here. I didn't tell you because I was afraid you wouldn't stop."

"We had no choice. Susan's condition was desperate," she added quickly, regretting her rude words.

"I know. It's rough on my self-esteem to know it took an emergency to make you set foot on Matador land again."

"Please, don't," Eliza begged. "I'm sure it's disagreeable to you for me to be here, but there seemed to be no other choice."

"It's not the least bit unpleasant," Cord said with his

eternal control. "If I'd known an emergency would bring you here, I'd have arranged one weeks ago."

Eliza felt as if she were sinking helplessly in quicksand.

"I still think about you, and dream of you here, waiting for me to come home."

Dear God, me too, thought Eliza, close to losing control. It was a recurring nightmare that destroyed her peace and reduced her nights to fitful periods of rest.

"I even make believe I've just come home, and we're having dinner, like we do every evening."

"Stop!" Eliza nearly screamed. Her hands closed like talons around her napkin, crushing the carefully ironed linen. She forced her frozen features to relax and with a great effort she pulled herself under control.

"I *cannot* remain here if you insist upon dwelling upon the past. It was an extremely painful interlude for me, and unlike you, I can't talk about it as though it were some perfectly ordinary experience."

Cord studied her face with apparent emotionless calm, his fork still in his hand, resting on his plate. "I won't mention it again, but I want you to know losing you was the most terrible thing that ever happened to me. I'd have given away every steer on the place if I'd known what that first one was going to cost me."

Eliza was shaken by a sob, and would have fled from the room if Sam hadn't entered, driven from Susan's side to his dinner by a harassed Ginny.

"How's your wife?" Cord asked, giving Eliza an opportunity to collect herself.

"I don't know," Sam said, too distracted to sense the tension in the room. "Mrs. Church has the arm back inside, but she's having a difficult time turning the baby around. She says it's going to be terribly painful." As though to reinforce his words, a scream from upstairs reverberated through the house. Sam came to his feet and headed out of the room, but Cord stood in front of him.

"I'm sure she's all right, or Ginny wouldn't have sent you away, especially not to eat your dinner."

"No, she wouldn't, would she?" mumbled Sam, trying to convince himself. He stumbled back to his chair, but the screams that penetrated to the farthest corner of the house destroyed everyone's appetite.

"I'm going to see if I can help," Eliza said, getting up with sudden decision. "It's better than sitting down here doing nothing."

"Let me go," offered Sam.

"I think it would be better if Miss Smallwood went alone," Cord said calmly. "Women seem to get along better without men at times like this."

Eliza left the room without looking back.

"Why don't we move to my office," Cord suggested. "At least we won't have them in the room overhead." Sam was reluctant, but a piercing scream broke the last of his resolution, and he followed Cord without hesitation.

Cord tried to carry on a conversation, but Sam was too preoccupied to listen to more than half a sentence. Finally, Cord gave up, opened his desk, took out several ledgers, notebooks, and a supply of pens, and settled down to work. Sam continued to prowl about the room, pausing every now and then to ask Cord whether his wife was going to be all right, what he thought was going on now, or if he thought he ought to go up and see if they could use any help.

"No," Cord said to the last question, slamming down his pen in irritation. "If they want your help, they'll ask for it."

"But they may not know where we are."

"There're at least twenty men on this place, and any one of them can find us. Now stop asking me the same question every five minutes. Doing these books is hard enough, but it's impossible when you interrupt me every time I just about get these columns straight."

"Keeping books is easy," Sam said impatiently. "That's what Susan wants me to go back to doing."

"You're welcome to start with these," Cord said, offering Sam his seat. Sam hesitated only a moment before he sat down and allowed Cord to explain what he was doing. Gradually Sam's interest was caught, and fifteen minutes later he was hard at work on the only job Cord Stedman had ever found difficult. Cord continued to supply him with books and answer an occasional question, but Sam had a real talent for bookkeeping and an hour later he had completed nearly half the work.

Cord realized he had not heard the muffled screams for some time, and after making sure Sam was still busy, he quietly left the room. He met Eliza coming down the stairs. She looked pale and ready to faint any minute. Cord escorted her to the parlor and put a glass of brandy in her hands.

"Drink it. It'll make you feel better."

"I'd rather not."

"Drink it, or I'll pour it down your throat." It was said more roughly than Cord had spoken that evening and unsettled her somewhat, but she lifted the glass and took a small swallow of the fruit-flavored liquid. The taste was quite pleasant, but when it hit her stomach it exploded into a fireball radiating heat throughout her body.

"Drink it all. It's not enough to make you drunk. How are they doing upstairs?"

Eliza handed him the empty glass. "Ginny thinks she can turn the baby, but she's worried Susan is too weak to give birth." A silence fell between them. "How is Sam? Susan keeps asking about him."

Cord smiled unexpectedly. "Come with me."

Eliza followed Cord to his office and peeped in. Sam was still seated at the desk.

"He's been working on those books for close to two hours," said Cord.

"He used to be a bookkeeper. Susan's been trying to get him to go back."

"So he tells me." They slowly retraced their steps to the parlor.

"He likes living out here, though, and working in the saloon. I doubt he'll ever go back to Missouri. I don't think Susan means to ask it of him, but she wants a house instead of a cabin and neighbors instead of empty hills."

"Perhaps there's a way they can both get what they want," Cord said thoughtfully.

"Maybe." Eliza stopped when they reached the stairs. "But first we have to make sure nothing happens to Susan or the baby." Her body showed its fatigue as she climbed the broad stairs, but she stopped before reaching the top and turned and looked down at Cord. "It was kind of you to let us use your house." There was a perceptible pause. "I like it very much."

For a long while Cord remained standing at the foot of the stairs, staring at the spot where Eliza had stood; then much like a sleepwalker, he moved to the parlor and poured himself out a brandy. He rolled it around in his glass a few times before a faint smile broke the sternness of his features. He drained the glass in one swallow and left the room.

"It's a girl," Eliza announced, bursting into Cord's office. "A big healthy girl." Cord was writing letters, but Sam lay asleep across the finished books and Eliza had to shake him to wake him up. "Go on up," she said as Sam jumped to his feet. "She's waiting for you."

Sam took the stairs two at a time. Abruptly, she and Cord were alone, and Eliza was thankful she was too tired to feel either happiness or pain. She doubted she could have endured facing Cord again otherwise.

"You must have had quite a night."

"It was Ginny. I only helped."

"Franklin says the coffee is ready. Breakfast will be on the table any minute now."

Eliza hesitated.

"Ginny will be in as soon as she cleans up," Cord assured her. "Franklin says she plans to sleep the rest of the day."

Eliza was too tired to resist. At the moment, nothing seemed to matter very much except that Susan and the baby were fine.

Ginny and Franklin were already at the table, and they listened to Ginny's account as she hungrily stuffed her mouth with food. Sam came in as they finished.

"Susan asked me to tell you she's named the baby Virginia Elizabeth for both of you." Sam's eyes became watery. "She says it's only right because neither of them would be here if it weren't for the two of you."

"She's a sweet little thing and I'll be happy to have a namesake," Ginny replied prosaically, "but you better hope she grows up pretty like Miss Smallwood. She'll never get anyplace looking like me."

Cord rose from the table. "I'd like to see you in my office for a few minutes, Sam."

Eliza looked surprised, but Sam swallowed his coffee and hurried after Cord.

"When will Susan be able to go home?" Eliza asked.

Ginny was exhausted, but she had not forgiven Eliza and now that Cord was gone, she dropped her friendly manner. "I don't know. She's in no shape to be taking care of herself, much less that baby. And then there's the father and the boy to see to. *You* can't help."

"They can both eat at the saloon."

"We can keep the boy here," offered Franklin.

"That leaves Susan and the baby, but I'm too far away to come out every day."

"I'll look in on her when I can," volunteered Ginny, "but I can't be there all the time. Now you two can talk all you want," she said, preparing to rise, "but I've got to go to bed before I drop."

Sam burst into the room nearly colliding with Ginny. "He's going to let us stay here, all four of us, and all I have to do is keep those books of his." Sam was so elated he didn't notice the looks of complete mystification.

"Not forever," Cord corrected, entering the room on his heels. "I only offered until they can relocate in town."

"You've sold your land?" Eliza asked stunned.

"For enough money to build the kind of house Susan has always wanted. With what I earn from the books and the saloon, we won't have to worry about money any more. I've got to go tell Susan."

"You ought to let her sleep," said Ginny.

"She can sleep the rest of the day. She'll never forgive me if I don't tell her right away."

"That wasn't a bad night's work," Franklin said after Sam left. "You got the land you wanted and someone to do your books, and he's deliriously happy into the bargain."

"It just seemed to work out all around," Cord said, a faint smile on his face.

"This seems to be your day for good deeds, but you're going to have to celebrate without me," said Ginny. She and

Franklin went off, leaving Eliza alone with Cord.

"I want to see Susan before she goes to sleep, but I guess it's time for me to go back."

"You never did get a chance to sleep in that bed."

"There never seemed to be time. And I don't feel sleepy now."

"Won't you rest some before you go back?"

"I don't think I'd better. If you could have someone take me to pick up my buggy . . ."

"I'll take you myself."

Eliza looked at the face she loved so much. It was calm, determined, and so terribly handsome it tore at her heart to deny him. "I think it would be better if someone else took me." It was hard, but it seemed easier to face him in the light of day than it had been the night before. Perhaps the fact that she had not run away had given her the courage.

"You would refuse to go with me?" Cord asked, his face not quite so calm now.

"I hope I won't have to make that choice," Eliza said, looking him squarely in the eye. She swallowed hard when Cord did not respond, but her gaze remained steady. "It was very painful for me to break our engagement. It's not made any easier by being constantly reminded of what I gave up."

For a moment Cord looked at her with equal earnestness, and then his features relaxed. "Go see your friend. I'll have one of the boys ready when you come down." He paused. "It was nice having you here."

Eliza stood perfectly still; she was sure if she moved one muscle, she would call him back to her. The minute the door closed behind Cord she sank into a chair, too weak from the raging emotional torment within her to stay on her feet. She had faced Cord and refused him with calm determination, but it had cost her deeply. She felt like a piece of her had died; every time she denied him, she denied herself. She didn't know how many more times she could do it.

She had grown in confidence and maturity during the past year, and learned to do things she never thought possible, but it was Cord's love that had enabled her to see her own worth, it was Cord's intervention that had made a place for her in the community, and it was Cord's support that had

273

enabled her to realize she was neither helpless nor without power.

Everything she had become was tied to Cord, and turning her back on the very roots of her strength was like pulling herself apart. She could go on becoming more independent and more successful, but what for? Self-respect or an improved vision of herself wasn't enough. Cord had been her initial reason to want to enrich and improve her life. Now she discovered he was the *only* reason.

Chapter 29

Iris marched into Lucy's room, heels stabbing angrily at the wood floor. "I'm supposed to wear this dress tonight," she announced, throwing several pieces of bright material onto the table before Lucy. "You haven't even started to sew it together. How can you possibly get it done in time?"

"I won't," Lucy replied through a mouthful of pins.

"I've been working on this number for weeks. Croley's virtually promised it to the boys tonight."

"Then give it to them. I don't see why you've got to come bothering me about it."

"Because I can't do my act without this damned dress!"

"Then you're in trouble. I got this dress to do for Miss Eliza, and with the cooking and having to stay after those cleaning girls, I haven't had time to sew on these ruffles. Sure is a lot of them," she said, dipping her hand into the pile and letting them cascade back onto the table. "Don't know when I'll get done. Guess those cowboys will have to wait a bit longer for you to kick up your heels in a dress you ought to be ashamed to wear."

"So that's it. It isn't proper enough for you."

"No, that *isn't* it, but it's all you need to know."

"I'll speak to Mr. Blaine about this."

"And what do you think he's going to do? Find himself somebody else who'll cook up three meals a day, keep this place swept out, and sew shameful dresses for you to go chasing after Mr. Cord? You go and tell him, and don't be slow getting back here with his answer."

Iris changed her tactics. Lucy was a pearl beyond price and she knew Croley wouldn't do anything to cause her to

275

leave.

"I *knew* Eliza was at the bottom of this, but I never thought she'd stoop to such a low trick."

"You watch what you say about Miss Eliza," Lucy said, firing up. "She wouldn't do anything underhanded, not even when she ought to," she commented in disgust. "But I will," she declared in warlike tones.

"You won't get away with this," Iris fumed.

"With this and a whole lot more," Lucy taunted, smugly confident of her position. "Of course, things might be a lot different if you was to get your claws out of Mr. Cord. Who knows how many dresses I'd be willing to run up for you."

"You can't blackmail me, you old witch. Eliza threw Cord over. I even asked her if it was all right to go after him."

"What did you expect her to say? She ain't about to empty out her poor broken heart to a painted hussy like you."

"Call me a hussy once more, and I'll slap you silly."

"Not with a broken arm you won't."

"Croley will certainly hear about this."

"Tell anybody you want. It's just going to make you look foolish when I tell them I haven't got the slightest notion what you're talking about."

"Do you really think I'm going to give up on Cord just so you'll sew up some measly dress? If I were to marry him, I could buy up this whole damned saloon and throw you out into the street."

"There ain't no use in trying to bring down an eagle with a peashooter," Lucy said scornfully. "There ain't nothing about you Miss Eliza can't beat to flinders."

"I'm a damned good-looking woman."

"You'll do fine for the likes of Mr. Croley, but you can put Mr. Cord out of your mind. He loves Miss Eliza, and they're going to get married."

"They'll have to start talking to each other first."

"That'll happen a whole lot sooner if you don't show your face every time he comes around. It takes the bloom off things right smart."

"I imagine it does," said Iris with a satisfied grin. "Cord hasn't ignored me yet."

"He'd take notice of the kitchen garbage if it was dumped

at his feet. You wait till someone comes around *asking* to see you before you start to crow."

"I want this dress done by tomorrow," Iris demanded, livid with fury. "If not, I'll fasten your hide to the wall with your own pins."

"Ain't nobody put on this earth to have all her wants satisfied, but I'll see what I can do," Lucy relented, going back to her sewing and blatantly dismissing Iris, who turned on her heel and stormed down the hall, where she slammed the door so hard that downstairs the top row of glasses danced merrily along the shelf.

Cord followed the quaking clerk into the inner office of Sanford Burton's Buffalo National Bank. The man had never seen Cord before, but he had fed on the idle remarks made by waiting customers, and unable to separate the reasonable from the fantastic, believed everything he'd heard. Cord's imposing statue, his brusque demand for Mr. Burton, and the unmistakable air of dark displeasure made the clerk so nervous that, as he later told his wife, he was unable to swallow more than two bites of his lunch.

Cord came to a halt two steps inside the door and leisurely passed the occupants of the room under review. In an unconscious gesture, he pulled the brim of his hat a little lower over eyes that seemed to have already receded into his head. Cord had never been a member of the Association, but it only took him a few seconds to realize he was face to face with the owners or foremen of every major cattle operation in two counties, and every nerve in his body was alert.

"I'm not sure you all know Mr. Stedman," Burton said, rising to greet Cord, "but I asked him to join us."

"We've met," said Chet Winfield, the roundup boss who had gotten in trouble for selling Cord unbranded calves at prices reserved only for Association members.

"We've done business from time to time," said another. But most were meeting for the first time a man they had heard a lot about and one they had come to fear, distrust, or respect as their interests happened to agree with or run counter to Cord's. A somber, unattractive lot on the whole, they nodded a greeting without getting up to shake his hand. Cord returned their salute with an equally noncommittal nod and took a seat next to the door.

"The purpose of this meeting is to discuss the rustling that's a continual drain on your herds and is threatening to reduce your revenues to nothing," explained Sanford.

"I'm not here to discuss," grumbled one owner, rising to his feet. "I'm here to *do* something. Everybody knows the courts won't do a damned thing about the rustlers that infest Johnson and Natrona counties. It's time we took things into our own hands. You don't see Montana having trouble with rustlers, not after they hanged every one they could get their hands on."

"I don't think we should consider a vigilante action—"

"Then we might as well all go home. We've tried everything else and gotten nowhere."

"That's why I invited Mr. Stedman," Sanford interposed quickly. "I thought he might share some of his methods with us."

"Besides breaking arms," one man said derisively.

"Men with broken arms don't steal cows," Cord said simply.

"Yes, well, you have to catch them first, and they don't exactly stand."

"You have to be on the spot. Lying snug in your bed isn't going to catch rustlers."

"But our men can't be depended upon to do anything once we find them. Half the time they look the other way, and the other half they just let the rustlers run right over them."

"You've got to give them a reason to fight. No man is going to face death for somebody else's property unless he feels he has something to gain."

"What do you suggest?"

"A decent wage, year-round employment, and letting them have a piece of the game."

"What do you mean by that?" the first owner asked suspiciously.

"I let any man who can save enough money buy a few head and run them with mine."

"But they're using your grass."

278

"They're also watching my cows with sharpened vision."

"But you're already paying them to do that."

"No hand will face a rustler's gun for thirty dollars a month, but if he has his own cows to watch, he'll stay in the saddle an hour longer, ride over one more ridge, or inspect a boxed canyon even though it will make him late for supper. He tells me everything he sees because he identifies his cause with mine, and I have his expert skills year after year instead of losing him in the annual turnover."

"But what you're suggesting will cost a lot of money. We're losing too much already."

"This policy has enabled Cord to put together one of the largest spreads in our area."

"That and buying mavericks at ten dollars a head."

"You do it," countered Cord. "Why shouldn't I?"

"Because you're not a member of the Association," one man said boldly, "and I don't see any reason why you should have been taken off the blacklist."

"Just because I'm better at ranching than you is no reason to think I've done anything illegal, Gene. If you'd get off your ass, you'd be able to turn a profit too."

Gene started up from his chair, but when Cord calmly rose to his feet, contrasting his six-foot, four-inch, well-muscled body to Gene's shorter and fatter one, the man's fury sputtered ludicrously.

"You even allowed rustlers to invade your roundup last spring and cut out the best steers right from under your nose," added Cord.

"They were armed," Gene protested, "and they were gone before I could get my crew together."

"When that same gang stole one of my herds, I went after them *into Montana*. They were armed then too, but you can bet they won't try it a second time."

"That's fine for you, you don't have a wife and children, but the rest of us can't be throwing ourselves in front of a gun for the fun of it. I still say we ought to back the Association. They've promised to send help come spring."

"What are they planning to do?"

"That's still a secret, but the Association secretary assures me come fall there won't be any rustlers left in Wyoming."

"What's the cost?"

"No more than five or six hundred each, and that's less than the cost of two steers. Think how much we'll save."

A spirited discussion followed, but everyone agreed the cost would more than be made up for by their savings.

"Are you with us, Stedman?" Gene asked.

"I don't need help."

"Then you're against us."

"I'm not *against* anybody. I just don't need to pay outsiders to defend my property." He stood up. "You won't want me listening to your business, so I'll leave."

Sanford Burton hurried after him. "Don't turn your back on us, Cord."

"Why are you siding with them, Sanford? You don't have any cattle."

"They're my customers."

"If you don't unhitch your wagon from that runaway team, you're going to end up smashed to pieces. Sounds like they're up to something dangerous. This county is hot enough to blow sky high right now. All it needs is one fool with a match."

"But these are the men with power. You ought to be one of them. Remember what I said about being willing to help a son-in-law? That son-in-law would have to stick by me too."

"I'm not going to be your son-in-law, and if you keep bothering me about it, I'm liable to pull my money out of your bank and start my own. There're a lot of people who would welcome an alternative to doing business with the Buffalo National."

"Don't threaten me, Stedman. I can destroy you."

"I'm just saying I don't need your friends in there, but I'm not afraid to butt heads with you. I beat them, I can beat you."

"You're a fool to think you can stand alone against the Association."

Cord opened the door on the quaking clerk. "But not a stupid fool, Sanford. And you are."

He departed, leaving Sanford cursing and the clerk hopping with excitement. At last he was seeing the violence and passion of the West at first hand, and the excitement was almost too much for the clerk's thin blood.

"And I think every saloon in Buffalo should be closed on Sunday. It's disgraceful for our citizens to get drunk before Reverend Fry has even started his sermon." Jessica had invited Buffalo's most influential citizens to a special meeting to discuss the increasing rowdiness of the habitués of the town's many saloons, and her parlor was filled with a confused babble of protest and assent.

"And you men needn't think you can shout me down, and then proceed undeterred in your greedy attempts to extract the last possible dollar from those unfortunate men," Jessica said sternly, refusing to yield the floor. "Everyone, including the ladies, shall have their say before a decision is taken." There was a chorus of groans from the men.

Sanford Burton succinctly expressed the position of the saloon keepers when he said there was no point in closing their doors to dollars that were going to be spent "in Sheridan or Douglas, if not in Buffalo. The men need somewhere to eat and sleep. You ladies forget our saloons provide many more services than just access to fine liquor."

There were several derisive hoots at that, mostly from the men.

"What you say is all fine and good," said Ella Baylis, her powerful voice carrying easily throughout the noisy room, "but nobody's objecting to giving people dinner and a place to sleep. What we don't like is to see a street full of stumbling drunks on our way to church."

The women signified their agreement in chorus, and the battle was joined. The issue swayed back and forth, first toward the ladies and the moralists in the group, and then back toward the merchants and the business interests. Soon the lines were firmly drawn, and sharp words began to stray from the issue of saloons into the arena of personal remarks.

"I don't suppose I should be saying anything, not living anywhere near town," said Cord, taking advantage of a momentary lull, "but since it looks like neither side is going to budge, maybe some of us outsiders will be the ones to decide the issue.

281

"As you all know, there's a good bit of bad feeling between the big ranchers and the little ranchers and homesteaders. It's been a dividing factor in this county for nearly two years, and it's getting worse. Each seems to think the other is out to ruin him, and the two camps regard each other with open hostility. The big ranchers gather down in Cheyenne. The folks here gather in the saloons and talk of nothing but their wrongs, imagined slights, and what can be done to get even.

"This talk is bad at any time, bad for the men, bad for the community, but it's especially bad when the men doing the talking are too drunk to think straight. If everyone had at least one day to look at things with unclouded judgment, maybe this situation could be defused." Cord paused a moment. "I think it would be mighty interesting if Miss Smallwood would tell us what she thinks," he said, and sat down.

Eliza nearly jumped out of her skin. After what had happened between them, she was surprised Cord had any interest at all in her opinions. She had only attended the meeting at her uncle's insistence, and hadn't given the matter any serious thought, yet a brief look around showed everyone was waiting for her to speak. She rose to her feet desperately trying to think of something to say that wouldn't make her look like a fool.

"Mr. Stedman referred to outsiders, and that's very much how I feel," she began tentatively, "but I suppose people are the same everywhere, and their problems aren't much different. Maybe there is a way each side can give up a little in order to keep what's most important." Eliza paused, hardly daring to put the barely formed idea into words.

"Is it possible for the saloons to remain open on Sunday" — the murmur from the women nearly drowned her out — "but not serve spirits?" Now it was the men's turn to mutter. "The merchants could still make money, the citizens would still have a place to eat and sleep, and the ladies would be confronted by none but sober men."

"Why didn't we think of that?" Ella asked. "It's so simple one of the men could have come up with it."

"Let's have none of that, Ella," said Sanford, taking charge. "I think Miss Smallwood has given us an excellent suggestion."

"But we make twice as much money on liquor as everything else put together," protested one owner.

"You won't get a dime if we set a match to that firetrap you run, Craig Little," snapped Ella. "Take what you can get before we overturn the whole table in your lap."

Naturally that exchange couldn't be taken lying down, and it was several minutes before Sanford could be heard. However, when Colonel Davis, the commander of the army fort outside of town stood up, the noise abated quickly.

"I'm not a local citizen either, but since my soldiers are some of the most frequent patrons of your saloons, I think you should know I'm being forced to consider placing Buffalo off limits, at least during the weekend. I don't blame anyone here, but I can't afford to have my men coming back too drunk to be of any use."

A stunned silence fell over the gathering. There were only a couple of hundred soldiers at the fort, along with the wives and children of some of the officers, but the money they spent was a major prop to Buffalo's economy. Without it, some businesses would close up. Taking advantage of the silence, Sanford stated Eliza's suggestion as a motion, and it was voted on and accepted with only the most diehard holding out. There being no further business to discuss, they broke up into groups of like views, each determined to hold to its position while trying to belittle the opposition.

"That was an admirable speech, Miss Smallwood," said Sanford, cornering Eliza. "But then one expects a schoolteacher to be an arbiter in this kind of debate."

"Brains are where you find them," Ella told Sanford. "It's got nothing to do with teaching school."

"You were most impressive, Miss Smallwood," Jessica agreed primly. "I can see why the children admire you so much."

"I can see other reasons for her popularity," Cord said, coming up. "At least with the boys."

"That doesn't account for the success of her female pupils," Jessica said austerely.

"Don't fool yourself into thinking it's not easier for a girl to be taught by a pretty face than one screwed up like a sour

283

prune," Ella declared. "I can still remember the green persimmon who tried to terrorize me into learning my letters. Gave me such a distaste for books I can't stand to read more than a mail-order catalog to this day."

"A lot of women in Buffalo must have gone to the same school," noted Mr. Burton, chuckling.

"It's time to bid our guests good evening," Jessica said, bearing her husband away.

"Sanford won't be allowed to forget *that* remark any time soon," Ella declared.

"I'm surprised he supported our side," said Eliza.

"He thought it was the best he was likely to get," Cord explained. "Things have been getting a little rough lately, and it's not at all unlikely the ladies could have voted to close the saloons altogether. Since they vote in a block, he wasn't at all certain of the outcome."

"Is everything always decided by money?" Eliza asked, dismayed.

"No. Sometimes it's an unfortunate misunderstanding or a bad combination of circumstances—" Cord began.

"Or not knowing when to leave well enough alone," Ella finished up for him.

"You don't have to talk for him, Ella. I know what he's talking about." Eliza colored, and then continued. "I know I sometimes don't understand why people act the way they do, but I have come to realize there is more than one way to look at everything."

"And . . ." prompted Ella.

Eliza hesitated, and then faced Cord squarely. "Do not take this to mean I have changed my position, but I am aware I have been unfair to you. Your kindness to Sam and Susan and your sensitive stating of a very difficult situation prove that beyond question. Now I must go. Uncle Ira has threatened to come after me if I'm late."

Ella trod on Cord's toe before he opened his mouth. "Won't you ever learn when to shut up?" she whispered urgently as Eliza moved away.

"But she practically said she was changing her mind," Cord pointed out.

"I know what she said. I'm not deaf. Neither am I fool

enough to go rushing at her and scaring her off again."

"You think I was going to scare her?"

"Do you deny you were bursting your buttons to ask her to marry you?"

"I guess so," Cord admitted, smiling so charmingly a woman across the room who thoroughly disliked Ella almost decided to come over and inquire after her corns.

"You know you were, just like before when you couldn't wait to shove Ira's guilt in her face. Let her alone. She's as shy as can be, but she's not a frightened little girl anymore. You push her too far, and she's capable of leaving Wyoming altogether."

"But what would she do?"

"With her looks and voice she could perform almost anywhere she wants. Any place has got to be better than singing in a saloon in Buffalo, Wyoming."

Cord watched Eliza intently as, across the room, she said good night to Jessica. "She won't leave," Cord said finally.

"No, I don't think she will either, though the thought has crossed her mind, but neither will she jump through your hoop. She knows she can make her own way now, alone if she has to."

"No matter what way she has to make, she'll never do it alone," Cord replied.

Chapter 30

"Do you think you can talk him into it, Sam?" asked one of several men gathered around the cookstove in Sam's old cabin on one bitterly cold afternoon. The little stove glowed bright red in its effort to heat the small room.

"How do we know we can trust him?" objected another.

"When are you people ever going to learn?" Sam asked in disgust. "Stedman was just where you are when he bought the Matador, but he's a lot smarter, he works a lot harder, and he's gambled everything he has over and over again to build up his spread. Sure he's a big rancher now, but has any of you ever forgotten what it was like to ride roundup for somebody else?"

"Of course we haven't, but Cord's never been one of us. He keeps to himself, and nobody's at all sure where he stands on things."

"He keeps to himself because he's too busy to stand around talking. Besides, what do you expect a man to do when you back away every time he comes up to the bar."

"Who wants to drink with a man who hardly says two words and stares at that singer like there weren't nobody else in the room?"

"And if you say something he doesn't like, he looks like he's going to take you apart right there."

"You're making a big mistake not to trust him," Sam insisted.

"Why should we trust *you?* You're taking his money? You're even living in his house."

"And I'm also taking Croley Blaine's money," Sam said, aware every one present knew of Croley's attempt to steal

Cord's herd on Christmas day, "but I don't see any of you accusing me of taking his side."

"I don't trust Blaine either."

"I'm not asking you to. I'm saying you're a fool to keep distrusting Stedman just because he's got more cows than you. You'll never find a better leader for your roundup. *He's* not about to back down before rustlers or the Association foremen, and if you think they're not going to come down on you when they hear you'll be dividing up the mavericks, then you don't know the Association."

"Well, I'm still not sure. I heard tell he attended a ranchers' meeting in Burton's office last week."

"If you heard that much, you ought to know he walked out on them. Go ask Burton's clerk. The man's dying to tell it to anyone who'll stand still long enough."

"I say we ask him," argued the first speaker. "Even if he does tell the Association, we haven't lost anything. They're going to hear it from somebody the minute it's announced, and there's nobody better able to stand up to that bunch of crooks than Stedman. And I'll tell you something else. I intend to ask him to take my steers to the railhead along with his this year. Those Association inspectors don't dare impound his herd and they know it. I'm still owed money for beeves I sold eighteen months ago. The only reason I haven't gone under yet is I borrowed money from Burton at enough interest to keep both his wife and daughter in furs."

"Then you want me to talk to him?" Sam asked. There was a discontented rumbling and a reluctant assent. "Make up your minds. I'm not sticking my neck out and having you change your minds. You need Stedman, but he can do without you."

Realizing the bitter truth of that statement, the men agreed to invite Cord to lead their independent roundup, thereby dividing northern Wyoming into two hostile camps.

"But I don't know anything about contracts."

Eliza was in a quandary. Lucy had come up twenty minutes earlier to tell her a theatrical agent was downstairs and insisted upon hearing her sing before he would even begin to talk about terms.

"They don't ever want to give you more than they have to. Make sure you do your best. Then tell him you want twice what he offers."

"I wouldn't know what to ask for."

"Then you let me do the talking. I know all about what to do."

"I imagine it will take a lot of money for both of us to live."

"You mean you're taking me with you?"

"I'd be lost without you."

"The agent will take care of you," Lucy said, trying to hide her pleasure.

"I can't trust a stranger."

"You can't trust anybody if he's a man," Lucy stated unequivocally. "Now you get warmed up while I'll talk to this fella and find out just what he's got in mind."

Eliza wasn't at all sure she wanted to go East. At first it seemed like a good way to get away from Cord, but she hadn't been wanting to get away from him so very much lately. Now that an agent was actually downstairs and she was faced with what leaving Buffalo would mean, she didn't know if she had enough courage to go to Chicago and meet all those strange people, even if it did help her to keep from thinking about Cord all the time.

But she knew she wouldn't forget him, not even if she traveled to every major city in the country. The more she thought about it, the less important their differences seemed to be.

The night he ruthlessly exposed her uncle and threatened Sam and Susan, he became a veritable demon in her eyes; he was awful, terrible, and she wanted nothing else to do with him. But when he let them invade his house to have Susan's baby and then gave Sam a job, he unquestionably blunted the cutting edge of her anger and disappointment. Seeing him at Mrs. Burton's meeting only stoked her great physical hunger and reminded her of how much she longed to be in his arms. She had no doubt that, in time, her heart and body would overrule her mind.

And it didn't help to have Susan Haughton singing his praises until Eliza almost dreaded to see her coming. Living in Cord's house and sharing confidences with Ginny, Susan knew how deeply he felt about Eliza and how greatly he suffered, and she had made it her special duty to mend the rift between them. Every time Susan came into town to supervise the construction of her new house, she took the opportunity to launch another attack on Eliza's crumbling defenses.

Eliza was such a soft-hearted creature her sympathy would have been engaged even if she hadn't liked Cord at all. But she still loved him, and she was finding it more and more difficult to remember why she had been so angry with him. When she ran into him outside the bank just this past week, she forgot completely. His mind was so completely taken up with something else he nearly walked past without seeing her. She was used to having to fend off Cord's attentions, and to have him practically ignore her knocked another prop from under her anger. Now there was a stranger downstairs waiting to listen to her sing, and she was less sure than ever what she was running from.

The agent was seated near the front of the empty room when Eliza came down. "I'm not going to let you say a word to him until he hears you sing," Lucy whispered. "He is even sharper than I remembered, and unless you surprise him out of his britches, he won't offer you enough to keep a bird alive." She glanced at the agent, and her eyes crinkled merrily.

"It seems that just looking at you has sparked his interest. Now give him your best. Don't let him catch his breath until your name's on that contract."

Eliza had already picked out the songs she intended to sing, but now she wondered if the simple, folk-like songs that appealed to the cowboys and soldiers were quite the right thing for a big-city theatrical agent. She was so nervous she had to take a deep breath before she could start.

She hadn't reached the end of the first verse when Cord walked in and sat down near the middle of the room. Her body was shaken by such a jolt of electricity she almost forgot her words, but she recovered quickly, and was pleased to see that the agent didn't seem to notice her stumble.

Even a casual observer could have noticed the single-minded intensity with which Cord listened to Eliza, but not the closest scrutiny yielded a clue to his thoughts. Eliza had often inveighed against the stone-like impassiveness of his countenance, and that quality was never more in evidence than now. She wondered what he was doing in town, why he had picked this morning to come to the saloon. She had been careful to choose the time when Croley and her uncle went over their business affairs with Sanford Burton. She didn't want them to know she was thinking about leaving, but it wouldn't hurt Cord Stedman to know. It would show him she hadn't forgiven him and didn't need to depend on him or anyone else anymore.

But just as she started the second song, Iris came in. Never once turning in Eliza's direction, she scanned the room swiftly until she found Cord, then moved quickly to his side. Eliza watched with gathering indignation as Iris began to whisper to Cord. Now they had their heads together, and even from a distance Eliza could tell he was no longer listening to her.

For the first time in her life, instead of being self-effacing and slinking off to hide her hurt, Eliza was eager to fight back. The accompanist had already begun the introduction to the third song, but Eliza stopped him and directed him to play a song they had been working on mostly for fun. She wasn't sure she could remember it, much less sing it without a mistake, but Iris still held Cord's attention and she was determined to get it back.

The song was full of runs, trills, and high notes. It had been fun to learn in spite of the wry faces Susan made. Susan didn't care for what she called *opera* singing, but she admitted that when Eliza sang it, it didn't sound half bad.

The agent thought it sounded a lot better than that. He sat up in his chair when Eliza performed the opening runs flawlessly, and leaned forward eagerly as she successfully executed one difficult passage after another, but Cord continued to ignore her, and Eliza redoubled her efforts, taking the last chorus even faster. The cadenza was coming up, one Eliza had never been able to sing to her satisfaction, and she needed all her concentration to get through it, but to her horror Cord and Iris got up and started toward the door.

Desperation and anger caused Eliza's adrenaline to flow more than ever; she tore into the cadenza, sang every flying note with a deft but true tone, and finished with a high note that astounded even Lucy. It brought the agent to his feet, but Cord didn't hear it. He was already gone.

Eliza tried to concentrate on what the agent was saying, but all she saw was Cord leaving with Iris. Lucy made one outrageous demand after another in her name, and the agent granted them almost without argument; Eliza's total lack of interest had unnerved him. He was used to people willing to do anything to attract his attention, yet this backwoods Jenny Lind seemed more interested in a couple of locals than the fact she could be singing in New York a year from now.

This girl was a sure thing. Her beauty and voice would place her in a class by herself, but she also possessed a quality of undemanding innocence that made her irresistible. She might even become a favorite of the ladies for she was not the type to steal their husbands or wear costumes designed to show more of her body than her talent.

"Miss Smallwood, I really must know what you think of my offer before I can draw up the contracts," said the agent.

"What do you think, Lucy?" Eliza asked, unable to remember anything the man had said.

"I'm not saying you can't get more money once the right people see what you can do, but you won't get a better contract now."

"Well, if you really think I should."

"What else do you want, Miss Smallwood? Just name it and you can have it," the agent added.

"I don't know that I want anything else—"

"Yes she does," interrupted Lucy. "She needs a room to herself. She doesn't want everybody tramping in while she's getting ready and using up her stuff the minute her back's turned."

"All the major theaters have private rooms."

"And she wants the best spot, the one next to closing."

"I'm not so sure of that."

"Yes, you are. You know if people are coming to see Miss Eliza, they'll put her anywhere on the program she wants to be."

"Okay, okay. I'll see she gets the best spot. Anything else?" he asked, feeling wrung out.

"Not just yet. You get those papers drawn up by one of your fancy lawyers, one who fixes it so you can't sneak out of paying her what you promised."

"My lawyer is the best—"

"Then we'll get *our* lawyer to give it a going-over. I don't trust you Easterners. I lived in New York too long to do a fool thing like that."

Eliza didn't know if Buffalo even had a lawyer, but she couldn't generate any interest in the contract. Why had Cord walked out? He couldn't have fallen in love with Iris, not when only last week he'd made it obvious he still wanted to marry her. Even Ella said Cord was hers for the asking.

But somehow that didn't make Eliza feel any more secure. For the first time she had exerted herself to attract a man, and she had failed miserably; he had walked out on her. Surely he wouldn't have done that if he still loved her.

Suddenly Eliza realized she was falling back into her old habits of self-doubt, and she gave herself a mental scolding. Cord *did* love her, and he must have had some perfectly good reason for leaving. But if she *had* waited too long and he *had* given up hoping she would change her mind, well, then she could still carry on. There were plenty of other men in the world—maybe not any she could love as much as Cord, but there had to be hundreds of handsome, rich, kind, loving men in a place like New York; she could find a dozen within six months.

But she had a growing suspicion that once she found the paragons, her treacherous heart wouldn't rest until it found a way to make them seem inferior to that stiff-necked cowboy.

Chapter 31

The first rumor raced through Buffalo with the speed of a galloping horse. The Cattlemen's Association had black-balled Cord Stedman again, and this time they'd taken pains to see the news was carried to every ranch in Wyoming. It meant Cord wouldn't be able to participate in the Association's roundup or buy unbranded maverick calves at ten dollars a head. No one expected it to bother him — he'd been blackballed before and survived — but it did remove any lingering suspicion that Cord was friendly with the hated organization the absentee landlords had set up to preserve their stranglehold on the Wyoming cattle industry. Now when he rode by a homestead, he was more likely to be met with a friendly greeting and an invitation to step inside for a cup of coffee. He never did, but instead of his refusal being viewed with resentment and suspicion, it now showed he was a man with too much on his mind to waste time talking.

The second rumor swept through the entire state faster than a prairie fire in a high wind: The small ranchers had joined together to hold a roundup of their own a month before the Association's scheduled roundup, and Cord Stedman was going to lead it. At stake was the ownership of uncounted thousands of mavericks, unbranded calves worth hundreds of thousands of dollars, and the confrontation everyone had long feared now seemed unavoidable. The Association couldn't possibly let such a challenge to its authority go unanswered, but no one in Buffalo or Cheyenne doubted Cord would be as good as his word; he and his men had a reputation for carrying the fight to the enemy instead of waiting for it to be brought to them.

Sanford Burton tried to reason with Cord, and then to apply financial pressure, even going so far as to say, when it was clear Cord wasn't going to change his mind, that he would squeeze the smaller ranchers and Cord could blame himself if they went under. The only result was that two days later Cord withdrew his money from Burton's bank, opened his own Northern Wyoming National Bank, and installed Sam Haughton as his cashier; before the end of the week he had talked fifty people into bringing their business to him, including the substantial account of Bayliss Hardware and Dry Goods.

"I can't think of a more harebrained thing to do," Ella told Cord, "but I don't see not supporting you against that grasping pinch-penny. Besides, I've been looking for a way to keep Jessica Burton from pestering the life out of me for nigh on ten years, and I'm willing to bet next month's receipts this has done the trick."

Ella's money was safe. Jessica did not speak to Ella, or anyone else who took their money out of her husband's bank. As for her intention to marry Melissa to Cord Stedman, Jessica would have preferred Melissa die an old maid rather than live a rich and happy life as the wife of a man she termed the greatest criminal west of the Mississippi. Ira and Croley were loud in their determination to stay with Burton, but the real blow came when the Army transferred its accounts. Sam offered to handle the payroll himself rather than have the Army cart the money out to the fort to pay the men and then bring it back to town to deposit. Burton had never agreed to do that because he said the soldiers' pay was quickly spent or sent back East, but Sam managed to see that enough of it stayed in his vaults to make a tidy profit.

But this upheaval only served to draw the lines more firmly: the larger ranchers, the merchants who had a common interest in serving them, and the town's *respectable* citizens sticking with Burton; the smaller ranchers, disgruntled merchants, farmers and homesteaders, plain cowboys, common soldiers, and Lavinia's girls changing to Cord. In a matter of days the antagonism was visible on the streets as citizens who had always greeted each other with friendly words either passed in silence or backed up their differing opinions with their fists. Sheriff Hooker had all he could do to see no one carried firearms within the town limits. He said if they wanted to kill each other outside his jurisdiction that was the U.S. marshal's business, but people were quietly building up their arsenals feeling that something—no one was quite sure what—was about to happen.

The only person who was unconditionally delighted was Susan Haughton. She had a new baby, a new house in town, and a husband who in a few short months had gone from a starving farmer to a respectable bank clerk who might possibly become a bank president some day. She knew if Eliza married Cord, the two of them could combine their efforts and become the most influential women within a hundred miles.

But Eliza wasn't enjoying it. Cord had come up to her the day after her audition, and still stinging from the humiliation of his walking out on her, she'd amazed both Cord and herself by turning her back and walking away from him.

She had regretted it immediately, but her pride wouldn't let her turn back, so she had proceeded on to the saloon, where Iris had completed her misery.

"I wanted to catch you before you saw Cord," Iris had said with unfeigned concern. "I doubt he'll tell you himself, but his mother just died and he's bound to be feeling it. I only came to know about it because we grew up in the same county and I wrote my mother that I'd met him out here. She wrote back to say his mother had died. I told him the day you were singing for that agent. I hadn't expected him to take it so hard. Not when she'd run away before he was six."

Eliza had wished the earth would open up and swallow her. She'd been barely able to mutter some reply before scurrying to her room. The first fit of temper she'd shown in her life, the *only* time she'd ever attempted to strike back when someone had hurt her, and she'd had to walk away from Cord when he needed her. She'd felt utterly crushed.

Unbeknownst to her, the last of her resistance had crumbled, and had Cord walked into the room at that moment she would have thrown herself into his arms and never remembered that only a few months before she had called him a cruel and heartless monster. Her heart had ached for his grief and the cruelty of her conduct. It received a further wrench the next day.

Eliza saw Cord across the street and made the unusual gesture of crossing the churned-up mud to speak to him. His eyes seemed to retreat into the back of his head when he saw her coming, but he stopped and waited. As she stood next to him with all her self-imposed barriers gone, it was almost impossible not to reach out and touch him, to stand within the circle of his arms. But even though her heart and mind were in considerable confusion, her tongue uttered the mundane, unexceptional words of condolence.

"Iris told me about your mother," she said in an unsteady voice. "I just wanted to tell you how sorry I am." His look seemed to harden, and he retreated further from her.

"I know it must be difficult," she hurried on, "losing someone who was so important to you."

"She wasn't much of a woman," Cord lashed out harshly. "I doubt she was a comfort to anyone." Two customers came up to the bank, signaling their need for his attention. "Keep your sympathy for the man she deserted this time." He tugged the brim of his hat as a sign of dismissal and walked inside the bank.

Eliza was almost too overcome to retrace her steps, and then she could barely restrain herself from running for the privacy of her own room. Terrible, wracking sobs welled up inside her; she hurried past two people who spoke to her, knowing if she stopped to say even one word she would burst into tears right there in the street. She made it to the saloon, but the tears wouldn't be restrained any longer, and Lucy and Iris came running up the stairs behind her.

"You go on back to what you were doing," Lucy ordered Iris peremptorily. "You can bet Mr. Cord is at the bottom of this, and if I find you had anything to do with it, you'd better pack your bags and get out of town. If I get my hands on you, there won't be enough left to feed a scrawny buzzard." She didn't wait for a reply, but hurried to Eliza's room, where she found her crying with huge, gusty sobs.

Lucy rocked Eliza in her arms while she poured out a story that made Lucy long to give Cord a piece of her mind and put Iris on a steamer bound for the Orient.

"Now you dry your eyes and listen to me," she scolded when Eliza grew calmer. "You are going to have to make up your mind what you want. You can't go changing it every week and expect people to put up with it. If you want to sing, you're going to have to forget Mr. Cord and everybody else in this town because you won't ever be coming back here. For when you get married, and a gal as pretty and sweet as you will surely get married, your husband isn't going to want to come out here and go riding about a dusty plain while you go sightseeing for old times' sake. He'll like it even less when he finds out one of the sights you're seeing is an old beau. I don't know of many men who can be put next to Mr. Cord without being made to look downright mangy.

"And if it *is* Mr. Cord you've set your heart on, then you'd better stop acting like a shameful tease and tell him. You can't turn your back on him and expect him to hang around for more of the same. Not even shiftless men—and I've seen enough of *them* to know what they're like—put up with that kind of treatment. There's too many females, and not all of them decent, just busting their stays to do for Cord what you won't. Now let me wash your face, for you don't dare go anywhere with tear stains all over it, and you can tell me what you intend to do."

Eliza submitted to Lucy's ministrations, but it didn't seem to clear her mind. "Three months ago I thought I knew what I wanted. Now I'm so confused I don't know."

"Then stay right here until you figure it out. I've had enough of your acting first one way and then another. It's got so people don't know what to expect from you next, and if you don't settle down soon, they're liable not to keep on caring." Eliza started to speak, but Lucy cut her off.

"Save your words for them that matters." She gave Eliza a swift hug. "I'm your friend no matter what, so put your mind to work on your other problem. Figure that one out, and everything else will take care of itself."

Eliza was only half listening to Croley and her uncle. She disliked the fact Croley had started taking his lunch in their rooms, even inviting Iris to join them at times, but Ira enjoyed the company and encouraged them to continue. Eliza retreated to her room as often as she dared, even on days when Iris was present, but she couldn't do it all the time. Besides, the short time she had to put up with them was nothing compared to Ira's black moods, which sometimes lasted for weeks. Iris and Lucy both thought there was something wrong with him, but whenever they mentioned it, Croley dismissed it as female foolishness. Eliza *knew* something was wrong with him, but he wouldn't listen to anything she said.

Eliza hadn't been able to get Cord out of her mind since he'd left her standing in front of his bank. Even when she was singing, she found her mind wandering back to the first few months after they met; it gave her songs a bittersweet quality the sentimental cowboys and soldiers found conducive to reminiscing about their own innocent youth. Since that encouraged them to drown their sorrows in even more drink, Croley did not tell her to change her material as he intended to at first.

She couldn't make up her mind how to approach Cord; her natural inclination was to shrink from initiating contact, but Eliza knew she had to take the first step. The possibility he had completely gotten over his love for her was too grim to be considered and she pushed it from her mind, but like a homesick dog, it kept returning to the place that had given it birth. She considered going to his ranch, but she wanted this meeting to be on neutral ground. If she saw him in private he was liable to demand the reason for her rudeness, and she doubted she could control the interview after that. At least he was too much of a gentleman to cut her dead in the street.

She toyed with the idea of asking him to visit her in their rooms, but there was no assurance Ira wouldn't walk in on them. Meeting him at Ella's smacked of the clandestine. It occurred to her she might ask him to meet her in the land office. She still intended to give him the land even if he never spoke to her again. Keeping it for herself, or selling it to someone who would use it against him, was an underhanded trick and she had never been capable of that, not even in the days when she had been so angry she would have welcomed any calamity not of her making.

Her thoughts, and Croley's conversation, were abruptly interrupted by the barman bursting into the room.

"An army of gunslingers has invaded Johnson County," he disclosed between gasps. "They're headed toward Buffalo to kill us all." All three inhabitants of the room stared at him in unbelieving shock.

"The man's drunk," Lucy declared as she came rushing up the steps behind the barman. "I told you never to trust an ex-cowpoke with liquor."

"I'm not drunk and I'm not lying either," the man said, real fear unmistakable in his face. "I swear to God, there's sixty or seventy of them, and they brought their horses and ammunition. In a railroad car too!"

"Then stop making up absurd stories and tell us what you're talking about," Croley ordered.

"And make sure you start at the beginning," prompted Lucy.

"I'm not sure of everything. I heard the tale at the livery stable, and they were arguing over it even then. But one thing's for certain: They killed Lem Poteet and Bucky Lloyd. Did it yesterday. They surrounded Lem's place at dawn and poured lead into the building all day. They got Bucky early, but they didn't get Lem until they set fire to the cabin and he made a run for it."

"You sure?" Croley asked, his face utterly drained of color.

"Yeah. They're headed toward Buffalo, and somebody said they have a list of people they're going to kill in cold blood."

"Who is *they?*" Eliza asked, hardly able to credit a word she heard.

"The Cattlemen's Association. There's been rumors around for a while they meant to do something, and this must be it. People are already packing up to get out of town."

"I never stole anybody's cows, and I'm not going anywhere," Lucy announced.

"I've heard the same rumors," Croley said. "And I also know there was a secret meeting at Burton's bank last month. Just in case it is true and Ira and I have to go help fight, you start packing some things for Miss Smallwood, Lucy. She can stay with Ella Baylis until this is over."

"But it can't be true," Eliza insisted, unbelieving. "What

reason could anybody have to send gunslingers to kill us?"

"It was your boyfriend's independent roundup that did it," exclaimed Ira, springing to his feet. "I told you he was one of them from the start. His offer to lead the roundup was just a ruse to give them an excuse to come down here and kill anybody they wanted."

"No," cried Eliza, denying a fact too logical to be completely ignored. "Cord would never do anything like that."

"How can you say that after what he did to me?" Ira said rounding on her.

"What he did to *you?*" exclaimed Eliza, groping for words. "Don't you mean what you did to him?"

"You two can keep chewing on this same old argument if you like, but I intend to find out what is going on," Croley said, interrupting. "I want the saloon kept open, but keep the doors to the upstairs locked," he said to the barman. "You ladies start packing. We may not have much time."

"Do you think we're really being invaded?" Eliza asked Lucy after the men had gone.

"If we are, it's Mr. Blaine's own hide he's worrying about. If there *is* a list, he's bound to know his name's near the top."

"Then you think there will be a fight?"

"I wouldn't put anything past men as full of meanness as some I've seen here. If everybody did what they were supposed to do, there wouldn't be any trouble. But I guess the Lord didn't aim to put us down here with nothing to do, so he made people like Mr. Blaine and that nasty man I see him talking to sometimes."

"Who's that?"

"I don't know his name, but it wouldn't make any difference. They're all the same. Now you and me had better get our packing done before those drunks downstairs start getting funny ideas."

Chapter 32

Watching from the balcony above, Eliza saw Croley go to his office instead of his room on his return and she waited a moment, undecided as to whether to wait in her own room or go down and see what she could find out. Before she could make up her mind, Ira entered from the back of the saloon and made straight for Croley's office. That decided the matter. Using great care not to make any sound, Eliza tiptoed down the stairs and along the hall. The door to Croley's office was closed, but she was able to slip into the office next to it that Sam had used to do the saloon's books before Croley fired him for going over to Cord.

"There's no doubt Stedman's with that gang of paid murderers," Ira was saying, a fanatical light in his eyes. "The sheriff said they were surrounded just before dawn at the Bar-T ranch house—one of the Association members. Not a one of them can get away."

"They won't be able to hold out long," Croley added. "We captured their baggage, and the only ammunition they have is what they carried with them."

"It should be gone already."

"Naw. Those Texas gunfighters carry belts of the stuff over their shoulders. And there was enough dynamite in those wagons to blow up half of Buffalo."

"Or enough to blow the whole Bar-T Ranch into Montana," Ira said with a shout.

"Don't get your hopes up. The sheriff has the wagons."

"All we need is one. We can load it up with dynamite and send it careening into the house. There won't be enough of those gunslingers left for the coyotes to find."

Eliza was afraid her gasp of horror had betrayed her presence, but the next sentence sent her scurrying back to her room.

"Get your niece over to the Baylis woman. There's a lot of men downstairs drinking themselves into a state fit to do anything. It'll be best not to have a female about to give them any ideas."

"What about Iris?"

"Let her take care of herself," Croley said coldly. "You just make sure Eliza stays put. There's going to be a lot of plans being made around here, plans she might not like, and I don't want her telling that Baylis woman or Sam Haughton."

"I'll see she doesn't say a word to anybody," Ira promised.

If Ira hadn't been so caught up in his own plans, he might have noticed Eliza was not acting like herself. That she meekly obeyed his rough command to follow him and not say a word to anybody should have been warning enough. Eliza's mind was already feverishly at work trying to figure out how she could get to the Bar-T Ranch and warn Cord. He might not love her any more, or want to marry her, but warning him was only a small repayment for the times he had helped her.

No one was at the Baylis home, but they found both Ella and Ed at the store doing a brisk business in firearms and ammunition. "Another few hours and there won't be a shell left in the place," she told Ira. "They've already cleaned out the other stores."

"Then you know why I want Eliza to stay with you," he said, being as ingratiating as he could. "Croley and I are going out to the Bar-T Ranch, and I'd feel a lot better if I knew she was safe."

"This is a lot of fuss and bother over nothing," huffed Ella. "She'd be more comfortable, and just as safe, in her own room, but if you want her to stay with me, I'll be happy to have her." She took off her apron. "I can't be gone from the store long, but I'll see that you get settled."

"I'm sorry to bother you," Eliza said when Ira had gone, "but Uncle and Mr. Blaine are worried the men at the saloon are drinking too heavily to be trusted in all this excitement."

302

"He might have something there, but not enough to drag you away from your own bed."

"Where is this place they're talking about?" Eliza inquired as innocently as she could. "I don't think I've ever heard of it."

"Probably not. It's about twenty-five miles south of here."

"Is it anywhere near the Matador?"

"No," Ella replied with a smile. "You know where the road out of town divides and the west fork leads past the Matador?" Eliza nodded. "Well, if you were to keep on the south fork another ten miles and then turn off to the left at the base of the red butte, you'd come across the Bar-T about five miles farther on."

"So they don't have any reason to go near the Matador?" Eliza asked.

"None at all. Now you stop worrying and make yourself comfortable. I'll be back as soon as I can. But with people rushing in to buy everything they can lay their hands on, it may be a while."

"Don't hurry on my account. I don't have to sing, so I can do anything I like. I might even take a nap."

Ella must have had even more on her mind than Ira, or she would have realized Eliza hadn't been up more than a few hours and couldn't possibly need a nap, especially since there would be no need to stay up late. But she pushed the whole thing out of her mind and hurried back to the store, worried over what this latest piece of violence would mean to the people of Buffalo.

Eliza waited just long enough to be sure Ella wouldn't come back. She knew she couldn't go to the livery stable without being seen, nor could she take the buggy without Croley or her father hearing about it before she got out of town. She was going to have to take one of the Baylis's horses, and she was going to have to ride rather than drive. That made her more than a little nervous, but this was no time to quibble. She would warn Cord if she had to ride bareback, and if she didn't hurry Croley and Ira might get there first.

Eliza hurried from the house and down to the barn where the Baylis's horses were stabled. Very few people kept their own horses in town, but the store had so many shipments to send out it was easier to maintain their own teams than rent

303

from the livery stable. "No point in making Chet Hadley rich out of my own pocket," Ed Baylis always said.

Eliza was dismayed to discover that not only did Ed Baylis use mules instead of horses to draw his wagons, they were not unattended; a lad of about sixteen leaned against the barn watching the half-dozen sturdy beasts in the corral. But Eliza didn't have time to look for another conveyance or wait until he went home. She pulled the broad-rimmed straw hat farther down over her face in hopes he wouldn't recognize her, and walked up to him with an air of feigned confidence.

"I have an urgent errand to run for Mrs. Baylis," she told the boy, trying to make her voice sound like it was giving a command rather than asking for a favor. "Pick out the gentlest mule and saddle it for me."

"These mules ain't exactly used to being saddled, ma'am," the boy said politely. "They ain't never been hitched to anything but a wagon that I know of."

"I don't have time to take a wagon," she insisted impatiently. "I must have one saddled as soon as possible."

"Maybe you ought to borrow Mr. Ed's saddle horse."

"Where is it?"

"Up at the store. He likes to have it handy in case he has to go out sudden. It frets him to have to send a boy to tell me and then wait while I saddle it up."

"Then he won't want me to use it. I may not get back for some time yet."

"I don't know about these mules," the boy said, hesitating. "They can be real ornery critters."

"Please hurry," Eliza almost shouted. "I can't wait forever."

"Okay," the boy said, taking a saddle off the wall. "I'll saddle that old jennet. She won't be very quick, but maybe she won't leave you in a draw either." The chosen animal did not regard the proceedings with a kind eye, but she did allow the saddle to be placed on her back.

"Maybe I'd better sit on her first, just in case," the boy offered. Eliza was profoundly thankful he did, for the animal threw back her head, delivered herself of a shattering heehaw, and proceeded to tear around the corral as fast as her legs would carry her, running into any animal that happened to be in her path and lashing out with her heels for good measure. Then just as suddenly as she started, she stopped and walked placidly toward the fence. The boy got down, opened up the gate, and lead the now-quiet beast over to Eliza.

"She's okay now, ma 'am. She just had a few fidgets to work out first."

"Thank you," Eliza said faintly, and allowed the boy to help her into the saddle. She fully expected to be sent sailing through the cold, clean air, but the jennet stood quietly, and then set off at a trot that threatened to rattle loose every bone in Eliza's body.

Yet Eliza felt better than she had for a long time. After weeks of indecision, it was a relief to have made up her mind about something, but she was tortured by the fear she might not arrive in time, or if she did, Cord might not still think well enough of her to heed her warning. Even worse, he might think she was acting with her uncle against him. And why shouldn't he? Hadn't she sided with Ira against him several times already?

No one besides Lucy and Ella knew of the months of anguish she had endured, the sleepless nights, the torturing doubt that never for one minute ceased to act upon her tender self-esteem like a corrosive acid, drop by scalding drop scarring her soul forever. No, her pride had forced her to keep this agonizing indecision to herself, to shield from Cord the only information which might have redeemed her in his eyes. She didn't care what anyone else might believe. They could think her the most heartless and capricious female in existence if only Cord would trust her once again, would open his arms to shelter her, would open his heart to give her sanctuary. Secure in the embrace of his love, she could and would endure anything, face anything, dare anything. Without it? Well, there wasn't much she could think of that mattered at all.

Eliza thought the trip would never end. For hours she saw no one at all, but after she turned away from the fork leading to the Matador, she was met and passed by several men, all heading toward the Bar-T Ranch. She kept her head low and answered any greeting with a shake or nod of her head, and the riders rode on, their horses quickly outdistancing her

305

mount.

Long before she could see the ranch buildings, Eliza heard the sounds of sporadic gunfire coming over the hills. There was nothing to stop the sound, and it rolled on for miles, teasing her into thinking she was much closer than she was.

When she at last came upon the scene she was nonplussed. There were men everywhere, hundreds of them, everyone armed and everyone firing into the small ranch house in the distance. Eliza rode around to the other side, but the cordon of men offered no break, no opening she could get through, and she ended up right back where she started, unable to get through to the man she now realized she loved above all loyalties and allegiances. In desperation, she approached a young man she had never seen before, hoping he'd never seen her either.

"I have to speak to someone inside that house," she said as the flabbergasted young man gaped to find himself face to face with a stunning beauty in the middle of a range war. "Can you ask them to stop shooting long enough for me to go in?" The poor man tried to gather his shattered wits.

"Go in there?" he echoed, aghast. "That'd be sure death. We've got these killers surrounded. Not a single one of them is going to get away."

Eliza's throat closed. "But you've got one man in there by mistake."

"Ain't nobody there by mistake, ma'am, and nobody's getting out. There's over two hundred men with rifles aimed at the house, and there'll be another hundred or so before this time tomorrow."

"But I've got to warn him," Eliza insisted. She tried to move past the young man, but he pulled her back. Eliza's hat fell off, revealing the full extent of her beauty, and he was so shocked he nearly let her go.

"You can't go in there," he stammered.

"But he'll be killed," Eliza groaned, near hysterics.

"Nobody's going to get killed unless they do something foolish. We're just holding them here until the sheriff can decide what to do with them. He's still over at the Lazy C." He cast an eye in the direction of some of the men. "He'd better get here soon, though. Some of the boys are so riled up they might not remember when to stop."

"But they *are* going to kill him. I heard them talking about blowing them up with dynamite."

"They can't do nothing like that. Even if they had the sticks, there isn't a man alive that could heave it that far."

"You've got to let me go," Eliza said, her voice breaking with sobs. "My fiancé's in there, and I've got to get him out."

"A nice lady like you can't be engaged to any of those rascals."

"I told you, he was in there by mistake."

"How?" he demanded, looking older than his few years. "Who could come to be in there by mistake?"

"Cord Stedman," she said at last. "I don't know how he came to be here, but I've got to talk to him."

"I thought I knew you. You're Belle Sage," he said, pleased at his feat of memory. "But I heard tell you and him busted up."

"That was all a mistake," Eliza answered, becoming more frantic by the minute.

"You can relax, ma'am. There's nothing to worry about."

"Relax? You don't know my uncle's friends. They're on their way here right now. I know, because I heard them."

"That's as may be, but they ain't going to do Cord Stedman any harm, no matter what they do."

"But who's going to stop them?"

"Nobody." He could see that Eliza was coming dangerously close to the end of her rope. "Cord Stedman ain't anywhere near here. As far as I know, he's at the Matador getting ready to set down to his supper. Something I could do with a little of myself. It's been a long day."

"Are you sure?" she demanded, miraculously revived. "I've got to know for *sure*."

"I don't know for sure he's setting down to supper, but I do know he ain't here, because I asked him to come and he said he wouldn't."

"Where did you see him? When was it?"

"Sometime this morning when I rode by his place. I told him what was happening and asked him to come help. He said he'd help us round up our cattle, but he wanted no part of people taking shots at each other like it was a turkey shoot."

307

"How do I get to the Matador?"

"You go back along the road until you come to the fork going west."

"That's nearly twenty miles. Isn't there a shorter way?"

"You could go over those hills, but there's no track to follow, and it's real easy to get lost."

"I'll chance it." The boy continued to protest, but when he saw that Eliza was determined, he gave in and described the route as carefully as he could. Eliza was so impatient to be on her way she had difficulty paying attention, but he made her repeat the directions, and wouldn't let her go until he was satisfied she knew them by memory.

"You tell him he's better off staying at home," the young man called after her. "I wish to hell I'd done the same."

Eliza set off, urging her reluctant mount into a canter. The sun was getting low, turning the endless sky brilliant shades of orange and purple, but its beauty was lost on Eliza. All she could think of was reaching Cord as soon as possible. The flood of relief that swept over her when she learned he was still at the Matador had washed away all of her doubt, and she could hardly wait to see him, to throw herself in his arms and pour out all the love that had been stored up inside her like water behind a dam.

She followed the light track until she came to a shallow creek. At that point the trail turned abruptly south and Eliza struck out over the hills, looking for the landmarks so carefully described by the young man and trying to keep herself pointed directly into the setting sun.

But Eliza soon discovered that every hill, rise, or gully looked the same to her, and even when she had to go hundreds of yards out of her way to go around some obstacle, she still seemed to be heading directly into the sun. She tried in vain to decide whether she had passed the dip with the twenty-degree rise, or whether it was still ahead. She kept urging her tired mount on, but the poor beast had traveled over thirty miles and was rapidly nearing exhaustion.

At last the jennet stopped and Eliza didn't try to force her to go on. She studied the landscape for anything resembling the landmarks the young man described, but could see nothing besides endless hills, each exactly like the other. A coyote howled in the distance and chills ran down her spine; she was completely lost, her mount was exhausted, and she had no idea how to survive a night on the open plains.

Chapter 33

Eliza slid off the jennet. There was still another hour of sunlight, enough time to make one last attempt to find the road. She chose the highest hill and began walking toward it. The jennet followed willingly enough when it discovered it didn't have to carry its human burden. The climb was long and tiring, but the view from the summit was truly magnificent, and for a moment Eliza forgot her fear in awe of the panorama of the open plain all around her. Rolling hills, turned blue by the evening dusk, stretched before her as far as she could see, and scattered cows grazed contentedly, unmindful of the coming night or the cold that caused Eliza to shiver.

The darkening sky convinced Eliza rain was likely and she must find shelter for herself and some way to secure her mule; if it wandered off she would never get back to town. Already her shoes were badly torn and blisters were forming on her feet, but to her surprise, she didn't feel like she wanted to cry or give up. She was furious with herself for having no more ability to distinguish landmarks than the rankest tenderfoot, and afraid of what might happen to her during the long night, but she was keenly alert and spilling over with energy.

The first thing she had to do was find a stream. Both she and her mount needed water. Eliza remounted, but she had gone only a short distance when she saw a man suddenly appear atop the crest of a distant hill and ride swiftly along its ridge. She was of two minds whether to attract his attention, but common sense told her she'd most likely be better off with a stranger than sleeping in the open. She applied the reins to her mount's rump, dug her heels into its sides, and set off hoping to intercept the rider before he could disappear.

But he saw her long before she was within calling distance and pulled up; then seeing her progress was slow, he galloped in her direction.

"Miss Sage," Royce exclaimed upon getting close enough to recognize her, for it was the same cowboy who had terrified Eliza at the creek. "What are you doing out here by yourself?"

"Getting lost," admitted Eliza, trying not to show her tremendous relief. "I was given the most careful directions, but all these ridges and canyons look alike. I can't find the road I was assured would take me to the ranch without any possibility of a wrong turn."

"You're too far south. You should have turned at the red butte."

"That's what I tried to do, but every butte I passed was the same rusty orange. Not one of them looked the least bit red."

Royce laughed. "I guess they *do* look alike. Never mind. Come with me." He looked inquisitively at the jennet. "Why are you riding a mule?"

"Every horse in town was already taken by somebody rushing off to the Bar-T Ranch."

Royce's mood changed swiftly. "You shouldn't be out here alone."

"I know, but I have an important message for Mr. Stedman, and I was told he was at the Bar-T." The boy's face grew stern.

"Mr. Stedman won't have any part of that fight. He says if those fools want to kill each other, who's he to try and stop them."

"Certainly a practical point of view, but not very civic-minded."

"There ain't nobody takes an interest in Mr. Stedman unless they want something from him. The rest of the time one side tries to steal his cattle with the help of the law, and the other side tries to take them without. But he beat them both, and now he's so powerful they're both after his help.

Mr. Stedman said they got into this mess by themselves, so they could get themselves out." Royce continued to deliver more opinions than Cord had been known to express in a lifetime, and Eliza had begun to wonder just where truth and fiction met when they topped a rise and the Matador came into view.

"Do you mean I was barely a mile away all the time, and I was already trying to figure out how to get through the night without freezing?"

"You'd be more likely to catch pneumonia," said Royce, pointing to the deep purple sky and the stirring tree limbs. "We're in for some rain."

"I'd race you to the house, but I don't think this poor beast could stay on her feet that long."

"I'm surprised you managed to get this far," Royce said with the natural scorn of a cowboy for anything other than a true cow pony, but the mule had borne Eliza faithfully and she gave it a friendly pat on the neck.

The rain started before they reached the house, and Ginny greeted a dripping Eliza with such loud exclamations Cord emerged from his office to discover the cause of the commotion.

Eliza heard the sound of his boots on the polished wood floors and she froze. Without looking up she knew it was Cord; the electricity of his presence was unmistakable. For a split second she panicked, afraid of what he might do, of what she might see in his eyes, but when she looked up, there was none of the hardness she feared. Inexplicably, there was the same warm smile of invitation, the same look of hunger, that same quiet, unconquerable strength; there were no questions, just acceptance.

"I got lost," she said, losing control over her brain. His fixed gaze, his absolute immobility, further unhinged her. "Then I got wet, which seemed an unnecessary reminder not to travel the plains at night."

"You've got to get out of those wet things this minute," Ginny said, cutting off any response Cord might have made. "I'll have the food heated and back on the table before you can turn around. Nothing of mine will fit you, but some of Susan's things are still here." Apparently Susan

312

had also given Ginny a more favorable view of Eliza because there was none of the anger Ginny had displayed earlier.

Eliza followed Ginny up the stairs in a daze. Outside the thunder crashed around the house, lighting up the hills so often it seemed almost day. The rain came down in torrents, causing Eliza to remember the supperless young man at the Bar-T Ranch who had helped her and to hope he had found shelter for the night.

But she had few thoughts for anyone else tonight except the huge, silent man waiting downstairs who could grant or deny all that she had ever wanted. There was little to do beyond dry her hair and try to make the borrowed dress look as though it fit her, yet she lingered over her preparations, putting off the final moment when she would come face to face with Cord. What could she say? How should she tell him of her change of heart?

He was waiting at the bottom of the stairs for her. The aromas coming from the steaming dishes momentarily distracted her attention from his powerful presence and radiating sexuality, but it didn't take her long to take the edge off her hunger, and when Ginny placed coffee on the table and disappeared to the kitchen, she could delay no longer.

"I suppose you're wondering what I'm doing out there alone," she began.

"No." That monosyllable threw her thoughts into disarray. Was his love so completely dead he was no longer interested in what happened to her?

"I suppose I deserve that, especially after the way I treated you in town last week. I was angry, but I guess you knew that. I wouldn't blame you if you never cared what happened to me again."

"I'll always care what happens to you," Cord said, in the same even, contained voice Eliza had come to dislike. Why couldn't he lose control just once? Why did he have to maintain that Spartan front while she made a fool of herself? "I don't care what brought you here as long as you're here."

"I can't stay," Eliza said foolishly, knowing the dark and the rain made the trip back to town utterly out of the

313

question.

"I've imagined us sitting like this, discussing the little things that happened during the day, knowing tomorrow and the day after would be the same."

Eliza swallowed too much of her coffee and burned her throat. "I've been meaning to talk to you about Uncle Ira," she said, keeping her head lowered.

"It doesn't matter anymore."

"Yes, it does. This is terribly hard for me to say so please don't stop me until I finish. I'm not sure I'll get it said if I stop."

Cord nodded agreement.

"I was terribly confused and upset when you had Uncle Ira arrested. When he admitted his guilt, I was humiliated. Then you dragged me out to that corral and *proved* he was nothing but a common thief." Eliza shuddered at the memory. "I couldn't face that, and in my agony I struck out at you. *You* had done this to me, you had forced me to admit I was nothing but a cheap saloon singer and the niece of a common thief. I fell into a fit of self-pity and took it out on you. But you accepted every mean thing I did without a word of complaint, and I was so miserable that when the theatrical agent arrived, I made up my mind to leave Buffalo."

"What theatrical agent?" asked Cord, breaking his barely held silence.

"The one Lucy sent for. When you walked in, I knew I wanted to tell him I was going to stay and marry a big, stoic cowboy. But you left with Iris, and I was sure you didn't love me any longer. When I tried to tell you I was sorry your mother had died, I was sure of it. That's when Lucy told me I'd better make up my mind what I wanted."

"And did you?" Cord asked, a good bit of his stoic calm gone.

"I didn't have to," she said, looking up with a smile. "I fell in love with you the day you stopped those boys from burning our wagon, and even though I've acted like a fool, nothing has changed my mind."

Cord was out of his chair and dragging Eliza into a crushing embrace before she had time to rise to her feet.

She laughed and cried at the same time, but she clung to him with equal desperation, hardly able to believe his arms were around her once again, hardly able to credit how wonderful it felt.

"If Ella hadn't stopped me, I would have swooped down and carried you away."

"You should have. I would have been furious, but I think I would have recovered more quickly."

"Are you really sure?"

"Don't ever ask me that again. Don't let me have room for doubts. Fill my mind with so many wonderful memories nothing can ever make me leave you again."

"I'm glad you two have finally made up your differences," Ginny said, entering the dining room wearing a broad grin of satisfaction. "But what with being worn out and soaked to the skin, it's time Miss Smallwood went to bed. We don't want her sick on our hands and her uncle at the door accusing us of trying to murder her."

Cord let her go, but no more reluctantly than Eliza wanted to go. The brief moments had hardly been enough to reassure her everything was well between them at last. Everything within her cried out to return to his embrace, to nestle in the safety of his arms, but Ginny stood in their way.

"Don't stand gawking at each other. I've got her clothes laid out. It's time I got home to my own bed or you'll have Franklin up here looking for me. You two will have plenty of time to talk tomorrow."

Eliza allowed herself to be ushered upstairs, feeling as though ropes were tied to her body trying to pull her down again. Ginny was kind and helpful, but she talked too much; Eliza wanted to savor the few, brief moments she had been allowed with Cord, and to look forward to tomorrow and the many days to follow.

When at last she was safely tucked in, the lights were out, and Ginny was gone, she found her thoughts were too chaotic to sort out. Her mind was like a whirlwind, everything inside it being blown about at such a speed she couldn't grasp hold of anything. She didn't know how long she lay there, unable to think, unable to sleep, when the door to her room opened silently and the well-known silhouette filled the opening. As if by a miracle, her mind cleared and she knew exactly what she wanted.

"I've been waiting for you," she said softly, and drew back the covers to welcome Cord into her arms.

There was no time for words; there was no *need* for them. Their bodies spoke more eloquently than words of their longing for each other, of the rightness of their love. The passion they had held in check burst its bonds and carried them away with the swiftness of a flash flood racing down a narrow canyon. Eliza's whole body felt buffeted and bruised, like a raft going over a waterfall. The stinging pang of need and the painful release of months of tension were transformed by the blissful feel of his body against hers, of his lips and hands caressing her with feverish intensity, of his raging need of her, and her body exploded in a star-burst of aching desire.

Cord could not wait to tease her senses into bloom, to bring her slowly and tantalizingly to full sensual enjoyment of their union; he flung himself at her like floodwater at a boulder, wrapping himself around her, burying her in his surging, tumultuous need to reach his destination. He drove into her with knifing strokes, catapulting them toward a ragged, jarring release. It did not satisfy and it did not relieve, but it destroyed the ugliness between them and left them free to begin again.

"Iris was right," Cord said when he at last lay quiet beside her. "The third time was lucky."

"How can you lie next to me and talk about another woman?" she asked rolling up on one elbow. She playfully punched him in the side and he chuckled.

"Iris thought she was talking about herself, after you and Eugenia, but she didn't know the first love of my life was my mother. She was the first woman to turn her back on me." Eliza felt his body grow less pliant under her caressing fingertips. Afraid of saying the wrong thing, she waited for him to tell her what he wanted her to know.

"She was very beautiful, almost as beautiful as you, but very unhappy. My father owned a small hardware store he'd inherited from his father and he needed Mother to

316

work with him. For a while she was content, but soon after I was born her desire for pretty things drove my father to enlarge the store. He was killed in a fall from the roof. Mother had to work very hard to make a living by herself. We moved in with Grandpa, but she became discontented. I remember her warm and soft, clinging to me when she was most unhappy. Then a man came through town and filled her head with stories of the stage. The last memory I have is her telling me she was going on a trip and I was to be sure to obey Grandpa and not get into trouble. She ran away that night and none of us ever saw her again. She wrote a few letters at first, telling of her success and enclosing a little money for me, but soon those stopped and we heard nothing.

"She was Grandpa's only child, and it broke his heart. In a way I think he held himself responsible for my father's death. I watched him die little by little for ten long years; I left home the day he was buried. I never wanted anything to do with that town again. I sold everything we owned and used the money to take over the Matador loan.

"I never heard any more about her until Iris's mother wrote she died of consumption in some hotel, deserted by the last in a long line of men who kept her. She lived in Buffalo too. Buffalo, New York. Isn't that a joke?"

Tears were streaming down Eliza's face and she held tightly to Cord. For a while he did not respond, just lay in her arms like a wood carving, but slowly her warmth penetrated the shield he had erected around himself and he turned and clung tightly. Moments rolled by without any change of position, but Eliza was sure she could sense a letting go of the past, a release of the poison he had kept buried deep within, a poison that had miraculously failed to ruin this highly principled son of a tramp.

"Maybe you can understand now why I couldn't let you go no matter how many times you told me to go away. After Mother and Eugenia, I would never have had the courage to try again. Besides, I knew if you rejected me, it would be because of something wrong with me."

"There's nothing wrong with you," Eliza said, kissing him gently. "I learned that when, knowing it was my own fault I wasn't already your wife, I had to watch half the women of Buffalo panting after you."

"We can change that."

"Soon, but not tonight," she whispered provocatively, biting his ear. "I can think of other things I'd rather do." Cord tumbled her over and kissed her with such fervor it left her breathless. Then they made love again, but this time with the molten fire of two people who had found each other after a long struggle and knew they would never be separated again.

"And the only thing anybody can talk about is that blessed fight at the Bar-T," Ginny said as she took away the last of the breakfast dishes. "Seems the storm didn't do a thing to cool off their tempers."

"They'll soon get bored and let the sheriff take over," Cord said. "It's no fun sitting for hours waiting for someone else to make a move."

"If they don't kill each other first."

"I doubt anybody will get hurt much," Cord assured her. "They'll just keep sinking bullets into the wood until somebody calls the whole thing off. If the outlaws are surrounded, they'll have to give up before long. They'll soon be out of food and ammunition."

"I completely forgot why I came," Eliza acknowledged. "Uncle Ira and Mr. Blaine think you're in the Bar-T ranch house. They plan to kill you."

"How?"

"Someone captured a lot of dynamite. Uncle plans to put some in a wagon and run it into the house. It would break through the doors, wouldn't it?"

"It would reduce the whole place to match sticks," Cord said getting to his feet. "I've got to stop them. Shooting at each other isn't going to cause much trouble, but if they start blowing up people, we're in for a real bad time."

"But why do you have to go?" asked Eliza. "Why can't the marshal stop them?"

"Sometimes he's a worse hothead than the rest. He runs a few head of cattle himself, and if he gets to imagining

318

himself being wronged, no telling what he's liable to do. Some of those men don't have much sense, certainly not enough to know when to go home." He gave orders for Franklin to have two horses saddled immediately.

"I want you to ride to Fort McKinley and bring the Army," he told Eliza. "Then go straight back to town. I don't want anybody to know you've been here." Eliza begged, pleaded, and argued, but Cord would not be moved.

"But you don't owe them a thing, not after the way they've treated you."

"Maybe, but I feel partly responsible. If I hadn't agreed to lead this separate roundup, maybe this gang of vigilantes wouldn't have been sent here. God only knows there's plenty of rustlers I'd just as soon see swinging from the nearest tree, but starting a shooting war isn't the way to get rid of them." He gave her a swift kiss and lifted her up into the saddle. "Give this letter to Colonel Davis. Then go straight back to Ella and tell her I said to keep a better watch over you this time." Cord slapped the rump of the horse he'd exchanged for Eliza's jennet and sent the animal down the road at a smart gallop.

Eliza rejected the temptation to turn around and try to persuade one of Cord's men to take the message for her. Cord might have decided against taking his crew with him, but he would certainly have ordered them to see she didn't return to the Bar-T Ranch.

The road was easy to follow, and she must have ridden for nearly an hour, still arguing with herself, when she came upon a boy riding out with his dog and rifle in hopes of bagging some game for the supper pot. With sudden decision, Eliza called out to him. The boy, startled to find himself being hailed by a stranger, and a beautiful young female at that, showed such a pronounced tendency to stare Eliza lost her patience and spoke rather sharply.

"Do you know how to get to Fort McKinley?" she asked. He nodded in response. "Then take this letter to Colonel Davis. You're not to give it to anyone else, understand?"

"Yes, ma'am," the bemused youth answered.

"Tell him the invaders are surrounded at the Bar-T

319

ranch, and if he doesn't hurry, someone's going to get killed." The boy's eyes grew wider and wider. Eliza dug into her pocket. "Here's a dollar. Will that be enough for your dinner?"

"Yes, ma'am," the youth replied, looking more stunned than ever.

"Then be off. There's not much time." For a moment the boy was too dazed to move, but then he called to his dog, dug his heels into his horse's sides, and set off at a gallop. Eliza did the same in the opposite direction.

When Eliza at last came in sight of the encampment around the Bar-T Ranch, she could hear an occasional shot, but everything seemed quiet. She rode around the perimeter, looking for someone she knew and hoping Cord had decided not to come, but she had hardly gone five hundred yards when she saw a tight knot of men gathered around a peculiar-looking contraption of timbers built upon two stripped wagon beds. Using it as a shield, several men were slowly pushing it toward a steep decline in front of the besieged ranch house. Eliza rode closer and suddenly her heart leaped into her throat. Cord was tied to the front and exposed to the bullets of the invading force. With a scream of pure terror, Eliza drove her horse into the center of the gathering.

Chapter 34

Cord arrived at the Bar-T to find the men in a desultory mood. Some of them were beginning their third day and their enthusiasm was waning. The invaders had hastily nailed over the doors and windows at the first sign of attack, and the men's bullets buried themselves harmlessly in the thick boards; the outlaws were safe as long as their ammunition lasted. Some of the men hailed Cord's arrival, assuming he was going to join them, but they were disappointed when he advised them to turn their prisoners over to the sheriff or the marshal.

The message was not popular, but it was sensible, and common sense was beginning to return to men who, for two days and nights, had suffered miserably from lack of food and water and been soaked to the skin by icy rains. Cord worked his way around most of the circle, convincing the men they would be doing themselves a disservice if they lynched the trapped invaders. Then he came upon a group of men building a strange contraption under Ira Smallwood's direction, and the whole tenor of the situation changed quite suddenly.

One glance at Cord was enough to break the last bonds of Ira's restraint. "There's the man who's responsible for bringing these killers among us," he yelled. "We ought to kill him where he stands." Ira pulled his gun, apparently intending to do just that, but a man next to him pinned his arm behind him and took his gun away.

"You can't go shooting people in cold blood," the man said, but he eyed Cord with obvious distrust.

"That's how they killed Lem and Bucky. They burned them out and shot them like cornered rabbits."

"That's how Keller and Frater died," another added. "Only they was shot in the back."

"I had nothing to do with those killings, and you know it," Cord said, engaging Ira's eyes with his own. "I hadn't even intended to come out here until I heard you planned to blow up the ranch house. I had to try and put a stop to that."

"Why?" asked one of the men suspiciously.

"Because you'll be doing yourselves and Johnson County a disservice if you kill these men."

"That's what they were meaning to do to us."

"It doesn't matter to the law what they intended to do. They're only guilty when they've done it."

"They killed Lem and Bucky."

"Then turn them over to Sheriff Hooker and let the courts decide what to do with them."

"Nobody's been hung for those other murders yet."

"You still can't take the law into your own hands. We've only been a state for two years, and if we start hanging people without a trial, Washington is going to do something we won't like." Cord had been looking about him as he talked and he didn't like what he saw. He recognized a few honest farmers, but the others were members of Croley's gang, and Croley had an even more substantial score to settle with Cord than Ira. Cord was beginning to wish he'd stuck by his original decision to bring his men along; he didn't like the odds against him.

"Don't listen to a word he says," Ira raged. "He's an agent for the Association. He's just trying to save his own men."

"I'm on their blacklist at the moment. And that was even before I agreed to lead the independent roundup."

"That's right."

"It's all a trick to make you think he was on your side when all the while he was working for the Association."

"How do you figure that?" asked one of the small number of faces not in Croley's pay.

"If he leads that roundup, the Association has an excuse to send in their hired murderers and tell the Governor they

322

were only saving themselves from being robbed."

"That's just your hatred talking, Ira. Everybody knows you've been against me since you came to town."

"He makes a lot of sense to me," said a man Cord didn't recognize. There was a good deal of mumbling, but no one seemed sure what to do next.

"You know you have no proof," Cord said, boldly facing the tightening circle. "I've stuck to my own because neither side trusted me, and you both tried to pick my bones." His eyes bored into Ira. "And you have twice tried to steal from me."

"You're just trying to make us forget you're the Association's spy," stormed Ira, not the least abashed.

"Can you prove it?"

"Can you deny Sanford Burton invited you to a secret meeting in his back room last month?" The cold, ironical voice belonged to Croley, and with his arrival came a deepening chill in the mood. "Can you deny that meeting took place just before a second meeting where you agreed to lead the independent roundup? Can you deny the second meeting was called and presided over by your friend and employee Sam Haughton?" The mood was turning ugly fast. Even the few who had been willing to give Cord the benefit of the doubt were beginning to wonder now.

"I walked out of that first meeting," Cord said fearlessly. "I didn't know what they had in mind, but I wanted no part of it."

"And you expect us to believe you?" thundered Ira.

"Why shouldn't you? I've done nothing except defend my own property." The unshakable quality of his voice gave pause to some.

"You've driven helpless farmers off any land you wanted, your men have nearly killed innocent cowboys, and now you've given these hired killers a list of our names, names of people to murder in *cold blood!*"

"If there is such a list, your name must be near the top."

"Tie him to the wagon," screamed Ira. The men surged forward, then stopped almost as quickly. Cord held a gun in each hand, one pointed at Ira and the other at Croley.

"There are too many of you, but I'll get you two before

anyone lays a hand on me. Those of you who are honest farmers and homesteaders look around. Do you recognize more than half a dozen faces? Do you wonder who these men are, and why strangers should be so interested in defending you? They're Croley's men, a paid gang of rustlers, who have been systematically preying on all our herds, large and small. They kill at night and sell the meat the next day. How many times have you have found a butchered cow or steer? These are the men responsible."

Several pairs of eyes rolled nervously from side to side, but rustlers outnumbered honest men, and Cord's guns held them as firmly in place as they did the rustlers. Then a shot sounded from behind Cord and he fell to the ground, his guns falling uselessly at his side.

"Shot in the back like he deserves," crowed Ira, triumphant at last.

Croley bent over the body. "Your aim's no better than it ever was, Roy," he said to a man stepping up from a small depression where he had been asleep after standing the night watch. "You only hit him in the shoulder."

"Tie him to the wagon," Ira said. "He won't escape this time."

"We ain't got no right to do that," said one of the farmers, plucking up enough courage to speak up.

"Anybody who doesn't like what he sees had better watch the fight from another ridge," Croley said, facing the group around him. "And anybody getting in the way is liable to find himself sitting next to Stedman." Nobody moved, but when Croley turned his attention to moving Cord's inert body, several men wandered away from the group as inconspicuously as possible.

They had just finished securing Cord to the wagon when Eliza saw them. Her terrified scream and the confusion created by her riding her horse into the heart of the group arrested their motion.

"Stop!" she cried, falling from the saddle of the rearing horse. "This is murder."

"Stay out of the way," Ira ordered, attempting to grab hold of her. "He's finally going to get what's been coming to him."

"You'll all be hanged," she called, evading her uncle's clutches.

"There won't be any evidence," Croley said quietly. Eliza gaped at Croley and then her uncle, truly horrified at what they intended to do.

"Are all of you so heartless that you can watch a man be killed for no reason at all?" she implored, turning to the impassive faces around her.

"You're wasting your time," Croley told her. "These are my men."

"You mean your *rustlers*, don't you?" she spat, turning on him like a wildcat. "Men you pay to steal what other men work for." Scorn dripped from her voice. "The money from the saloon wasn't enough. You had to have more."

"It started before you came, when the saloon was losing money. Just think, if you'd come a little sooner, you might have saved me," Croley said sarcastically.

"No one can save you because no one made you steal."

"We're wasting time," Ira said impatiently. "Let's get on with it."

"Don't be in such a hurry," Croley said. "I'd like to negotiate a little. Maybe your niece would like to bargain for her boyfriend's life."

"What do you want?" Eliza asked, dread in her heart.

"You, my dear."

"I'll never marry you," Eliza shouted, recoiling in revulsion. "I'd rather die first."

"But you won't be the one to die. It'll be your boyfriend." Eliza looked at Cord, bound and bleeding, and knew if she didn't do something he would soon be dead. She didn't trust Croley to keep his promise, but nothing would matter if Cord were dead.

"I can give her to you if you want her that bad," Ira said. "She's underage. One of your crooked judges won't mind hearing her say *I do* even if she is in a dead faint. Now come on. I've been wanting to see Stedman dead for close to a year now."

"Looks like you've lost your bargaining chip," Croley drawled, grinning wickedly. "Your uncle offers a better bargain."

"You would murder him?" she asked Ira. "After he let you get away twice?"

"I would murder him with my own hands if necessary." Eliza realized from the look in her uncle's eye he didn't know what he was doing. He had nursed his hatred for Cord so long, prompted by Croley, he couldn't see reason. If he wasn't completely mad, he was perilously close.

"Then you'll have to kill me too," she informed him, and began to climb up on the wagon. A gathering audience watched from a distance. They were horrified when Eliza climbed up on the wagon, but no less so when Croley pulled her down so roughly she stumbled and fell.

"Keep her out of the way," Croley ordered one of his men, and a large, burly man pulled Eliza to her feet and held her firmly while Croley attached fuses to a dozen sticks of dynamite. "Now let's get this thing to the top of the ridge. We can't light it till it's rolling down the other side."

Eliza begged and pleaded, but the men laboriously pushed the double wagon up the incline. The gathering circle of onlookers followed, muttering among themselves; Eliza's efforts only seemed to drive Ira to greater frenzy.

"You ought to be ashamed to let people know you prefer Cord Stedman to your own flesh and blood," Ira told her.

"I'd prefer a rattlesnake to you," Eliza shouted at him. "You're a liar, a thief, and now a murderer. I'll tell the sheriff. I'll even go to the governor if I have to go to."

"You'd better give some thought for your own safety," growled Croley, his beady eyes full of evil.

"I don't care. Nothing, do you hear me, *nothing* will stop me!"

"Everyone can be stopped, one way or another," Croley snarled dangerously, and turned back to his work; no one took notice of two more horses arriving at a gallop. People had been coming and going for days; the most compelling drama of the siege was happening right before their eyes.

"Halt!" The order was given by a voice used to being obeyed, and even Ira paused. The gathering looked up in shocked surprise to see Colonel Davis, commander of Fort McKinley, dismounting from a badly lathered horse; Iris O'Sullivan was right behind him.

"The United States Army is in charge now," he said, "and no one on either side will be harmed."

"And how do you proposed to enforce that order, you being but one man among twenty?" Ira demanded, infuriated by the unexpected interference.

"That's how," Colonel Davis said, pointing to a long column of soldiers coming across the ridge a mile or so distant. "Now clear away that dynamite, and untie that man."

"No," screamed Ira. "I won't be cheated now." He sprang for the wagon and released the break, snapping the handle as he did so. Then as the wagon started to roll down the hill, he lit the fuses; at once they began to sparkle brightly.

"You're too late," he yelled, a fanatical light in his eyes.

With a scream that raised the hair on the necks of everyone present, Eliza bit into the arm of the man holding her, and the instant his grip relaxed she broke away and raced down the hill after the runaway wagon.

"Eliza, don't!" screamed Iris.

"Somebody stop that woman," Colonel Davis ordered, but no one wanted to risk his life chasing after a wagon careening down a hill and loaded with a dozen sticks of dynamite. They watched incredulously as Eliza raced after the wagon until she was able to grab hold of the low rail. Heedless of the stones and brambles that bruised and tore at her flesh, Eliza pulled herself up on to the wagon bed. It was almost impossible to stay on the wagon as it lurched over stones and uneven ground, but she clawed her way toward the sparks, moving ever closer to the dynamite. With one clean jerk, she pulled the fuses out, caps and all, and flung them to the ground, where they went off in a series of harmless pops. Then, after having thrown the dynamite from the wagon, she stood up and embraced the still-unconscious Cord, ready to die at his side.

Chapter 35

Eliza sat propped up on five pillows in Ella's spare bedroom while Lucy fed her a thick soup. Standing guard at the end of the bed with arms akimbo, Ella superintended the proceedings, a look of motherly pride on her broad face.

"For a gal who used to be too shy to open her mouth in public, you sure set Buffalo on its ear this time. Every household in three counties is talking about what you did."

"They're not talking of anything else in the saloon either," added Lucy. "There's almost more people down there now than used to come hear you sing. You're more popular than Annie Oakley."

"But are you sure Cord's all right?" Eliza asked, arresting Lucy's spoon long enough to get the question out.

"I don't imagine it's too comfortable to be going around with a bullet hole in his shoulder, but he was tied so tight to that contraption nothing could have pried him loose. It was you who went flying through the air and has been lying here with a concussion for three days."

"I shouldn't be lying here at all," she said with a vain effort to sit up. "Who's going to take care of him?"

"Ginny Franklin, and she can do a better job of it than you can in your condition," Ella stated uncompromisingly. "If I know Cord, he's already up and around. You lie back and eat your soup. If you don't stay quiet, you'll have scrambled brains for the rest of your life."

"What about the invaders?"

"The soldiers hauled them off to the fort. But the colonel says he can't do anything except keep those gun-toting renegades in protective custody, just like they weren't the ones

328

who started all the trouble in the first place."

"What did they do to Uncle Ira?" Eliza had to know.

"Not a blessed thing!" Ella declared, utterly disgusted. "There's not a man in Buffalo who seems to know *how* Cord got tied to that rig. To hear them tell it, he must have tied himself up before he passed out, and that hole in his shoulder just appeared by magic. Spineless cowards is what they are, afraid of I don't know what. The colonel and Iris saw Ira light the dynamite, but the colonel insists he has his hands full with the invaders, and it's up to Joe Hooker to deal with Croley and your uncle. But the sheriff didn't do a thing when he had the chance, and now that the county's gone crazy all around him, he *can't* do anything."

"What do you mean, gone crazy?"

"I don't know what I mean because I don't stick my nose outside the store unless I have to, but I hear tell a lot of shiftless scalawags are coming in from all around and running off whole herds and nobody dares stop them. They also ransacked a few ranch houses and stole anything that took their fancy. You don't see our good sheriff—or the marshal, for that matter—trying to put a stop to it. I'm afraid some of the local boys have joined in on the scavenging, but then I'm not too surprised. If they're going to be taken for rustlers, they figure they might as well act like it."

"Are they stealing Cord's cows?"

"Nobody's that crazy. Cord's men are so spitting mad at what Croley and Ira did, not to mention feeling guilty over letting Cord go out there by himself, they'd shoot anybody who came near one of their steers and forget the questions altogether."

Eliza settled back. "It seems things are no better than they were before."

"They're worse, but that was to be expected. The Army taking those killers away when everybody had the smell of blood in their nostrils made just about everybody crazy. They're getting even any way they can."

"And then getting drunk," added Lucy. "The Sweetwater's never been so full." A knock sounded at the door.

"It's open," thundered Ella, as though the door were a half mile away.

"I thought I'd drop by to see how you were doing," Iris said, presenting Eliza with a small bouquet of spring flowers. "Lucy told me you'd finally come around."

"I'm glad you came," Eliza said, smiling warmly. "I've been wanting to thank you for bringing the colonel in such a hurry."

"Forget it. I was there when the boy reached the fort, and I knew that if he really had seen you riding at a gallop, matters must be in desperate shape. I didn't know you *could* ride astride!"

"I never had before, but I got in a lot of practice in a hurry," Eliza said, smiling shyly.

"When's that colonel going to string up those foreigners?" Ella demanded, referring to the Texas gunmen. "He ought to hang every one of them."

"He doesn't have that kind of authority—that's for the civil courts to decide—so he's transferring them to Fort Russell for greater security."

"Great jumping Jehoshaphat," Ella exclaimed. "I never heard the like before. I hope I get that kind of treatment if I ever take to murdering honest people just because I'm paid to." She paused in midthought, and fixed her keen gaze on Iris. "And just what were you doing so handy to that Fort, Miss O'Sullivan?"

"I was visiting my little girl. She stays with the wife of one of the enlisted men."

"Seems to me she stayed in town when you first came here. And don't give me that old song and dance about fresh air. You had other fish to fry that day, and don't think I don't know it." Eliza was surprised to see Iris turn pink.

"Well, it's not general knowledge yet, but Colonel Davis has asked me to marry him," said Iris.

"So you did get your claws outa Mr. Cord," Lucy said.

"I never got them in, not even with Eliza's permission. If I hadn't grown up eight miles from Cord's hometown, he would never have bothered to speak to me except to ask about you," she said, turning to Eliza. "I know I'm nowhere near as pretty as you are—"

"Miss Eliza is *beautiful*," Lucy stated emphatically.

"Beautiful then. But it's not good for a girl's morale to

know she can do her best and a big hunk like Cord wouldn't notice whether she was male or female. I can take rejection, but I don't crave it."

"I suppose that means you'll stop working in the saloon?"

"Not right away, but it wouldn't be suitable for a colonel's wife. And of course there's the possibility he'll be given a new post."

"Then you make sure you get the knot tied first," Ella advised her. "Men have a mighty poor memory when they can't keep their eye on what it is they're supposed to be remembering."

"It didn't seem to bother Cord."

"Cord's just the opposite. The only thing he *can* see is what he wants, and telling him he can't have it is only going to make him try harder. But that's just like a man, always blowing too hot or too cold for comfort."

"Looks like we both get what we wanted," Iris said to Eliza.

"Looks like you did," agreed Ella, "but it's time we let Eliza get some rest, or she won't be leaving this bed for a month."

"I'll be up tomorrow," Eliza promised.

But Eliza was mistaken. Both Cord and Ira came to see her the next day, and the visits so depleted her strength she was thankful to have Ella announce she would have no further visitors until she was stronger.

Cord looked worn down and worried. "I'm glad I was out cold," he said with the reluctance of a man who made it a habit not to be indebted to anyone. "I would have blushed like a girl to see what you were put to to save my hide." Eliza tried to demur, but he wouldn't let her.

"I've had your exploits described by nearly every man at the Bar-T, and a few I suspect were safe at home, so you can save yourself the trouble of denying you took an awful risk. I'd give a lot to see you leap on a moving wagon, but I hope you never have any more dealings with dynamite. Do you know how close you came to getting killed?"

"All I could think of was getting rid of the dynamite." She didn't add that nothing would have mattered if he had died; he could see that in the way she stared at him and in the way her hands gripped the sheets.

"Apparently you have greater strength than you know. That first dynamite stick landed in a group of Croley's men. They scattered like a flock of prairie chickens, all the while straining their necks to see what you were going to do next." Eliza tried to smile, but Cord didn't miss the signs of fatigue.

"How is your shoulder?" she asked. "It's not good for you to be up so much."

"It's still a mite stiff, but as long as I don't try to spend the whole day in the saddle, it doesn't pain me too much. I was forced to use a buckboard for two days." A ghost of a smile lightened his expression. "I was almost ashamed to be seen in such a contraption, but the worst was when Ginny offered to drive me about."

Eliza's grin of response was a weak imitation of her usual smile.

"You need your rest," Cord said, bringing his visit to an end, "and I need to get back to the Matador before they send out a search party." He took Eliza's hands in his. "I don't want to embarrass you with my gratitude, but it's the first time anyone ever put my life before theirs, and I won't forget it." He kissed Eliza roughly and quickly, leaving her shaken but radiant.

Ira did not show similar restraint. Less than five minutes after he'd closed the door behind him, his upraised voice brought Ella and Lucy down upon him, and their combined fury drove him from the room, Ella giving him the strictest orders not to "set foot on my property again, or I'll take a shotgun to you faster than to a coyote in a henhouse."

"I have a right to see my own niece," he objected.

"As far as I'm concerned, Eliza doesn't have any relations," Ella decreed. "She sure doesn't need one that acts like a mad dog, biting and snapping at her until she's worse off than when she arrived here."

"I want her home where I can watch her."

"She's not setting foot out of this house until I say so," Ella informed him. "It was you and your hateful vengeance that put her here in the first place."

"I know why you're so anxious to have her back," said Lucy, pointing an accusing finger. "You want to make her sing."

"It can't hurt her to sing a few songs," Ira complained. "She can sit down if she wants."

"You're afraid you won't get much business without Eliza. I know what people are saying about you, and I heard Mr. Blaine gave you orders not to show your face downstairs. Miss Eliza kept telling you to leave Mr. Cord alone, but you wouldn't listen."

"It's Eliza's responsibility to sing—" Ira began, but Ella cut him off.

"You don't deserve a niece like Eliza! She's too kindhearted to tell you what a miserable little dab you are, but I'm not. You've bullied her for the last time. She's not singing one note until she's good and ready. And if she takes my advice, she'll never set foot in that saloon again. Now you get out and don't come pestering her again, or I won't let her out of bed for a month."

"You can't keep my own niece from me," Ira announced, firing up.

"See if you can get that sheriff to do something about it. *You* come around here again, and Eliza's going to be an orphan."

Eliza was much improved the next day, but Ella thought it was better to tell Susan Haughton to wait one more day. As it turned out, even though Eliza was anxious for visitors, things weren't any better. All anyone could talk about was the cold-blooded murder of the new foreman of one of the big ranches.

"And the worst of it is he hadn't set foot on the ranch. He hadn't even reached Buffalo," Susan added for emphasis. "Somebody shot him just for meanness. They shot him in the back too."

"I don't know what things are coming to," Ella lamented, finally forced to abandon her customary sanguine outlook. "I've lived through the War Between the States and more Indian wars than I care to remember, but never have I see men kill for sheer devilment. I always said people out here were rough and took a little getting used to, but they were honest and upright. I'm not so sure anymore."

"People are crazy with fear," Susan said. "Every day there's a new rumor. Either it's an invasion twice as big as the first on the way, or half the county is going to be arrested and hauled off to Cheyenne to stand trial."

"But that's no reason to go crazy. The fighting's over. The Association is defeated."

"Not yet. Ever since their hired guns got arrested, they've been trying to get President Harrison to declare martial law. Sam and I both have talked ourselves blue in the face, but people are still so mad about the invasion we can't get them to see this kind of lawlessness is playing into the Association's hands."

"What's martial law?" asked Eliza.

"They send in the Army with permission to shoot anybody who resists and hang people without a trial. The sheriff and the courts would be completely powerless. They've sent six hundred additional troops to the fort just this week."

"But that's worse than the invasion," Eliza exclaimed.

"You try and tell that to those hotheads, especially after they've been in the saloon for a couple of hours."

"You can be sure I won't be selling them any more ammunition," said Ella. "They can shoot each other to pieces if they must, but they won't do it with my bullets."

Two days later Cord came again. "I wanted to tell you I would be away for a few days."

Suddenly Eliza's heart was beating too rapidly. "Where are you going?" she asked uneasily.

"I'm taking two herds to Montana. My boys have been in the saddle around the clock for over a week. I've got to do something before they start acting crazy. We've closed up several herds to make them easier to watch, but there's not enough grass to keep them in one spot for more than a few days."

"I had no idea it was that bad for you too," Ella said.

"Some of the boys have been shot at. One got hit in the arm. The other night someone took aim at me."

Eliza turned white. "Will it never stop?" she exclaimed. "Has everybody gone crazy?"

"Just about. I warned people this was coming, that they

ought to be looking for ways to solve their differences instead of creating more, but nobody wanted to listen. Now they got what they wanted, though it's a lot worse than I expected."

"It was that foolish invasion," declared Ella. "I know these people. They're good folks at heart."

"I'll take your word for it," said Cord. "Right now there're enough bad ones out there to make it nearly impossible to protect my herds." He stood up. "Sam knows where to reach me. I'd rather you stayed here," he said to Eliza. His eyes suddenly became warm, and Eliza longed to reach out and pull him down to her side.

"She's not setting foot outside that door until I say so," Ella informed him, "and Ira Smallwood can cry and moan for his lost customers all the way to Douglas for all I care."

"As long as there's a new rumor afoot, there'll be enough new customers to make up for the loss of any old ones," Cord said. "You stay here and let Ella take care of you," he said, bending over to kiss Eliza on the lips. "When I get back, I intend to make taking care of you my permanent job."

Eliza wanted to cry out, to say anything that would bring him back, but she knew she couldn't. This was his work, a job he had to do.

Eliza walked along the plank walkway that fronted a row of buildings that included the Sweetwater Saloon. She was almost well, but after being in bed for a week she was as weak as a kitten. It felt a little strange to be up without leaning on a chair, table, or Lucy's arm every few steps, but she couldn't stay inside any longer. She probably shouldn't have gone this far, and if Ella or Lucy had been around they most certainly wouldn't have allowed her to leave the house alone, but it felt good to be out and breathe in the fresh air, and the walk would not have bothered her at all if it had not been for her notoriety.

Eliza never considered herself a celebrity. Everyone knew her because of her singing and her beauty, but the fact that she was secretly ashamed of one and didn't put much value in the other did much to help her keep her equilibrium. But nothing in her twenty years had prepared her to be pointed at and followed by a group of untidy urchins and roundly applauded by men who came out of saloons as she passed. She was so rattled she instinctively headed toward the safety of her room in the saloon. By the time she realized what she was doing, she had covered two thirds of the distance, and nothing would have made her retrace her steps to Ella's house.

"Yoo-hoo, Miss Sage," Amelia Craig called, virtually catapulting herself out of a shop in Eliza's wake and leaving her purchases to the clerk who had attended her. "Though I suppose I really should call you Miss Smallwood, Miss Sage being your stage name and young *ladies* preferring to be addressed in a proper manner, at least when they're not working, not in a saloon, that is."

"Please call me Miss Smallwood," Eliza told her, trying to recover her composure after the unexpected barrage.

"It doesn't really matter what I call you, because you're such a heroine everybody will know who I'm talking about. You're just about the most talked-about person in Wyoming. Why, they've even heard about you in Cheyenne."

Eliza blanched.

"And they should," Amelia declared enthusiastically. "Any young lady who would leap onto a runaway wagon and defend her fiancé from a horrible death with her own body should be talked about. Not that young ladies usually are called upon to leap upon wagons, or consider it a proper thing to do, but it was very brave of you just the same. I don't know how you did it. *I* never would have had the courage. Why I get gooseflesh every time my Horace mentions traveling as far as his sister's place, and that's just ten miles away. But I dare say you consider that no more than a morning's jaunt, compared to riding across half the county on a mule. I know one has to take what one can find, but I will never understand how you kept your dignity on that horrid animal. And astride! Well, I realize these are terrible times and that heroes—I beg your pardon, I meant to say heroines—rise above every difficulty, not letting any consideration stop them, but me ride a mule! Well, I just couldn't. You may call me a poor creature, and indeed I know I am, but I think I would faint if I were even forced to touch one.

336

As for throwing myself on a wagon load of dynamite! Well, all I can say is you are an amazingly brave woman. I don't see how you did it."

"It really wasn't so terribly hard."

"Well, I can see that falling down on some dynamite doesn't take much skill, but you must admit that you haven't been in the habit of leaping onto racing wagons every day. You must tell me how you did it."

"It had just started to move . . . I wasn't very far away . . . I really didn't stop to think how I did it."

"I can assure you I wouldn't know how to do such a thing without a great deal of thought. Your resourcefulness must come from farm rearing. Us city-bred folks are at a serious disadvantage."

A particularly well-scrubbed urchin pulled at her skirt.

"Henry, you know I've told you never to interrupt Mama when she's talking."

"Mr. Huggins wants to know if you want the milk fresh, or are you going to wait till it's clabber?"

"You tell Murty I'll thank him to give me none of his sass."

"I must be going," Eliza said feebly. "This is the first time I've been up."

"Shame on me. I forgot you've been a great invalid. You run along back to your bed. I'm sure everyone in town will be calling to tell you how proud they are of your brave deed now that they know you're up and about."

Certain she would have a relapse if she were accosted by another person, Eliza hurried down the street, entered the saloon by the back stair, and tottered along the hall to her rooms, feeling very much like a cornered rabbit. She opened the door to her parlor and came face to face with her uncle.

Chapter 36

"So you've finally decided to come back," he sneered, looking anything but pleased. "Or did that old battle-ax kick you out?"

Eliza was no longer surprised by her uncle's cruelty. "I went out for a walk because I was tired of being cooped up all day. Do you know some little boys followed me singing a song that put my whole history into silly verse? Then I ran into that awful Mrs. Craig."

"It's disgusting the way people have been carrying on, just like you didn't turn your back on your own flesh and blood."

Eliza was tired of the old complaint, and didn't even bother to answer. "I need some more clothes. Mrs. Baylis has finally agreed to let me get out of bed for most of the day, and I'm tired of the same two dresses."

"You're not going back. I need you here. With Sam gone and Iris getting above herself, we don't have anyone to attract customers these days."

"I'm not very strong yet. I wouldn't have come this far if those people hadn't scared me half out of my wits. Cord said you had more business than ever." She hadn't meant to mention his name, but he was a natural part of her thinking and it just slipped out.

"So you've been seeing him again, have you?" Ira exploded. "You're too weak to help your own kin, but you're strong enough to chase after that cocky pair of britches."

"He came by to see how I was doing." Eliza was going to have to tell her uncle sometime she had changed her mind and was going to marry Cord, but she didn't feel up to it now.

"You swore you'd never see him again."

"Can't you forget your hatred for one minute?" she demanded angrily. "I was nearly killed, yet all that upsets you is Cord Stedman coming by to thank me for saving his life."

"You brought it on yourself."

"*You* brought it on me, you and your blind, unreasoning certainty that Cord is behind everything bad that happens in Johnson County."

"He *is!*"

"Even if he were and I never wanted to see him again, I'd have done exactly as I did."

"You only did it because you can't stop thinking about him."

"I couldn't let any man die unfairly, especially not at the hands of my own uncle," she added wearily. "Not after he'd made a fool of himself before the whole town."

"Nobody calls me a fool," Ira said, straightening his thin body and adjusting his fancy clothes. "I've grown too rich."

"Nobody cares about your money. It'll disappear as fast as it came if you continue to make yourself a laughing-stock."

"Don't you dare talk to me like that, girl," he shouted. "People in this town look up to me."

"Then why did Croley order you not to show your face in the saloon?"

"There are plenty of people who listen to me now, especially since Stedman tried to save those killers."

"What for? Trying to kill a man who'd been shot in the back and tied up while he was unconscious? When did it become a praiseworthy act to blow up a helpless person?"

"They're listening now that Stedman says he's taking his cows to Montana. I know it's a cover for turning tail and running like the rest of his kind," Ira continued, ignoring her questions. "Now everybody knows him for the miserable informer he's been all along."

"He's doing it so he can watch the rest of his herd more carefully. You're making a big mistake if you think he's running away."

"You're afraid he won't come back. Then everybody will know what a shameless spectacle you made of yourself over him."

"I'm not afraid anymore, not of you or anybody else. I'm going to marry Cord and never sing in this saloon again," she added with increasing earnestness. "I *hate* it. Even after I stopped shaking every time I got up from the dinner table, I only did it because you needed me. There were times when I was so frightened it made me sick, but you never saw that, and you never saw how the men stared at me, thinking things I didn't dare let myself imagine. And when Cord defended me, you insisted he was costing you money, even after Croley told you it brought in even more customers. All you've been able to think about since you came to Buffalo is the saloon and your hatred for Cord. You never thought of me, certainly not of what I wanted or what was good for me. And everything that interfered with what *you* wanted was either proof of Cord's diabolical nature or evidence of my degenerate character.

"I've always known you didn't love me," Eliza said, swallowing an involuntary sob. "I knew I could never take the place of Aunt Sarah or Grant, but all those years when I was growing up, I thought if I worked hard you would learn to like me. But nothing I did ever satisfied you, and you never made me feel like anything except a burden to you. When we came here and Cord Stedman fell in love with me, my whole life changed. For the first time since Aunt Sarah died I knew what it was like to have someone want to take care of me, to be concerned for my happiness. I found friends and made a place for myself with the school. I *was* somebody, not just a nameless shadow who cooked and cleaned and then vanished until needed again.

"I tried to stick with you, but you wouldn't let me. This *thing* you have against Cord has made you so sick in your mind you strike out at everybody around you. I think you've taken to hating me almost as much as you hate him. When you lit that dynamite, you forced me to choose, something I probably never would have done if it hadn't happened so fast. But I chose Cord, and I'm moving in with Ella until we can be married. I'm never coming back here again. I hope you will visit us, but not if you mean to disparage Cord. I won't let you run down my husband."

Listening to the longest speech Eliza had made in her entire life in stunned silence, Ira realized she meant every word she said. In his mind's eye, he could see Cord laughing at him, and with every word Eliza spoke, Cord laughed harder until Ira couldn't stand it.

"There won't be any ranch or rich cowboy for you to marry," he jeered in a kind of half-crazy triumph. "While Stedman and his crew are away, we're going to run off every head of cattle he has left. He'll be a pauper." He glared defiantly at Eliza, not even remembering Croley had threatened to break his neck if he said a word about their plans.

"Do you mean after failing twice, you're going to make a fool of yourself again?" demanded Eliza, thunderstruck.

"Croley's gathered a crew that's double the size of Stedman's," Ira announced furiously between grinding teeth. "And they won't shy away from putting a bullet into anyone who gets in their way."

"What crew?" Eliza stammered. "Even Croley wouldn't dare to hire the outlaws who have been running loose lately. They're the same madmen who shot that poor foreman before he reached town."

"He was shot by his own men."

Eliza gave him a blank look.

"It's an Association ranch. The owners paid one of their cowboys to shoot him so they could blame it on us. Then the governor would bring in the Army."

"You're mad," Eliza said, putting into words what others had felt for some time. "Your hatred has completely destroyed your common sense."

"Where are you going? Ira demanded sharply as she turned toward the door.

"I'm going to tell the sheriff of this extremely foolish plot before anybody else gets hurt."

"You mean you're going to warn Cord's men," Ira accused, grabbing her by the arm.

"I doubt I could ride that far, even in a buckboard,"

Eliza said, jerking and twisting her arm, but failing to free it from Ira's surprisingly strong grasp. "This is the sheriff's job."

"You're not going to the sheriff or anybody else," Ira said, half desperate, wholly furious. "You're going to stay right here."

"No I'm not," contradicted Eliza. Unable to free herself, Eliza jabbed the heel of her shoe into Ira's toes. Ira loosened his grip long enough for her to make a dash for the door, but he grabbed her from behind and slung her so hard toward the center of the room she stumbled over the rug and tumbled onto the sofa. Before she could get to her feet, he was on her, dragging her to her feet and shouting in her face.

"I'll beat you senseless before I let you spoil this plan. Stedman's fooled everybody for years, but at last he's going to pay."

"You'll have to hold me here yourself, because if you don't, I'm going to tell everybody I see my uncle is a thief, a shameless scoundrel. I'll shout it to every person on the street."

Ira struck Eliza hard, knocking her to the floor. She looked at him in unbelieving surprise, but when she put her hand to her mouth and saw the blood, her mind cleared and her bewilderment quickly vanished.

"You have just released me from my vow and any remaining loyalty I might have felt. From now on I'm going to treat you like any other senseless murderer."

"You won't do a damned thing," Ira swore, dragging her to her feet and pulling her, half walking and half stumbling after him, in the direction of her room. "I'm going to lock you up until I get back." He shoved Eliza through the doorway, intending to lock the door on her, but before he could find the key she was at the window. Ira yanked her back and slammed the window down so hard one of the panes cracked.

"Have it your way," he said roughly, and dragging her over to the bed, threw her down on it, and tied her hands behind her back through the brass tubes of the bedstead.

"You'll never get away with it," Eliza spat at him. "Cord

342

is smarter than all of you put together." Ira took a handkerchief out of his pocket and gagged her.

"His smartness won't help him if he's in Montana. And now you can't either. I'll untie you when I tell you how many cows *we* took to Montana, cows bearing the Matador brand." He slammed the door behind him and Eliza heard the key turn in the lock. He moved about in the parlor for the next few minutes, then left, locking the door to the apartment as well.

Eliza felt like kicking herself. Why hadn't she had the sense to keep quiet instead of announcing her intentions and giving him the opportunity to stop her. Her struggles caused her shoulders to ache unbearably, but every time she thought of quitting she remembered it was Cord who would suffer the most. However, she soon exhausted her limited strength and was forced to abandon the struggle. Tears rolled down her cheeks as she thought of Cord being robbed of all he had worked so hard to gain while she remained helpless.

Eliza had no idea how much time had passed when she was startled by a thunderous knocking at the door to their rooms. The gag prevented her from calling for help. She heard Ella Baylis's voice, soon joined by Iris's, calling her name, and all she could do was sit there, powerless, knowing the help she so desperately needed was just a few feet away. The voices stopped, and Eliza supposed Ella and Iris had decided to look elsewhere. How long would she have to wait until someone found her? Would it be too late to help Cord? She looked out the window; she couldn't see the sun from where she lay, but it must be getting on to midafternoon at least. It was doubtful anyone would come back before evening, if then, and by that time it might be too late to do anything at all.

Not many minutes had gone by when she again heard sounds at the door, but this time there was the turning of a key and several people entered the parlor.

"There's nobody here," said Ella, worried and clearly disappointed.

"But somebody's been here," Lucy declared. "That's Miss Eliza's jacket, and she's not in the habit of leaving her things on the floor." She looked around suspiciously. "Something else is not right either. I just feel it."

"Let's check the bedroom," suggested Iris. She was surprised to find the door locked.

"Whatever for?" wondered Lucy.

"Where's the key?" demanded Ella, whose suspicions were immediately aroused.

"I don't think there is one. Leastways, I never saw it."

"There's got to be one. The door's locked, isn't it?" That was undeniable. "Shush!" Ella said imperatively. "I think I hear something." Eliza was trying as hard as she could to throw her body about on the bed to make the springs or the bed frame squeak.

"She's in there," Ella stated. "That poor child is locked in her own room."

"But why?" asked Iris.

"There'll be time enough to ask that when we get her out. If there's no key, we'll have to break the door down."

"Don't you look at me like that," Lucy said, her voice rising in excitement. "I'm not throwing my old body against that door and breaking something that's not likely to ever get put right again."

"There must be some way we can bash it in."

"Wait," said Iris, struck by a thought. "If you never saw a key, maybe there wasn't one."

"The girl got too much sun riding back and forth to that fort," Ella said with a groan.

"I mean maybe the same key fits both doors."

"What did you do with your key?" Ella demanded, as Lucy took the key out of her pocket and put it in the lock. It turned effortlessly, and the three women stampeded into the room only to be brought up short by the sight of an exhausted and tearful Eliza gagged and bound to the bed.

"The beast!" exclaimed Iris as Lucy and Ella hurried to release Eliza.

"Find the sheriff at once," Eliza said as soon as the gag was out of her mouth. "Croley plans to run off Cord's herd while he's in Montana. I think they mean to try for tonight."

"Cord pays his men a good wage to look after his property," said Ella, untying the last bond on Eliza's wrists. "You let them worry about rustlers. I'm going to get you home and between sheets before you collapse of a brain fever."

"I can't, not until I've talked to the sheriff. Nobody at the Matador suspects anything, much less that it may come tonight. And Uncle Ira says they have twice as many men as Cord."

"You might as well see if you can find that worthless sheriff, Iris," Ella sniffed. "Though what good you think he can do is beyond me."

Eliza couldn't sit still or keep her mind on anything during the wait for the sheriff, but long before the reluctant steps of Sheriff Hooker could be heard following the more eager ones of Iris up the hall, Ella and Lucy had dragged everything belonging to Eliza from its closet, drawer, or wardrobe, packed it up, and sent it off to Ella's house.

"I don't want you to have any reason to set foot in this place ever again," Ella stated emphatically.

"I got the dratted man at last," Iris said, disgust rampant in her tone. "I could have brought the whole Army with less effort and in half the time." Susan Haughton followed in their wake.

"You've got to take as many men as you can and go straight to the Matador," Eliza stated, pouncing on Joe before the man was barely across the threshold. "Croley's gang is going to try to steal Cord's herd tonight."

"Like I told this lady," Sheriff Hooker said, pointing to a very exasperated Iris, "I can't go busting out to Stedman's place and arrest everybody who sets foot on his land. A man is free to ride anywhere he wants as long as he doesn't cause trouble." The sheriff shifted his weight from foot to foot, tugged at his collar with two fingers, and looked uncomfortable. His job had never been easy, but during the last month it had become nearly impossible.

"My uncle *told* me they were going to take Cord's cows while he's gone," Eliza repeated, with emphasis. "That

345

means they have to do it in the next few nights."

"And that's another thing," Joe added. "I can't ask a bunch of men to sit in the dark for several nights. They have their own cows to look after."

"And well they should, for it's very little looking after you've been doing, Joe Hooker," intoned Ella, entering the fray. "If you don't do something, you'll never be elected sheriff again."

"All it will take is a few men," Eliza pointed out.

"It's not all that easy to get men to volunteer," Joe replied, looking more and more harassed.

"Then deputize them and make them go," urged Ella.

"I know Cord's men won't let their herds be taken without a fight," Eliza said, thinking of Franklin, and Royce and Sturgis. "They're likely to follow them all the way to Montana."

"Family men aren't anxious to get into the middle of a gunfight," Joe said.

"You're all cowards," Ella said emphatically. "Ever since that no-good bunch of cutthroats rolled into Johnson County, stealing and burning for the fun of it, you and every other so-called decent man in town have taken to hiding behind closed doors. You're going to have a hard time explaining what you've been doing when that scum turns on the law-abiding citizens."

"I'll go for the Army," volunteered Iris.

"You'd better get your men together and go with Eliza, Joe," Susan advised him. "A second gunfight is all Washington needs to be convinced the state's in rebellion. If the Army comes in, you'll lose any authority you have."

"And the Association will be just as mad at Cord as everyone else because he agreed to lead that roundup," Eliza said earnestly. "If they succeed in ruining him, you know there's nothing to stop them from smashing the rest of the ranchers and homesteaders and farmers around here."

Joe Hooker felt helpless and surrounded. He wasn't *afraid* to round up a posse; he doubted that he *could*.

"If you can't, or *won't*," Eliza stated, at last roused to fury by the sheriff's reluctance to take action, "then I'll go into every saloon in this town myself. I'll find out whether there are any men of courage left, or if they prefer talking and drinking to living up to their word. You can go back to your office and board up your door, Mr. Hooker. I will take them to the Matador myself."

"Now just a moment, Miss—"

"You're not setting one foot out of this town, Eliza Smallwood," Ella told her sternly. "You're going straight to bed."

"Not until I've warned Cord. Uncle Ira is the cause of all this trouble. If I hadn't sided with him against Cord, he'd probably be in jail right now, so in a way I'm responsible. I'd better get started now if I want to find enough men."

"I'm coming with you," declared Susan. "I know most of them already, and if you can't convince them, maybe I can shame them."

"And I'll see the colonel has the Army ready in case it's needed," Iris chimed in.

"How does it feel to see your job done by a pack of females, Joe?" Ella sneered, her contempt cutting through to the man's soul. "You're not going to be able to hold your head up when this gets out, and I'll make *sure* it does. Don't fool yourself by thinking they'll fail. Eliza's so popular right now she could raise an army to fight Sitting Bull all over again."

"You don't have to say any more, Ella," Joe said, pushed to the limit at last. "I'll get some men together."

"You've got to have at least twenty."

Joe hesitated.

"I'll come along if you think you'll need help," Eliza added.

"Of course he will," said Ella, rubbing salt into his wounded pride. "The man can't even get his deputies to do their job."

"I'll have two dozen men at the edge of town an hour before sundown, and I'll do it by myself."

"I'm coming along," said Susan. "I have a family here now. I have just a much of a stake as Eliza."

Joe didn't want any woman's help, but it was obvious

Susan was not going to be stopped.

"I'm going to the Matador," Eliza said, looking at Ella and Lucy rather than Joe.

"Then I'm coming too, 'cause you're gonna faint sure enough," declared Lucy.

"And I'm going to drive," stated Ella. "You're too weak, and I wouldn't trust Lucy with a pony cart."

"That's a good thing," agreed Lucy. "Cooking, sewing, and cleaning I can do, but I'm not sitting behind no horse and telling it to start running. I don't know how to talk to horses, and I've never been around one yet that didn't want to slow down when he ought to hurry up, or turn off to the right when any fool could see he ought to go to the left."

Joe Hooker gave up and fled. The companionship of Susan, however undesirable, was preferable to being surrounded by four women, not one of whom he could understand.

Chapter 37

The wait sorely tried Eliza's patience, but Ella forced her to spend the time resting.

"I'm letting you go because I can't stop you," Ella said brusquely "but I won't allow you to kill yourself over a few cows. The men have been trying to do that to themselves for years, so it'd be a shame to deny them their fun after all this time. You, however, are a female and you ought to have more sense."

"But they will soon be my cows," Eliza objected.

"When that's the case, you'll have a husband to keep you from dashing off after I don't know what kind of ruffians. Until then you're stuck with me and Lucy, and I'm putting my foot down."

Lucy put *her* foot down too, and Eliza stayed in bed. Shortly before six o'clock Susan stopped by to report she and Joe had rounded up more than the two dozen men Eliza wanted.

"Joe wasn't too anxious to speak up at first, so I had to do most of the talking. But when they learned it was you who had asked for their help and that you were planning to take on the rustlers by yourself if you had to, it wasn't hard to get them to listen."

"I'm relieved to hear there are still some *men* in this town," Ella observed.

"A lot of people are tired of all the unruliness," Susan said. "Joe was surprised how many volunteered. He thinks the men are behind him at last."

"The question is how far they'll go."

But when Ella's buckboard pulled up at the edge of town

that evening, she was reassured to see the men were just as anxious to be off as the sheriff. There was also an element of face-saving in their participation. As one young man so succinctly put it as he pushed away the whiskey he had just ordered, "If a lady schoolteacher is willing to face those cutthroats, how can I stay here and still call myself a man?" Not everyone was inclined to go as far, but neither were they predisposed to continue drinking and advertise the fact that they were unwilling, or unable, to do what a mere schoolteacher could do. Without meaning to, Eliza had closed down every saloon in Buffalo for the night. Even Lavinia's girls went to bed early.

They made the long ride in the dark, and the late spring air turned chilly when the sun went down. Eliza never felt the cold, though she wasn't sure whether it was due to the excitement or the three blankets Lucy wrapped around her. She also had no idea who they would find at the ranch, or how she was going to convince them she was bringing help, not attacking them.

"Maybe one of you should ride ahead and tell them why we're here," Eliza suggested as they neared the ranch house.

"That ought to be you, miss," Joe said. "Not meaning to hide behind your skirts, but a buggy full of women coming to the door in the middle of the night isn't going to upset anybody. A crowd of armed men might unnerve some guy with an itchy finger."

But Eliza didn't find a stranger in charge.

"What are you doing here?" Cord demanded roughly, stepping out of the dark shadows.

"My God, you nearly scared me half to death," Ella gasped after stifling a scream that had already half slipped out of her throat. "What do you mean popping out at people from behind dark corners with a rifle in your hands." But at the first sight of Cord, Eliza had slipped out of the buggy and run into his arms. Safely folded to his chest, she felt all her apprehension melt away.

"I thought you had gone to Montana," she said as soon

350

as she escaped from his crushing embrace.

"I'm still too useless to make a trip like that," he confessed, chagrinned at the limitations imposed by his still-healing wound.

"If you'd gone to bed like a sensible person, you'd be fit as a fiddle by now," Ella scolded him.

"We all had better get inside before we get sick," said Lucy, tying the horse to the hitching post. "There's nothing like night air for making a body feel poorly."

"I've spent half my life sleeping in the open," Cord objected.

"And you ain't feeling too good now, are you?" demanded Lucy.

"No," Cord admitted with a chuckle. "But as soon as you tell me what brought you here in the middle of the night, I'll let you tuck me in bed."

"It's little sleep you'll be getting if Miss Eliza's right," Lucy warned ominously. Cord turn toward Eliza, a question in his eyes.

"We came ahead to warn you that the sheriff and a large group of volunteers will be here in a few minutes."

Cord looked at her without understanding, a dangerous tenseness about him.

"Everybody thinks you're in Montana, and Uncle Ira said Croley and his men are planning to steal the rest of your herd while you're gone."

"I've got men riding the range around the clock."

"Uncle said Croley has got more than twice as many men as you have, and some of them will be happy to shoot anybody who tries to stop them."

"So Croley has hired himself a gang of outlaws, has he?" mused Cord. "Chances are he won't be able to control them in the end."

"But you won't have any cows by then," Ella pointed out remorselessly.

"But what is Joe Hooker doing here?"

"I talked the sheriff into bringing some volunteers to help. I thought I could explain everything to Ginny and she would explain it to your men, and when the rustlers knew the sheriff and his men were here, they would go away again."

"And then the sheriff started acting like he was stuffed with cotton instead of a backbone, so Miss Eliza told him she would raise the men herself," Lucy related proudly. "She shamed him right good and proper."

"If I don't marry you soon, I'm going to be too much in debt to ask you to be my wife." Cord wrapped her in his arms and kissed her again.

"Ain't you asked her already, and you with your hands all over her?" demanded an outraged Lucy.

"Yes, and she's agreed, so you can put your hackles down. Let's go inside. Ginny will be delighted to have someone to entertain."

"But I want to help," Eliza insisted.

"This is not a game for girls, especially one who's still weak from a bump on the head."

"She ought to be lying down in her bed this minute," Ella scolded, "but I knew she'd never get a minute's rest if she didn't come herself."

"I've got plenty of beds, so you can all stay. It's out of the question to try and return to town at this time of night." He ushered the ladies inside and turned them over to an excited Ginny.

"No point in telling him we've been planning to stay all along," Ella whispered to Lucy.

"You'll come back before you leave?" Eliza asked.

"Of course. I couldn't go off without seeing you again," Cord reassured her.

Ginny was properly horrified when she learned the cause of the ladies' errand, but she was too excited at having female company to think of that for more than a few minutes. She took them into the parlor, beamed with pleasure when Ella praised everything in the room, and nearly burst with pride as she showed them over the whole house, telling them what had been in the rooms in the days when the Orr family had lived there and how Mr. Stedman's purchases were a great improvement.

"There was no reason to think he would know how to pick out furnishings, him being a man and more used to the outdoors than the inside of a house, so I was right amazed when all this stuff showed up, right down to the rugs and the curtains for the windows."

Eliza welcomed the additional proof that Cord was truly an extraordinary man, but she couldn't forget that close to fifty men were gathering outside, or that before dawn some of them might be dead, and her heart was heavy.

"We're going out to the herd now," Cord explained when he returned. "It'll be less dangerous if we're in position before the rustlers arrive."

"Will you be able to catch them?" Ella asked.

"You don't capture a gang like this without killing half of them first. That would mean risking my men, and frankly, I'd rather keep them alive."

"But not lose a single cow in the process," Ella added for him.

"No, ma'am," Cord said, breaking into a reluctant smile, "I don't aim to lose a single cow. I'll see you all at breakfast." He smothered Eliza in a rough embrace, and then was gone.

"That man is enough to make me forget I'm a married lady," Ella sighed. "If I was thirty years younger, I'd fight you for him myself," she told Eliza.

"That man is so in love with Miss Eliza, he wouldn't notice you even if you were *forty* years younger," said Lucy coming nearer to the mark.

"You don't have to tell me what I can see with my own eyes." Ella laughed good-naturedly. "You also don't have to tell me when I was *thirty* years younger I didn't look half as good as Eliza, because I know that too. Now stop trying to depress me and put a little more of that brandy liqueur in my coffee. I declare, I never knew spirits could taste so good."

"Your husband won't like it," Lucy cautioned.

"Then I won't tell him. Don't pour so much in your cup. I don't want to have to carry you to bed."

No one had to help either lady upstairs. After their long day, they looked forward to a luxurious bed piled with feather mattresses. Eliza reluctantly decided against staying up another hour because she knew Ella and Lucy would insist upon sitting up with her.

"There's nothing you can do sitting down here," Ginny told her, understanding in her heavily lined face. "If you marry Cord, you're going to have to get used to waiting. It's never easy, but the first times are the worst. You should have let me put some brandy in your coffee."

Eliza still hadn't fully recovered her strength and she had no trouble falling asleep, but about one o'clock she sat up in the bed with a start; she was wide awake and shaking like a leaf. She had been having a nightmare, a horrible, senseless kaleidoscope of terrifying scenes. Out of the mishmash, two chilling pictures battled for supremacy, one of Cord killing Ira and another of Ira murdering Cord; in the end, the one of Cord shooting her uncle emerged the victor. Eliza was too unnerved to even consider going back to sleep. At least wakefulness would keep the nightmares at bay.

The moon was shining in her face, and she got up and pulled the heavy curtains over the window, but she didn't feel like going back to bed. When her uncle told her of Croley's plans, her only thought had been to stop his stealing Cord's cows, but now the specter of death rose up as an even more appalling menace. She couldn't let Cord kill Ira any more than she could let Ira kill Cord.

She knew she wasn't released from her vow; she never would be as long as her uncle was alive. No matter what he had done to her, no matter how sick with hate he had become, she had to help him. She could not live with herself if she didn't.

More importantly, she didn't know how she could live with Cord if he killed Ira. It seemed so unfair that just when her vow to Aunt Sarah no longer had the power to separate her from Cord, Ira should have the power to drive a potentially fatal wedge between them. She couldn't allow that to happen. There had to be some way to prevent it, some way to avoid an event that would always gnaw at the very foundations of their love.

Eliza dressed quickly and tiptoed downstairs. The silence of the big house was eerie; the thick carpets deadened her footsteps as she moved soundlessly through the hall to the front parlor, but Eliza didn't remain in the hall for long. She had made up her mind to go look for Cord.

Cord pointed to a narrow pass leading from the plain where most of his herd was gathered. "They'll have to come through here if they intend to take the herd to Montana," he told the sheriff. "They're pretty well scattered over the plain, but they ought to be easy to move in one direction if Croley's men are skillful."

"You can depend upon it they are."

"Then the best thing will be to let them gather the herd unopposed until they try to take them through the pass. You take half your men and block the other end. Sturgis can show you where best to station them."

"I can command my own men," Joe said, his feelings still raw because of the rough treatment he'd endured that day.

"I'm sure you can, but my men know every foot of this ground, day or night, and we've had a good of bit of experience at waiting in ambush."

Joe had to agree, with no particular enthusiasm, to accept Sturgis's help.

"The rest of us will close the trap at this end."

"Won't that trap the cows as well?"

"Some, but I hope not many. They're bound to have some men ride ahead, but once the cows enter the pass, they can't do anything except go forward. I'm hoping most of the men will be at this end and you and Sturgis will be able to capture those at the head without giving warning to the rest. I don't want a single one to escape."

Joe looked up sharply. "You told Mrs. Baylis you weren't planning to capture this gang."

"I didn't want the women to worry. Rustling isn't the only cause of the trouble we've been having, but it's caused most of it and it has done more to prolong and intensify it than anything else. If we can eliminate this pernicious gang of thieves, the casual rustlers will be too afraid to operate openly and the hardened criminals will look for easier pickings somewhere else."

"So you're set on capturing everyone, huh?"

"Alive or dead," Cord said grimly. "And I don't have any prejudice against the latter condition."

Eliza drove steadily on, but she was no longer sure of where she was. Cord had told her the herd was being held near the pass to the high plain; she'd been there once before, but in the dark everything looked different. It seemed hours since she'd gone to the corral and harnessed the horse to the buggy herself. She'd never done that before, but it wasn't very different from hitching a horse to a wagon. In any case, there were no unused buckles or dangling straps when she finished, and after bouncing over half the stones in Wyoming, the horse was still connected to the buggy. She knew she should still be at the ranch house soundly asleep in her bed, but she was glad she had come. Even if she was lost, it was better than lying in bed waiting to be told Cord or Ira was dead.

Suddenly she halted the buggy; she thought she'd heard a shot, but no other sound followed. Still, she was certain if she followed the sound it would somehow lead her to Cord, so she turned her buggy and headed off in that direction.

The trap closed on Croley's men with jarring suddenness. One moment they were moving the herd along without a hint of trouble, and the next they found themselves surrounded, their route of escape cut off by the herd ahead and by a cordon of men, led by Stedman himself, who had suddenly loomed up out of the silent shadows behind them. Croley had never paid much attention when he'd heard it said Cord materialized from nowhere, but now he understood why some men refused to ride across Matador land after dark.

"We've got to look for someplace to hole up," he said, thinking hard.

"Why don't we push through the herd and out the other end?"

"Unless I misjudge my man, . Stedman has clamped

356

down on that end as well."

"Do you mean we're trapped in this goddamned canyon like cornered coyotes?" demanded one of the criminals he'd hired.

"For the time being at least."

"You were a fool not to know Stedman wasn't in Montana. You led us into this trap, you mother—" The single shot Eliza heard ripped the silence of the night. The man, a huge, ugly-tempered bully, had started for his gun, but Croley put a bullet through his heart before the gun had cleared the holster.

"Anybody looking for more of the same?" Croley threatened, looking around him with an ugly glare, his gun moving in a slow arc. "Nobody's going to be captured unless we start fighting among ourselves. I don't aim to be caught because there's a hanging tree waiting for me this time. I can't get hung any more for killing a dozen men than for one." No one showed any inclination to argue the point.

"Now sit tight while I do some thinking. Nobody's caught me yet, and I've been at this for more than ten years." Croley sent Harker forward with four men to see what was ahead and stationed nearly a dozen at his rear to hold that end of the canyon. He took the two left, Ira and Les, to look for a place to dig in if the trap closed on them from both ends. To the south the river glimmered in the moonlight like mother-of-pearl, but a sheer wall on its far side made it of no interest to Croley. There was no way out across the river.

Croley made his way through the canyon along with the plodding cows until he came to a place where the north wall of the canyon looked as if it had been worn down by rains. It just might be worn enough to allow them to climb out. In case they had to fight it out, several large boulders offered some cover.

"We'll hole up here if we have to, but I want you to find a way up to that rim," Croley said to Les. "It may be our only way out."

Eliza pulled her buggy to stop at the rim of the pass. She was unable to see anything from where she sat, so she climbed down, walked over to the edge, and peered down. The sight that met her eyes was extraordinarily beautiful. The river lay more than a hundred feet below, a torrent of molten silver in the moonlight as it wound through the pass, cascading over falls and surging between rocks as it dropped the two hundred feet between the high and low plains in little more than a mile. A few cows plodded soundlessly along the trail, leaving the empty silence of the night unbroken. Eliza walked a short way along the rim, but there was no way down and no one in sight. Just as she was about to conclude her ears had deceived her, a man jumped out of the dark at the canyon's edge and was on her in a few strides.

"Croley will be mighty glad to see you, Miss Sage," he growled. "It'll give him something to talk to your boyfriend about." Eliza made a spirited attempt to escape, but Les knew she was the best chance they had of getting out of the canyon alive.

"What are you going to do with me?" Eliza asked when she realized it was useless to struggle any longer.

"We're going to talk to Croley," he said, pointing to a spot that seemed to fall *straight* down. It took all her courage not to panic, but she knew her impetuosity had caused her capture and possibly endangered Cord. She couldn't afford to act foolishly now.

"Where is my uncle?" she asked as calmly as she could.

"Down there too."

"Then let's go, only not so fast. I've never tried to climb down a canyon wall before."

Les looked at her uncertainly. If she really did want to see Ira, she might be useless after all, but it was best to make sure.

"Don't try to get away again," he warned in a gruff voice.

"You frightened me," she said, trying to reassure him. Frantically, Eliza racked her brain for ways to escape, but every thought fled her mind the moment she looked over the rim of the cliff and realized she would have to follow.

Her body froze.

"Come on," Les urged. "It's not as bad as it looks."

"It l-looks horrible, stammered Eliza, and only the knowledge she had to warn Cord enabled her to throw her legs over the edge. She closed her eyes and slowly lowered her body, seeking a foothold in the hard clay that formed the side of the canyon, but a large chunk broke away under her weight and she pitched forward into space.

Chapter 38

Eliza didn't have time to scream. Before she could open her mouth, her body catapulted into Les and the breath was knocked out of her; the two of them went end over end down the slope, like rocks in a landslide, until they came to a jarring halt against a large boulder. They lay there, one atop the other, momentarily stunned.

"You trying to kill me?" Les growled, pushing her off him with ungentlemanly swiftness. He picked himself up, bruised and sore, but neither had any broken bones.

"The bank caved in," Eliza gasped, her wits nearly paralyzed with fear.

"Hold on to me then. I don't want to fall the rest of the way down." He grasped her hand tightly and began the descent.

The fall had completely shattered Eliza's nerve, but each time she made it to the next rock, it seemed a little shorter. Certainly the distance to the bottom was less. Again Eliza tried to think of some plan, but it was impossible to concentrate with the ground steadily falling away in the dark at such an alarming rate. It took all her concentration just to stay on her feet.

The two half ran, half stumbled the last twenty yards, coming to a halt virtually in front of Croley.

"And where did you find this little keepsake?" he inquired, eying Eliza with a mixture of fury and lust.

"She was driving about up above."

"You seem to take an extraordinary delight in riding about in the dark," he said, coming so close Eliza could see the moonlight reflected in his eyes. "What do you find so

360

interesting out there? Or should I ask *whom*?"

"Don't be insulting," Eliza said, attempting to brazen it out and searching frantically for some explanation that might allay his suspicions. "Uncle Ira told me you were planning to steal Cord's herd tonight, and I came to tell him the sheriff was on his way here with a posse."

"We've already found that out. But how do I know you weren't the one who organized it?"

"That was Susan Haughton."

"And I suppose you want me to think you had nothing to do with it?"

"I do wish all this killing would stop." That didn't sound very convincing.

"So you came to warn your uncle?" Croley inquired in a falsely sweet voice.

"I didn't want him to get hurt."

"Liar!" Croley shouted, and struck her hard, knocking her down. "I suppose that's why he had to lock you up?"

"I warned him last time his life was in danger," she said, staying on the ground safely out of his reach.

"Let's see whose life you're more interested in," Croley growled, pulling her to her feet and dragging her down to the trail through the pass. He fired into the air twice, but the sound was covered by sporadic gunfire from both ends of the canyon. "Son of a bitch!" he swore savagely, and headed down the canyon. When he came within sight of the men who were trying to hold the bottom of the canyon against Cord's steady advance, he pushed Eliza in front of him, and using her as a shield, he moved past his men and into the space between the opposing lines of fire.

"Stedman," he shouted, "I've got your woman. Show yourself."

"He'll kill you," Eliza yelled. Croley clamped his hand over her mouth, but Eliza sank her teeth into his bony fingers; with a howl of pain, he struck her a glancing blow with the butt of his gun. Everything went hazy and she slumped against Croley for support, but Eliza fought to keep from passing out.

"Show yourself, Stedman, or I'll shoot her right here."

"You're bluffing, Croley." Cord's voice was uncannily

near. "You harm her and you'll have a hundred bullet holes in your hide before it hits the ground."

"You wouldn't dare take that chance," Croley shouted back furiously.

"For me, it's a chance. For you, it's a dead certainty."

Croley ground his teeth in impotent fury. She *was* his only chance, and he wasn't about to waste it on empty revenge. "I want your men to clear this canyon by sunrise," Croley shouted. "I'll let the girl go when my men are safely out."

"Let her go now. There's nothing against you except rustling. Touch her, and you'll hang, *if* you make it to your trial."

Croley's blood ran cold in spite of his iron nerve. Over and over Cord had proved he *never* made empty promises. "You have till morning," Croley shouted back. "Clear your men out of the canyon, or the girl dies."

"Let her go unharmed, or you won't see the dawn."

"Those are empty words, Stedman. As long as I have Eliza, you can't do a damned thing." But Croley hurried back through his lines more rapidly than his men thought a confident man would have done.

Eliza's mind was consumed by fear and confusion as they traveled back up the canyon more quickly than they came. Didn't Cord love her enough to try to save her? She knew Croley wasn't going to let her go just because Cord told him to, and her interference had not only jeopardized her life and the success of the ambush, but would force Cord to risk his life in an attempt to save her, if he *did* attempt to save her. He didn't sound like he was too upset she was a pawn in Croley's grasp. She would have been begging and pleading if their positions had been reversed; she had already risked her life for him once. Surely he would do as much for her.

But she didn't know what he could do. Croley's men had plenty of cover, while Cord and the others would have to come down the open trail. Well, it was her own fault she was in this mess, so she had no one to blame but herself. It was beginning to look like she had no one else to depend on, so she'd better think of something quick.

"How did you let her get past you?" Cord thundered at a cowhand whose neck he threatened to break with one wrench of his powerful hands.

"You told me not to worry about the plain until the trap was down at both ends," the unfortunate boy managed to gasp. "You said there wouldn't be anybody trying to get up the rim until they knew there was no other way out."

Cord didn't slacken his grip.

"She was already out of the buggy when I got there. I was just in time to see her go over the edge." He didn't dare tell his infuriated employer the girl seemed to have gone willingly.

"I ought to skin you alive," Cord swore, releasing him at last. "Find J.D. and tell him I want him at once." The boy staggered to his feet and disappeared. Cord had hardly taken more than a few turns before a boy, barely older than the first, came hurrying up to him.

"Do you know the crack in the river wall, the one right above the falls?" The boy nodded. "Do you think you could get down it and cross upriver from where the canyon wall has eroded?"

"Sure," the boy answered with easy confidence.

"Then crawl on your hands and knees until you're opposite where Croley's hiding?"

"The river's nearly up to its banks. That would mean I'd barely have my head out of water."

"Maybe not that much."

"And it's icy cold."

"If you can't do it, I'll send someone else."

"I can do it," the boy promised, caught between wanting to and not wanting to. "I just ain't looking forward to it."

"Can you talk two more into going with you?"

"Chrissakes! You don't like asking easy things of a man, do you?"

"Men don't expect to be asked easy things."

The boy swallowed hard. "Give me a hour."

"I'll give you thirty minutes. Maybe less."

The young man looked dumfounded, but said nothing.

363

"I'm going down the opposite side to bring Miss Smallwood out. I'll have to go a little slowly because I don't want to start a rock slide, but when I give you the signal or you hear any unexpected activity, be ready to stand up and fire point-blank."

"But we'll be naked in their fire. There's not even a pebble out there to cover our asses."

"Then make sure you don't miss. The others will be closing in from both ends. Once I have Miss Smallwood safe, the bastards will be covered on all four sides."

"Okay, thirty minutes, but I want a double bonus for this."

"But I *don't* know what he plans to do. I haven't even seen him." Eliza's face was bruised, and blood trickled from her mouth. Croley had been interrogating her for several minutes and was enraged at her refusal to divulge Cord's plans.

When he had returned from his confrontation with Cord, Croley had thrown Eliza behind a rock, ordered Les to watch her, and stomped off to see about positioning his men. At first Eliza had thought she might be safe, that he would be so busy defending himself he would forget about her altogether, but it wasn't long before she discovered how wrong she was. Croley was determined to break her no matter what it took.

"Leave her alone, Croley," Ira said. "Can't you see she doesn't know anything?" Ira had been shocked out of his habitual inability to think of anything except his hatred for Cord by Croley's cold-blooded murder of one of his own men. The brutal beating of his niece, along with the utter collapse of their plans, had thoroughly shaken his confidence, and the little world he had built for himself had begun to break apart. Dazed, he tried to get between Croley and Eliza, but Croley shoved him out of the way.

"You stupid jackass," Croley growled contemptuously. "You're so dazzled by your clothes and money you can't see what a pitiful little pissant you are."

Ira couldn't have been more staggered if Croley's words

had been a fist.

"I've put up with your strutting about like a bantam rooster, making a goddamned fool of yourself, because of your hatred for Stedman. Nobody believed a word you said, but it kept the pressure on him. I don't need you anymore, so don't push me."

It wrung Eliza's heart to see her uncle's pride wither and die under Croley's cruel words, but to her surprise, Ira didn't cower before his tormentor.

"Let my niece go, and neither of us will ever bother you again," said Ira.

Croley threw back his head and laughed, but it was a cruel, mocking laughter. "Look at the little peacock trying to crow at last. You waited too long, old man. I'm going to get the information I want if I have to beat your niece's beautiful face to a pulp."

Instinctively, Eliza's hand flew to her cheeks.

"But I won't do it just yet," Croley said, pulling her closer to him. "I'll save that for later. I'd rather try a different kind of persuasion." His free hand snaked out and roughly covered Eliza's bosom. "I'd like to sample what you're so determined to save for Stedman. Doesn't seem to me like he values it very highly." He squeezed her breast painfully. "I just might value it a lot," he said trying to kiss her.

Eliza nearly panicked when Croley first touched her, and she twisted away, avoiding his lips, but his hand squeezed her breast so brutally she was unable to check a grunt of pain.

"Just a small exchange," he purred. "Not much to ask in exchange for your life."

"Take your hands off my niece," Ira said, trying once more to force his way in between Croley and Eliza, his own convoluted moral code so outraged by this conduct he finally saw Croley for the cold-blooded killer he was. This time Croley released Eliza long enough to send Ira sprawling from a savage right to the jaw. Eliza tried to run, but Croley was on her almost immediately, pulling at her clothes, trying to get his hands in her bodice. Eliza fought with all her strength, but she was no match for him.

"Take your hands off her, or I'll shoot," Ira shouted, a small pistol held shakily in his hands. Croley halted only briefly. Before either of them could move, he whirled Eliza between him and her uncle. Then as Ira danced around trying to keep Eliza out of the line of fire, Croley calmly pulled his gun and shot him; Ira fell to the ground in a crumpled heap. With a terrified scream, Eliza broke free and raced to him.

He lay on his side, blood oozing from a wound in his chest. A sudden burst of gunfire, intense and much nearer, deflected Croley's attention, and he ran off in its direction.

"I'm sorry, Eliza," Ira said with difficulty. "I never realized what kind of man he was."

"Don't think about that now. Can you stand up? We've got to get up the slope while he's occupied. It's our only chance." She searched for and found the pistol with its single unspent bullet and tucked it in her pocket. It was the only weapon they had.

"I don't know if I can move."

"You've got to. Here, lean on me." Ira put his arm about Eliza's neck, and got to his knees. "Now bring one foot up," Eliza coaxed.

"I can't."

"You must. Croley will kill us." With a superhuman effort Ira got to his feet, and straining every muscle, Eliza helped him reach the cover of the first of the large boulders. If they could just get far enough up the cliff before Croley came back, they might escape. The first steep climb taxed Ira's strength, but Eliza wouldn't let him give up.

"I can't make it. Try to get out yourself. After what I've done, I don't deserve to escape. How could I have been so blind?"

"Hush. Save your strength."

"I let the money go to my head," he said, beginning to climb again. "I told myself it was *my* success. I refused to admit it was all due to you."

"Keep climbing. We've got to get higher," Eliza urged, lifting the thin man by her own strength when his failed.

"I've got to rest for just a minute," he panted. "I

shouldn't have hated Cord," he said when he finally got his breath. "But I had to have somebody to blame for all my failures. I couldn't accept them myself."

"We can't stop. We're still not high enough." Eliza forced the nearly exhausted man to keep going. The path was much steeper now, and she barely had the strength to keep her uncle on his feet.

"He was the kind of man I wanted to be and never was," Ira continued. "But he wanted the only thing I had left, and I couldn't let him have you."

"You never really wanted me," Eliza said between gasps. "You never loved me." They were both almost too exhausted to move, but getting away from Croley was their only chance.

"I never forgave you for still being alive when Sarah and Grant died. At times I think I was so angry I almost hated you, but I never did."

"But I can be hurt too," Eliza said, her aroused anger giving her the strength to continue to climb. "I can be lonely and I can cry, but I can also love and laugh."

"I was too bitter to see that, or even want to. It took Cord to see it in you, and I hated him all the more for it." He stopped, gasping for breath as he slid to the ground. "We can't stop now. We're almost out of reach."

"You go on without me. I can't go any farther."

"Yes, you can," Eliza said fiercely, tears streaming down her face. "I waited ten years to have you offer me just one scrap of affection, and now that I have it I'm not going to let Croley Blaine take it away. We're going to get out of here if I have to carry you on my back."

"Ira! Eliza!" It was Croley screaming down below.

"Stay down," Eliza whispered urgently.

"If you don't come down, I'll come after you."

"Go on, get out if you can," Ira urged. "I'll see if I can hold him off." He took her hands in his and kissed them. "I've been a great fool. It took that beast down there to make me see what I should have seen ten years ago, but it's too late now. Don't make the cost of my stupidity any greater than it already is."

Eliza could hardly see for the tears. "You can straighten

367

this out after we get out of here," she said, forcing him to his feet.

"I can't," he said pitifully.

"You must," Eliza commanded harshly.

Croley spotted them when they moved out into the open, but they were beyond the range of his gun and his bullets expended themselves harmlessly on the rocks.

"I'll kill you when I get my hands on you," Croley shouted, and began to climb up after them.

"I can't go any farther," Ira said kneeling in the dust. "You've got to go for help. Listen to me," he insisted when Eliza started to refuse once more.

"It's you he wants, and it's you he'll hurt. Get out and bring help. That man of yours can't be far away. He'll know what to do. He always has."

Still Eliza hesitated. They were little more than half the way up the canyon wall.

"You know it's the only way."

"Hide," Eliza said. "He'll never catch me once I get to the top. I brought a buggy." She gave her uncle a quick kiss and began climbing as fast as she could. Below Croley climbed rapidly up after her, bellowing his fury as he went. Eliza climbed frantically, but she was exhausted from carrying Ira, and the last of the climb was so steep, she was barely able to make any progress and Croley gained on her. She looked back often to gauge his progress, to see if she could gain the rim before he reached her, but he was gaining much too fast. He would catch her.

The pistol! It was still in her pocket. She pulled it out and stared at it stupidly. She had never fired any kind of gun, but she had only one bullet and it was her only chance. She leaned against a rock and steadied her shaking hand against its surface. There was no time to remember that it was another human being she was trying to kill, no time to force down the bile rising in her throat. There was only time for one shot, and she had to make it count. Carefully, she took aim and squeezed the trigger. The shock of the recoil caused the pistol to fly from her hands, but it didn't matter; the bullet had missed Croley and he

368

was climbing with redoubled fury.

"Run, Eliza," her uncle's voice called out. "I'll stop him." With the last of his strength, Ira raised a rock above his head and threw it at Croley. It fell uselessly short.

"Nobody's going to stop me," Croley spat, and shot Ira again. This time Ira did not move. Eliza screamed, caught between her desire to go back to her uncle and the realization she must still try to escape, knowing Croley was bound to catch her either way. She was only twenty feet from the rim of the canyon, but Croley was less than that distance away from her and climbing twice as fast. Eliza's strength was gone; she was trapped.

In that instant a huge body came catapulting over the rim of the canyon, leaping down the side with the agility of a mountain goat, his enormous strength providing the only inspiration Eliza needed.

"Cord!" It was at once a cry of relief, exultation, and warning. He stopped only long enough to see her bruised and bloodied face before descending on Croley in a whirlwind of fury. Blaine saw death staring him in the face and his anger turned to fear; the repeated click of his gun told him he had used his last bullet on Ira. The old man had saved both Eliza and Cord.

Cord's hurtling body hit Croley with the force of a charging steer, knocked him to the ground, and drove every ounce of breath from his body. Cord's hands closed around Croley's throat as they rolled over and over sending rocks catapulting down the cliff into the pass. They came to a jarring halt, lodged behind a rock a short distance above Ira, yet Cord's hands still encircled Croley's throat; Croley's face turned black and his body thrashed about in its death agony, but the remorseless grip did not lessen, and the last thing Croley Blaine saw was the face of the one man he had never been able to defeat.

The body went limp, and Cord stood up, the mask of murderous rage relaxed at last. He returned quickly to Eliza, but she sped past him to where Ira lay. She knelt beside the inert body and gently smoothed the hair from his brow; miraculously his eyes opened once more.

"Croley?" he asked as she cradled his head in her arms.

"He's dead," she told him.

"And Cord?"

"He's right here. He's all right."

Ira closed his eyes. "Then I haven't been a failure at everything," he whispered, and breathed his last.

Wracking sobs shook Eliza's exhausted body. None of his selfishness and cruelty mattered now. He was the man she had lived with for ten years, the person who had protected her and provided for her as she grew to womanhood, and his death was a grievous loss.

Cord came up behind her, but he made no attempt to comfort her. She was grieving for years he had taken no part in, and she must do it alone.

Somehow Eliza sensed his presence, and her weeping abated. "He looks peaceful now," she said without looking up, "like he's glad to be free of this world." She dabbed uncaringly at her eyes with her torn sleeve. "I guess that's what he wanted all along. All his anger was just unhappiness at being separated from Aunt Sarah and Grant."

Mechanically she straightened his tie. "He saved our lives, you know, me down there and you up here." His fancy coat was bunched under him, and she tugged at it until it was free, then took great care to make sure it was straight. "He said he was sorry for what he did to both of us. He tried to help me get away, even though he knew Croley would kill him." She raised her eyes to Cord, and her lips started to tremble uncontrollably. "I guess maybe he loved me after all."

"Just about every rustler we were looking for is here," Franklin observed as the column of bound men paraded past.

"They were easy to catch after Mr. Stedman started that rock slide," Sheriff Hooker said. "Those boys by the river had them in their sights when they came running out from behind the boulders. Simple as rounding up milk cows after that. And no more than a few flesh wounds to show for it."

Franklin gestured to Eliza and Joe Hooker fell silent. It

was impossible for any of the men to enjoy their triumph in the face of Eliza's grief. He'd never seen anyone look so pitiful as she did when she stumbled down that hill, following behind Cord as he carried her uncle's lifeless body in his arms. They could fetch Croley's body later. It would be indecent to force her to carry her uncle's murderer in the same wagon. Poor girl. With someone she loved on both sides of the conflict, she was bound to get hurt, but he couldn't see any call for Croley to beat her like that. And her not the kind to hurt a fly.

He sighed. Oh, well, she was about to be married. She'd get over it. It was often violent in Wyoming, and people learned to recover from their losses quickly. She would too.

Chapter 39

Eliza continued to be listless. Her uncle had been buried a week earlier and nearly all traces of her brutal beating were healed, but there seemed to be a wound inside her that would not respond to any kind of treatment. The whole town had turned out for the funeral, and she had had as many visitors as Ella and Lucy would allow, but she'd continued to be uninterested in anything.

Cord had come to see her every day, making plans for the biggest wedding ever seen in Buffalo, and she'd languidly agreed to everything he said.

"I don't know what's wrong with her," Ella told Cord for the dozenth time. "From the way she's carrying on, you'd think that old man treated her like a precious treasure instead of a slave."

"He made his peace with her before he died."

"It's easy to say nice words when you know you're not going to have to live up to them," Ella said uncharitably. "He was nasty when he was alive, and I don't see any reason to think he would have been any different now."

"I don't care about Ira, then or now," Cord replied shortly. "I just want Eliza back on her feet again. I never saw her look so miserable."

"You never saw her lose her only living relative before either."

"I suppose you're anxiously awaiting your wedding day," Jessica Burton said coldly, sitting rigidly across the width of Ella's parlor from Eliza.

"Of course she is," Ella answered for her. "Every girl looks forward to her wedding."

"You couldn't tell it to look at her," Jessica replied with a tight smile. "She looks positively haggard. Not at all like someone who has just cornered the most eligible bachelor in the state."

"She did that long ago, when you were still thinking he was just a cowboy grown too big for his britches."

"Gossip has it Cord had lost interest, that she got up that posse to keep from losing him."

Eliza looked stricken.

"Who dared to spread such a lie?" Ella demanded, rising majestically from her chair. "Just tell me their name and I'll see they don't spread any more."

"My dear Ella," Jessica tittered with false sympathy, "you may be able to intimidate people with your overpowering personality, but you can't stop them from talking. And they always say, where there's smoke, there's fire."

"The only fire you're going to see is the one I light under your tail feathers, Jessica Burton, if you repeat one word of that malicious gossip."

"How dare you," retorted Jessica, swelling with indignation.

"Easy," Ella fired back. "Especially when you come into my house intending to mortify this child just because she got the man you couldn't trap for Melissa. Yes, you can color up, but everybody's been gossiping about *that* too. You got your own back when Cord started his own bank and took away half your customers. After what he's done now, I expect he'll get the other half."

"Sanford's customers are most loyal," Jessica said emphatically.

"What you mean is Cord wouldn't do business with the half of them. You don't fool me, Jessica Burton. You came here meaning to be nasty because you know you won't be undisputed queen of Buffalo any longer. Eliza's gone and pushed you right off that pedestal you built for yourself. Well, you've got no one but yourself to thank for putting her there, you with your pushing and shoving ways and Sanford's determination to corner every dollar in the county."

"Please," begged Eliza, feeling like her head was going to burst. "I don't want to replace anybody, and I don't want to be queen of anything. All I want is to be left alone."

"I can assure you that *I* shall grant your wish," declaimed Jessica, slamming out of the house with none of her habitual majesty.

"Forget everything that old biddy said," Ella ordered, shepherding Eliza off to bed. "You get a nice nap and then I'll fix you some supper."

"You don't have to watch over me so. I can still take care of myself."

"I know that, but your ideas and mine don't seem to fit too well these days. You used to be the sweetest, most biddable gal, but here lately you've become as slippery as a cake of wet soap. All I have to do is turn my back, and you're up to your neck in trouble."

"Is there ever going to be any peace here, Ella? It seems ever since I came to this town, everyone's been fighting everybody else. I'm sick of the killing and I'm sick of living in fear of what's going to happen next. My uncle is dead, but he might still be alive if I hadn't fallen in love with the one man he hated. I saw Cord kill a man, and not just some stranger. He killed a man I knew, a man who talked to me and even shared meals with me. And who knows when he'll have to do it again. Now, just when I think the fighting's all over, it's starting all over, only it's a different kind. Does it ever end?"

"Not for the likes of Jessica. She won't ever forgive you for being more beautiful than her daughter and getting the man she wanted for a son-in-law. And she won't forgive Cord for taking away her husband's customers and choosing you for his wife. Jessica will never be happy unless everything about her family is better than anything anybody else has."

"All I want is to be left alone to marry Cord and have his children. I don't want to lead society or have people coming to me for things."

"Neither you nor Cord is the kind to go after fame—or money, for that matter. All he wanted was his own ranch

374

and you. All you wanted was Cord. But Fate put both of you in the way of great things, and when others were backing away or hurrying to do nothing, you pushed ahead and emerged the winners. You have so much courage and talent and determination you're always going to be successful at what you do, and people will just naturally look up to you."

"I don't think I can stand it," Eliza said with a hiccupping sob. "This country makes everybody hard and brutal, killing before they can be killed, thinking only of their possessions instead of the human lives being wasted on every side. I can't live like this. It'll drive me crazy."

"You will because you must," Ella assured her. "You're still in low spirits because of your uncle, and unless I miss my guess, you're feeling guilty at finding yourself the owner of a prosperous saloon and rooming house. You can soothe your conscience knowing you had nothing to do with your uncle's death, and there wouldn't be any saloon or rooming house if it wasn't for your singing. Now you get some sleep. You've got to stop tormenting yourself with all this thinking and worrying. I don't say it's not a bitter draught to swallow, but swallow it you must."

But after she had gone, Eliza drew a thick, folded paper from under her pillow and reread its contents. "But I *do* have a choice," she stated vehemently as she searched for a pen to sign the contract. "And I'm going to take it."

Cord would follow her, she was sure of it, and she would talk him into selling the ranch. It wouldn't be easy, but they could be together and there would be no more shooting and hating and violence in their lives. She would miss Ella and Susan, and she knew Cord would miss the Matador, but if he loved her, he would leave Wyoming behind forever.

Two days later Iris came into the Baylis's store, her agitation obvious from the way she walked. "Have you seen Eliza?" she demanded immediately.

"She went to visit Susan. I was hoping the baby would help get her mind off things."

"Susan hasn't seen her."

"Ask Lucy. She's been at her side nearly every waking minute."

"I can't find Lucy either, and no one at the saloon has seen her since early this morning."

"Well where do you think she's gotten to? She's not mooning about over at the schoolhouse, is she?"

"No, I've been there too. I think she's left town."

"What!"

"I think she's accepted that agent's offer to go East. She's been overwhelmed by everything since she saved Cord from that dynamite. And now with the capture of those rustlers, her uncle's death, and this enormous wedding, I think it's scared her to death."

"And I know who's responsible," Ella intoned, storm clouds gathering in her eyes. "Have you seen Jessica Burton hanging about Eliza?"

"No, but Susan said Eliza came up to her yesterday when she was out walking, and she looked like she'd seen a ghost. She mumbled something about gossip, but wouldn't say any more."

"Blast that old crone," Ella said, pulling her apron over her head. "Ed!" she called over her shoulder. "I'm going out, and I don't know when I'll be back."

"Where are you going?"

"To the stage office. If she's gone any place, they'll know."

"Sold her two tickets to Douglas first thing this morning," the station master told Ella. "Wanted to get there in time to take the evening train to Chicago."

"Gus Lewis, you're the biggest fool that ever a woman birthed, and if I had the time, I'd bash your face in for you." Ella stormed out of the office, Iris in her wake, leaving the stunned man staring after her with bulging eyes.

"You go see if that colonel of yours can telegraph Douglas and have the stage detained."

"What am I supposed to tell him?"

"Do I have to think of everything? Tell him she's got small pox. Tell them she's robbed the bank and gotten away with all the money. For God's sake, girl can't you think of anything?"

"I hope I can do a little better than that." Iris grinned. "But what are you going to do?"

"I'm going to drive out to the Matador and put a flea in Cord Stedman's ear. If that man hadn't held back, trying to treat her kindly and not rush her, everything would be fine. I swear, you can't ever depend upon a man to know the right time to do a thing. When I told him to sit still, he couldn't help jumping into the fire every time he got a chance. Now when we could use some action, what does he do but sit at the ranch of his, politely refusing to hurry her and planning a wedding big enough to give one of Lavinia's floozies palpitations. If he had just swooped down and carried her off, none of this would have happened."

"You told him to do that?"

"Certainly not," Ella replied, shocked. "You'd think the man could come up with something on his own. After all, he's not helpless."

Ella arrived at the Matador expecting to have to contain all the things she'd spent hours planning to say while someone was sent to find Cord, but he was at the house, standing speechless with an envelope in his hands.

"What's that?" demanded Ella, marching into the parlor and pouring herself a brandy.

"The deed to the piece of land on Bear Creek I've been trying to get my hands on for years. Eliza claimed it for me."

"Did she include a note?"

"No, not a word."

"Then if you don't saddle your fastest horse and intercept the stage to Douglas before seven o'clock, that's the last thing you'll ever get from her," Ella stated before draining her brandy.

"What are you talking about?" demanded Cord.

"I don't stutter, man," Ella snapped, and poured herself some more brandy. "She's on the stage to Douglas and she intends to take the evening train to Chicago."

"What for?"

"There isn't a particle bit of good asking me that question when she's the one with the answer."

"What are you going to do?"

"I think I'll see if I can get drunk on this brandy liqueur of yours. I don't see why you men should have all the fun." Cord stared at her. "Don't stand there gaping, boy. I wouldn't hurt myself if I was to drink the rest of it, which I promise I won't. But if you don't catch that stage, a whole cabinet full of brandy won't drown the hurt you'll be feeling."

Cord ran from the room, and minutes later Ella saw him bowling down the road with a light buggy drawn by the two fastest horses in his stables. "It's taken a lot of work, Ella honey, but I think we may just pull this one off yet." She laughed to herself and drank her brandy.

Eliza sat quietly in the corner of the stage as it bounced along the uneven road. She had spent most of her time staring out the window at the passing landscape, trying to tell herself she wouldn't miss the wide open spaces, the loneliness bred into the land. She also tried to tell herself she was looking forward to the opportunities offered by a big city like Chicago, but she'd never been in a town of more than a few hundred and had no concept of what a city was really like. After spending her entire life on the plains, she doubted she could ever get used to streets that, according to Lucy, were considered empty when they were more crowded than Buffalo on its busiest day.

Lucy had been delighted when Eliza had told her she was going to accept the agent's offer. She looked forward to resuming her old life, especially since she was positive Eliza would soon become a sensational success, but it wasn't very long before she began to question whether Eliza really wanted to leave Buffalo. She hadn't spoken more than a few sentences since they left. Lucy had tried to cheer her up, but after about an hour it was clear Eliza was not going to be cheered, and Lucy thought it best to leave her to her thoughts. "You made your bed, child," Lucy said, breaking the silence at last. "You mean to tell me now you don't want to lie in it?"

"I never wanted to go to Chicago," Eliza told her. "I just

378

couldn't stay in Buffalo."

"You're running away," Lucy asserted. "You know that, don't you? You can say what you like to other people, but there's no point in telling lies to your own self."

"That's what Ella says too."

"Sure she does. Everybody thinks the same thing."

"And you think I shouldn't go?"

"Depends on what you're running toward."

"There's not a thing in Chicago I want," Eliza said bleakly.

"Then you ought to tell that driver to let you off right here. There ain't enough money in Chicago for me to let some dragon-faced banker's wife drive me off if I didn't want to go."

"You know about Mrs. Burton?"

"Everybody knows about Miss Jessie. She hasn't shut her mouth since you became the main topic of conversation. That woman can't stand not to be the center of everything, and you pushed her into the shade right smart."

"But she said such terrible things."

"Let her. What harm can it do? Ain't nobody believing her, so why should anything she says bother you?"

"But people listen to her."

"Not anymore. It's you, and maybe Miss Ella, they want to hear from. Miss Jessie was on the wrong side. Besides, she was setting on her broad behind when you were out there raising a ruckus. People pay attention to things like that, and they look up to you."

"It sounds like you've been talking to Ella."

"Of course it does. Anybody but a newborn babe can see that with one eye closed."

"And you think I'm failing those people?"

"I ain't worried about those people. They took care of themselves before you got here, and they'll go right on no matter what. The one you're failing is yourself."

"And Cord," added Eliza.

"No, just yourself. You think you're still a little girl, but you're a woman now, and it's time you started acting like one. Mr. Cord doesn't want to be married to a pretty doll

379

baby all his life. No matter what men say, they want a woman to be able to do everything they can. They just don't want the knowledge shoved in their faces all the time."

Eliza laughed in spite of herself.

"You're just hurt now," Lucy added in a milder voice. "You want to hide and lick your wounds, but what better place than a pair of arms like Mr. Cord's. Hmmm, hmmm! That's mighty powerful medicine."

"After all the hate and the killing, I wanted to get as far away from Wyoming as I could. I kept telling myself I couldn't live in a place where that kind of misery never stopped. I was sure I would find the kind of life I was looking for in the city, but it's not that way, is it?"

Lucy shook her head.

"I didn't think so. I suppose I realized it about twenty minutes after we pulled out of Buffalo. I also realized I couldn't do it to Cord."

"What do you mean?" asked Lucy, puzzled.

"I told myself if he loved me, he would sell the ranch and stay with me. You don't have to look so astonished. I wasn't stupid enough to think that for longer than ten minutes. Now you'd better tell the driver to turn around. If I get too far away from my medicine man, I might never get well."

"Do you mean it?" Lucy asked, beaming hopefully. "I mean, for real?"

"Yes, I mean it, for real." Lucy leaned her head out the window.

"Turn this dad-blamed contraption around," she ordered in commanding accents. "We are going back to Buffalo."

"I can't do that."

"Turn it around before I climb up and give you a good rap with this umbrella stick I'm carrying."

"Lady, this is a stagecoach, not a private carriage. If you want to go back to Buffalo, you're going to have to go on to Douglas and buy a return ticket."

"No, we ain't," Lucy shouted, jumping up and down so the stage rocked dangerously. "I see a cloud of dust coming up behind us, and if that isn't Mr. Cord come to fetch his gal you can call me a cross-eyed hound dog."

"Cord?" stammered Eliza, suddenly vibrantly live. "Are you sure?"

"It's either him or the Army, and I think Miss Iris already has that one tied up." Eliza stuck her head out the window, holding on to her bonnet to keep it from being blown away. "I can't tell yet," she said, peering hard in the distance. "I don't know the horses."

"It ain't the horses that's coming after you, gal. It's the man driving them."

But now Eliza was able to make out the shape of the man driving the pair at a gallop, and there was no doubt in her mind it was Cord.

"Stop, you fool," Lucy said, using her umbrella stick to get the driver's attention. "You are just about to lose the only business you've got."

"Please stop," Eliza said, adding her entreaties to those of Lucy. "I've made a terrible mistake and you've got to let me out."

"I already told you, lady. I don't stop this stage for *nobody*."

"Then you're about to meet *somebody* who's going to make you change your mind."

Cord had set his horses into a gallop when the stage came into view, but when he saw Eliza leaning out the window, unmistakably beckoning to him, he whipped them into a hard drive. The stage driver didn't seem to have any intention of slowing down, but when Cord pulled his buggy in front of him and then slowed his own horses until they came to a standstill, he had no choice.

"You can't interfere with stage business," he said, considerably offended, but Cord paid him no attention. He jumped down and ran around to the side of the stage just in time for Eliza to leap into his arms.

"I don't want to run away ever again," she said, emerging from his embrace.

"You don't mind being the wife of a half-civilized cowboy?"

"I wouldn't consider marrying you if you weren't," she said, laughing. "And I want to form committees, hold charity balls, and tell *everybody* what to do."

"Lord, that child never does anything, but what she goes overboard," moaned Lucy.

"You know you don't have to do anything like that," Cord said, making her look at him quite seriously. "You can stay on the ranch and never go into town if you don't want to."

"I think I would prefer living on the ranch instead of in town, but I don't want to bury myself. I'm not afraid anymore."

"Are you sure? There's bound to be a lot of pressure on you."

"Then I'll stay at the Matador until it goes away." She smiled at his slight pucker. "I'm teasing. With Lucy and Ella telling me what to do, and Susan making me do it, I'm going to have to depend on you for protection. You do want to take care of me, don't you?"

"Forever, but you must obey me implicitly."

"How?" Eliza asked suspiciously.

"You can keep on with your teaching—I don't think you'd be happy if you gave that up—but I want you to turn the saloon and boarding house over to Lucy and marry me the minute I find the preacher."

"Any more orders?" she asked meekly.

"Just one. Kiss me."

Eliza threw her arms around Cord's neck and he buried her in his embrace. Then Cord swept her up into his arms and carried her to his buggy.

"You can stop staring like a bare-bottomed sharecropper's brat, and throw those bags down," Lucy ordered the driver, who had listened open-mouthed to the whole exchange. "Then you can head on to Douglas if you're so hot to get there. We ain't got no use for you anymore."

Cord and Eliza seemed to have no use for anyone except each other. She nestled within the circle of his arms as he took up the reins and turned the buggy toward home. The driver, watching as though mesmerized, stared after the retreating buggy until their silhouettes merged into one inseparable whole.

Author's Note

The Johnson County War is the name usually given to the confrontation that took place in northern Wyoming in April 1892. Tension had been growing for some time between the large absentee owners who controlled the cattle industry through the Wyoming Stock Growers Association in Cheyenne and the small ranchers whom they saw as competitors, the homesteaders who fenced off grazing land and water, and rustlers. Originally the issue was control of the mavericks and the open range, but it turned into one of survival after the rustlers became very active. Nearly two hundred cases of rustling were brought to court, with only one conviction. On the other hand, at least five "little" people were killed before the invasion; in one instance the killers were known by name, but no one was ever convicted. An army of seventy paid gunmen *did* arrive in Casper on April 6th, *did* kill two suspected rustlers at the KC Ranch on April 9th, and were surrounded at the TA Ranch on the 11th, where they were rescued by the Army on the 13th. They were later transferred to Cheyenne, and all were allowed to go free without a trial.

To this day there is a great deal that is not known about what happened or who was involved, and much of what is known is disputed. There are many firsthand accounts of the early days of the cattle industry in Wyoming, and most give their side of the Johnson County War, but perhaps the most objective presentation of the facts is Helena Huntington Smith's *The War on Powder River*, published by McGraw-Hill in 1969.

I have tried to fit my story into the historical framework

and have my characters reflect the sentiments of the time *as I imagined them to be,* but my characters are fictional and their actions are from my own imagination. When I have referred to actual events, such as the killings before Christmas of 1891, I have used fictional names.